REBEL OF RALEIGH HIGH

Copyright © 2019 by Callie Hart

All rights reserved.

No part of this book may be reproduced in any form or by any electronic or mechanical means, including information storage and retrieval systems, without written permission from the author, except for the use of brief quotations in a book review.

THEY BROKE HER WINGS, BUT STILL SHE FLEW

PROLOGUE

Grave robbery has never been that high on my to-do list, but tonight, with a frigid Washington wind blowing in off Lake Cushman, I find myself up to my waist in dirt with a shovel in my hand. Weird how life likes to fuck with you sometimes. There are plenty of other places I could be tonight, and yet here I am, the muscles in my back aching like a bitch as I lift the haft of the shovel over my head and I pile-drive the steel blade into the unforgiving, frozen earth.

"Dorme, Passerotto. Shhh. Time to go to sleep."

I ignore the soft whisper in my ear. That voice is long gone now. It doesn't serve me to remember it, but…forgetting wouldn't be right. Forgetting would feel like a betrayal.

The cut, scrape, swish of my work fills the night air, and a river of sweat courses down my spine. My body's no stranger to physical labor, and I'm grateful for the fact as I press forward, hurling clods of icy dirt over my bare shoulder and out of the deepening hole. This task would be way shittier if I weren't in shape. Scratch that…it'd probably be impossible.

I don't believe in zombies, vampires, ghosts, or any other kind of apparition, but there's something about this place that creeps me out. *Yeah, it's a graveyard, Poindexter. You're surrounded by rotting bodies.* I roll my eyes at my own inner monologue, again lobbing loose grave soil out onto the well-manicured grass to my right. It's only natural that this place would have a sinister edge to it. It's abandoned, not a soul in sight (very convenient for me), and yet there are signs of the living everywhere—laminated cards bearing the smiling faces of children; floral tributes, tinged with the first signs of fading decay; stuffed animals, fur matted and crusted over with frost. The people who left these trinkets and treasures are safe in their own warm houses now, though. It feels like the end of the world out here, a neglected place, filled with neglected memories. The moon overhead, round and fat in the clear September sky, casts long shadows, making spears out of the headstones.

I wipe at my forehead with the back of my forearm, grit and clay smearing my skin, and I consider how much further down I need to go. They bury people deeper than usual here in Grays Harbor County. I read that on the cemetery website yesterday morning when I was scoping the place. They said it was because of the bears. Seriously fucked up. I try not to think about that as I quicken my pace, eager to accomplish my goal and get the hell out of here.

A loud, metallic clang eventually signals that I've come to the end of the road, I've found what I'm looking for, and that hard part, the disturbing-as-fuck part of this evening's adventure has finally arrived. Takes some time to clear off the coffin and figure out how to open the damn thing. This kind of thing is always made to look so easy in the movies, but it's not. Far from it. I nearly rip the damn nail from my index finger as I try to heave back the lid.

"*Figlio di puttana!* Fucking piece of shit." I nearly shove my finger into my mouth to suck on it, but then I remember the fucking grave dirt underneath the nail of the finger in question and I decide against it. Dirt is dirt is dirt, but grave dirt? No, thanks.

Upon close inspection, I conclude there's no way to finesse the coffin open, so I resort to brute force, heaving on the wood until the coffin makes a splintering sound and the lid frees, groaning as it yawns reluctantly open.

Inside: the body of a man in his late fifties, dressed in a red button-down shirt and a black tie. No suit jacket. His face, a face I know all too well, is as severe and downturned in death as it was in life. Hooked nose; pronounced brow; deep, cavernous lines carved into the flesh of his cheeks, bracketing his thin-lipped, angry-looking mouth. His hands have been stacked on top of his chest. Beneath them: a copy of the Gideon's Bible. The cheap, generic kind you might find in the drawer of a nightstand in a Motel 6. I scowl at the sight, a familiar, slick, oily knot tightening in my chest. Ahh, rage, my friend. Fancy seeing you here, you sly old fuck.

Speaking to a dead body isn't nearly as weird as you might think. "Well, Gary. Looks like the piper wanted to be paid, huh?" Sweat stings at my eyes. Crouching down, feet balanced on either side of the coffin, I take my t-shirt from my back pocket where I hung it for safe keeping, and I use it to wipe at my face. Before I arrived here tonight, I'd prepared myself for the sickly-sweet odor of death, was ready to face it, but two feet away from Gary, the only thing I can smell are the winter pine trees on the wind. "Figured we'd end up here eventually," I tell him. "Didn't think it would be so soon, but hey...I'm not complaining."

Unsurprisingly, Gary has very little say in return.

I contemplate his face. His sallow, sunken in cheeks and his pinched, withered features. When did he get so gaunt? Was he always like that, or did the process of dying shave twenty pounds off the guy? I suppose it's a mystery I'll never solve now. It's been six months since I saw him last; there's every chance the bastard joined Jenny Craig during that time.

I stoop low over him and reach out a finger, prodding at his cheek, expecting to find some give in him, but there's nothing. He's solid. Stiff, like a calcified husk. Like I said, I didn't come here unprepared. Gary's been dead for four days, so it seemed prudent to read up on what kind of shape the motherfucker was going to be in when I unearthed him. His corpse isn't bloated, though. His tongue isn't protruding from between his teeth. He looks…he looks kind of normal. Even the makeup they must have put on him at the funeral home still looks like it's holding up.

It's the cold. Has to be. There's no way he'd be so perfectly preserved otherwise. Honestly, I'm a little disappointed. A part of me was looking forward to seeing the bastard's skin sloughing from his bones.

With quick hands I get to work, first grabbing the Bible and tossing it out of the grave, hissing between my teeth. Gary's hands are next. I wrench them apart, then hinge his arms down by his sides, giving me room to unbutton his shirt and fold the material back. He's wearing a vest, but that's no big deal. I stand briefly so I can get my hand in my pocket, and then the short blade of my flick knife is gleaming brilliantly in the moonlight. The sharpened steel cuts through the thin polyester in two seconds flat.

Gary's narrow, twisted pigeon chest hasn't been rouged up like his face, and here I find the evidence of decay I was looking for. His skin's pale, tinged an unhealthy blue, mottled like a fine-veined marble. And just off center of his torso, a little up and to the right, a small, neat, black hole with puckered edges punctures his skin.

Do morticians charge for sewing gunshot wounds closed? If they do, then Gary's penny-pinching brother from Mississauga declined to cover the added expense. I never met him—the brother. In the three years I lived under the roof of Gary Quincy's doublewide trailer, I only ever heard his brother's voice on the other end of a telephone, and even then I knew I didn't like the fucker.

"Had to make sure, Gaz," I say. "Needed to see with my own

two eyes. Now. Where'd you put it, hmm?" I pat down the pockets of his cheap suit pants, feeling around carefully...

I didn't just come here to make sure Gary Quincy was dead, though that was a big part of this. I've spent the last two hours laboring in the dirt, digging his ass up, because he has something that belongs to me, something he took from me, and I want it back.

His pockets are empty. Juuuust fucking perfect. I lift his head, checking his throat, just to make sure, but it's not there, either.

"You swallow it, Gary?" I ask, glancing at the knife I rested on the edge of the coffin. "Wouldn't put it past you, you fucking psycho." I take up the knife, dread lacing my bones as I survey the concave shell of his stomach, wondering if I have the stones to even proceed with such a fucking crazy idea. Cutting Gary open, unraveling his intestines, feeling around inside the cavities, nooks and crannies of his insides will not be something I'll ever be able to forget. Something like that changes a person, I'm betting, and I don't really feel like undertaking that type of a transformation right now. I like being able to sleep at night.

"Dorme, Passerotto. Shhh. Time to go to sleep."

Fuck. No, not here. Not now. I push the voice aside, shivering away from the comforting warmth of it, and I'm left chilled to my core, a cold, angry fist closing around my heart.

"Fuck you, Gary," I growl under my breath. "It wasn't yours. You should have known I wouldn't let you keep it." Steeling myself, I pick up the knife and lower the blade, its shining tip hovering an inch above Gary's stomach. I'm ready. I can do this. I'll gut him from stem to sternum if it means I can reclaim what's mine.

The knife meets Gary's skin, and...

The moonlight strengthens for a second, the shadows inside the grave peeling back, and I catch an unexpected flash of gold out of the corner of my eye. A brisk gust of wind moans through the trees, and I stop dead.

There...in Gary's right hand.

"Motherfucker," I hiss. "I knew it. Couldn't just leave it for me, could you? Had to make sure I never found it." Prizing Gary's fingers open takes work. I don't even flinch when I feel the snap of his middle finger breaking, though. I actually have to fight the macabre urge to break even more of his bones as I pluck the small gold medallion attached to the delicate gold chain out of his palm and close my own hand around it.

Suddenly, I'm five years old again, watching owl-eyed as a woman with hair the color of sunshine kisses the small, golden medallion and tucks it inside her shirt. "St. Christopher, holy patron of travelers, protect and lead me safely on my journey."

Jesus, the past is hitting hard tonight. It's as if my close proximity to Gary's empty carcass is opening all kinds of doors to the dead, and I can't fucking take it a moment longer. Standing, freezing cold now that I've been still for a while and my sweat has cooled, I adopt a wide stance with my feet still planted on either side of the coffin, and I unzip my fly. "Sorry, Gary. But you and I both know you deserve this."

Steam rises from the coffin as my piss splashes down onto Gary's chest. I've been waiting for this for a long, long time. It feels…Damn, it feels fucking—

"Hold it right there, kid. Stop what you're doing this instant!"

Oh, come on.

I tense, freezing in place, every part of me rigid.

The female voice behind me is alive with anger as she repeats her command. "I said stop what you're doing, asshole!"

I risk a glance over my shoulder and my stomach sinks when I see the uniform. The badge. The gun aimed at the back of my head. "If you're referring to the fact that I'm still pissing, Officer, then I'm afraid there's nothing I can do. Stopping mid-flow is bad for the prostate." I smile to myself, knowing I'm not helping matters. Fuck it though, right? I am going to be arrested. No doubt about it. And if my ass is getting thrown in jail for this, then I'll be damned if I don't finish what I started.

"Kid, if you don't quit right now and put your dick away, you're gonna get Tazed. You understand me?"

Ahh. Tazer, not a gun. Well, I guess that's something. I surrender a long, resigned sigh. I do not stop.

"Last chance, dumbass."

There are worst things to be in this life than stubborn and dedicated to a cause. And let's face it…this opportunity will never present itself again. I brace, even though bracing is pointless, and I wait for the pain.

When it comes, lancing into my back, striking like lightning down my arms and into my legs, I retain just enough control to make sure I sag sideways into Gary's grave and not forwards.

After all, the very last thing I need, on the back of such a long and successful night, is to find myself slumped over the deceased remains of the man who repeatedly beat me while lying in a pool of my own piss.

Somehow, through my gritted teeth, my tensed muscles, and the blinding ball of pain that's lashed itself to my back, I manage to choke out a single, bitter burst of laughter.

The sound echoes like a gunshot over midnight Lake Cushman.

1
SILVER

Silver Parisi: most likely to suck dick for dollar.

I stare down at the slip of paper on the table, creased and stained on the back by something that looks suspiciously like mustard, and my temper riots. This, right here, is some fucking bullshit. I'm used to detention, I'm a regular attendee, and I'm used to the chores we're tasked with, but tallying the nominations for yearbook has turned out to be a rather cruel and unusual form of punishment. Because this isn't cleaning erasers or scrubbing graffiti from the girl's bathroom stalls. This is fucking personal.

Silver Parisi: most likely to contract syphilis.
Silver Parisi: most likely to cook meth.
Silver Parisi: most likely to fuck your boyfriend behind your back.

The suggestions are colorful and aplenty. I already know who's behind the offensive, hate-filled superlatives: the football team, the cheer squad, and the sheep who follow the Raleigh High elite around with their noses pinched firmly between their pampered, trust fund ass cheeks. I'd say the spiteful nominations stacked on the desk in front of me right now are innumerable, but I've actually had to count them, and I know exactly how many there are. And of the twenty-three vile suggestions that have been made in my honor, so far there's one clear winner.

Silver Parisi: most likely to die on prom night.

The Raleigh High Year Book Committee is going to replace this. No way they'll allow such a terrible thing to be printed beneath the photo of one of their graduating class students. In fifteen years' time, anyone who just so happens to be flipping through the pages of their dusty old high school yearbook will see a photo of a pale, seventeen-year-old girl with solemn, intense blue eyes, mousy brown hair, and an unusual shaped birthmark on her neck, wearing a Billy Joel T-shirt, and they'll read:

Silver Parisi: most likely to learn a foreign language.

I can already see it now. Fucking foreign language. No one will remember me. No one will come across my picture and suddenly recall all of the fun, amazing times they shared with me. No, they're going to take one look at my stern, unhappy face, and they're gonna recoil. Jesus Christ, who was that girl, again? And why the fuck was she so damn miserable all the time?

They won't remember the shit they all put me through in the final year of high school. Most conveniently of all, they'll have forgotten all about the fact that they subtly threatened my life and implied they were going to murder my ass on the night of prom.

Assholes.

I snatch up the slip of paper and scrunch it in my hand, then toss it across the room. I'm aiming for the trash can, but I'm a terrible shot. I miss, and the balled-up nomination slip ends up on the floor with all the other anonymous threats to my life.

Out of the corner of my eye, Jacob Weaving hunches over his desk, scribbling furiously into his notebook. He's supposed to be writing an essay on the Cuban Missile Crisis, but I can picture the scrawled mess he's drawn instead—a manga fuck doll with giant, bare tits and parted lips, legs spread wide open. Anime porn is Jacob's specialty. Out of the corner of his eye, he catches me watching him, and a smug, infuriating smirk fishhooks his mouth, pulling it up at one side. "Need a ride home later, Sil? Cillian and Sam are waiting in the lot. We really enjoyed the last time we all hung out."

"I'd rather crawl on broken glass."

Jacob feigns shock. "No need to overreact. Just thought you might like to play us a few songs or something. No harm, no foul."

But there has been harm. There's been more than one foul on Jacob Weaving's part. He's a pig. A psycho. An evil, twisted, disgusting excuse for a human being, and I hate him with every fiber of my seventeen-year-old being. I grab the purple sparkly ballot box Mr. French thrust at me when I arrived at detention thirty minutes ago, swing my bag onto my back, and I get to my feet. A loud screeching sound fills the room as my chair legs scrape the floor, and Jacob sits back, lacing his fingers together, stacking them on top of his stomach as he observes me heading for the door.

"Abandoning detention before you've been dismissed? So brave, Parisi. Your courage makes my dick hard."

I kick at the screwed-up paper littering the floor by French's desk. Yanking open the door, I pause before I leave, casting a disgusted look back at him over my shoulder. "We both know it isn't my courage that makes your shriveled-up dick hard, Jake. You prefer it when I'm screaming and afraid, don't you?"

A cold, detached viciousness settles into the handsome lines of his face. Because Jacob Weaving is handsome. He's the hottest guy at Raleigh. He's tall, and he's ripped, and there was once a time when the sight of him smiling would have made me weak at the knees. Not anymore, though. Now, when he smiles, all I see are the many lies and the secrets, lurking just beneath the surface of his privileged, All-American demi-god charm, and it makes me want to puke. It makes me want to claw my way, broken and bleeding out of my own skin, so that I no longer have to be me anymore.

"Careful, Parisi," he snarls under his breath. "Your fall from grace has been pretty hard already. Wouldn't wanna go making things worse for yourself."

My own smile is a ruined, sour thing. "Worse?" I want to laugh, but I'm afraid to. My body's been betraying me lately; It can't be trusted to carry out the simplest of tasks. No matter what emotion I try to project, I end up displaying the exact opposite, and I cannot afford to cry in front of Jake Weaving right now. I draw in a deep breath, stepping out into the empty hallway, and I let the door swing closed behind me. Jake's eyes remain on me, burning into my skin like twin brands, until the door clicks shut and he's gone.

I'm going to be in shit for bailing on detention, but I don't care. Sometimes, it's as though even the Raleigh faculty are in on this sick, twisted game I've found myself caught up in. They know about Jake. They know about our history, and yet they're still willing to leave us alone, unsupervised in a room together after school hours?

Madness.

Pure and absolute madness.

I check the watch at my wrist, Mickey Mouse on its face, grinning, one arm longer than the other, pointing out the hour and the minutes, and I hiss between my teeth. It's almost four p.m. which means Mr. French will be coming by to cut us loose any moment. My boots ring out, my footfall echoing loudly off the unending row of scuffed grey lockers that line the hallway, and I fight the urge to run head-on for the exit. This always happens. I'm terrified the corridor will never end. That I'll find myself striving toward it forever, reaching out to push the chipped pale blue painted door open, but it's always just out of reach. Or when I get there, it's locked, and no matter how hard I push, rattle it, or plead with it to open, I'm stuck inside this hellhole of a building for the rest of time.

I do reach the door, though. When I push on it, palms pressed flat against the wood, it inches back quickly, and a jolt of relief makes my body feel momentarily numb. Outside, the late autumnal air smells like freedom. I can taste it. On the other side of the emptied-out parking lot, my old Nova is sitting there, waiting for me to climb inside, start the engine, and get the hell out of here, but—

I can hear voices.

Principle Darhower's deep baritone voice has been a daily staple of my life for the past four years; it's easily recognizable. I don't know the woman's voice, though—firm and authoritative—nor the male voice, thick with a southern accent, that speaks after her.

"We understand this isn't an ideal situation. For you or your faculty. If it were up to us, the boy'd already be in for a couple of years over in Swanson County, but the judge ruled he was still classed as a minor."

"What about juvenile detention?" Principle Darhower says, his tone tight with tension.

I creep back from the exit, allowing the portal to my freedom to fall closed. I'm silent as a church mouse as I tiptoe along the hallway to my left. No one notices me as I peer around the corner, into the hallway that branches off toward Darhower's office. There, Darhower's ramrod straight in his trademark stance, arms folded across his chest, head canted to one side, the stark strip lighting overhead bouncing off the small bald patch at the back of his skull that he's always so diligently trying to hide. Opposite him, a thin, tall woman in a grey pantsuit is leafing through a stack of papers, frowning as she tries to find something. The man next to her is wearing a uniform. The 'Grays Harbor County Sherriff's Department' badge on the sleeve of his dark green bomber jacket tells me everything I need to know about him.

The Deputy sighs, removing his hat and scrubbing the back of his hand against his forehead. He looks stressed. "Juvie's not an option in this particular case. The facility in Wellson Falls has been shut down. We'd have to transfer him out of state if we really wanted to pursue the charges, and the paperwork alone is just..." He trails off, and Principle Darhower heaves a sigh of his own.

"I don't need to tell you how disruptive something like this is to our students. The school year might have only just started, but our seniors are already buckling down and prepping for college. We have plenty of our own bad apples. Another trouble maker stalking the halls of Raleigh is only going to make life harder for the good kids."

"Jim, we know, believe me." The woman in the grey pantsuit seems to have found what she was looking for. She holds out a green file to Darhower, and I take a look at her face properly for the first time. Mid to late thirties. Dark hair. Dark eyes. I suppose she's quite pretty. There's a sad, tiredness to her that makes her look like a kicked puppy, though. I can picture her opening a bottle of wine when she gets home at night, telling herself she deserves a glass after the day she's had, and then before she knows it, she's polished off the entire bottle. She's a social worker, no doubt about it.

She called Darhower by his first name, which means she's dealt with him before. Darhower grimaces as he takes the file from her, briefly opening it and glancing at the first page, then closing it quickly, as if he can't face its contents. "I guess I don't really have a say in the matter then," Darhower says. "He starts on Monday."

The social worker and the sheriff's deputy trade a glance that looks relieved even from where I'm standing. All three of them shift as if some unspoken command has been issued to them, and they head toward the door that leads to the principal's office. That's when I realize there's been a fourth person there the entire time. With Darhower and the deputy standing so close together, blocking my view, I just hadn't seen the guy sitting on the chair to their right.

He's young. My age. His dark hair is almost black, shaved close at the sides, longer on top, thick and wavy. He's both stretched out and slumped in the chair at the same time, artfully arranged into a position of careless boredom, the soles of his booted feet almost reaching the opposite wall of the hallway. His clothes are dark and simple—grey jeans, and a plain black t-shirt. Tattoos stain the skin of his bare arms. To the left of his chair, a black motorcycle helmet sits on the floor, along with a beaten, ratty looking canvas bag, covered in patches. I only see his face in profile. His eyes are closed, his fingers pressing into his brow like he's nursing a headache. The cut of his jawline is strong, as is the high slope of his cheekbone. His mouth…I can't really see his mouth.

He's silent, he's still—unbelievably still, actually—but there's something about the shape and the cut of the guy that fills me with panic. The vibe he's silently giving off at the other end of the hallway feels dangerous. He's nothing like Jacob and the other guys on the football team. Jacob's an instrument of chaos, and that's precisely what he incites in his dumb ass buddies. They thrive on manipulation and deception, half-grown and on the brink of graduating into their adult bodies, hopped up on testosterone, convinced they own the world, that they're entitled to it, and god help anyone who tries to prevent them from claiming it.

This stranger, though…

He's an unknown. An outside threat. There's nothing about the way he's sprawled out in that chair that tells me what motivates or drives him. He holds himself with a kind of self-possessed arrogance that makes me want to climb inside my locker and hide there until the end of term. From the sounds of things, he's up to his neck in trouble, and whatever he did almost landed him in prison.

As if he senses that he's being watched, the guy slowly opens his eyes, lowering his hand from his face. I suck in a startled breath, kicking myself for lingering so long when I should have slipped away three minutes ago. He doesn't turn to look at me, though; he only turns his head a little, slightly angling it in my direction. His eyes remain glued to the floor, but I can feel him notice me. The ghost of a smile plays over his mouth, which I can now see is full and perfectly fucking formed.

Great.

Just…great.

Before I can turn and flee for my life, the social worker reemerges from Darhower's office and stands in front of the guy with one hand on her hip. She looks down at him with clear and obvious frustration. "All right, Alex. I'm not gonna bother with the talk. We both know there's no point. You need to be here Monday morning, eight a.m. You need to register for your classes, and then you need to show up for them. Understand?"

The guy's still frozen in place, his head slightly tilted in my direction. His smile forms properly now, a little lopsided, a little off-center, more than a little sardonic. He slowly turns his face up to look her in the eye. "You got it, Maeve. Monday morning. Loud and clear. Nowhere else I'd rather be."

He has an accent, but nothing so evident as the deputy's southern twang. The subtle, faint lilt to his words makes his voice sound almost musical, and the hairs on the back of my neck stand to attention.

We haven't had a new kid at Raleigh for well over three years. My existence here is a living hell, and has been for some time, but it's a predictable hell. I'm not safe within the walls of this building, but at least I know what to expect. I know who I need to avoid, and I know which corridors I just can't walk down. Come Monday morning, a new element will have been introduced to my already complicated, fragile ecosystem of hate, and I already know this Alex person is going to make things harder for me.

The entire football team is going to be on canvasing hard for him. He's tall, he's broad, and he looks like he doesn't take any shit. Jacob will want him on the team, no matter what. Whoever he is, this new guy looks like he could pose a threat to Jacob, and he will not like that. He won't like that one bit. He'll want to control him, the way he controls everyone else. Jacob will want this Alex guy inducted into the Raleigh Roughnecks crew quickly, which can mean only one thing: one more person to despise me. Another mindless member, added to their ranks, charged with the task of making my life as unbearable as physically possible.

I pull back, turn, and finally head for the exit, a cold, oily dread settling in my veins. This isn't good. I can feel it in my bones. I really shouldn't be all that surprised, though. Just when I thought things can't get worse…they do.

They always do. That's just how things at Raleigh go.

2
SILVER

For the most hated girl at school, my home life is surprisingly normal. My parents are still together—increasingly rare—and I have a younger brother, who interferes in my shit twenty-four seven, as little brothers like to do. Mom works at a local accounting firm, and Dad is an architectural engineer. We have some money. Not a lot, but enough. We live in a good neighborhood. Our house is a beautiful old Colonial with a wraparound porch and painted blue shutters. Every Sunday, we visit my grandmother at the Regency Park Retirement Community, and she feeds me baked ziti and tells me stories about 'The Old Country,' otherwise known as Italy.

Between the hours of eight in the morning and two thirty in the afternoon, I might be a social pariah, scorned, laughed at, shoved and tripped. But at home, I'm just Sil: much-loved daughter, goofy older sister, and doted on granddaughter. One more year and I'll be able to get the hell out of Raleigh and start at a college where no one knows my name. I don't even care which college I end up going to, so long as I don't know a single fucking soul there.

Saturday morning brings an early acceptance letter that has my mom dancing around the kitchen, singing my praises before we've even eaten breakfast. I get back from my morning run, and she's still in her pinstriped pajamas, her hair all ruffled and sticking up from her pillow, and the smile on her face makes me want to hurl myself up the stairs and lock myself in my bedroom for the rest of time. She doesn't know. I haven't told her a thing about what's been happening with me for the past nine months, and I'm not planning on telling her, either. She has enough on her plate with work and with Max, and I don't want to add to her troubles.

The signs are all there, though. I used to go out on the weekends. I used to hang out at my friends' houses. Every now and again, a cute boy used to wait out front for me in a pick-up every morning to take me to school. Now I spend my weekends studying, playing guitar, and reading books. Now, I drive myself to school in the beaten-up old Nova dad bought for me at the beginning of summer. Now, I don't smile anywhere near as often as I used to.

A part of me is angry that she hasn't noticed.

"Jesus, Sil. You didn't tell us you were applying to Dartmouth." Mom holds up a torn open envelope and a sheet of paper, waving it in my face. "Can you believe this? I can't believe this." She clears her throat. "Dear Ms. Parisi. Upon reviewing your application, we are pleased to announce that we have chosen to confer a 'likely' status upon you. Please note, our final acceptance of your application will not be confirmed until March of next year, but you can assume your 'likely' status will ensure your entrance to Dartmouth, should you maintain your current record of achievement and personal integrity!"

She speaks normally to begin with but then slips into an English accent part way through. By the end of the statement, she's talking like Kate Middleton and screaming with excitement. "Silver!" She grabs me by the shoulders, shaking me. "I can't believe you got a 'likely' letter from fucking Dartmouth."

"Mom! No swearing!" Max's high, reedy voice calls from the living room.

"Sorry, sweetheart, that is a bad word," she calls. "I got carried away. Did you know that your sister's a genius?"

"I did begin to suspect when she walked into that glass door at Olive Garden," he replies flatly. Little bastard. I'm gonna have to tickle the crap out of him later. For an eleven-year-old, he really does possess a surprisingly accurate understanding of sarcasm.

I take the paper from Mom's hand, scanning the words there, printed in black and white, plain as day. I wait for the wave of triumph that should wash over me (this is a seriously big deal, after all) but it doesn't come. Somehow, I feel even emptier than I did before I walked in through the front door.

"Aren't you happy, Honey?" Mom asks, tucking a rogue strand of hair back behind my ear. "I thought there was going to be more...I don't know, hysterical jumping around?" She turns, heading for the kitchen counter, where it looks like she was in the process of making pancake batter.

"You shouldn't have opened it," I say quietly.

"Hmm?"

"It was addressed to me, right? The letter? You shouldn't have opened it."

Her head whips up, and I see her instant guilt. Her eyes are the same color as mine, blue as cornflowers and spring skies. The excitement in them fades, and it's as if her entire face has clouded over. "God, you're right. I just went out of my head when I saw the address stamp. I've been opening mail for you your entire life. I forget sometimes that you're almost an adult now. I'm sorry, Sil. I won't do that again."

Damn. I feel shitty now. I didn't mean to make her feel bad. It's not a big deal, and I wouldn't have usually even said anything, but the twisted, gnarled knot of anxiety that I woke up with this morning only worsened while I was out on my run, and I feel like I'm edging toward a complete nervous break right now. I don't say any of this to Mom, naturally. I give her a tight-lipped smile, placing the letter from Dartmouth down on the kitchen counter, and I head for the stairs.

"Where are you off to, sweetheart?"

"I need to shower. I'm covered in sweat."

"Okay, well hurry up, okay. Dan asked me to finish up on an urgent account. They need their third quarter paperwork first thing on Monday, so I have to head to the office for a couple of hours. I thought we could eat together before I leave."

"Okay." I feel numb as I trudge up to the second floor. Luckily, my room has an en-suite, and I get to shower without Max banging on the door, harassing me. Once I'm dressed, I go back down to the kitchen, where the table is heaving under the weight of all the food Mom's laid out for us.

"Cute outfit," she says when she sees me. "Overalls were crazy popular when I was your age, too. Are dreads back yet? I always wanted dreads. Didn't think I could pull them off. I used to sing in a Bob Marley tribute band. D'you know that?" She belts out the first line of 'Buffalo Soldier,' and I smile despite myself. I thank my lucky stars that I have her as a parent most days. She could be an uptight, overbearing, maniacal overlord type, but she's pretty laid back as it goes. She doesn't try too hard. She's not watching me like a hawk twenty-four hours a day, firing out orders and telling me what I can and can't do. She's also not constantly trying to be my best friend. She's just her. She's just Mom, secure in her role, typically fair and reasonable. But yeah. Also weird.

"You might have mentioned that a couple of times before." I snake a pancake from the stack in the middle of the table, biting into it, and Mom slaps my hand.

"Neanderthal. Sit down and eat with a knife and fork like a civilized human being. Are you gonna go over to Kacey's and celebrate today or something?"

I sit. I use my knife and fork as directed. "No. I have a bunch of homework."

"Do it tomorrow, love. It's not every day you get into Dartmouth."

"I didn't actually get in. I got a 'likely.' And you read the letter. If my grades slip, they'll rescind the offer anyway. I can't start slacking off now."

"Silver, one day won't kill you. I'm sure Kacey's mom hasn't drained the pool for winter yet. You should put on a bathing suit and go get some sun this afternoon. You spend way too much time indoors these days. You're looking a little vampish. You'll start to glow in the dark if you're not careful."

"Gee. Thanks, Mom." Max isn't the only Parisi child with a Ph.D. in sarcasm.

"I'm just saying. A little R and R never hurt anybody. It's good for the soul."

"Ah, then I'm okay, then. Vampires don't have souls."

Mom points her fork at me, talking around a mouthful of food. "That has not been proven. Countless books and movies would have us believe otherwise. Now can you please lighten up a little? I'm trying to live vicariously through you, and you're making it really boring." She winks, and I consider hurling a pancake at her.

"Aren't you going to be late?" I ask, checking with Mickey Mouse. "It's almost quarter to nine. You aren't even dressed."

Her eyes go wide. Scrambling to her feet, she grabs her plate. "Shit! I am. I am so going to be late!"

"Jeez! No swearing, Mom!" Max hollers.

"Sorry, honey!" She flies out of the kitchen, her hair streaming out like a honey gold banner behind her, and I breathe a sigh of relief.

I'm glad the conversation ended when it did. Somehow, Mom hasn't even noticed that Kacey and I aren't friends anymore…and I wouldn't have the faintest clue how to begin explaining that one to her.

3

SILVER

I used to love Monday Mornings. It's normal to love them when you're at the top of the socio-economic food chain. Attending high school never felt like a chore, because people worshipped me there. Once upon a time, other students tripped over themselves to make my life as blissful and easy as possible.

"SILVER GEORGINA PARISI, GET YOUR ASS OUT OF YOUR PIT BEFORE I COME UP THERE AND DRAG YOU OUT OF IT MYSELF!"

Now, on a Monday morning, however, I pull the duvet up over my head like every other ordinary student at Raleigh High, and I block out the world, cursing miserably that the weekend isn't longer. "I'M NOT GOING, DAD!" I holler. "SCHOOL IS FOR LOSERS!"

There's a thunderous crash in the room below me—Dad's office—and the sound of a door slamming closed. Then comes the drumbeat of hurried feet charging up the stairs. My bedroom door opens, and I can feel my father standing there, staring at my misshapen, lumpy duvet cocoon. "Don't you want to be remarkable today, Silver?" he asks.

"I'm remarkable every day. Everyone else's just too stupid to notice."

"I know, Kiddo. But the powers that be will fine my ass and take Max away if I don't enforce a pointless secondary school education on you. So can you do me a solid and take one for the team? Your mom and I really can't afford to lose Max."

I throw back the covers, glaring at him. "Wow. I feel really valued. Thanks, Dad."

He's leaning against the door jamb, arms folded across his chest, wearing a plaid button-down shirt and the horn-rimmed, round glasses that he thinks make him look like a hipster. His dark hair, touched with grey at his temples is swept back, and…god. I squint at him, trying to decide if my eyes are playing tricks on me. Is he rocking stubble?

He winks at me. "Come on. We both know you're gonna fly the coop and be working on the International Space Station way sooner than any of us are anticipating. You're too intelligent to wind up stuck here in Raleigh, working at the observatory. Your brother, on the other hand, possesses an average intelligence. He's our insurance policy. If he gets taken away, who the hell's gonna look after us when we're old?"

"Dad." I'm deadpan, my voice muted to a whisper. "That's really messed up. Tell me something."

"What?"

"Please tell me that you're not trying to grow a beard."

He thrusts out his jaw, rubbing a hand over the dark whiskers that are jutting out of his face. "Huh? You don't like it? Simon and I have a bet. Whoever has the most impressive, manliest beard by the end of the month wins a hundred bucks."

"I'll give you a hundred bucks right now if you get in the bathroom and shave that off. I'm serious. Beards are for hot fitness models on Instagram, not middle-aged architects."

His eyebrows rise in unison. "First, you'd better save your money. That Nova's gonna need a gearbox eventually and that shit ain't cheap. Second, beards are for carpenters and rugged naval captains. Everybody knows this. Third, I could be a fitness model on Instagram. I run marathons. I have abs on top of my abs. And last but not least, dearest daughter…middle-aged? How old do you think I am?"

I smirk wickedly. "From the crow's feet and all that salt and pepper in your hair, I'm gonna say sixty-seven."

Dad's face is a mask of mock outrage. "Witch. Get up. Now, before I pay your brother to come in here and fart all over you. And if you're not up, dressed, fed and out of the door in the next forty-five minutes, I'm gonna start uploading your baby pictures onto your precious Instagram, and I'm gonna tag all of your friends. Sixty fucking seven. Jesus Christ."

He spins around and leaves, running back down the stairs, heavy footed and making enough noise to wake the dead, so he doesn't see my expression of abject panic. He wouldn't dare. He wouldn't fucking dare upload my embarrassing baby photos. Dad's reckless, though, and tends to follow through on his threats. Unluckily for me, he's nowhere near sixty-seven; my parents were practically kids themselves when they had me, and he won't be celebrating his fortieth birthday for another six months, which means he definitely has his own Insta account and he knows perfectly well how to use it.

Reluctantly, I drag myself out of bed and haul ass into the bathroom. My father could have threatened me with many things, but having him tag my 'friends' in embarrassing photos of me online? Yeah, that's not something I can afford to even joke about.

∽

Dad really shouldn't have mentioned anything about the Nova's transmission. The engine sounds rough and throaty the entire way across town, and I begin to worry that it's gonna quit on me about a mile from school. Miraculously, it makes it, but I'm still gripping the steering wheel, praying under my breath that it doesn't stall out in front of the entire Roughnecks cheerleading squad as I drive all the way to the back of the school parking lot.

I ignore the hard, unwelcoming eyes that follow me as I pass by the building's entrance; I barely even notice them staring anymore, though the girls I used to hang around with, girls I've known since I was seven-years-old, don't seem to care if I respond to their mean-girl act either way.

It's started to rain as I jump out of the Nova, grab my backpack from the backseat and hurry across the lot, avoiding the puddles of standing water as I go. It's still fifteen minutes to the bell, which means there are plenty of other students loitering outside, sitting on the trunks of their cars, rough-housing and gossiping with one another. This is the perfect time to arrive—amongst all of the other students hunched against the cold, laughing and shouting, I'm almost invisible. Anonymous. It's easy enough to slip through the clustered groups of my peers without drawing too much attention.

There's no avoiding the girls, though.

Melody, Zen, Halliday, and, of course, Kacey. Once upon a time, I knew all of their secrets, and they knew mine. When my world combusted into a fiery ball of shit nine months ago, they were pretty quick to make sure everyone knew every single one of my secrets, while stupidly or otherwise, I clamped my mouth shut and kept theirs. I can't even count how many hours I've spent lying in bed at night, imagining their faces if some of their skeletons were to come to life and leap out of their closets. It'd be so fucking satisfying to watch them scramble, to see them frantically trying to hold the pieces of their lives together after all the pain and suffering they visited on me.

But...

I don't do it. I like to tell myself those bitches will get what's coming to them. Karma will show up on their doorsteps one day, and they'll pay the price for their actions, but honestly, the simple, quiet, sad truth is that I don't want them to suffer. I miss my friends. The dumb practical jokes we used to play on each other. The sleepovers, and the silly traditions we used to share. I miss the late-night laughter, and swooning over boys, and...fuck. I miss being part of a ride-or-die group of friends who would do anything for each other.

I suppose now, in hindsight, it's stupid to miss that. As it turns out, I never really had it. I thought I did. I would have bet money on the girls having my back. In the end, they are the ones who betrayed me the hardest, though.

I have to pass them to get into the building. I already have my headphones in, so I crank up my music and make sure to keep my chin high as I stroll past them. I will not hurry. I will not look away. I will not look ashamed. I will not give them the satisfaction.

Zen says something to Halliday, obviously about me. Her mouth is turned down, her nostrils flared, and I remember that same look being on her face the day she found that her dad had been cheating on her mom for a year—the fury and the disgust had poured off her like heat from a flame. I'd been the one to soothe her pain that night, and many nights after, too. I'd brought over gallon tubs of Ben & Jerry's, and watched lame teen dramas, and listened to her while she'd ranted. The other girls had come by too, but I was there every night. I was a constant source of comfort to her when it felt like her life was ending, and the tear in her heart would never heal. And now she's looking at me, the same way she looked at her father.

Halliday—silly, sweet, strawberry blonde Halliday—giggles, furtive eyes cast in my direction, and I recognize malice and spite there, where before there was only ever empathy and kindness. I don't know what's wrought this drastic change in her, but I'm brimming over with sadness as I take the first step up the stairs that lead into Raleigh High.

Billy Joel sings into my ears about rainy nights in Paris and the sitting by the Seine in the European rain, and out of nowhere I feel something hit my arm—light, barely a contact at all. I almost ignore it, but out of the corner of my eye, I see whatever hit me fall to the ground...and it's a cigarette butt. Still lit, though smoked down to the filter. The cherry glows, flaring red, before the rainwater on the ground soaks along the paper, putting it out.

What the fuck?

I look back at the girls. I can't help myself. My gaze meets Kacey's, and my ribcage squeezes like a vice as a curl of smoke slips out of her mouth. Melody titters, elbowing Kace, and my ex-best friend fucking winks at me. Her green eyes are blazing with defiance, and I'm reminded very clearly that Kacey Winters earned her nickname: if you're lucky enough to find yourself on the right side of the Ice Queen, life can be a marvelous thing. Find yourself on the other side of the line she's drawn in the sand, however, and you'll quickly be suffering from frostbite.

My expression's appalled, I know it is, but I can't keep it from my face. Slowly, I stoop down and pick up the cigarette butt. My feet carry me towards the girls, unbidden. I can't fucking stop them. Billy Joel falls quiet as I remove the earbuds and clear my throat. I address Kacey. "You smoke now? Leon must love that."

Leon's been her boyfriend since freshman year. Already on track for a swimming scholarship, Leon's the clean-cut, extraordinarily focused, wholesome type. No alcohol. No drugs. Definitely no smoking. Since he was fourteen years old, his only vice has been Kacey.

Melody rolls her eyes, inspecting her French polish. "Fuck. She's so out of touch. It's a miracle she even knows what day of the week it is."

"Grow up, Mel," I snap. "The rest of the world grew out of talking about people and pretending they weren't there back in middle school."

She looks stung. Immaculately dressed, thick auburn hair styled in flawless beach waves, Melody has always spent way more time on her appearance than she ever spent developing a mind of her own. She looks to Kacey to see if she should retaliate, but Kacey doesn't spare her a sideways glance. She's far too busy lasering holes into my skull.

"Leon and I broke up. I'm with Jacob now. Hope you don't mind."

Bile rises in my throat. My reaction hits me hard, too quick to rein it in. I can't fucking breathe. "You aren't serious?" The words are little more than a startled gasp.

A cunning, sour smile tugs at Kacey's mouth. Mom used to call her Snow White when we were little. All that jet-black hair, her rosebud lips, and the permanent pretty red blush to her porcelain-skinned cheeks. If she could see her now, she wouldn't call her that anymore. Kacey bears more of a resemblance to Cruella de Vil with this nasty sneer plastered across her face. "Why wouldn't I be? Jacob's hot. He's captain of the—"

"You know what he did, Kacey. You were there."

Her shoulders are tense, and for a second I see something shift in her—a fleeting shadow of doubt in her otherwise steely eyes. In a split second, it's gone, though. She opens her mouth, about to speak, but—

Thunder rolls across the parking lot. Deep, reverberating thunder that vibrates up through the soles of my boots.

Kacey looks over my shoulder, and the other girls follow suit. Halliday's mouth actually falls open as another rumbling, rolling wall of sound splits apart the morning air, and I realize that it's not thunder after all, but the snarl of a powerful engine. The sound cuts off, and I grind my teeth together, already knowing what I'll see when I turn around.

"Monday morning. Loud and clear. Nowhere else I'd rather be."

He'd had a motorcycle helmet at his feet in the hallway.

"Who the fuck is that?" Zen mutters. She's pouting, which means she's seen something she likes and she's about to lay claim to it.

At the end of the day, I'm a flawed human being, so I bite. I turn, even though I don't want to, and I see him there, less than fifty feet away, sitting astride a matte-black Indian motorcycle with his helmet resting on top of the tank. He's wearing a leather jacket and faded scruffy black jeans—I can tell from here they're not the kind of 'distressed' pants you buy that way. They're scruffy from extensive wear and tear, which is a little more respectable, I guess.

His dark hair is thick and full of waves, shielding his face from view as he looks down at the phone he's holding in his hand. I'm locked in place, feet cemented to the ground, breath lodged in my throat, waiting for him to lift his head. For his hair to fall back and give me a proper look at him…but then I'm flooded with a strange sense of panic, and I'm moving, fingernails digging into my palms as I hurry away from the girls and I hurtle up the steps, and into the building.

Zen shouts something behind me, but I don't know if it's at me or to the guy sitting on the motorcycle; her words are nothing more than a blur of sound. Inside, weaving my way through the heaving press of bodies in the hallway, I can feel my pulse all over my body, pounding like a determined fist against a wall, trying to break its way through.

I have no clue why I had to run.

I just couldn't stand there, waiting to see his face. It felt like pure torture. It felt like waiting for the world to end.

～

By lunchtime, the whole school's buzzing with the news: not only has a new student enrolled, but he looks like the frontman of a rock band. He's covered in tattoos. He had a knife confiscated from his bag in first period. He squared up to Travis McCormick in the locker room and threatened to knock his teeth out.

The rumors grow wilder and wilder with every retelling, and I know I'm on borrowed time. I am going to run into him at some point. The population of Raleigh High isn't all that big, and the guy who showed up on that motorcycle was no junior. He was a senior, which means we're in the same year and bound to be in at least one class together. I do not, however, expect it to be my A.P. physics class.

I was never a front row kind of student. Before, I was always most comfortable sitting in the middle row, in the middle of the room, where I had plenty of room to see and be seen. Now, thanks to the fact that my classmates like to throw shit at my back and launch spitballs into my hair, I can be found on the very back row, tucked out of the way, usually in a corner if I can help it. I arrive early to class whenever I can, and I bolt for the door first, too. Easier to get in and out as quickly and quietly as possible.

I arrive at the last class of the day, my brain a little foggy from the overheated library where I ate lunch, and I don't even look up as I make my way into the back-left corner of the room. I nearly have a heart attack when I dump my bag on the desk, seconds from sitting down, when I look up to find someone sitting there… at my desk.

His leather jacket is hung over the back of the chair, and his legs—how the fuck did I not notice his legs?—are stretched out in front of him, protruding into the aisle. Christ, I must have stepped over them in order to plunk my backpack down on the surface in front of him.

His t-shirt is grey, plain, with the sleeves cuffed, rolled up a couple of times, and the thin material is pulled taut across his chest. There really are tattoos all up his arms—dark swirls of ink that my eyes snag on as they travel up to his face.

High, pronounced cheekbones. Strong, cut jawline. Arrow straight nose. His lower lip is slightly fuller than the top. A pair of dark, intense eyes stare up at me, and it's all I can do not to squeak like a fucking church mouse. Making eye contact with him is like staring into a bottomless well, inexplicably being stuck with vertigo and almost falling in. He's exactly as I imagined he'd be.

He's nothing like I imagined he would be. Fuck, I just dumped my fucking bag down on the desk, right in front of him like an insane person, when every single other desk in the room is empty.

His dark eyebrow slowly curves itself into a question.

My brain short circuits. "Ah, shit. Sorry. I—I didn't—" I reach out and grab my bag, snatching it back from the desk. "I—" I don't know what the hell to say. I don't know what to do, either. I stagger back, bumping into the desk behind me, and all the while he just stares at me with those steady, penetrating brown eyes of his.

Jesus wept, Silver, pull yourself together.

"I usually sit there. Is what I meant to say," I clarify. "And I didn't see you…sitting there." For fuck's sake. That did not go well.

The new guy's mouth lifts up into an amused smirk. "I'm kinda hard to miss," he says quietly.

"Yeah, well. I wasn't paying attention, so…"

He angles his head to one side, studying me from the boots up. He looks confused. "Name?" he demands.

Okay, now that's just fucking rude. I'm suddenly not so shocked that he's in my seat anymore. I'm more…mad. Narrowing my eyes, I half-scowl at him. "Nope."

Now it's his turn to act surprised. "Nope?"

"That's right. No."

"You're not going to tell me your name?"

"Maybe if you asked for it properly, like a normal fucking person and not some sergeant major asshole handing out an order, I would tell you."

This earns me a swift bark of laughter. "All right, fine. Please, Oh Angry One, would you do me the honor of telling me your name?"

Mercifully, Professor Cline enters through the door and not a moment too soon. The towering stack of texts books in his hands wobbles, threatening to fall any moment. He curses under his breath, then curses again when he sees that two of his students have already arrived. "Sorry, guys. Sorry. Here, Silver, grab this for me, would you? I'm gonna lose it in a sec—woah!" The top book in his pile clatters to the floor. Looks like the rest of them are going to go any second, too. I lunge forward, rushing to help him.

Students file in while I help him unload the textbooks onto his desk, and the tension in the room ramps up; the guy sitting in the corner might as well be dressed as a circus clown with a face full of makeup for all the attention he's getting.

Marjorie Chen's looking at me like I've grown another head. David Moss—a guy who once told me I was breathtaking and begged me to go to spring formal with him, is now wrinkling his nose at me like I'm an apple he's bitten into and discovered to be rotten. Everyone else is casually glancing at the stranger in the corner, though, whispering furiously to each other behind the backs of their hands.

"All right, thank you, Silver. You can take your seat." Professor Cline extends his hand, about to touch me between my shoulder blades—a casual gesture to usher me toward a desk—but he stops himself at the last second, apparently thinking better of it. He gives me a tight-lipped, uncomfortable smile, then quickly looks away. In a louder voice, he addresses the rest of the room. "Yes, yes, I'm glad to see all of you are still mentally alert for this highly anticipated last session of the day. You are indeed correct. We have a new student amongst us this afternoon. Yes, he looks quite imposing. Yes, he rides a motorcycle. Please, get your behinds in your seats, or we're going to be here all day. Silver Parisi, where are you going? Take the desk next to our new friend. You're holding up traffic."

God damn it.

I had just retrieved my bag, eyes firmly glued to the floor, and was attempting to weave my way over to the other side of the room, but now I'm fucked. Now I have to sit right next to New Boy, two feet away from him; I can feel his intense eyes glide over me, inspecting me distractedly as the chorus of chatter around us slowly begins to die down. Professor Cline removes his grey blazer and hangs it from a hook on the wall behind his desk. I've never been a great judge of age, but I'd say Cline's in his mid-forties. I overheard Karen, Principle Darhower's assistant, on the phone once, telling someone that Cline used to teach at UCLA. That he'd been involved in some sort of scandal and had been relegated to teaching high school physics here at Raleigh because of it.

"All right. Let's get it all out of the way," he says, splaying his fingers in a supplicating gesture toward the group. Cline's gaze lands on the guy sitting next to me, and he sends an apologetic smile his way. "Alessandro Moretti. I said that right, yes? I'm guessing you'd rather poke both your own eyes out than stand at the front of the class and tell us all a little bit about yourself?"

My skin feels like it's on fire; my neck is prickling like crazy as I cautiously look to my right. The guy—Alessandro Moretti—clears his throat. For one eternally long second, I can't seem to rip my eyes away from the sight of his Adam's apple shifting in his throat. "Alex," he says. "And no. If it's all the same to you." The timbre of his voice is a lot like the rumble of his motorcycle's engine—deep, rich and resonant.

"Fair enough. Alex it is. We'll do a seated quick-fire round and move on, then. Guessing you're seventeen?"

Alex's dark eyes rove over the wall next to him, picking over the posters and the notices with mild disinterest. "Yes," he answers.

"You're built like you bench more than my body weight. Are you a linebacker?"

"No."

"Did you burn down your last school?"

I wouldn't call Alex's expression surprised, but he does look away from the wall; Cline's managed to snare his attention at least. "No."

"Married?"

"No."

"Kids?"

The suggestion of a smile pulls at Alex's mouth. "Not that I'm aware of."

"Ooh, careful, ladies," Cline says, laughing. "This one's got game. Are you planning on causing trouble in my classroom, Mr. Moretti?"

Alex seems to really consider his answer. After a moment's pause, he answers, "No."

"Fantastic. That's all I needed to hear. Okay, class, you have the rest of the academic year to piece together the mysterious, bad boy puzzle that is our friend Alex Moretti. Quiz him on your own time. For now, let's focus on Sir Isaac Newton. Fun fact. According to the Julian calendar in use in England at the time of old Ike's birth, he was officially born on Christmas Day. Unlucky, right? Probably hated only getting one gift at the holidays. And, Isaac Newton lived until he was eighty-five. People were dropping like flies in their late thirties back then, so in the grand scheme of things, Isaac was basically a million years old when he kicked the bucket..."

I sit through the rest of class, numb. I don't raise my hand to answer questions, but then again, I never do. Why draw attention to myself when I can just blend into the background? Cline doesn't call on me once and doesn't call on Alex, either. Fifty minutes crawl by, and my neck actually grows stiff thanks to the fact that I'm staring straight ahead so rigidly. When the bell rings, Cline blocks the doorway, holding out his hands. "Test at the end of the week, guys. It's a doozy, so study everything. I mean it. Everything. You are welcome. See you all on Friday."

A chorus of groaning floods the room, but I don't participate. My books are already packed up in my bag, and I'm ducking around Cline, bolting from the classroom like I'm fleeing a crime scene. The doors to all the other rooms are only just opening as I fly down the hall, making a break for the exit.

Once I'm in my car, I lean my forehead against the steering wheel, relief soothing my frayed nerves; I made it out unscathed.

Today was just one day, though. I pull out my cell phone and open up the calendar, doing the math. It takes a while to factor in all of the public and school holidays, but time is something I have right now. Since Mom and Dad still think I'm on the cheer squad, I have a full ninety minutes to kill before I can show up at home without raising any red flags. Eventually, I come up with a number—a large, soul-destroying number that makes me want to weep. One hundred and sixty-nine days. That's how many school days there are left between now and graduation. Reaching my car without mishap just now felt like a victory, but in the grand scheme of things, it was nothing. I'm going to have to repeat this whole, shitty, frustrating process another one hundred and sixty-nine times before I can walk away from this place for good.

I almost drop my phone, jumping at the sound of the deep rumble across the other side of the parking lot; it can only be Alessandro Moretti's motorcycle, roaring to life. Two weeks ago, I started off this academic year, determined to make it through the other side in a dignified manner, with a straight back and a defiant 'fuck you' in my eyes.

What a joke. I've been in detention once already, and the arrival of some jumped up bad boy wannabe has sent me down some weird helter-skelter of anxiety for absolutely no goddamn reason. I need to be stronger than this. I am fucking stronger than this. I need to remember who I am, the girl I used to be before one terrible night changed everything and my life disintegrated before my eyes. The old Silver would never have sulked in her car, hiding from the world, feeling sorry for herself. She would have grabbed today by the balls and forced it into submission. And if it hadn't obeyed? The old Silver would have forced it to conform, or there would have been dire consequences.

It's strange to me now that I used to be so confident. I remember feeling that way—self-assured, poised and assertive—as I stalked the halls of Raleigh High like some kind of apex predator, comfortable in the knowledge that I was untouchable. Those days feel like another lifetime. They feel like a very vivid dream I had once upon a time, real for a time during the hours I was asleep but gone the moment I awoke and found myself here, wearing the skin of someone deeply and profoundly crippled by self-doubt.

I close my eyes, thumping the back of my head against the headrest behind me a total of three times before I realize that it actually hurts, and I should stop. Fuck…this…shit. I could go to the library. I could hit up Giacomo's for a slice and do my homework in a booth, but Mom sometimes picks up a pie for Dan's kids after they finish school. If she saw me there, well, it wouldn't be the end of the world. I know I can't keep this up forever. There will come a time over the next one hundred and sixty-nine days when Mom or Dad finds out that I've been shirking the after-school activities that helped bolster my college applications, and I already know how they're going to react. They're going to freak the fuck out. Part of me thinks I should just tell them everything and get it over with. But then I imagine the look on mom's face when I delve into the finer details of my outcast status, and I just can't do it. It'll fucking kill her. She won't be able to take it.

I crack my eyes, checking Mickey, and I see that it's only ten to three. Still almost another hour to go until I can leave. Man, time really does seem to slow inside the Nova when I'm—

"Fuck!" A loud rap on the window, right next to my head, startles the living shit out of me. I slam my knee into the console, scraping the bare skin that's showing through the rip in my jeans. Damn, that hurts like a bitch. I can see blood, for fuck's sake. I'm boiling mad as I quickly wind down the window and glare at the person standing beside the car, ready to rip them a new one, when…

Alessandro Moretti slowly bends down and rests his forearms against the side of the Nova, curving a dark eyebrow at me. His bottom lip is sucked into his mouth. His leather jacket is nowhere to be seen, even though it's fucking freezing out, and it looks like it's starting to rain. Quick, intelligent, demanding brown eyes meet mine, and I react by stuttering out a jumble of syllables that don't make any sense.

"*Ju—ne—wha—do—waiiiiiiit. Youuuuu...*" I shake my head, throwing my hands up in defeat when I run out of potential sentence starters.

A deep frown forms between his charcoal eyebrows. "*Non sembrava Italiano. Doveva essere Italiano?*"

I just blink at him. "Excuse me?"

His lips purse, his mouth lifting up at one side. Am I imagining it, or does he look weirdly disappointed? His eyes aren't just brown; they're full of cinnamon, gold, honey, and caramel—all warm tones. So how the fuck do they somehow manage to look frosty as his gaze flits around the inside of the Nova, settling on the guitar case that's sitting on the back seat. He huffs down his nose, then pulls away from the window. "Never mind," he says in English.

He spins around and walks away, the back of his grey t-shirt spattered with rain, clinging to his back, and I'm left staring after him with my mouth hanging open.

Never mind?

What does that mean, never mind?

Did I just fail some sort of test? He was asking me if I spoke Italian or something; I heard the word 'Italiano' twice in pretty quick succession. But to just bail when I don't understand? That seems like a bit of a dick move. In my mind, I lean out of the window, and I yell after him in the rain. I call him an asshole. I ask him what the hell he wanted. But I don't do that, because I'm a coward. I'm fucking scar—

Oh, shit.

He's turned around. He's coming back.

I sink back into my seat, sliding down the leather, but then I force myself to sit up straight as he arrives back at the window. "Why don't you speak Italian?" he demands.

"I'm sorry? I didn't realize it was mandatory now."

"Your last name's Parisi, right? That's what Cline called you."

"Yes?" I'm not sure what his point is, but his impossibly deep voice is rough with anger. Why the hell is he so agitated?

"Who? Who in your family is Italian?"

"Can I ask what this is about, please?"

"I'm trying to wrap my head around the fact that you have an Italian family member who didn't teach a lick of the language."

"Look, I'm not really interested in this…cultural shaming, or… whatever. I'm just… gonna… go…" I start to wind up the window. The Nova was manufactured in 1969, which means I have to do it by hand. I'm sure I'd look way cooler if I were just able to hit a button and block him out electronically, but I'm stuck with what I've got.

It's raining much heavier now. Large, fat droplets of water explode on the windshield, blocking out the looming grey shape of the single-story school building crouched on the other side of the lot. I can see the shape of Alessandro perfectly well as he walks around the front of the car, around the passenger side, opens the door, and…

…and gets in!

"What do you think you're doing?"

"I don't ride in the rain," he rumbles, as though that's answer enough.

"I can appreciate that. Motorcycles are dangerous at the best of times. What I meant to say was, what do you think you're doing getting into my car?"

He points at the school. "Better than waiting out the weather inside the cell block."

"Look, I know you're new and all, but—"

He pivots, twisting his torso to face me. His damned t-shirt is drenched, a much darker grey across his shoulders and down his chest. There are rivulets of water running down his neck, soaking into the collar of the cotton. God, what does he smell like? A light, fresh scent has flooded the car, like clean laundry and soap. It's a masculine smell, though, teasing the back of my nose, making me want to lean in...

"It was you, last Friday. In the hall. Watching me," he states.

"I wasn't watching you. I just heard voices."

"And then you stood there, in the shadows, watching me. You heard what a bad boy I've been."

"That you nearly got sent to jail? Yes." I'm not thinking about my responses before I give them. I'm just saying the first thing that presents itself to me. If I start to analyze what I'm going to say or try and be clever, my words are going to get jammed up in my throat, and I'll end up stumbling over every vowel and consonant, or worse, I won't be able to make a sound at all.

Get out of the car. Get out of the car. God damn it, Alessandro Moretti, get out of my car right now.

He looks at me, stares into me, picking over my face as if he's deciding which parts he likes, which he doesn't, and how he could improve me. I wrestle myself into stillness. Hardly the quiet stillness of the content and at ease. No, I am a possum, playing dead, in the hopes that the creature stalking me will lose interest and move on.

Alessandro doesn't go anywhere. He narrows his eyes at me. The rain drives harder against the glass, the downpour suddenly torrential, and the hammering roar of the water drums against the roof over our heads, almost deafening. Distracted by the sound, he looks away, head craned back, eyes unfocused as he listens, and the electric pressure that's been building inside the car subsides. So fucking strange that such a weight is lifted from me as Alessandro's attention slips for a second.

The sensation's a lot like finally reaching the surface of dark, deep water and urgently sucking in a lungful of much-needed oxygen. Or a brilliant light, shining straight into your eyes, blinding you to anything but its brightness, going out, leaving you blinking as you try to adjust to the world around you again.

"This place is a fucking disaster. You can sense it sucking the life out of everyone dumb enough to venture too close to it," he says absently.

"Welcome to Raleigh High, Alex Moretti," I whisper back. "Glad to hear you're settling in." Since we're here together, and it doesn't seem like he's going anywhere any time soon, I voice the burning question that's been niggling at me since last Friday. "What did you do to land yourself here, Alex? What was so bad that almost got you sent to prison. Are any of the rumors people are saying about you true?"

He stops listening to the rain. The pressure returns, pressing in on all sides, though he doesn't turn his head toward me. He faces the windscreen, eyes burning holes into the glass. "I did what had needed to be done. And I don't know if any of the rumors are true. No one's said any of them to my face."

"Yeah. Well…" I shift uncomfortably, leaning my elbow against the car door, chewing on my thumbnail. "Consider yourself lucky."

"That's right. A fellow black sheep." I hear the sharp-edged smile in his voice. "Are any of the rumors about you true, Silver?"

Heat flares in my cheeks. I'm used to all the major high school players of Raleigh High spreading the lies and hurtful gossip about me, laughing at my story of woe, disbelieving me, calling me every name under the sun, but not one of them has actually come and asked me what really happened.

The truth will set you free. I'm not a churchy person; I don't believe in God. I've read sections of the Bible in religious studies, however, and I've experienced enough of life in Grays Harbor County's tiny little backwater towns to know that this piece of scripture should come with a caveat: the truth will not always set you free. Sometimes, the truth will ruin your damn life. Sometimes, the truth will make your life a living hell, and you'll wish you kept your goddamn mouth shut.

New Boy's asking me for the truth now though, just as I asked him a second ago, and I'm torn between giving it to him and making something up. Something fantastical and unbelievable.

Something outrageous. At this point, what the fuck does it matter anyway? When it did matter, no one listened. No one cared.

I blow a frustrated breath down my nose, digging my fingernails into the top of my thigh, feel the bite of pain there and reveling in it. Needing it to calm my nerves. "I'm sure half of whatever you've heard is true. I'm sure the other half is bullshit."

"Which half is which?"

"Take your pick. It doesn't even matter anymore."

His eyes are on me. I feel his scrutiny like I might feel a hand on my shoulder—a very physical, very real thing. "Do you sell coke out of your locker?" he asks.

I bite back laughter. "Look at me. Do I look like some kind of drug kingpin to you?"

He shrugs one shoulder, looking me over. His gaze diverts from my face, down to my band tee and my plain blue jeans. He pauses on my scruffy, worn high tops and smirks. "Tough call. Some drug dealers are tattoo-covered, motorcycle-riding degenerates. Some are librarian grandmothers with RSI and a weed card."

God, he's infuriating.

"No, I do not sell coke out of my locker. If that's the real reason you came over here to harass me, then I'm afraid you're shit out of luck."

"I don't want to buy drugs from you, Silver. Remember, I'm a tattoo-covered, motorcycle-riding degenerate. I can find my own coke."

"Awesome. Why am I not surprised that you're a drug user?"

"D'you turn tricks for cash?" Alessandro doesn't even blink. From his expression, it looks as though he just asked me what fucking day of the week it is.

An uneasiness begins to creep into my bones. Surely, he didn't come here for that. "No. I don't. I'm not a whore."

He nods. "And what about the rape thing? Did you wrongly accuse a bunch of students of raping you last year?"

Ashen, my heart beating faster than it has in a long time, I force myself into making eye contact with him as I slowly shake my head. "No. I didn't," I whisper. Alessandro doesn't move a muscle. A water droplet, beaded on the end of his dark hair, falls and lands on the leather upholstery of his seat. Outside somewhere, on the other side of the parking lot, a girl shrieks, laughing, presumably running from the school building to her car in the rain. I steady myself, laying myself bare as I rebelliously stare down the abrasive boy with the slightest, softest lilt of an Italian accent to his rough, resounding voice.

Lightning flashes overhead, and three long, unbearable seconds draw out before an explosion of thunder crashes overhead. Alessandro takes a deep breath. "Not wrongly accused, then," he says. There's no accusation in his tone. No recrimination, or disbelief. He's just stating a fact. That makes it easier to admit, somehow.

"No. They weren't wrongly accused."

Alessandro turns away. He sinks back into his seat, his body relaxing—I hadn't realized he was holding himself so tensely until the moment he let himself go. The flat, even look on his face is confusing as fuck. During our very first conversation, I've essentially just told him—the guy I planned on avoiding the entire school year, on pain of death, no matter what—that I was sexually assaulted by a group of people, and...he doesn't look like the information has impacted him in any way whatsoever.

"The rain's stopping," he says after a while.

I can practically taste my own stupidity. I shake my head, reaching for the key in the ignition. I start the Nova's engine, gunning the gas. "Great. You don't believe me," I say.

"Why wouldn't I?"

"Just get out of the car please, Alessandro."

"Alex. You didn't answer my question."

I slam my fist into the steering wheel—it feels like my chest is cracking open, and a river of molten anger is pouring out like lava. "Get out of the fucking car!"

"Pretty Princess Silver. Too good for all of us. Too fucking special. Don't bite. Don't kick. Don't scream. Spread your legs and keep your mouth shut, bitch, and we'll see if we can make this quick."

Alex opens the car door, but he doesn't get out. His expression is tough to read, but none of this has unsettled him. He breathes out, slow, steady, even; it's as though the world could be ending, and he would take the whole thing in stride, without the faintest flicker of emotion.

He looks at me, and I want to smash my fist into his face. "I mean it. Get out," I snap. "It's better for you if we're not seen together anyway."

"What makes you think that?"

"You've only been here one day, so I'm sure they'll forgive the faux pas. I'm the pariah of Raleigh High. Sitting anywhere with me is the quickest, most efficient way to commit social suicide. I am broken, Alex."

To my surprise, he actually gets out. When I try and lean over to close his door, he catches hold of me by the wrist. "It's okay to be broken. You have every right to be. Just don't let them keep on breaking you. That's not how you win this particular game."

I wrench my hand free. "This isn't a fucking game."

Looking around the parking lot, as if he's seeing his surroundings for the very first time. "Of course it is," he says. "This is high school, Silver. This is the biggest game there is."

4

ALEX

Two weeks later

Let me be clear. Silver Parisi is *not* my type.

The oversized shirts and the frayed jeans aren't really sexy, per se. The Chucks make her look like a tom boy. She doesn't do anything with her hair as far as I can tell, and the touch of eyeliner and mascara she wears is hardly worth mentioning.

In the past, I've been drawn to women who take care of themselves. Girls who spend time making sure they look their best before they step foot outside the house. Recently, though, the barbie doll look hasn't been doing it for me. I used to find tight skirts and heels a turn on, but the past year or so I've found myself seriously fucking irritated by the vanity and shallow nature of the girls who've flocked around me. Sure, they might look good, but nine times out of ten they're dumber than dumb, void of any personality or opinion, and boring enough to reduce a guy to fucking tears.

Silver Parisi, on the other hand…

I felt her watching me in that hallway with Maeve and the Deputy. I felt her eyes on me and knew I was being judged. The way she refused to tell me her name in Cline's class, and the fierce defiance that blazed in her eyes when she ordered me out of her car made me really *notice* her. Now it's two weeks later, and I haven't been able to *un*-notice her ever since.

I've done everything in my power to avoid thinking about Silver. Difficult, though, when she's in at least one of my classes every day, and we usually end up seated side by side at the back of the classroom.

I haven't said one word to her since I got out of her car. Not one single word uttered. I've observed her plenty, though. There have been times when it's looked like she's preparing to talk to me, planning out what to say, but then she seems to think better of it and disappears into the crowded hallways without even opening her mouth to me.

In fairness, no one really speaks to me during my first few weeks at Raleigh. A black cloud hangs over my head, my temper ready to flare at any given moment, and the other students make a point of keeping their distance.

I'm pissed that I've been transferred from Bellingham. I'm pissed that I have to skate on such thin ice at precious, pretentious Raleigh High, and I'm extra pissed at myself that I can't seem to get my fucking head screwed on straight. See, I can't stop thinking about the girl with the baggy t-shirts and the scruffy high-tops. I can't get her unruly golden-brown hair and her intense, penetrating blue eyes out of my head. Whenever I'm walking from one class to the next, I make a point of not looking, but I always *know* where she is.

And, most fucked up of all, the more rumors I hear about her… the angrier I get. The girl's fierce. She's baring her teeth at the world every time I see her, head held high, a threat in her eyes, like a wolf backed into a corner, ready to fight at the drop of a hat.

I'm getting used to holding my breath around her. Wherever Silver goes, an oppressive tension follows her; you can feel it prickling against your skin like electricity. Without even knowing why or when I made the decision, I've realized I'm waiting for something to happen, for a match to strike or a fist to be thrown in her direction…and I'm preparing to raze the whole fucking school to the ground in her defense.

It's *so* fucking stupid.

I shouldn't get involved.

It's none of my fucking business.

I should walk away and let her deal with her own shit.

Because, as far as I can tell, from all of my silent watching and waiting, it's pretty clear that Silver Parisi hates me.

"Alex? *Hello?* What day is it today, hon? 'Cause according to my schedule, it's Monday, and Mondays are not on your visitation roster."

Goddamnit. I shake Silver out of my head, trying to focus on the woman in front of me instead, but it's difficult to really see the social worker. They're all the same. This woman, Rhonda, is wearing a flamboyant pink shirt with flowers printed all over it, and her earrings are so big they're resting on the tops of her shoulders, which does separate her from the other clones I've had to deal with in the past. At least Rhonda has some sort of personality, which makes for a change, but at the end of the day, she's still an administrator. A glorified pencil pusher, ticking boxes, thinking in the straightest of lines, unwilling to bend even the slightest amount to accommodate someone else.

"I have to work Wednesdays now, and that bitch won't let me come by on the weekends."

Rhonda makes a show of pulling a face; her earrings sway wildly as she jerks in mock surprise. "Firstly, do you think the title, '*Bitch*' is appropriate when referring to the woman who so graciously agreed to take Ben into her home and care for him like he is her own son?"

I huff out a blast of laughter that can only be described as scathing, shaking my head. "That bitch doesn't care about Ben. We both know she's only letting him stay with her because of the paycheck you guys give her at the beginning of every month. And no one asked her to treat him like he's her son. He's not her son. I'm his blood, and I should be able to see him whenever I fucking feel like it."

Rhonda pouts, displeased. I have a knack of displeasing people like Rhonda. Quite a talent, in fact. I can do it without even trying. "You are frighteningly clever, Alex. I know you're not delusional. I know you're more than acquainted with the harsh realities of the world we find ourselves in, which is why I'm so confused by the fact that you still expect life to be fair. I am a college graduate with a masters in human psychology. I should be a college professor by now, commanding a ridiculous salary, but because I'm not only black but a woman, I'm entirely unsurprised that I'm sitting here across a table from you, explaining that you cannot just do whatever the hell you please, whenever the hell you feel like it. Why did Jackie tell you not to go over there on the weekend?"

I slump back in my chair, crossing my arms over my chest. Outside, it's snowing. The view from the third-floor window of this shitbox is, admittedly, quite pretty. The stand of trees at the bottom of the hill that rolls away from the building are all dusted white. Briefly, I'm transported back to another time and another place, a smaller version of me, standing impatiently next to an old woman with cloudy eyes as she pats the side of a sieve, sending clouds of icing sugar cascading down on the wedding cookies we just made together.

"The bike. She said it makes too much noise," I tell her. "She doesn't want to disturb the neighbors."

Rhonda taps the end of her pen against the notebook on the table in front of her. "Can't you just take the bus?"

"No, I cannot just take the fucking bus! I have a means of transport. I shouldn't have to ride a bus twenty-five miles away, just to keep fucking Jackie happy. What is this, Nazi fucking Germany?"

Rhonda arches an eyebrow. "This has nothing to do with Nazis. Jesus Christ. I despair of you sometimes, boy, I really do. This is about your brother. He's ten years old, and it's good for him to have you in his life. If you need to make a few compromises in order to do the right thing by him, then—"

"Compromise? To settle a dispute by mutual concession." I push back in the chair, leaning so that the front feet hover off the floor.

"And? Your point being?"

"Me not riding my motorcycle isn't a compromise. There is no mutual concession. Jackie isn't meeting me halfway. She's just getting her own way. Sets a terrible precedent, Rhonda. Makes her think I'll bend over backward to whatever random, stupid demand she makes next. And that….is not going to happen."

Rhonda throws down her pen, sighing in frustration. She turns an open, weary look on me, and I finally do see her. She's tired. This is a thankless job at the best of times, I know that. That's why every single social worker I've ever met is jaded and completely resigned to the fact that the system is broken. "Haven't you learned how to pick your battles yet, Alex?"

I shrug a shoulder, unwilling to surrender my point of view. "If I concede on any ground, I ultimately lose. And I won't lose Ben to her. He's the only family I have in the world. As soon as I turn eighteen, I'm petitioning for custody of him. I'll take him to live with me, and I won't have to worry about Jackie's bullshit anymore."

Rhonda isn't surprised by this statement. This isn't an idea I've just snatched out of the thin air. It's always been the plan to take Ben as soon as I'm old enough. I've been waiting seven years, and now the end is in sight. Now, I only have seven more months to wait before I can become Ben's legal guardian, and we can get the flying fuck out of Washington altogether.

"Baby boy, right now, I'd say the chances of any judge awarding you custody of that child are sitting at a big fat zero," Rhonda informs me. "Take a look at yourself. You do ride a motorcycle. Your arms are more ink than skin—"

"Oh, is that how it is? I expected better from you. Given that you're not only black but a woman, I'd have thought you'd be a little less judgmental than—"

Rhonda holds up a hand, cutting me off. "Don't even try and pull that shit with me, boy. I don't have to be sitting here, wasting my time on you. I have a kid of my own, and I finished work twenty-five minutes ago. I am free to walk outta here at any time, and you can sit here with your bad attitude in silence if that's what you want. Or you can shut the hell up and listen to me."

She waits; from the look on her face, she really will get up and walk out if I say one more word, so I keep my mouth shut. At the end of the day, loathe as I am to admit it, I need Rhonda on side.

"Hmm. That's what I thought," she mutters under her breath. "I don't give a shit if you have tattoos on your damn eyeballs, Alex. I don't care if you drive a repurposed garbage truck around and refer to yourself in the third person all day like a goddamn lunatic. The only thing that matters to me is Ben's welfare. If I thought that you were mature, responsible and serious enough to take care of a ten-year-old boy, then I wouldn't hesitate in recommending Ben be placed with you once you're eighteen."

Heat prickles at the back of my neck. I grind my teeth together, wrestling to keep my temper in check. One heated, angry word and I'll only be proving her point. Somehow, I manage to affect some level of calm as I force out the words that are burning at the back of my throat. "I've been looking after myself for years, okay? Me. I worked. I bought my own food. I cooked my own meals. I learned to look out for my own wellbeing when the guy you people placed me with got wasted and beat the shit out me every night of the week that ended in the letter Y. I am more than capable of looking after my own little brother. And guess what? I'll do it for free. You won't have to pay me a goddamn dime—"

"This isn't about money, Alex—"

"And what do you mean, if you thought I was serious enough about taking Ben? I'm serious as a heart attack. The day after my birthday, I will be walking away from Jackie's place with my little brother, and there won't be a damn thing she can do about it. So please. Go ahead and tell me how that isn't serious enough for you."

"You are treating him like he's a PlayStation, Alex. Despite how you may feel, Ben is not an object or a piece of property that was confiscated from you. You don't deserve to have him handed over to you once you meet the barest of criteria, just because you share a mother and a father. That is not how this works."

Oh, god. If I even part my lips right now, I am going to fucking explode. I grind my teeth together as hard as I can, but the rage doesn't subside. I have to look away from her, back out of the window and onto the winter landscape beyond as I silently fume.

Inhale.
One. Two. Three. Four.
Exhale.
One. Two. Three. Four.
Inhale.
One. Two. Three. Four.
Exhale.

Rhonda huffs—she's obviously having trouble letting go of her own anger. Her voice is much calmer when she speaks again, though. "At the end of the day, a stuffy old man is gonna review your case. He's going to take into account your age, and the way you've chosen to decorate your body, and the fact that you ride around on a fucking deathtrap, and he's gonna form an opinion real quick. And then, he's going to look down at your file in front of him, and he's going to read that you were Tazed in an open grave ten days ago, while you were pissing on a dead man. What do you think he's going to say about that?"

I can already feel my hackles rising again. I do my level best to keep my shit together as I return my gaze to her. "I don't know. Maybe the old bastard will have a sense of humor. Or some sense of justice?"

Rhonda slowly pushes away from the table, sliding back her chair. She gets to her feet and crosses her pokey office, collecting her purse from a hook on the back of the door. "I like you, Alex. I really do. You're a smart kid. Your grades are…" She throws her hands up, her eyes rolling to the ceiling. "If you wanted to go to college, I do not doubt for one second that you'd get a scholarship based on your grades. I'm not going to bother wasting my breath trying to lead a charge on that campaign, though. Instead, I'll give you some sound advice. You need to fix your attendance. You need to start building up some extra credit. You need to create a stable, clean, safe home environment. You need to get a job—"

"I have a job."

"Shut your mouth and listen to me for five minutes. You do not have a job. You bus tables at a dive bar until the early hours of the morning, which is nothing but a huge, giant black check mark against you. Have you thought about who's gonna be there to watch Ben while you're out until two in the morning on a school night? No. Uh uh, Sweetheart. You need a proper job, with reasonable hours, and the potential to build a career for yourself out of it. If you want to stand a cat's chance in hell of becoming Ben's legal guardian, then none, I repeat, none of this is negotiable. You have seven months to accomplish all of that. You think you can handle it?"

My tongue is stuck to the roof of my fucking mouth. I feel like smashing every stick of furniture in Rhonda's office into kindling, but instead, I calmly stand, grabbing my jacket from the back of the chair. "I guess I don't have much choice, do I?"

5

SILVER

"You need to be home by four to watch Max, Sil. I have to work late, and your dad's in Spokane for some conference. Neither of us will be back before midnight." My mom's in a rush, frantically sifting through her bag in search of something. I stab a knife into the butter dish, absently smearing some onto my toast. "Can you give him dinner, Honey? And I don't mean pizza. A proper meal that has at least one green thing in it. There's forty bucks on the mail stand if you wanna go grab some groceries."

This is becoming more and more frequent, this palming-off of Max. Could be that all seventeen-year-olds end up playing stand-in parent once they get old enough, but my parents would never have dreamed of asking me to cart him around or feed him at the beginning of last year. It feels as though something's changed, and not just all my shit at school. There's been some kind of dynamic shift inside my home that feels distinctly unpleasant. Barely noticeable, but wrong.

"I'm teaching tonight. Gregory and Lou. Every Wednesday, remember?"

She stops what she's doing, her hands falling slack, the open-heart surgery she was performing on her purse suddenly forgotten. "Shit. Uhh..." She closes her eyes; the cogs inside her head work overtime for a moment as she tries to come up with a solution to this problem. "I'm sorry. How much do they pay you again? Fifty bucks? I can just give you the cash instead to make up for it."

"The money's not the problem. Dr. Coombes drops them here so he can visit their mom. She's still at St. Jude's. I can't just cancel at the last second."

"Gail's in a coma, Silver. She's not going to notice if David doesn't show up tonight."

"Mom! Jesus Christ!"

She reacts to my tone, her head jerking around, finally looking at me with wide eyes. She looks like she's about to yell at me, but then she stops herself. She pinches the bridge of her nose between her fingers, taking a deep breath. "God, I am...that was really insensitive. I don't even know what's wrong with me this morning. I'm sorry. Of course David needs to go and see Gail. And yes, you need to take the twins. Don't worry about it. I'll figure something out while I'm at work."

I say nothing. When I tear a chunk out of my toast, it feels like I'm biting into a healthy slice of guilt, though. I drop my cold breakfast onto my plate, pushing it away. "I'll pick Max up before the boys the arrive. He can play Halo while I do the class. I'll take him with me to the store afterward."

My mom nearly sags with relief. She slides across the kitchen in her sock feet, wrapping her arms around me, enveloping me in a Gucci scented hug. "Silver, you are officially the freaking best. I'm sorry to lay that on you, but I do appreciate it. Your dad and I are gonna do better at making sure one of us is always here in the evening from now on, okay? This was just an unavoidable situation." She plants a kiss on top of my head, squeezing my shoulder, and then she's back at her bag, singing under her breath as she rummages, the entire thing completely forgotten about.

Gregory and Lou's mom was T-boned at the intersection by Costco a month ago, and she's been in a coma ever since. Before the accident, Gail used to be the one who brought the boys over for their guitar lesson, and she and Mom—best friends since high school—would sit in the kitchen at the breakfast counter and drink glasses of Sauvignon Blanc until the class was over.

Mom cried for three days straight after Gail's accident. A black cloud descended on the house, and no one could breathe a word in Mom's direction without causing a fresh barrage of tears. After the third day, when Gail looked like she wasn't going to die, but everyone was unsure when, or if, she was going to wake up, Mom just…stopped crying.

She hasn't been to visit her once.

~

It's been a while since I put any real thought into what I wear to school, but for the past few weeks, ever since Alex Moretti showed up and ruined everything, I've been making changes. Every day, there's been some small concession made. It started with matching socks, even though no one was going to see them. Then matching underwear. A pretty hair-tie. Lip balm, and then actual lip *gloss*. Last week, I pulled my favorite Billy Joel shirt out of rotation because it was looking a little threadbare and ratty.

Today, though, I've done something unthinkable. As I walk through the entrance to school, my head down, I feel incredibly self-conscious in the strappy black top with the lace trim I'm wearing underneath my hoodie. It was fucking stupid to wear something that doesn't completely cover my skin. Extra, *extra* stupid to wear it for Alex Moretti's benefit, when he hasn't even looked in my general direction for the past two weeks, and I decided on day one that I didn't *want* him to notice me, either, but…

When I was eleven, there was a full solar eclipse, and everyone warned me not to look up at the sun without wearing the special glasses they gave out to us at school. I knew it would potentially damage my eyes, but I couldn't help myself. I had to take a peek.

I am *that* person.

And now here I am in a strappy black top, hoping rather recklessly that Alex might actually see *me* today, even though…

"Well, would you look at that. Parisi bothered to look in a mirror before she got dressed this morning. Boys, is…is she wearing makeup?" Jacob Weaving's voice calls from across the hall. I can feel his eyes crawling over me, and I have to fight the urge to throw up inside my locker. As always, he's hovering with Cillian and Sam in front of his locker, joking and rough-housing—they're like a bunch of fucking Neanderthals, guffawing and shoving one another as if they're somehow impressing the rest of the school with their brainless antics.

"Wonders will never cease," he continues. "Honestly, I was beginning to think you were gonna start showing up in a garbage bag. Are the short skirts and the knee-high socks gonna be making a comeback, too, Silver?"

I press my lips together, biting back the cutting retort that's just begging to be unleashed. This is nothing new. I'm used to the taunting and the sly digs he sends my way across this hallway. Some days, ignoring him is harder than others, though.

"Come on, Sil. We all miss those thighs of yours. I'm getting bored of diving into the spank bank every time I wanna jerk off. You used to love putting on a show for us."

"Gross, Jake. Why would you even bother with that hag when you have me to tempt you now?"

The cool, mocking voice belongs to none other than Kacey. I catch a glimpse of her in the mirror I have glued to the inside of my locker door, and I see the spite in her eyes as she stares at my back. Her hip is popped, jutting out to one side as she leans provocatively against the bank of lockers next to her new monster of a boyfriend. She's pouting, her lips heavily glossed, her demeanor confident and commanding, but I recognize the jealousy in her gaze. She hates me; she hates that she just caught Jake talking about my body even more.

I huff out a breath of bitter laughter under my breath as I grab my calculus book for first period and slam my locker door closed. There will come a time when she won't be desperate for that sick motherfucker's attention...

"Ahh, don't get precious on me now, baby," Jake croons. "She's got nothing on you. You are one hundred percent right. Why would I want Second Place Silver when you are first place gold?"

This seems to pacify her. God, Kacey was never a straight-A student, but she was never this stupid either. I sling the strap of my backpack over my shoulder, peeling away, hurrying down the hallway, making sure to keep my eyes on my shoes; I'm almost past them when Jake's voice echoes above the chatter of the other students.

"Hey! Hey, man. Alex, right? Has Coach talked to you about trying out for the team yet?"

God, do not look up. Do not look up.

At some point, Alex has arrived, and he's standing somewhere behind me. I quicken my pace, not wanting to witness the moment when Jake makes his move, trying to induct Raleigh's newest student into his entourage, but my progress is halted when a hand lands on my shoulder. My instant response is to whirl around, fist raised, ready to defend myself—

—but then Alex's voice is in my ear. "Steady there, *Argento*. My street cred'll be in ruins if my first fight at this shit hole is with a chick."

He places a hand in the small of my back, setting pace beside me as he urges me away from Jake and the others. I look up at him disbelievingly, daring a glance out of the corner of my eye, and there he is, dressed in black, looking like the devastatingly handsome villain of a story that I can feel being written even as he ushers me toward the women's bathrooms. He gives me a shove, and I stumble through the door, a protest already on my lips. "Dude, you can *not* be in here. Karen'll have a fit if she finds out—"

"Who's Karen?"

"Darhower's assistant."

"All right, well fuck Karen. I don't care about Karen."

I spin, so mentally turned around that I dump my bag into the wet sink beside me without thinking. Against my own better judgment, I've wanted to speak to him again. I didn't think he'd be shoving me into the bathrooms before first period this morning, though.

The black long-sleeved sweater he's wearing pulls taut across his chest; he's not as built as some of the guys on the football team. He's broad in the shoulders, though, and his biceps are defined. His jeans hang low on his hips, tight enough to be fashionable, but not that tight. His white sneakers are Adidas—Stan Smiths if I'm not mistaken. The green flash on the tongue gives them away. For the first time since he showed up at Raleigh, I really see the tattoos on the backs of his hands. On the left, a huge, intricate, black rose with vines snarled around it, thorny, winding their way around his wrist and his fingers; on his right hand, the face of a wolf, or a lion, baring its teeth in a savage snarl. I can't really make out which—

"You done?" he asks, voice hard. He slides his hands into his pockets.

"Done what?"

"Picking over me like I'm standing in a fucking line-up."

"I was just looking at your tattoos, asshole."

"I'd rather you didn't."

"They're hard to miss."

"Try harder."

"Try not to make yourself stand out from the crowd so much. Try not to cover your skin in artwork that invites people to look." I throw my hands up in the air. "You asked for people to stare at you when you did that to yourself. Don't get on my case because I'm a fucking normal, curious human being."

His scowl seems to darken the room, even though the stark fluorescent lighting overhead remains constant. "I need a favor," he rumbles under his breath.

"Hah!" I cast around, looking for the hidden camera. This guy has *got* to be joking. "You want a favor. You've ignored me for two solid weeks, after breaking into my car and insulting me for no apparent reason, and now you want something? You know, people usually try and ingratiate themselves with someone before they hit them up for something."

Alex's gaze catches on the black lace of my top. His expression remains blank. I find myself straining against the urge to pull my hoodie around myself and zip it closed. "You want me to act fake? Bullshit you?" he asks.

"No."

"Then excuse me while I don't blow smoke up your ass. I need extra credit, but I'm not joining the fucking debate team."

"So?"

"I need you to teach me to play guitar."

I reel back, caught off guard. That's not what I expected him to say. "I don't think so, Alex. I have a lot of shit going on, and this… this isn't some kind of *'bad boy tutored by the outsider, cue cute makeover and the unlikely pair are suddenly an item'* situation. That's far too fucking cliché. Plus, I don't need a damn makeover. Or a rebel boyfriend."

Oh my fucking god. Why did I even say that? That was probably the dumbest thing anyone has ever blurted out in front of a guy.

A detached, cold, hard look forms on Alex's face. There's a cold, flatness in his eyes that suddenly makes me feel very, very stupid. "I'm not *interested* in you, Argento. I definitely have zero interest in being your rebel boyfriend. All I want's the extra credit and none of the fucking drama. If you think you can help with that, then great. I can pay you in cash. If not, no big deal. I'll pay that Harriet Rosenfeld chick to teach me fucking trumpet instead. Makes no difference to me. Be under no illusions. You're nothing but a means to an end."

If he'd slapped me across the face, I'd feel less scalded right now. I roll back my shoulders, reeling through a mental Rolodex of insults to hurl at him, searching for the perfect one, but then it occurs to me that he's probably expecting me to be hurt by the words he just flung at me, and I won't play into his heavily inked hands like that. No fucking way. I grab my bag, pulling my cell phone out of the front pocket, then I hold it out to him.

"My rate's sixty bucks an hour. I have time to teach on Thursdays and Mondays, right after school. Take your pick."

"I'll take both. Has to look like I'm learning fast on paper." He eyes my phone like it's an unexploded bomb. "Am I expected to do something with that?"

"Put your number in it. I have to send you learning materials, and you're going to text me an hour before our classes to confirm that you're coming. I'm not going to waste my time, waiting around on you if you're not gonna show."

He curves a dark eyebrow at me but takes the phone and taps his number into it all the same. When he hands it back to me, he catches hold of my wrist, and I fall still. Slowly, he turns my arm so that the back of his own hand is face up, clear for me to see now. He's showing me the ink I was studying just now—it *is* a wolf. A fierce, angry looking, feral creature, with anger in its eyes. He drops his hold on me, letting my arm fall, but leans in a little closer, his gaze dipping down toward my black lacy top again. This time I can't help myself: I instinctively cover myself.

"What the hell are you doing?" I growl.

A curved, almost cruel smile lifts Alex's mouth up to one side. "You asked for people to stare at you when you dressed like that, Silver. Don't get on my case because I'm a fucking normal, curious human being."

He slaps something else into my hand, then spins on the balls of his feet and smoothly exits the girl's bathroom as if he had every right to be in here. I grimace down at the money he just gave me, then, numb and frankly a little shocked, I follow him out of the bathroom. Jacob and his crew are still standing there, taking up too much real estate in the hallway, acting like morons even though the bell's about to ring. I watch as Alex walks right up to Jake and stops in front of him, back straight, eyes flashing with sharpened steel. Surprised, I note that Alex stands a good two inches taller than Jake—something that looks like it doesn't sit well with the King of Raleigh High. Jake laughs under his breath, glancing at his boys as if Alex's intense stare isn't unnerving him in the slightest.

"Hey, man. There a problem?" He folds his arms across his chest. "You didn't seem like you wanted to talk a moment ago. Now you look like you're about to ask me for the next dance."

"Tell your coach I'll join the team," Alex bites out.

Amused, Jake makes a show of looking Alex up and down. "That's not how it works, Homie. Just 'cause you're new doesn't mean you're special. You gotta try out, just like everyone else."

A muscle pops in Alex's jaw. The air is laden with tension, to the point where my feet feel like they're glued to the ground. Horror courses through the highways and byways of my nervous system, making me vibrate with uneasy energy as Alex swipes a wave of his hair back out of his face, his nostrils flaring. "When?" he grinds out.

"Coach'll probably put you through your paces over lunch if you think you're ready for it."

Alex doesn't say anything further. He just smirks and walks away.

6

ALEX

Pretending to learn guitar is a complete and utter waste of time, and playing a sport is pretty much identical to signing up for voluntary torture, but I have no other choice. There really is no way I'm joining the fucking debate team, and I have to make an effort to show Rhonda that I'm taking this shit seriously. If that means I have to strum out a few chords and bulldoze a handful of jocks on a football field, then so fucking be it.

The apartment issue's going to have to wait for now. I have a roof over my head, but Rhonda was right; no judge in their right mind is going to look at the trailer I call home and sign off on it as a safe, secure place for a child. I'm going to need to bust my ass to make some cash for a deposit on a better place, in a better neighborhood, but that's not really a concern right now. The money's there to be made if I want it. And that in itself is my main problem. Getting another job that pays as well as my position at the bar is going to be challenging to say the least.

If only I could get paid to *lie* for a living, I'd be rolling in cold, hard cash by the end of the fucking week. I barely even blinked back in that bathroom when I told her I wasn't interested in her. I sounded seriously unimpressed by the very idea that I might be into Silver, that I was laughing at the very concept of an attraction between the two of us. I managed to sound that way, even as I was fighting the urge to pick her up, wrap her legs around my waist, pin her to that vile yellow tiled wall behind her and shove my tongue down her throat.

From the moment she dumped that bag on the desk in front of me, she's been plaguing my thoughts, day and night. I tried to tell myself on the way to Raleigh this morning that guitar lessons were nothing but an easy way to get where I need to be with the family court, but I'm no fool. There are other reasons why I chose her…

I saw the embarrassment creeping into her expression when I cut her down; I know I got a rise out of her. And inside, in the very pit of my stomach, that hadn't *exactly* felt good. I did tell her the truth, though. I don't want any drama, which means no romantic bullshit, no miscommunication, no stupid, childish games, and absolutely no distractions. Ben's the only thing that matters right now, and I can't afford to deviate from this course of action, no matter how weirdly drawn to her I feel.

Silver.

Who calls their kid Silver? I read about a kid named Bus Shelter in New Zealand once, so I suppose it could have been much worse, but still…

I make a conscious effort not to speak to another living soul for the rest of the morning. I'm so accustomed to existing in a heavy, sullen silence that having to string so many sentences together the moment I stepped foot inside the building this morning has put me in a bad fucking mood, and so I button my lip and keep myself to myself. Sam Hawthorne, one of the meatheads that was hanging out with that Weaving asshole in the hallway, tries to start shit with me. As I make my way to a back-row seat in Spanish class, second period, he shoves me, standing in the way, but I hold the fucker's gaze, making it plain what'll happen to him if he doesn't move. He deflates like a popped balloon and scuttles off to sit by the window on the other side of the room.

After that, I wait for lunch to roll around, boiling away on a constant simmer. My best friend, Anger, has an issue with personal boundaries. It shows up uninvited nearly every day and makes a nuisance of itself, roaring in my ears, too brash, too loud, until I can't hear anything over it. I've come to accept anger as a constant in life, just as I've accepted that the sky is blue (or rather grey, here in Washington), and that night follows day; it feels completely normal to be consumed by my own bubbling rage as I forge a path down the hallway once midday arrives, heading for the locker rooms.

This might actually be fun. Get out onto the field. Run so hard your lungs hurt. Feel your muscles burn. Remember you're alive.

The track pants and the red 'Raleigh High, Home of the Roughnecks' t-shirt Maeve gave me fit well enough. I'd tossed them into my locker, fully intending never to use them, and yet here I am, two weeks into my Raleigh career, donning them in the hopes that I'll be accepted onto the football team. At Bellingham, I did more than scorn the football team. I made it my own personal mission to disrupt as many of their games as possible. I flooded the field, stole the posts, spread manure from goal line to goal line, put Ipecac in the team's Gatorade, until the principal finally began to suspect I had something to do with the repeat incidents and banned me from attending events or going within a hundred feet of the field. So now, stepping out onto Raleigh's pristine, highly manicured field, this is all beginning to feel a little…hypocritical.

A tall guy with a ginger mustache is yelling at a kid on the other side of the grass, getting in his face as the kid stares down into the football helmet in his hands. He has to be a freshman. Must be. He's reedy. Small, even for a fourteen-year-old. His immature physique isn't helped any by the fact that he looks like he's about to cry.

"How you're related to your brother, I don't fucking know. Your mom always was a little free with her affections. She spread her legs for a different dude every week when she attended Raleigh. Maybe she fucked the mailman and you, Oliver, are the unhappy byproduct. I don't wanna see you back on this field until you've grown some fucking balls. You hear me? I don't care if your brother runs this entire school. You won't be embarrassing me by wearing that uniform until you've damn well earned it." The coach glimpses me off to the right, watching the exchange, and he sets his jaw.

I learned at a young age to assess men very quickly; when you're passed from pillar to post as often as I was, performing an accurate threat assessment on the guy who's supposed to be looking out for you becomes a vital skill. This man is one of the worst kinds. I read a lot on him in the first three seconds when he straightens and faces me: power hungry, because inside he feels unvalued and worthless; ex-military, was probably deployed but sent home on health grounds. Mental health, I'm guessing. Guys like him don't accept a fifty-one-fifty lying down. He probably fought it. Railed against the decision that he was unfit for service, and then became embittered and soured against the world when they forcefully ejected him from active duty.

He grew up without a father, which is how he inadvertently ended up here, pretending to be one to all of us poor, misguided miscreant youths. In the morning, when this harrowed, worn, rejected man gets out of bed and looks at himself in the mirror… he's so unhappy with what he finds staring back at him that he takes it out on the world around him.

I have met his type before, and let's just say this: it has never ended well.

"Alessandro Moretti. You don't look Italian to me," he says. There's a large embroidered 'Q' on the left breast pocket of his ultra-white polo shirt. Presumably, this stands for Quentin—I already know this is the guy's last name. It's plastered all over the local newspaper clippings that are tacked to the notice board inside the locker room.

"Coach Bobby Quentin leads Raleigh Roughnecks to State."

"Raleigh local, Coach Quentin, whips Roughnecks into shape pre-spring training."

It all seemed pretty masturbatory. Grab a blue light and shine it on that notice board, and I'm fairly sure the whole thing'd be covered in Coach Bobby Quentin's jizz.

I sigh down my nose. "What does an Italian look like?" I offer. "Isn't that the same as telling someone they don't look American?"

Quentin's top lip curls up, signaling his confusion. "Don't get smart with me, boy. You know what I mean. You've seen an Italian on T.V."

This…is just about the strangest, weirdest, dumbest…fucking… thing I've ever heard in my life. "So…I'm supposed to look like Tony from the Sopranos? Five foot seven? Pudgy 'round the belly? Balding? Spaghetti sauce around my mouth?" I pretend to wipe something from my lip.

Quentin eyes me like he's trying to figure out if I'm fucking with him or being serious. Man, the guy must have played football in high school himself. He's definitely taken a few knocks to the head. After a long pause, his eyes narrowing further and further until they're nothing more than slits, the coach slides his clipboard underneath his arm and points a finger at me. "I don't appreciate your attitude, boy. And I didn't like the Sopranos either. If you want to be a member of this football team, the sass has gotta go. Is it permanent, or is there an off switch? 'Cause if it's permanent, you might as well walk off this field right now and don't come back."

Holy shit, I'd fucking love to do it—walk off this field and never come back. But I think of Ben, stuck at that bitch's house, waiting for me to go get him, thinking I fucking abandoned him there and just left him, and I swallow down the fire in my throat.

Hard. It's really fucking hard to do. "I'm just here to try out. Nothing more. You won't get any trouble from me."

Quentin squints. Funnily enough, he looks just like James Gandolfini when he does it. "You a team guy?" he asks.

The winning smile I send his way must dazzle the shit out of him. "Sure am." I refrain from mentioning that Maeve's file on me clearly states, 'Does Not Play Well With Others' in big, bold letters on the very first page.

"Alright, then. Suicides. Move. And don't you dare stop running 'til I say you can stop."

∽

SILVER

I'm sure he can't see me, but I feel the need to duck down behind the bleachers all the same. Pathetic, really. Technically, the fact that I'm here, watching Alex try out for the football team is not my fault. I can't help it if I just so happened to decide to eat my lunch here today…

This should be the last place I'd want to come, really, what with this being Jacob's territory, but the team is rarely out here during lunch. On the odd occasion Coach has them out here running drills, I make sure I'm far, far away, usually in the library, or taking refuge in my car. Today, I figured I would risk an unwelcome encounter in the hopes that I could watch what goes down with New Guy.

I keep calling him that in my head, hoping the tactic will force some mental space between Alex and me, but so far it hasn't been all that successful.

I don't even know why I care about him. Yeah, he's attractive, but before, when I was hanging out with Kacey and the girls, I would have screwed up my nose at him, deeming him too low on the social food chain to warrant my attention. The tattoos alone would have had me hugging the opposite walls of the hallways whenever he was around, purely so the other girls wouldn't have thought I was interested in any way. There was a lot of that kind of stuff before—me acting in particular ways, to make sure I was always seen in a particular light by Kacey and the Sirens. Mostly Kacey.

But now…it's almost freeing in a way, my exile from the glory of Kacey Winters' good graces. I find that I'm learning more and more about myself every day, now that I'm no longer trying to be her. And it turns out, for better or for worse, that I'm reluctantly attracted to the hostile bastard that's currently sprinting back and forth up and down the length of the football field.

I unwrap the sub I made myself this morning and take a bite. I relish the burn of the hot sauce I slathered all over the sandwich, enjoying the reaction in my mouth as Coach halts Alex and sets him to linemen drills, getting him to alternate between hitting and blocking on the padded blocking sled he's set up on the field. Alex doesn't even break a sweat. Correction: Alex does break a sweat. A large, dark patch forms in the red material of his t-shirt, right between his shoulder blades, and I find myself transfixed by the idea that he would fall prey to such a regular, normal physical response; it feels as though he should be exempt from all mundane, everyday bodily functions.

What I mean to say is that he makes every single challenge Coach Quentin throws his way look easy. Far too easy. He's going to ace this tryout, and then he's going to be on the fucking football team. Alex may have made a show of being disagreeable with Jacob this morning, but there's no way he can join the football team and not be in Jake's back pocket. Literally no way. Jake's father paid for the damn college-level field Alex is standing on right now. Mr. Weaving also pays for a team nutritionist, a sport's physiotherapist, and a masseuse for the players before especially big, critical games. Darhower would never allow anything to jeopardize that. Alex could be the best football player in the world, and he would still be booted from the team if Jake decreed it so.

I look down, finding to my surprise that my sub is gone. I've eaten every last bite without registering it, as I've followed Alex's form up and down the field. My cold brew coffee's vanished, too. Should have paid more attention. The cold brew's usually my favorite part of lunch, and now I'm just sitting here with the sour, metallic taste of unease in my mouth. Justified, it seems, when Coach Quentin reaches out to shake Alex's hand. If I needed a sign that this was a done deal, then the handshake is it.

Coach Quentin gives Alex several papers—probably the team practice schedule and their calendar of preliminary games—then he stalks off the field, leaving Alex standing there, staring down at the papers with a bewildered, unhappy look on his face that I find instantly confusing. He was determined to gain extra credit. Like, determined. A guy like him, on his last warning before jail? There's a reason why he needs that extra credit, and it's an important one. I would have thought making it onto the team would have made him happy, but the look on his face is far from it as he clenches his hand around the papers and he slowly makes his way back toward the locker rooms.

It's lucky that I made him put his cell number into my phone earlier in the bathroom. I'm going to need to give him the bad news. It doesn't matter if I'm attracted to him or not: if he's going to wind up being just another one of Jacob's puppets, then I won't be teaching him guitar. I doubt he'll lose a moment's peace over it, but I also won't be associating myself with him again. Whatever brief acquaintanceship was forged between us during our two, equally brief encounters just fizzled out and died an irreparable death. I, Silver Parisi, will never be speaking to Alessandro Moretti again.

7
ALEX

I find the piece of paper wedged inside the vents of my locker door; I almost don't even bother to unfold and read it, but my own damned curiosity gets the better of me. It's a flyer. An invite, really.

'Scuntapalooza – Chez Leon. Friday night @ 8. BYOB!'

Scuntapalooza? I'm not even gonna pretend to know what the fuck that means. Printed on the red paper in black ink is a crude drawing of Big Foot smoking a giant joint, with veiny, bloodshot eyes. I laugh to myself at the BYOB remark. I haven't been introduced to a Leon yet, but he's a fucking sad sack if he hasn't figured out how the hell to get his hands on a keg or two at the ripe old age of seventeen. I ball up the flyer in my hand and I lob it at the trash can; the projectile arcs perfectly through the air and disappears.

"Nice. Didn't even touch the sides."

I turn toward the female voice, half expecting to find Silver standing beside me, but it isn't her. Instead, a girl with bright, startling green eyes and skin the color of honeyed cinnamon is leaning against the locker next to mine, her head resting up against the locker door. Her hair's a wild mass of corkscrew curls, tumbling around her face to her shoulders. First thought: *you're pretty enough.* Second thought: *now go the fuck away.*

She smiles broadly, expectantly, like she's waiting for me to drop down to my knees and worship her. I'm sure guys do that a lot around her. She could have been an Egyptian Goddess in a past life. "Shouldn't be so quick to turn down an invite like that, though," she tells me. "They don't come around very often."

"Doubt I'm missing anything." I dump my notebook in my locker and slam the door closed, pushing away. I'm hoping she won't follow…but she does.

"I'm Zen, by the way." She rolls her eyes playfully. "I know. Weird name, right? My parents are the biggest hippies."

"They must be really disappointed in you then."

She falters, irritation flashing in her cat-like eyes. "I'm sorry?"

"Hippies don't often bring up daughters to lust after three-hundred-dollar purses." I point down at the black leather obscenity dangling off her arm, and she slaps a hand to a chest, feigning surprise like she just noticed the damn thing hanging there.

"Oh, wow. Yeah, this was expensive. Thank you. You get what you pay for with products like this though, right?"

I grind to a halt, unable to keep the incredulity from my face. I'm about to ask her how the fuck she just took my backhanded insult as a fucking compliment, when I register the way she's preening and figure it wouldn't be worth it. "Can I help you with something? I'm trying to get to my next allotted torture session."

"Allotted torture session. Hah. That's funny."

God, she's one of those people. The *I'm-going-to-tell-you-that-you-said-something-funny-instead-of-just-fucking-laughing* people. I am so turned off right now.

Zen flutters her eyelashes, pouting a little. "You know, Kacey might be off the table now that she's dating Jake, but there are still three other Sirens for you to choose from. I just wanted to introduce myself, and, y'know. Mark your card."

I stare at her blankly. "I have no idea what you're talking about."

"Come on, Alessandro." She blushes in a way that feels practiced. "This is the twentieth century. We're progressive here at Raleigh." She reaches out and lays her palm against my chest. "Most guys consider it a compliment when a Siren hits on them."

Oh, my good god. What the fuck is happening right now? This has got to be a joke. Gingerly, I take hold of her hand and remove it from my chest. "*Alex*," I say. "My name is *Alex*. And…you do know it's the twenty-*first* century, right?"

She blinks, her brows pulling together. "Dude. Of course. That's what I said."

"All right. Well…" I don't have time for this. Or the fucking energy. I turn around and walk away, leaving her standing there. This time, mercifully, she has enough common sense to let me go.

8
SILVER

Wrangling Max during the twins' lesson is easier than I anticipated. It costs me five bucks and a Hot Pocket, but it's a price I'm willing to pay. When Dr. Coombes arrives to collect the boys, flustered and all over the place, I feel so bad for him that I offer him a cup of coffee and a chance to sit down for a second. It never occurs to me that he might accept, but when he looks at me, his eyes a little wild and distant, I realize that he probably hasn't simply sat down to drink a cup of coffee in a very long time.

He's way older than Mom and Dad, somewhere in his midforties. Mom always used to take me to him to get my eyes tested when I was a kid. Everything about him is normal. He wears regular, smart clothes. His hair is a medium brown, and his eyes are a steady, reassuring blue. He was calm, and always nice to me—and in return, I was always terrified of him. I hated going for eye exams. I hated having to put my chin on the metal stirrup. I hated having a light shone in my eyes until I could see the alien, weirdly textured back of my own retina. Most of all, I was afraid that I was going to fail, that Dr. Coombes was going to tell my mom those three, awful words that would signal the end of my life as I knew it: 'She needs glasses.'

Sitting at the counter now, staring into his coffee, Dr. Coombes' presence no longer fills me with a deep sense of dread. I just...I feel sorry for the guy. I shift awkwardly from one foot to the other. "I'm so sorry about Mrs. Coombes. Have they said anything? Is she getting better?"

Dr. Coombes scans the kitchen, as though he's misplaced something, but he can't quite remember what. "Uh, no. No, they haven't said anything. Just that she's stable. They're not really sure what's going on with her."

I don't know what to say to this. Outside, Max is showing Gregory and Lou the fort he made two summers ago. It's raining, the sky a roiling mass of grey, and it feels as though the weight of the heavy clouds overhead is pressing down on top of the house and the walls are about to buckle under the strain. "I'm sorry to hear that, Dr. Coombes."

He waves me off with a flick of his wrist. "You can call me David now, Silver. You're, what? Sixteen?"

"Seventeen."

He nods. "Seventeen. Okay. Wow. Time seems to be speeding up every goddamn day."

"Yeah. My Nona keeps warning me that it only gets quicker, too. She keeps on telling me, Appreciate your youth, Silver." I imitate Nona's heavily accented, raspy voice. "Appreciate your figure. Appreciate your health—"

"Forget that shit," Dr. Coombes says. "The thing you really need to treasure, the only thing you should value above anything else at your age is the complete and utter lack of responsibility. No mortgage. No bills. No taxes. No impossible decisions, or people looking to you for comfort. Shit gets real, Silver, and it gets real fast. Nothing in here really changes." He taps the side of his head. "You start finding grey hairs. You notice a few more lines on your face.

Your back starts to ache when you sit down for too long. But everything else...the whole 'older and wiser' line they spin you in high school. Don't believe a fucking word of it. It doesn't matter how old any of us get. We're all still fumbling around in the dark, pretending like we know what the fuck is going on. What the fuck we're supposed to do. But when we climb into bed at night, we're still gripped by the same sense of panic we felt when we were teenagers. Believe me. We are all just making this shit up as we go along."

"Well. That's one way to make a girl feel optimistic for the future." I take a sip of my own coffee, wanting to hide my entire face inside the mug.

"God, I'm sorry. I didn't mean to be such a downer. I'm just... I'm so fucking tired." He looks it, too. The large, puffy bags under his eyes have aged him at least ten years. He lifts his head, watching his sons out of the kitchen window as they follow my brother into the copse of trees that marks the boundary of our yard and the beginning of the Walker Forest. Max's yellow rain jacket is easy enough to spot through the bare, spindly trunks of the trees. Gregory and Lou's matching green jackets are a little harder to see, though. I go to the back door and yell their names into the impending dusk.

When I turn around, Dr. Coombes is on his feet, putting his own coat on. Out of nowhere, he pulls me into a quick, tight hug and then releases me just as quickly. "Thank you for listening, Silver. It's nice to be heard for a couple of minutes."

The boys barrel into the kitchen, whooping, full of energy, tracking mud all over the tiles. "Oh, Jesus, I'm sorry. Where are your paper towels?" Dr. Coombes scans the kitchen counters, but I stop him before he can get carried away.

"It's fine. Please. Get on the road before the rain worsens. I've got this. It's no problem."

He sags with relief, as if I've just told him I've seen the future and his wife is going to wake up, happy and healthy next Tuesday, and his life is going to go back to normal really, really soon. "Thanks again, Silver. You're a good girl."

Absently, he places down three twenty-dollar bills on the kitchen table, and it feels as though he isn't paying for the guitar lesson I just gave to the twins. It's as though he's paying me for something else: the moment of peace and quiet I gave to him, while I let him sit in the kitchen and stare into an untouched cup of coffee.

Later, I sit with Max on the couch, watching Jeopardy, thankful that he's oblivious to most of the shit that's going on around him. He's small for his age—almost the shortest kid in his class. He's still obsessed with comics and loves animals. If Max could have a dog, his life would basically be fucking made. His hair is fine like Mom's but dark like Dad's. There's something delicate about him. He isn't rough and tumble like other boys. I worry sometimes that something hard will happen to him one day, the same as something happened to me, but it won't galvanize him. It will break him instead, and I will have gone off to college and left him here alone with our absentee parents.

Max wriggles his toes, digging his feet underneath my legs—something he's always done when his feet are cold. "Do you think Greg and Lou's mom's going to die?" he asks. He's still fixed on the television screen, still scooping melted ice cream onto his spoon and ladling it into his mouth, but I can feel that his attention is now on me. This question's obviously troubling him.

I squeeze his calf, and he grumbles, jerking his leg away. Turns out physical reassurance from his big sister isn't cool anymore. "I don't know, Maxie. I don't think the doctors know, either."

"How can the doctors not know? They know everything."

I remember still believing that doctors were infallible, all knowing, all powerful beings that never put a foot wrong. It wasn't too long ago that I still believed that, if someone was sick and they went to the hospital, then they were sure to get fixed and be just fine afterward. It came as a shock to me to realize that, just because it was a doctor's job to fix people, didn't mean it was possible every single time.

Sometimes, there's nothing that can be done. Sometimes, people just fucking die and no matter how hard we object, or fight, or battle with that, it can't be changed.

I don't want to be the person to tell Max any of that. Our parents brought Max into the world. They need to be the ones to break it to him that occasionally it's a cruel, hurtful, horrible, fucked up place, where sometimes Moms get hit by cars, and they don't wake up from comas.

"I don't know all the answers, Maxie," I murmur. "Things are complicated sometimes. Would it make you feel better if I called Mom?"

He blinks owlishly at the T.V. "No. It's okay. It's just really sad for Greg and Lou. That's all."

I move his legs and scoot across the sofa, drawing him into my side. He doesn't shrug me off this time. "I know, Bud. It is, isn't it?"

9

ALEX

The bar's heaving, packed to the rafters, the smell of damp lying heavy in the air. Every time a new customer walks in through the door, a good-natured roar goes up inside the Rock, the patrons already parked at the bar and crowded around the pool tables hurling a shower of peanut shells at the offenders guilty of letting the heat out.

The jukebox has been cycling through White Snake and ACDC all night, sporadically interrupted by the sounds of The Eagles and Creedence Clearwater Revival. Behind the altar, the name the Rock's locals call the huge, sticky slab of mahogany that forms the length of the bar, Angela and Maisy have been busting their asses for the last six hours, working their hardest to make sure everyone has a drink in front of them at all times.

And me? I've been clearing tables, running food, watching the drunkest guys for any signs of hostility, and fielding the unwelcome advances of at least three middle-aged women who all seem intent on 'making me a man.' This always happens when I'm working at the Rock. Women get it into their heads that, because I'm young, I'm still a retiring wallflower virgin who's never had his dick touched. Little do they know I could spend the night teasing them into fits of hysteria if I wanted to. They'd forget their own fucking names and lose all motor function if any of them could coax me to slide in between their bedsheets. They won't, though. Unlike other guys my age, I'm capable of maintaining focus once the subject of potential sex comes up, and besides…I don't shit where I eat. I have nothing against older women. Older women can be sexy as hell. But I like my job, and I like bringing in a paycheck, and I'm not dumb enough to risk any of that for one night getting my dick sucked.

"Hey, Alex! Alex, Montgomery's asking for you!" Maia hollers across the bar. She's in the middle of pouring three different drinks but she still somehow manages to hold up a black, corded handset to show me that the owner of the bar is waiting for me on the other end of the line. I spit out the toothpick I've been toying with between my teeth and vault over the altar, accepting the phone from her.

"Hey, man. What's up?"

"Got a girl out back. Wants to try out," a gruff voice informs me. "She's young. Probably too young. Get out there and clock her. Tell me if you know her face."

Montgomery runs with a club. A dangerous one. On the weekends, it amuses him to have girls strip for his buddies, and sometimes he calls on me to wait with the girls, to make sure none of his boys gets too handsy with them. Every once in a while, he has me head out back to see if I recognize them before he lets them out onto the bar floor to perform. Bad for business, he says, if a chick below the age of eighteen shows up, trying to earn herself a cool grand by artlessly taking her clothes off on a Wednesday night. Doesn't work out in anyone's favor, especially if the cops show up and shut the place down. It's happened before.

"Sure thing." I hang up the phone and head through the back, stepping over a pile of empty Corona boxes that have been tossed back here by the girls. Past the kitchen, and then past Monty's office, I hurry down the corridor and boot the back emergency exit open, throwing my shoulder into the door when it sticks.

In the alleyway behind the Rockwell, a startled girl with bright blonde hair nearly jumps out of her skin when the door swings back and hits the wall by the dumpsters. Her dark eyes shine brightly. She's wearing a coat with a fur trim around the collar and red PVC knee-high boots with a heel that could be used as a fucking prison shank. She nearly shits herself when she sees me.

For once, I do recognize her, and I don't know what she's told Montgomery, but she is not eighteen. This girl is in my fucking biology class; her name is… fuck, it's right on the tip of my tongue. She pales when our eyes meet. "Oh, shit. It's you."

"Likewise." I turn to head back inside. "Look, I can't lie to the boss. He wants to know if you're old enough to dance, and you're not, so…"

"Please. Wait. Alex, right? I need the money, okay. My mom's blown her entire paycheck at the casino. Again. We can't be late with the rent this month, or our asshole landlord's going to kick us out. I can—"

"Stop. You have to be eighteen. There's nothing I can do."

Her eyes have grown round. Bright with unshed tears. This is obviously not an act; I've borne witness to enough of those before to see this for what it is: sheer desperation. I'm not unsympathetic to her situation. Far from it. I've been corralled into some seriously dark corners when I've been struggling to make ends meet, too, but lying to Monty is just something that I cannot, will not do. She looks like she's about to burst into tears. "Look. I can take you in to see Monty. Maybe there's some other way for you to earn out tonight, but I'm going to be honest with him. You read me?"

Somehow, I've conjured hope into her eyes with this suggestion. I immediately kick myself. Monty's hardly a bleeding heart. Definitely not one for sob stories. Still, this is all I can do for her, so it is what it is. She follows me into the building, unsteady in her stripper heels. I have to catch hold of her at one point to make sure she doesn't topple over. She shoots me a grateful smile, but not a single word is passed between us as I lead her back up the corridor toward Monty's office. I knock once and wait for him to call us in before I push the door open.

Montgomery's office is not what you might expect. It's clean, for starters, while everything else at the Rockwell bears a patina of grease and sticky, spilled alcohol. On the wall, landscape paintings depict balmy summer scenes from Tuscany and Provence. Behind Monty's white marble desk (completely clear, besides a computer screen and a single framed photograph of Montgomery's dear departed mother, Babs), the man himself sits, wearing a bright red Christmas sweater with Rudolph emblazoned across the front of it.

"S'up, Kid," Monty mutters. He's yet to look up at me from his computer screen. His bright hair is long, tied back into a ponytail with a leather thong. Angela always says he reminds her of Brad Pitt from 'Legend of the Falls.' For a nearly sixty-year-old guy, he's in pretty decent shape.

"Well?" he asks.

"Seventeen. Senior at Raleigh," I tell him.

Montgomery huffs. He finally looks up, his eyebrows forming one, bushy line. He quickly glances at the girl beside me and sighs. "What are you doing here, sweetheart? You're still a baby. This place ain't for you."

The girl takes a deep breath and shrugs. "I don't have any other choice. This is the end of the road. I either come in here and I make money, or my family is out on the street. End of story."

"I don't like when need drives young women to my doorstep. If they don't want to dance, then they're not gonna be good at it."

"I am good at it. And I can fake enthusiasm just like all the other women you've ever met, believe me." Her voice doesn't shake, which is pretty fucking impressive.

Montgomery leans forward across his desk. "Forgive me for

saying so, Sweet Thing, but you don't look like you got much meat on you."

"Forgive me for saying so, but you're wrong." She unfastens the fur-trimmed coat and lets it drop from her shoulders, revealing a heavily doctored Raleigh High cheerleading outfit. The skirt barely covers the top of her thighs, and the cropped top had been hacked low around the neck, displaying her considerable cleavage. The girl has tits, that's for sure. Montgomery's eyes her critically, like he's assessing a horse before buying it, testing to see if it's sound.

"All right. Point made," he concedes. "When's your birthday?"

"December eleventh," the girl replies.

"Fine. You can dance here, starting tonight, but you don't get naked until December twelfth. Understand?"

She nods, covering herself with her coat again.

"And you dance upstairs only. No dancing down in the basement."

"Why, what's in the basement?"

Monty squints at her. He's deciding whether or not to tell her the truth, but in the end, he doesn't have much of a choice. If she's gonna dance here at all, she's gonna find out all of the Rock's secrets soon enough. "A club. A *kink* club. People go down there to fuck. If you're smart, you'll give the place and the customers a wide berth. You stay upstairs on the bar floor, you strip down to your underwear, and then you take whatever tips you make and get out of here. I see so much as a nipple and you're done. Have I made myself clear?"

"Yes, Sir."

"Polite. Good. I like that. What's your name?"

"Halliday, Sir."

Monty grunts. "Whenever you walk through the door of this establishment, you're no longer Halliday. You're Billie. Your very first stripper name. Lucky you. Consider yourself christened. Now get the hell out of here before I change my mind."

"Thank you, Mr. Montgomery." Looking a little nervous, Halliday quickly backs out of his office.

Monty shoots me a weary look that speaks volumes. He thinks I'm a moron for even bringing her before him and he's not afraid to show it. "Keep an eye on her, Moron. You vouched for her. She's your responsibility now."

Great. Just what I fucking need.

I'm back out on the bar floor and Halliday, or rather Billie is set up on the stage, when I feel my phone buzz in my back pocket. The text is from a number I don't recognize.

(253) 441 9678. Sorry, classes are off. I can't teach you. Harriet's a great trumpet teacher. Best of luck – S.

10

SILVER

I was prepared for some fallout after the message I sent to Alex last night, but I'm hardly expecting him to be waiting at the foot of the stairs for me first thing this morning. He's wearing a Billy Joel t-shirt and a face like thunder. I manage a warped smirk as I walk past him, into the building. "If you think you're gonna win me over with a t-shirt, you're sorely mistaken."

"What?"

"The Billy Joel…never mind. Look, I'm sorry, but I'm in the same boat as you. I don't want any drama either, and if you're gonna be rubbing shoulders with the football team, then as far as I'm concerned, you're damaged goods."

"Of course I'm damaged goods. What does the football team have to do with—" He stops short, as if he's *just* pieced together why I hate them so much. "Oh."

"Yeah. *Oh.*"

"Why didn't you say something?"

I screech to a halt, and he nearly walks right into my back. I'm fizzing with the beginnings of anger as I face him. "I'm sorry, do I owe you an explanation for anything I do? Am I indebted to you in some way?"

His expression is stony. The muscles in his jaw tic like crazy as he flips a set of keys over and over in his hand. "Play nice, *Argento*. What makes you think I'll be rubbing shoulders with any of those meatheads?"

"Because that's how things work around here, okay. If you're on the team, you are *on the team*. I can't help you."

"You can't, or you won't?"

"I won't."

"Okay. Fine. But I already paid for my first two lessons. You have to get me started at least."

God, the gall of this guy. I've already put the money he gave me in an envelope. I take it out of my jacket pocket and thrust it at him. "I was gonna slide it into your locker, but I guess this saves me the trouble. Here. Take it back."

He doesn't take it back. "That's not how this works. You agreed to two lessons. I'm getting them."

I let my hand fall slack. "Jesus, Alex. Why is everything so damned difficult with you? Just take the money and leave me alone, okay. I just want to get through this year, graduate, and get the fuck out of here. Please. You're making a scene."

"Two lessons. Then I'll be out of your hair, and you won't have to worry about me complicating your plans. I promise."

"What does it even matter? Do you think I'm gonna change my mind or something? Because I won't. I will out-stubborn you every step of the way, believe me."

"Oh, I believe you."

"Moretti!" The shout rings out across the parking lot. It's Jake. Every single muscle in my body tenses at the sound of his boisterous voice. Alex frowns when he sees my reaction to the guy, and a dark, ominous look spreads over him.

"Him?" he says.

"Yeah, *him*. Now, please, just take the money…"

"I'll see you after school, *Argento*. Don't stand me up. You won't like what happens if you do."

"Alex. *Alex!*" It's too late. He's jogging off down the steps, towards Jacob and his crew, and my heart is plummeting in my chest like a lead weight. It feels like it's about to fucking explode when Alex reaches out and accepts Jake's bro handshake like they're suddenly the best of fucking friends. My mouth is hanging open.

Horrific timing, really, since Kacey and the girls choose right now to saunter up the steps. My ex-best-friend sneers as she shoulders her way past me. "Catching flies again, Silver? I'd watch out if I were you. One of these guys might find something to slip in there again if you're not careful."

The girls all titter like the mindless mannequins that they are. I glare after them, which is the only reason why I catch Halliday looking back over her shoulder, her face the very picture of conflict. At first, I think she's staring at me. But then, I realize with a sick weight pressing down on my chest, that she's actually looking at Alex.

11

ALEX

I make nice with the kid who hurt Silver, and it costs me dearly. I fucking hated him before I knew what he did to her, but now...

Now, I want to fucking *kill* the bastard.

"Leon's parties are legendary, man," he tells me, throwing his arm around me as we head inside. "Half the school's still talking about the last one, and that went down, like, nine months ago. His cousin's a DJ in L.A. He always comes up here to play a set. There's plenty of booze, and the girls..." He shakes his head, laughing. "The girls get fucking crazy, man. You're guaranteed to get laid, no matter who you are. Last time, I fucked three different girls and they were all hot for it."

He spins a sordid, repulsive tale of Leon Wickman's spring fling party that took place last year, as I try to make a beeline for History. Unlucky for me, turns out Jake is in my class, so I have to listen to him brag on and on about how some chick was blowing him under a table while he made out with a different girl, who had no idea what was happening.

"There'll definitely be some action for you there, Moretti, if you're into it." My face feels fucking numb. Jacob sits down next to me on the back row. "Any of them caught your eye so far?" he asks, as Mr. Biltmore, a skinny guy with a wispy, half-assed beard begins scribbling something on the chalkboard at the front of the class.

"Hmm?"

I'd ignore Jake if I could, but the motherfucker is persistent. "Any of the girls here in school?" he presses. "You into any of them?"

"God, no."

"It's cool, it's cool. I know Zen's diggin' on *you*. She's one of Kacey's friends. Gives amazing head, and I heard she let Taylor Elliot stick it in her ass. She'd be a freaky first conquest."

"Told you. I'm not interested."

"Hey, okay, okay. Didn't mean to stick my nose where it's not wanted. I just felt like I had to say something because…well, I hate to speak badly, but I saw you hanging 'round with Silver Parisi a couple of times, and *pssshh*…" He widens his eyes, making a crazy face. "That one is certifiable, my man. Bitch has mental problems."

I press the nib of my pen into the notepad in front of me so hard, the plastic buckles and cracks between my fingers. "Oh yeah?"

"She's a manipulator. Worse, she's a super bad lay. Take whatever she says with a pinch of salt, dude. If Silver's mouth is moving, then she's fucking lying. She's always been that way. Took a long time for any of us to see it, but now…I'm telling you the truth, man. There isn't a single person at Raleigh stupid enough to look twice at her."

"All right. Open your books to page fifty-eight, people. Today we're learning about, you guessed it…the United Nations Treaty Series! One of the most important international docu—ahh, who am I kidding?" Mr. Biltmore calls from the front of the class. "We're going over the American Civil War again, ladies and gentlemen! Are you pumped for the Battle of Gettysburg or what?"

His sarcasm goes mostly unnoticed, but I appreciate it. Slowly, I turn my head a full forty-five degrees to the left, until I'm staring coldly at Jacob Weaving's profile. "Duly noted," I tell him. "Silver's a liar. I'll give her a wide berth."

Jake grins at me, an All-American football hero in the making, complete with perfectly white, perfectly straight teeth. "Good man, Moretti. Good man. Now, are you gonna come to Leon's party on Friday or what?"

My pen cracks again. The entire thing breaks in two. I clench my fist around the broken pieces, enjoying the feel of the sharp edges digging into the flesh of my palm. "Sure. Why not. Wouldn't miss it for the world."

When class ends, Jake thumps the top of my arm, telling me he'll catch me later, and just like that, I'm dismissed. It's a relief. All I can think about is slamming my fist into the fucker's throat; finding myself free of him is like finding myself free of a persistent and particularly nasty bout of Chlamydia. I do not like the dynamic Weaving's trying to cement between us—one where he assumes the role of alpha, with me playing along as the good subordinate.

Jacob really has to be the stupidest fucking person I have ever met. Or maybe not. Maybe he really is this sure of himself. Either way, he seems to be missing all the warning signs where I'm concerned: the rap sheet; the tattoos; the motorcycle; the murder in my eyes whenever I look at the piece of shit. I'm gonna go right ahead and blame this one on Instagram. They made guys like me popular. They made it fashionable to look like me, to dress like me, to talk and walk like me. But these Insta famous fuck boys have no idea what the hell they're doing when they pick a gang tattoo from a wall in a hipster den in Seattle and pay to have it driven into their skin. They have no idea what a knife feels like in their hands. They sure as fuck don't know what it feels like to drive that into someone else's skin.

In the end, they don't have a clue how to really walk this walk or talk this talk. The fact that you can buy my 'style' in H&M might have robbed me of my threatening reputation...but that doesn't mean that I am *not* a threat.

~

I spend the day on the look-out for Silver. She's not an easy person to keep track of, let me tell you. I swear I see the same repeating faces in the hallway, over and over again between classes, but not the girl with the haunted look in her eyes. Seems as though she's a ghost from the moment she walks into Raleigh High to the moment she books it out of here. I'm unsurprised to find her noticeably missing in the cafeteria at lunch. I normally leave school grounds and eat at a diner nearby myself, but not today.

I'm headed for the exit, about to go in search of something more palatable than cafeteria fare, when I catch sight of the food and realize that it's actually a far cry from the garbage they dished up at Bellingham. Grabbing a loaded tray of food—burger, wedge of lasagna, cup of chocolate pudding—I find an empty table and park myself, ready to hoe in. I'm unimpressed when I sense someone to my right, lowering themselves onto the bench beside me. One, single, solitary banana appears on the table next to my tray, and an overpowering smell, saccharine sweet, hits the back of my nose.

"Wow. You starved at home or something?"

I sigh, annoyance snapping at my back. It's her again—the Walking Fenty Purse. Zen straddles the bench, facing me, smiling suggestively as she peels her banana and takes a bite. Has this chick never seen a fucking movie? Doesn't she know that she's a walking cliché? Aside from the obnoxious perfume she's doused herself in, she also reeks of desperation. Highly unattractive. She eyes my lunch like it's both the most disgusting and most enticing thing she's ever seen in her life. "Seriously, though. Do you live in an orphanage?" She clears her throat and then speaks, affecting a terrible English accent. "Please, Sir. May I have some more?"

Stupid, ignorant, stuck up bitch.

"Oliver. Nice. No, I didn't grow up in an orphanage."

Zen beams. "Oh, I know. I was only messing around. I—"

"They call them 'homes for boys' now. I stayed in one from the age of six until I was eleven. After that, I bounced around in the foster system for a while. *That was fun.*"

The girl looks bewildered. Her mouth falls open wide enough to tell me that she can't figure out if I'm fucking with her or not. I should put her out of her misery. Tell her it was a joke. That would be the kind, if dishonest, thing to do, but fuck…I've never been accused of being kind.

She shifts awkwardly on the bench, swiveling around to face the table properly. "That sounds like an interesting childhood."

"Oh, yeah. Fucking fascinating." I jam the burger into my mouth, taking a massive bite. Zen watches me, horrified, as I plow through my meal. I don't bother looking up from my tray, even when three other people—two guys and a girl—come and sit with us. Eventually, I surface from my food and lock eyes with Halliday; she gives me a warning glare, nostrils flared, and the look conveys her thoughts perfectly: *Please, dear God, do not breathe a single word about what happened last night. Please, please, fucking* please.

I give her a single raise of my eyebrows, mentally telling her to chill the fuck out, then I grab my tray and stand.

"Hey, dude. What kind of motorcycle is that anyway?" the guy on the left asks. His name is David, or Daniel, or Diego or something.

"It's an Indian. A Scout."

"Huh. My old man says anyone who rides a motorcycle must have a death wish."

I grunt as I leave the table. "Yeah. Your old man's probably right."

It feels like an eternity passes after lunch. I'm torn; I can't wait to get the fuck out of this hell hole, with its clean bathrooms, and horribly healthy, wholesome-looking students who smile way too damn much, but I'm also looking forward to staying, too. Because once that bell rings at two-thirty, all of these assholes are gonna file out of here and I'll get to spend an hour with Silver.

She's going to follow through on the lesson. She will. I know she will. I'm so confident that she's going to be there when I enter the music room at two thirty-five that I'm honestly a little confused when I show up only to find the place deserted. I even check the sound booth cubicles to see if she's waiting for me in there. It takes me a second to really understand that she's stood me up. I run my tongue over my teeth, leaving the music room, heading in the direction of the admin office, where all the student records are kept.

Okay, Silver.
It's like that, is it?
Well, two can play that game.

12

SILVER

"Hey, Maxie! For real, dude. Where the hell are your shorts? We're gonna be late!" I've already run all over the house, searching for Max's soccer uniform, but the boy loses everything he touches, and thus far he's been more interested in 'Call of Duty' than helping me hunt down his shit.

I'm not even supposed to be taking him to practice tonight, but Dad managed to talk me into it—uninterrupted time for him to continue working on his piece for The Architect's Digest. In exchange, he promised I could have the keys to the cabin this weekend since it's Labor Day on Monday, plus a full tank of gas so I can drive myself up to the lake. The thought of being up there, alone, with only my guitar and my books for company? Seventy-two blissful hours of solitude? Yeah, it's gonna be heaven on earth. Of course, Dad has no idea I'll be going up there alone. I didn't lie to him, per se. Okay, well it's potentially a lie by omission, but it's hardly my fault if he doesn't do his due diligence. For the past two years, I've been allowed to use the cabin at the lake because the girls always used to come with me. A group of five girls, together in the woods, armed with pepper spray, made it possible for my parents to sign off on unsupervised trips to the tiny log cabin my grandfather built on the shore of Lake Cushman back in the sixties.

Since last spring, I've been going there by myself, though, and neither Mom or Dad have bothered to ask if any of my friends were going with me. They've assumed, which is to say…they've been too wrapped up in their own separate shit to adequately parent their only daughter.

For once, their total lack of interest in my life has worked out in my favor.

"MAX! I swear to god, I will burn your PlayStation if you don't give me some sort of clue here, Bud!"

Downstairs, there's a loud crash, followed by a thud, and then the sound of footsteps hammering up the stairs. My brother bursts into his room, where I'm ankle deep in the clothes that have been dumped on his bedroom floor; his cheeks are flushed, eyes flashing with irritation. Like most eleven-year-old boys, Max takes threats to his PlayStation very seriously. "I don't even care about soccer anymore. I basically told Dad I wasn't going to go, so you might as well stop."

"Well Dad *basically* told me you *basically* had to go, so find your shorts. If you're not in the car in five minutes, there'll be consequences."

Growling like a little fucking savage, Max begins to kick through his clothes in search of his elusive soccer shorts. I grab my bag and head downstairs, trying to decide which book to read while I wait for Max's practice to be over. I don't blame the kid for not wanting to go. It's raining again, layers of mist skating through the tops of the trees that cover the mountainside opposite the house, and the cold feels like it's seeping into my bones.

I'll be safe and dry in the car, but Maxie will be soaked to the skin and covered in mud in less than five minutes flat. Which reminds me…

"I'm taking the van, Dad!"

"Can't you take him in your car?" he calls from his office.

"No dice, hombre. Last time I did that, it took a week to get the dirt out of the seats. Pretty sure it's all still ground into the carpet, too. I'm not dealing with that again."

"Come on, Sil. I don't have time to clean the van!"

"I appreciate that. But you're an adult with the six-figure salary. You can afford to have someone detail it for you. See you in an hour!" I snatch up his keys, ignoring the sound of his grumbling coming from underneath his office door, and I go wait in the van for Max. I'm getting ready to lean on the horn when he comes running out of the house, red-cheeked but dressed in his full kit, soccer cleats and all. He slams the car door behind him and slumps down into his seat, arms folded across his chest. "I need your cell phone," he informs me.

I throw the van into reverse and clear the drive. "Why?"

"I was s'posed to hang out with Colton and Jamie in the game. I need to let them know I've been kidnapped."

For all their faults, my parents have stuck to their guns on this one thing: Max doesn't get a cell phone until high school. I had to live by this same rule, so I sympathize with him. The little monster has memorized all of his friend's number's, though, and he constantly has his hand out for my phone. Beyond annoying. If I don't give it to him, the next hour is going to be brutal. I opt for the quickest, easiest route to a peaceful life and I hand it over.

He begins typing furiously. "Mom was crying this morning," he says.

"What? What do you mean, she was crying?"

"I heard her in the shower."

The sky's darkening. I haven't bothered to turn any music on, so there's nothing to obscure the deep, low rumble of thunder that rolls in the distance. "I'm sure she wasn't crying, Max. She might have been humming or something. It's tough to tell what's going on when the water's running."

"Silver. I'm eleven, not a moron. I know what it sounds like when someone's crying. She was crying just like when Grandpa died."

When our grandfather died three years ago, Mom didn't just cry. She sobbed inconsolably, and the sound of her pain stole the very last fragments of my innocence. I'd never seen such agony on anyone's face, or heard it in that way before, and I knew for a fact that I was witnessing the lowest, most harrowing moment of my mother's life as she lay in the fetal position, collapsed on the hallway floor, clutching the phone to her chest.

If she was crying like that in the shower, then…No. There's just no way. I would have heard her. And besides, something monumentally bad would have had to have happened to make her that distraught. Dad would have pulled me aside and given me a heads up, even if Mom had tried to hide it from me. "Could have been a video, Bud. Or maybe a song."

Max huffs, stabbing at the phone's screen ever faster. "Whatever you say." He hates not being believed. It's his thing, his trigger, the one thing that makes him snap and act like he's fucking possessed. Mom always says we should never discount or dismiss him out of hand, and that sometimes it's best to just humor him. I'm about to do just that when I hear the shooping sound of his message being sent. "Who's Alex?" he asks.

"What?"

"Alex. You got a message from him."

I nearly swerve the car off the road. "Give me the phone. Give it to me, Max!"

"Don't freak out. He just said he was going to hang at the house with Dad until we get back. Did you forget he was coming over?"

"Oh my god. Oh my fucking god. Nope. *Noooooo. No, no. no.*" My vision's blurring. Holy shit, my vision is blurring. I can't fucking see.

"Windshield wipers, Sil," Max says.

Oh. The rain's worsened. I'm not going blind from sheer panic after all. I turn the windshield wipers on, and they beat frantically across the glass, sweeping a river of water aside as I pull into the parking lot of Max's soccer club. I throw the van into park and snatch my phone from my brother, my hands shaking as I read the message lit up on the screen.

Alex: Just missed you. Ready and waiting for our lesson. Your dad seems cool. Very interested in my ride. We're gonna hang in the garage until you get back.

Fuck me fucking sideways. Fuck. What the hell is happening right now? How in the name of Celine Dion has *this* come about? Alex is there? At the house? He's with my dad, and they're…they're hanging out in the fucking *garage*? Dad hasn't stepped foot in the garage for years. I can only imagine what he's thinking right now. I can barely feel my fingers as I type out a message to him and fire it off, utterly dismayed.

Me: Sorry, Dad. You can tell Alex to leave. I canceled our lesson. He must have forgotten.

Ha. Forgotten. More like he got pissed that I refused to bow down to his demands, and now he's trying to fuck with me. I can picture the scene all too freaking well—Alex, leaning up against Dad's rusting workbench, hands in his pockets, sexy as hell with his ridiculous smile and his ridiculous eyes, and…a cold knot of fear begins to form in my stomach. What the hell are they even talking about right now? Alex and I have barely spoken ourselves, and our stilted conversations have revolved heavily around the fact that I was sexually assaulted.

He wouldn't bring that up to my dad.

He wouldn't…

Would he?

Sweet fucking Jesus.

"We can just go back if you want," Max says. "It's freezing. At this point, it's safe to say neither of us wants to be here."

I sit very still, considering that option for a second. Should we go back? Every part of me is screaming at me to burn rubber back home and roll out the damage control, but there's also a part of me that's railing against that option. If I go running back there, panicked and freaking out, I'm giving Alex precisely what he wants. I'll be reacting the way he's undoubtedly expecting me to react, and I don't want to give him that satisfaction. It'd mean he won, and Alex Moretti is never going to fucking win with me. I will sit here in the car, and I will make Max play in the rain if it means I get to be the stronger person.

"Sorry, Maxie. If your coach still thinks you guys can play, then I do, too. Out you go."

Disappointed, he shoots me a betrayed grimace as he opens the car door and steps out into the wild weather. Before he slams the door closed behind him, in his most serious tone, he says, "If I die of pneumonia, it'll be your fault. I will haunt you, Silver. And I'll be really good at it, too. You'll be so scared, you'll probably choke on your own tongue and die."

The threat's kind of endearing, really. I'm not really worried about it, since it seems I'm being haunted by a real life, living monster now anyway, and he's dead set on ruining my entire fucking life. Once Max is gone, I open up the message Alex sent, and I tap out a reply.

Me: If you think this is cute, you're sorely mistaken. Do NOT say anything weird to my dad. About ANYTHING.

Max's coach must be a hard ass because he makes the kids play even when the rain is hammering on the roof of the van like a drum. I sit in the driver's seat, unable to do anything but nervously sweat and dig my fingernail into the cord to my headphones until

I've stripped the plastic from the copper wires inside and I've ruined them beyond repair.

Max groans and shivers all the way home, smearing mud and mangled blades of grass all over the place. My pulse rises at an alarmingly rapid rate when I pull into our driveway, bracing myself for the scene I'm about to stumble across in the garage, but…the door is up, the lights are on, and there's no one there.

I was kind of hoping Alex would get bored, realize he'd made his point and leave, but his motorcycle's still sitting in the drive, so looks like I'm shit out of luck there. That can mean only one thing: *Alex Moretti has made it inside my house.*

13

SILVER

"Cut the shit. You're lying." My heart bottoms out at the hard edge to my father's voice. *"There is absolutely no way—"*

I nearly trip over my own feet as I hurry into the kitchen, my pulse thumping urgently in all of my extremities. I feel like I'm going to pass the fuck out. When I throw myself through the doorway, miracle upon miracles, Dad's hand isn't wrapped around Alex's throat. I barely know what to do with myself as Alex, leaning up against the fridge, perfectly at home, like he's been here a thousand times before, looks over at me and winks. The majority of his ink is hidden by his long-sleeved shirt, but the intricately woven design—looks like vines and thorns—sprawling up the right-hand side of his neck is still very visible, as are the backs of his hands. There's just no hiding *that* ink. Not that Alex looks even remotely fazed by the fact that his artwork is on show.

"Silver!" Dad grins over his shoulder when he notices me standing behind him. "Sorry, honey, I only just got your message. Your friend Alex here has been telling me that he met Paul Ryder from Denver Blues at a concert last year. Remember, your mom and I went to see Denver Blues play last year, too? I would have lost my cool if I'd gotten to shake Paul's hand. Silver isn't such a huge fan. I don't know what I did to deserve a daughter that doesn't appreciate good music."

At any other time, I'd never let a sly dig like that from Dad fly, but I barely even hear it today. I'm far too busy boring holes into the side of Alex's head. "What are you doing here, Alex?" I try and keep my voice steady, but my anxiety is tussling with my anger, and the battle between the two warring emotions is making it difficult to feign calm.

"We had an agreement. I paid for two lessons. We agreed we'd have the first today after school."

Do not make a scene in front of Dad. Do not make a scene in front of Dad. I'm prickling all over. Pretty sure there's a vein pulsing in my temple, too. "I told you I couldn't fit you into my schedule. I have too much going on at the moment. I tried to give you back your money this morning, remember?"

Dad takes a long pull from the bottle of beer he's holding. "Thought you were trying to save up for a new paint job for the Nova, Sil. Now you're turning down cash? And, come on. You're hardly busy. You spend most of your time moping around the place with your nose buried in a book."

I smile at him grimly, lips pressed into an unimpressed line. "And I thought I had to take Max to practice because *you* had work you needed to do. Now you're talking music, drinking beer, and kicking back with an absolute stranger?"

Dad laughs. "Just trying to get to know your friends, honey. And if you're gonna be riding around on the back of a motorcycle, I figured there was no harm in meeting the guy who'd be operating it."

"Dad! I'm not going to be riding around on the back of a motorcycle! Alex and I don't even really know each other."

Dad doesn't bother to hide his amused disbelief. "All right, kiddo. Whatever you say. Well, Alex, it was nice to meet you. I hope you guys have a nice lesson. I cleared out some space for you in the garage. Don't make too much noise, though. Your mom'll kill me if the neighbors start complaining."

∽

The garage is cold with the door open, but ain't no way I'm closing it. I do *not* want to be trapped inside a secluded space with any boy, let alone one who thinks it's okay to fuck with me like this. Sitting on the edge of Dad's ancient pool table, I'm livid as I set up the spare guitar I use for teaching, resting the waist of the instrument against the top of my leg, twisting each tuning peg in turn and then strumming, listening for a moment when I bend the sound to find the perfect note.

Alex watches me, arms across his chest, his head a little dipped, his dark eyes unreadable. In my mind, a thousand burning insults present themselves to me like weapons, each one begging to be thrown, hurled or thrust, but instead, I keep a leash on my temper, quickly working to prep for this damned lesson. The sooner we can get started, the sooner I can put an end to this nonsense and get this over with.

"*Silver.*" The rain thunders down onto the flat roof of the garage, rushing down the drainpipes, tinging against the copper windchimes hanging from the eaves by the front door, but Alex's voice is so clear, as if his mouth is pressed against the shell of my ear and the exhale of his breath is all I'm capable of hearing. The expression I set on my face as I raise my gaze to meet his is less than friendly.

"What?"

"I'm nobody's bitch, okay? If you think I'd ever bow down to Weaving, then you've got me all wrong."

I slide off the edge of the pool table and shove the guitar into Alex's chest. "I don't care what you do."

"Sure you do."

"Nope." I unfasten the catches on my hard guitar case, taking out my own instrument. I just played it this morning, but it's habitual—I still check to make sure every string is perfectly in tune. Alex pulls up Dad's rolling stool, taking a seat on it and resting the guitar I've given to him on his knee. A bright flash of lightning flickers in the sky over Hunter Mountain, briefly illuminating the heavy, swollen clouds. The world beyond the mouth of the garage is the color of iron, seething purples and flashes of silver as the snap of electricity turns all of the puddles to molten lead.

As if by some unspoken agreement, Alex and I wait for the thunder. Neither of us breaks the silence until the booming crash of sound shakes both the sky and the ground beneath our feet.

"We're starting from the very beginning," I say in a professional tone—my teaching voice. "The anatomy of a guitar." I spin my guitar around in my hands so that its base is resting on top of my legs. "This is the headstock." I point to the top of the guitar, where the tuning pegs attach to the strings. "These are the fingerboards. These steel bands are the frets. You change the tone and key of whatever you're playing by—"

"You care more than you're willing to admit," Alex says.

I look up from the guitar. "If you're not gonna pay attention to even the most basic part of this lesson, then you're not going to learn anything."

"You watch me, Silver. I feel your eyes on me all the time. You think I didn't know you were there on the football field, sitting underneath the bleachers?"

My usual reaction would be instantaneous embarrassment, but not this time. He crossed a line coming here. I don't have to be anything other than angry. "What do you want me to say? When a car's hurtling toward the edge of a cliff and you know it's about to crash through the safety barrier and explode in a fiery ball of flames on the rocks below, it's impossible to look away, Alex."

"It wasn't just yesterday, though, was it? You've been keeping an eye on me for the past two weeks."

"You'd only know that if *you'd* been watching *me*," I snap back.

He smirks. Hair tousled, skin pale, eyes as dark as sin. His mouth twitches as he breathes steadily down his nose. "I have a brother. A little brother. He's in care right now. I want to be his legal guardian when I turn eighteen, but I need to impress the crap out of Darhower first. I'm asking for your help."

So, there is a reason behind this. I knew there had to be, but I didn't expect it to be this. He has a little brother, and he wants to take care of him. I just...I can't picture it. Not for a second. Alex doesn't exactly give off the responsible, stand-in-father kind of vibe.

"I have seven months to get my shit together. If you sign off on my lesson sheet twice a week, that'd be a huge step in the right direction."

I laugh, massaging the pads of my fingers into my forehead. Seems I've developed a bastard of a headache all of a sudden. "Sign off on the lessons? Say you've done them when you actually haven't? Right. So, you want me to lie for you. What are you gonna do when you have to sit the end of year music exam, genius?"

A secret, amused smile makes it all the way to the corners of his eyes. "You don't need to worry about that. I've got it handled."

"This is some fucking bullshit, Alex." If he doesn't register the frustration and annoyance in my voice, then he's mentally fucking compromised. He's been wasting my time, playing some sort of weird game with me ever since he decided to climb into my car, and I don't know why. Whatever his reasoning, I'm sick of it.

Another round of thunder growls in the distance. "Fine. Just go. I'll sign off on your lessons. Whatever you want me to do. Let's just minimize contact as much as possible. I'm not willing to make my life any harder than it already is."

He stares at me, unblinking. His eyes run me through like dark blades. "I think you'll change your mind about that one, Silver."

Exasperated, I get up, hurriedly putting away my guitar. My fingers find the catches on my hard case, but it takes three attempts to close them. "I don't understand what your game plan is here, but you're not making any sense. You stood there in the bathrooms the other day and told me in no uncertain terms that you weren't interested in me. But by the way you're talking now, it sure as hell doesn't sound that way." I continue to fluster, snatching the other guitar from him and sliding into the gig bag, zipping it up in quick, angry movements.

"How does it sound to you, Silver?" The timbre of his voice mimics the thunder, gravel, rough, deep enough to make me quake.

Rounding on him, my chest rising and falling way too quickly, I ball my hands into fists, fighting the urge to scream. "Like you realized it might be fun to try and mess with me. Like you saw a broken, vulnerable person, just trying to get through her last shitty, miserable days of high school, and you thought to yourself, "Hmm, graduation's a long way off, Alex. Maybe you should toy with that girl as a source of entertainment to stem your own selfish fucking boredom."

He stands perfectly still, frozen in place. The only small movement he makes is that of his shoulders rising slowly. As always, he appears annoyingly unaffected by what I've just said to him. His gaze is as hard as ever, impenetrable and distant. For one insane, awful moment, I think I'm actually going to pick up one of Dad's barely used tools and smash him over the head with it. That would be satisfying, at least, and I'd feel a little relieved for a moment before the remorse kicked in.

"You think you're so fucking clever, don't you?" I snap. "Nothing touches you. Nothing reaches you. You're… you're…"

"I'm what?"

"You're a void, Alex. A vast, beautiful fucking black hole that sucks everything into it and gives nothing back. Ever. Even the goddamn daylight can't escape you. A dark cloud follows you wherever you go. It's impossible to miss. You *see* everything. You *judge* everyone. You think you *know* everything. And, underneath all of that, you *feel* nothing."

For the very first time, a small flicker of emotion flashes over his features. I haven't angered him, though. His composure doesn't falter even for a heartbeat. He simply looks…confused. With careful, measured, even steps, he moves towards me, and a kernel of fear begins to take root inside me. What…what the hell is he going to do?

"I have a temper," he grinds out. "A bad one. I had to master it a long time ago, otherwise it was going to master me. So, yeah. I'm not exactly the most reactive person you'll ever meet. But that doesn't mean there's nothing going on in here," he says, tapping the side of his head. "I'm not aloof. I'm not cold. I'm not distant. I'm learning. And I feel *everything*, Silver." He pauses, an unfamiliar edge of uncertainty smoldering in his eyes. It looks like he's battling with himself over what he should say next. He speaks quickly, then, rushing the words out, as if he wants to expel them from his body before he can change his mind.

"You're right. I told you that you were a means to an end in the bathroom, that I wasn't interested in you, and that wasn't true. I am not trying to use you as a source of entertainment, though. I'm trying to figure you out. I'm intrigued by you."

"Why the hell would I intrigue you, for Christ's sake?"

He doesn't miss a beat. "Because you're still standing. Because, after everything you went through, you didn't fucking break."

He's so close to me now. Closer than he's ever been before. I'm unsteady on my feet, and my heart is rioting against my ribs, as though it's trying to break free from its cage and flee the scene of a crime.

"Strength is drawn to strength, Silver, and I think there's a chance that you might be the strongest person I have ever met." His warm breath skates over my collar bone and the shiver that follows doesn't just slide over my skin—it sinks deep down into the marrow of my bones. With excruciatingly slow movements,

Alex reaches out a tentative hand and takes hold of the curl of hair that's fallen free from my sloppy ponytail. He gently winds it around the end of his finger, pupils blown, his lips parted, fixated on his finger and my hair that's wrapped around it. He whispers the words that follow. "It isn't just that. I also happen to think that you're the most beautiful fucking thing I have ever witnessed with my own two eyes. I *am* watching you just as much as you're watching me…and I don't trust myself to look away."

Ho…ly….shiiiiiiit.

I am seventeen-years-old. The world is changing around me so rapidly that I worry I might never find my place in it. Just a few short years ago, I was so sure of everything. I loved boybands, and horses, drawing and playing my guitar. Then, almost overnight, nothing was certain anymore, and things I thought I knew to be true no longer were. It was as though I was a caterpillar, happy, learning and growing, and then without warning I began to transform into something else. There has been no chrysalis, though, no cocoon to hide away inside, safe, until I'm ready to reemerge into the world, new and fresh and complete. No, all of my transformations have taken place out in the open, in public, for all to see, and the process has been horrific.

In the past year alone, I've had to endure more trauma and heartache than most people are asked to endure in their entire lifetimes. Something precious was taken from me, ripped away, stolen with greedy hands and whiskey-soaked breath, and I felt it inside me—that bottomless, dark chasm that swallowed any hope of me ever having a normal teenage life. I've believed, since the moment I rolled over onto my side on the bathroom floor of Leon Wickman's father's bathroom with my insides all torn up, blood making the insides of my thighs sticky, the smell of copper hanging heavy in the air, that I would never be capable of feeling affection for a guy ever again.

And yet…

Here I am, seventeen-years-old, unbroken…and the way Alex

Moretti is looking at me now has kindled something in the hollow of my chest that I thought had perished.

Alex swallows, his eyes on fire, and I can read his intentions on his face: he's going to kiss me. He's going to press his mouth on mine, and he's going to bury his hands into my hair, and he's going to steal my breath, and my heart and the tattered remnants of my fragile soul…and I'm going to let him, because I'm intrigued by him, too, and—

"*Get out.*"

I hate the words even as I whisper them, but I can't. I can't fucking do this.

Alex's eyes, half lowered, open wide at the command. He immediately takes a step back. Next thing I know, he's sliding on his leather jacket, which has been sitting on Dad's workbench this entire time, and he's leaving the garage. He swings his leg over his motorcycle and then sits there for a second, staring at me. "I'm not going to force you to fall for me, Silver. You've already been forced to do too much. But don't blame me if I try and change your mind."

"You've got more chance of pulling down the moon." My throat throbs, aching against the words, but they're the truth.

Alex turns the key in the ignition, and the motorcycle's engine roars to life. The single beam of its headlight feels like a tractor beam, pulling me toward him, tugging at the very cells of my body, but I stay absolutely still as he backs down the driveway, out onto the street, and rides off into the rain.

14

ALEX

Another shift at the Rock. Halliday doesn't show, which is a relief. I don't want to deal with anyone from Raleigh right now, least of all a member of Kacey Winters' Sirens. Montgomery has me make a run for him just before midnight. I hand off the bag and accept the envelope all without looking up at the person I'm making the deal with. I don't want any faces sticking in my memory, and this has never felt good to me. I don't know what's in the bag, but it's probably drugs. Coke, maybe. Hopefully not meth or heroine. I don't like the idea of being Monty's mule any more than I like the idea of losing out on the cash if I tell him I won't do it anymore, so I try and get the job done as quickly and painlessly as possible.

Monty gives me a six-pack and my own little envelope containing our agreed upon amount. Once my shift's over and I'm back at the trailer, the green neon digits of the alarm clock next to the T.V. reading two twenty-three in the morning, I squirrel the envelope away in the box behind the water heater. Then, I drink the six-pack in silence, staring at the static on the television screen, thinking about Silver. The over-sized t-shirts she wears are a shield. A defense. She uses all that extra fabric to hide her body from hungry eyes. I should know—I couldn't take mine off her when I saw her in that black lacey number she was sporting yesterday. She wore that for me, to impress me, to catch my attention, and when she got it...

She was afraid.

She was afraid of *me*, which is not okay. I'm a piece of shit, sure. I've done plenty of things I'm not proud of. I still do things I'm not proud of on a regular basis, running Monty's deliveries being a prime example, but I have never, *ever* hurt a girl. I've never laid my hands on a girl unless she's begged me to do it, and then it's only been to bring her pleasure. I've never encouraged a chick to do anything she didn't want to do. Damn it, I don't even disrespect women when I open my fucking mouth.

Silver doesn't know this. She doesn't know me, so her reluctance to give me a shot is understandable.

I fall asleep on the couch—nothing new there—and my neck's killing me when I wake up. I shower while the coffee's brewing, hurrying because I don't want to miss Silver before she disappears through Raleigh's doors and manages to give me the slip for the rest of the day. But when I open the trailer door...it's fucking raining so hard I can barely see three feet in front of my own face.

No way I can ride to Raleigh in this. I'm going to have to drive the old Camaro, and it's been so long since I even started the engine it's bound to be fucking dead. When I throw my ass inside the car, slide the key into the ignition, and turn it over, I'm met with the straining sounds of one very unhappy combustion engine. It stutters, catches, almost strengthens, and then dies. Fuck, I hate when I'm right.

I've been fixing cars since I was old enough to hold a wrench, so it doesn't take long to hook the Camaro up to the neighbor's car and zap some life into the old girl. It does mean the bell's already rung by the time I jog inside the school building and Silver's nowhere to be seen, though.

I think about missing homeroom altogether and just waiting for her outside her room; I need to have my attendance marked even if I am late, though, otherwise Rhonda *and* Maeve are gonna shit themselves, and I can't be fucked dealing with that right now. Besides, hunting Silver down and lurking in the hallway until she appears is pretty fucking close to stalking, and I doubt that will help.

At lunch, Jake informs me that my presence is required after school for my first training session with the team, even though the schedule Coach Quentin gave me doesn't have me down until next week. "All good, though, Man. We're all gonna be on a massive high for Leon's party and no extra sit-ups or push-ups required to make our shirts look good. Plus, that first beer is gonna taste so fucking good if we've earned it on the field."

I really fucking hate the way he throws his arm around my shoulder and grins at me, laughing like a hyena, but I allow it. Jacob needs to believe I'm toeing the line with him for more than one reason. I'm still working out the details, but there will come a day when Jakey Boy's crown slips, and I'll make sure the whole school is on hand to witness it. His fall from grace will make Silver's descent look like she tripped and landed on the world's most comfortable feather mattress.

∼

Training's brutal. My lungs are scorched, and my legs are on fire before we're even halfway through warm-ups, but I hide it well. Can't let these motherfuckers think for one second that I can't keep up. I can, and I do. But I also make a personal note to start running every morning. My cardio could be better.

Jacob's as subtle as a sledgehammer to the head as he whispers into his buddy's ears, encouraging them to put me through my paces. I'm tripped, punched in the back, and bombarded with a series of late hits that Coach Quentin ignores with a level of skill that I find pretty damn impressive. I was expecting this kind of shit, though. I'm the new guy. This probably won't be the last training session I walk away from covered in bruises, and it won't be the last time my new teammates give me the rough treatment. In their eyes, I'll need to prove myself. Make them trust me.

And I've decided that maybe I do want them to trust me, too.

"Stai attentio, mi amore. Stai attento."

I hear her voice, the whisperings of a ghost, as I shower, my body singing with pain. I try not to hear. I try not to pay attention, but it's hard to turn the memory of my mother away. These memories are all I have left of her. I know how these things work. If I keep blocking the soft lilting melody of her voice from my ears, eventually I'll stop hearing it altogether. There will come a day, maybe years from now, that I can no longer remember what she sounded like at all. I fucking dread that day's arrival, it's my worst nightmare, but I can't lose myself in dark memories right now. I have no choice but to banish them from my mind. Later. There will be time for remembering later, when I'm alone, back in the trailer, when I'm grateful for the company of the dead.

"Might as well follow us over to Harry's, Moretti," Cillian Dupris calls across the locker room. "We're grabbing burgers before we head over to Leon's."

Fuck. I was hoping I'd have a moment to slip away between the end of practice and the start of Leon's party, but it doesn't look like I'm going to be able to escape.

As we drive over to Harry's diner, my head's spinning. Connections are being made, pieces of a plan slowly coming together. In the background of my mind, images of Silver present themselves to me, one after the other, my subconscious thrusting memories of her to the forefront of my mind. These memories are recent, though. Unlike the echoes of my mother, the girl with the haunted blue eyes burns vividly in my head.

She's there, sitting beside me in the booth as I make short work of a burger, the guys tossing fries at each other, chugging milkshakes that Jake spikes from a scuffed hipflask. She's there, silent, judging me morosely as I make a point of joking and laughing along with my teammates. On the way over to Leon's place, she's sitting next to me in the Camaro, her head resting sadly against my shoulder. I can feel a resigned sorrow pouring from her and into me as I pull down a driveway after Jake's tricked out Jeep Cherokee, and I know she thinks this is a bad idea.

Except, Silver isn't really here. She's probably locked away in a bedroom I've spent a considerable amount of time imagining in great detail, studying, her head buried inside a textbook, hair gathered in a messy ponytail, her quick, bright eyes devouring the information on the pages before her. She's probably playing her guitar. She's probably not struggling to shove the memory of *me* out of her head. She probably hasn't even thought about me at all since last night, when she told me I'd tasked myself with the impossible challenge of pulling down the moon.

Leon's family are predictably wealthy. The driveway turns out to be a mile long. From the outside, the house is a sprawling jigsaw puzzle of a building, all odd angles and jutting overhangs; an architect designed this building to mimic the shape of the land that surrounds it, complementing the steep, unforgiving buttress of the cliff face that forms the western wall of the valley the house is nestled into. The soft, liquid lines of the sloped roof seem to open themselves to the sky. Everywhere, vast stretches of glass reflect the green of the trees that gather around the structure. The subtle grey-blue of the slate exterior blends into the landscape with artistic precision. That's how the whole place feels actually: that it wasn't just designed. That it emerged or was wished into existence, right out of an artist's dream.

"Pretty badass, right?" Jake asks, jerking his chin toward the house. "Leon's dad's rich as fuck. He's a defense attorney in Seattle. He's never here." Jake shrugs. "Leaves Leon alone with his platinum Amex and the keys to his jag most of the time. Leon's basically the luckiest bastard in the world."

"Where's his mom?" The question comes out unbidden.

"Dead."

I flinch away from the word.

"Oh, it's okay, man. Leon was just a kid when she offed herself. You ask me, he's better off without her. My mom's a major pain in the ass. Don't get me wrong. I'm not saying I wish she'd kill herself of anything. That'd be super fucked up. But…you can't deny it. Leon's got it fucking easy here. And he wouldn't be able to throw such killer parties if he had a bored, self-medicated yoga instructor mom hovering over him, prying into his shit, right?"

It feels like the gold chain around my neck is choking the life out of me. Thank fuck it doesn't seem like Jake actually expects an answer out of me, because I don't trust myself to speak right now. I ignore the heat rising up the back of my neck, giving Jacob a tight smile. If he were concerned with anything but his own shitty perspective, his own self-centered point of view, then he might notice the cutting edge that's crept into my voice.

"Yeah, you're right. He's far better off without anyone giving him shit. It'd suck if he couldn't throw parties anymore."

I would *kill* to have my mother back.

I would kill to know where my father was, if only so I could throat punch the fuck for abandoning us all after Ben was born.

Jacob's probably never even considered the possibility that Leon might sacrifice this house and his unfettered freedom if it meant that he could have his mother back in his life. He grins at me like I'm seeing things his way, we're cut from the same cloth, and he's pleased that we're so much alike. "Come on, man. Let's get this fucker started before the others show up. Leon's dad's got a stash of high-end Japanese whiskey, and I know where the key to the liquor cabinet is."

∽

Everywhere I look, I keep seeing her face. The place is thumping, loud, bassy music echoing around the cavernous interior of the house, but everything feels very quiet and very still inside my head. I know she's not here. This is the last place on earth Silver would appear, but still my eyes continue to play tricks on me, making the back of every head of long golden-brown hair look like hers. I can feel the slight buzz of alcohol jittering through my veins, but I'm far from drunk. I'm used to drinking. I've been knocking back stuff way harder than the pissy beer one of the guys on the football team managed to scrounge up for a very long time now. Even Leon's dad's whiskey didn't have any real impact on me. I laugh and joke along with the other revelers, though, pretending to be as fucked up as them, and all the while I'm biting my tongue, hating every second of this bullshit, tasting blood in my mouth.

Leon's not like Jake and his brainless cohorts. I'm not sure how I haven't run into him until now, but I think, under different circumstances, I'd like the guy. He's quiet and steady, thinking a lot as he looks around, watching our school mates treat his father's pad with complete disregard. He flinches every time something breaks, but he doesn't do or say anything about it. When a large, expensive looking painting hanging over the fireplace is hit with a flying football and the canvas tears, he just walks blankly into the kitchen, his eyes glazed over. The guy looks like a teenaged ken doll in his stiff, button-down shirt and his khakis. On the outside, he and I couldn't be more unlike. But when I catch the look of open disgust on his face when he finds three guys in the hallway, gathered around a phone, rapt, talking about someone's wet pussy, I get the feeling we're pretty fucking similar on the inside.

I spend an hour dodging both Zen and Halliday for different reasons and wind up in the kitchen, back to the wall, observing the drunken debauchery that's taking place in every direction with a cold, unimpressed mask of indifference on my face. The mask's a warning, a threat: come within five feet of me and expect to lose a limb. For the most part, it's an efficient way of making sure no one bothers me, but Leon seems impervious to it. He enters the kitchen, hands empty when everyone else is holding at least two drinks, and when he sees me, he actually looks *relieved*. He heads straight for me, smiling tightly, and I wonder what he's going to say; he wasn't all that talkative earlier when Jake introduced me to him as his new 'boy'—a title that I resent beyond words. Somehow makes me feel complicit with him.

When Leon reaches me, he spins around and sags against the wall beside me. "Just like every cliched movie you've ever seen, right?" he says wearily. "We are the children of America. The country's brightest and most promising." He seems resigned as a girl with bright green hair runs into the kitchen, diving for the sink, leaning over it and retching her guts up. The moment couldn't have been timed better. Neither could the roar of laughter and cheering that goes up as everyone turns toward the spectacle and begins to celebrate the fact that the party's arrived at its drunken zenith.

A series of high fives are traded around the kitchen. A grinning, slack-faced girl with lipstick on her teeth laughs like a hyena, turning to me, holding her hand up for me to join in. The icy, unamused lift of my left eyebrow is all I require to decline. The girl's smile falters. She lowers her hand and turns away, hiding her face in her red solo cup.

"Impressive." Leon laughs softly, scratching at his jaw. "Think you could teach me how to do that sometime? I use way too many words to tell people to fuck off. Very ineffectual."

This earns him a wry smile. "It's a gift," I admit.

"You're hating this," Leon observes, tucking his hands into the pockets of his jeans.

I throw back a mouthful of beer, draining my cup. "Whatever gave you that impression. Aren't I the life of the party?"

"I've seen nuns have more fun."

A full smile this time. "Hey, I bet those broads are freaky as fuck underneath those habits." And then, "You don't seem to be having the best time yourself."

Leon lets out a derisive huff of laughter. "Yeah, well, I'm sure I'd be just as moronic as those idiots if I drank, but I'm not quite as enamored with the whole 'typical high school experience,' as my father calls it."

"Your dad encourages this?" I say, empty cup in hand, pointing at the ceiling, encompassing the entire party in one circle of my finger.

Leon pulls a face. "Yeah, well, high school was the best time of his life, apparently. He expects these blow-outs. Means I'm enjoying my life, even though he's never around to witness it. If I don't throw the occasional rager, he tells me I'm working too hard and threatens to ban me from the swim team, so…" He holds out his hands, palms up, shaking his head a little as he takes in the scene in his kitchen. Two guys are holding teaspoons to their mouths, a challenge in both their eyes as they count down from three. Once they reach one, they both shove the spoons into their mouths, attempting to swallow back what looks like a heaping mound of cinnamon. A hale of choking follows after, spluttered brown clouds of fragrant spice coughed up as they both struggle to gasp around the cinnamon. It's the most moronic thing I've ever seen.

"*…here we are*," Leon says, finishing his sentence with an air of resignation. "I swear, I have no idea how people can get dumber as they get older."

"These guys certainly make it look real fucking easy."

Outside. Apart. I feel *other* than these people, I always have, and it sounds to me like Leon feels the same. He takes my solo cup from me and heads to the large marble island in the center of the kitchen, punching Austin, one of the guys in my History class, in the shoulder when he tries to give him a tittie twister. Looks like the slug hurt, but Austin laughs it off, slapping Leon on the back. Leon ducks his head, quickly pouring a number of different liquids from a number of different bottles into the cup he took from me and then adding a splash of coke at the end.

I can smell the liquor fumes rising out of the cup as he passes it back to me; I'm gonna be in trouble if I drink this. I sure as shit won't be riding home, that's for sure. I can scheme and bust my ass all I like to get Ben back, but if I end up with a DUI on my record, I can kiss goodbye to any hopes of getting guardianship of Ben. Even *I'm* not that stupid.

"Come on," Leon says, jerking his chin toward the large set of sliding glass doors to his right. "These assholes are giving me a headache. I wanna show you something."

I don't argue. Any excuse to get the fuck away from the party, really, and I'm curious. What this guy wants to show me in particular, I have no clue, but it's got to be better than watching two dickheads choke on cinnamon.

I haven't been out the back yet. A manicured lawn stretches down a slope toward a few outbuildings, and I can hear water running somewhere. Lord knows why anyone would bother with a fountain when the sky is basically a permanent water feature. Leon walks off down the slope into the looming dark without saying a word. I sniff the contents of my solo cup as I follow after him, risking a sip and then wincing at the sheer volume of alcohol within the drink. It's Long Island Iced Tea level shit.

"My dad has trouble finding new and interesting ways to spend his money. He set this up for me a couple of years ago, I guess back when he was trying to inspire some sort of masculine, boy's club attitude in me." His face is pale and solemn as he looks back over his shoulder. "As usual, I disappointed him."

I knock back a mouthful of the drink, my insides burning as the alcohol slides down my throat. "Wouldn't worry about it. Sons are born to disappoint their fathers."

We reach the first of the outbuildings—a large, white, corrugated steel structure with a flat roof, the size of a small barn—and Leon takes out a set of keys, unfastening a weighty, industrial sized lock that secures a large steel sliding door. A moment later, Leon steps inside and hits a light, and bank after bank of strip lighting blinks to life inside.

It's a workshop. Not just a workshop; it's a monstrous space, with two bays to work on vehicles, and countless metal shelving units, packed high with just about every tool and piece of equipment known to man. Everything is meticulously clean, organized and in its place. Wrenches, spanners, and screwdrivers hang from the walls, ascending in size. And along the right-hand side of the workshop, three motorcycles are parked one beside the other. All of them are classics—two Harleys and a Honda. They're immaculate. The kind of bikes a guy dreams about. They must have cost a cool twenty grand a piece.

I whistle, shoving past Leon into the workshop. "Shit. You just have these sitting here? In a workshop behind your house? You don't ride them?"

Leon shakes his head. "I put the Honda together. My father had one of his guys come in here and take it apart, down to the nuts and bolts. And then he told me, if I wanted to keep my trainer over the summer break, I had to figure out how to put it back together inside a week."

"YouTube?" I ask.

"YouTube," he confirms.

"Can I take a look?"

He holds his hand out, a rueful smile on his face. "Be my guest. You'll be the first person besides me to lay eyes on them since Dad dumped them here."

Closer, the bikes are fucking beautiful. I love my Indian—there was a time when I spent every single spare dime that came my way on hulking that thing out—but let's face it. My bike is nowhere near as lovely as these machines. I run my hand over the Harley Roadster, imagining I can feel the purr of the engine beneath my palm. It would be so, so fucking sweet to put this baby through her paces. "You haven't shown these to Jake and his friends, then?"

Leon's expression warps; if I'm not mistaken, it's anger that I see flaring in his eyes. "No way, dude. Jake thinks anything and everything is put in front of him for his own amusement. If he saw these, he'd have one of them wrapped around a fucking street sign in five minutes flat. And he'd probably walk away unscathed, of course. Jake and his friends seem to have nine lives."

There's a bitter edge to his voice that makes me look up at him. "I thought you were tight with Jake."

"Jake thinks he's tight with everyone. Truth is, he's a fucking asshole, and no one's brave enough to call him on his shit. Jake kind of stole my girlfriend from me, and yet here we are..." He throws his hands up, frustrated. "He shows up, ready to party. He makes himself at home without a second fucking thought. Right now, I'm pretty sure he's upstairs with Kacey, for fuck's sake, and I'm just supposed to...*let it slide.* Just like everyone else, I'm supposed to pat him on the back and tell him his shitty behavior is totally fine because he is the great Jacob Weaving, master of everything the light touches."

I smirk. "Was that a Lion King reference?"

"Kinda," he replies glumly.

I hold out my solo cup to him, and he takes it for me so I can throw my leg over the Roadster and push the bike upright. The shape of it's much like my Scout, but it's heavier, more substantial. The key's in the ignition. I point at it, asking a silent question, and Leon nods. When I start the engine, the bike explodes into life, and I get the same, familiar burst of adrenalin I always get when I start up any motorcycle. A smile spreads on my face, so broad and wide that my cheeks begin to hurt. "Fuck, man. This thing really sings."

Leon folds his arms over his chest, nodding, but I can see it in his eyes—the sound of this engine doesn't light a match inside him the way it does with me. It goes without saying that Leon's not really a greaser; if he were, he'd be raving about these bikes right now, pointing out every small detail of their engines and their specifications, a fire burning in his eyes. The way he looks at them, they could be interesting ornaments on a mantlepiece.

I kill the engine, still grinning. "So, Jake stole that girl from you? Don't take this the wrong way," I tell him, "but honestly…I thought you were gay, man."

Leon's tenses up, his spine straightening, eyes widening a fraction. "What? I mean, why would you say that?"

"I don't know. I just…" I shrug, patting the bike's gas tank. "Sorry if I'm way off. It's just what I figured when I met you earlier."

His eyes narrow. He doesn't seem angry, though. Accuse some guys of being gay, and you'll earn yourself a split lip and a trip to the emergency room. Leon just seems confused. "Am I super effeminate or something?"

"No, man. You're just…you're a guy. You're you. Whatever."

Leon rocks on his heels. There really isn't any physical reason I would have thought he was into dudes. You meet some people and you know instantly, because of the way they speak or gesticulate, or because of the specific things they say. That didn't happen with Leon. It just seemed true. "No one's ever said that to me before," he says tightly.

I begin to think I might have overstepped, which kinda sucks. I don't want to fight him. He's a big guy, but I'm more than capable of kicking his ass. Leon's big and broad with a huge fucking reach on him, but he's not a brawler. No fucking way. He shifts from one foot to the other, his eyes sharp, searching my face. "You don't give a shit, do you?" he says, the statement an accusation.

"I'm sorry?"

"You wouldn't give a shit if I were gay, would you?"

I jerk my head back, my mouth turning down as I consider what he's just said. "No. Of course not. Why would I?" I wait for him to say something back, but he doesn't. He doesn't move for a second. He just stands there, hands still in his pockets, eyes boring into me…and I realize that he's holding his breath. Eventually, he shakes himself, as if he's coming back to life, and scuffs the sole of his shoe against the buffed concrete floor.

"Well I'm not *gay* gay," he says stiffly. "Obviously, otherwise I wouldn't have been with Kacey. I like guys and girls. Anyway, let me know if you wanna use this place to work on your bike sometime," he adds, changing the subject rather clunkily. "I'm never in here. Seems like a shame to let everything just…sit."

I recognize that as our cue to leave. I climb off the back of the bike and take my drink from him, swallowing down half the liquor inside in one go. I finally feel the effects of the booze, my legs beginning to feel heavier and heavier as we walk back up the slope toward the house.

"You ask me, you're better off without that Kacey chick, anyway," I tell him. "She's a piece of work. Probably would have bitten your dick off if you'd put a foot wrong."

Leon glances at me out of the corner of his eye. "You're more right than you know. Kacey's beautiful. Popular. Fun. But Jesus fucking Christ, her teeth are sharp. Cross her or any of the other girls at your own peril."

I laugh under my breath, draining the last dregs of the punishing drink. "Don't worry. I'm not interested in any of those dumpster fire bitches."

"No. You're only interested in the weird, quirky, indie outcasts, I s'pose?"

I say nothing, but we trade dry looks and it's very obvious who and what he's referring to.

"I won't tell you to be careful of that one," Leon says, rubbing at the back of his neck awkwardly. "I know Jake's already done that."

"Do I really *need* a warning?"

For a moment, Leon looks uncomfortable. "I don't know the details. I can't say either way. That night just got…it got really fucking crazy, and when the shit hit the fan, Kacey still had her claws in my back so deep, I'm ashamed to say I just did whatever the fuck she told me. All I do know is that Silver used to be one of them…and something really horrible must have happened between her and Kacey for everything to have blown up the way it did."

I frown, crushing the solo cup in my hand. We're almost back to the kitchen's sliding doors. The sounds of the party have reached a fever pitch, the music pulsing like an angry heartbeat. Someone opens the door, throwing an oblong shard of golden light out into the darkness. Inside, someone screams raucously at the top of their lungs, but I'm not focused on what they're shouting. I'm still trying to process what Leon just said. "Wait, what do you mean, she used to be *one of them?*"

Leon nods, rocking his head from side to side, as if he finds the idea of Silver and Kacey being friends absolutely un-fucking-believable, too. "Yeah, I know. Kacey and Silver were inseparable not too long ago. You couldn't say one of their names without the other. Kacey and I were in a relationship for years, but you'd never hear the names 'Kacey and Leon' put together. It was only ever Kacey and Silver. You couldn't picture it now if you tried."

I *am* trying. I'm trying to picture it, and he's right. I can't fucking do it.

He gives a brittle, hollow laugh. "I guess now it's not Kacey and Leon, or Kacey and Silver, anyway. It's Kacey and fucking *Jacob*. I wonder how long *that's* gonna last."

15
ALEX

Leon goes back inside, but I need a moment to clear my mind. I can't face the football team right now. All I really wanna do is think for a second, to try and wrap my head around the idea that Silver used to align herself with Kacey and her clones. I don't hate Halliday, but the rest of them are vacuous witches without an independent thought between them, and it's strangely unbearable to think Silver used to be like that. Like *them*.

Around the side of the house, I'm unsurprised to come across a swimming pool. Steam rises off the illuminated body of water, up toward the night sky. Leon made it seem as though his father didn't want to support his commitment to his swimming, wanted him to do anything else but swim, but this makes a different statement altogether. Usually, people have modest pools in their back yards, kidney-shaped, maybe with a fountain or a waterfall. Not Leon's, though. Leon's pool was clearly not put here for relaxation purposes. It's an Olympic sized pool, fiercely rectangular, long and thin with only three lanes. Leon must come out here every morning and swim a thousand fucking laps to justify such a huge, obnoxious body of water.

There are sun loungers to one side of the pool, though they look like they've never been used. I sit my ass down on one and then lie back, staring up at the clear sky. Up there, the heavens are a midnight blue, the color of deep, dark water. The stars are incredibly bright, like burning pinpricks of silver.

Silver.

Silver.

My phone feels like a lead weight in the inside pocket of my leather jacket. I pat my hands against my chest, contemplating taking it out and pulling up her phone number. Maybe hitting the dial button. I wonder briefly where she is. What she's doing. It's late, almost one thirty in the morning, so the likeliest answer to those questions is that she's in bed, asleep, and she wouldn't appreciate a drunk dial from *me*.

A burst of giggled laughter disrupts the quiet behind me, to my right, and I hear the sound of a door closing. The hurried padding of feet follows, and I know immediately that someone's headed this way, toward the pool. I close my eyes, annoyance rippling beneath the calm surface of my exterior. It's too late to get up and get the fuck out of here without being seen, and I don't feel like I should have to move to make room for a gaggle of Raleigh High's social elite anyway. However, when I crack my eyes and realize who's coming running around the side of the building, wrapped in nothing but towels, I wish I had gotten to my feet and bolted.

Halliday, Kacey, Zen, and three other girls all study me with amused eyes as they tiptoe toward the pool. They all have wet hair, which makes it seem as though this isn't their first dip into the water. Halliday's expression tenses when our eyes meet, but Zen's on the other hand…There's something fucking wrong with that girl. She doesn't seem to be getting it, and I don't know of many more ways to tell her to fuck off without getting really hostile. She bounces on the balls of her feet when she sees me, covering her mouth with her hand as she leans over to whisper excitedly in Kacey's ear, and I swallow down a groan. Kacey's eyes cut to find me, and she arches an assessing eyebrow—she seems to be considering something. Zen clasps her hands in front of her chest, doing little hops from one foot to the other, her mouth stretched wide, bearing her teeth as she clearly says, "Pleeeeeeeeeease?"

Kacey sighs, rolling her eyes at Zen, but she nods all the same. Zen squeals like she just got something she desperately wanted for Christmas. Halliday dumps her towel on the tiles by the side of the pool—she's wearing a pink bikini and doesn't seem bothered by the fact that I'm here to witness it. But then, why would she? She's strutted around the stage at the Rock half naked, her tits hanging out of her doctored Raleigh High cheerleader uniform. One guy sitting by a pool isn't going to faze her now.

The other girls shed their towels, all of them wearing a scant, tiny swimsuit or bikini of some description. Zen makes a point of bending over, ass facing me, making sure I get a good look at her as she stoops to fiddle with the ankle straps of her sandals, taking her time to unfasten them. She's shit out of luck, though. I'm not interested, and I'm not looking. I go back to lying down on the lounger, my eyes firmly fixed on the stars overhead.

A series of loud splashes, along with girlish, high pitched squeals, signal that they've jumped into the water. Still, I don't look.

The door opens again, and Jake's voice carries on the fresh, autumnal air. "You girls better be naked," he calls. "My dick could break concrete right now."

Gross. I don't wanna think about Jake's boner, or what nightmarish catastrophe is about to take place in that pool. Gradually pulling myself up into a seating position, I'm about to get to my feet when Jake sidles past me wearing board shorts and slumps down on the lounger next to mine. He holds out a beer to me, grinning from ear to ear. "Saw you out of the window there. Looked like you needed this."

I don't want the beer. I specifically don't want it because he brought it out for me, but I can't be an asshole. Not if I want to put all of these moving pieces into place and get what I want out of this fucked up situation. The glass is beaded with condensation, cool in my hands. The night's growing colder, and it feels as though it's going to start raining any second now, but the beer's still somehow refreshing. I press the beveled rim to my mouth and allow the golden liquid to pour down the back of my throat, raising my eyebrows at the guy sitting across from me.

"There are some shorts inside for you if you want them, man. Leon has a thousand pairs. He doesn't mind us borrowing his shit at these things. Mind you, from what I heard earlier, both Zen and Halliday wouldn't mind if you jumped into the pool sans shorts."

"I'm actually gonna head home in a beat." I'm firm. My tone brooks no arguments. Not that Jake pays any attention to that.

"Ahh, come on, Moretti. The pool's a right of passage. It's gotta be done."

I pull on the beer again, draining half the bottle in one swift move. I could drain the whole thing right now and get the fuck out of here if I wanted to, but Jacob would probably see it as a slight against him. I need to draw this out at least a few more minutes before I get to my feet. "Sorry, man. I'm just not feelin' it. I got shit I have to take care of, anyway."

"Let me guess," Jake says, wagging the neck of his beer at me conspiratorially. "You can't swim, and you don't wanna embarrass yourself."

"I swim like a fish."

"Then, what? There are six beautiful women in that pool right now, and in about ten minutes none of them are gonna be wearing any clothes. Beautiful naked mermaid shit. Tell me you aren't just *dying* to see that. Don't you like tits?"

"I like tits just fine. But I have better things on the agenda."

"What does that even mean? What's better than tits? Hey, Zen!" Jake calls. "Your boy's talking about leaving. I suggest you do something to capture his attention and do it fast!"

It's Kacey that answers, not Zen. "Don't worry. We have something in mind for the newest student at Raleigh High. It'd be rude not to give him a proper welcome, don't you think, baby?"

Jake whoops, throwing his hands up in the air, spilling beer all over the place. "That's my girl. Come on, Kay Kay. Let's see what you got!"

I've never been a relationship guy. I've been around plenty of other guys in relationships, though, and as far as I can remember none of them have encouraged their girlfriends to get naked to impress another man. If I went to the trouble of committing to a girl, I'd destroy any motherfucker whose gaze lingered too long in her direction. This just feels gross on so many fucking levels.

"Watch, man," Jake says, laughing. "Just fucking watch. These girls are dirty as fuck."

Sure enough, Kacey and Zen are stroking and caressing each other, unfastening each other's bikini tops. It happens all too quickly. One second, they're nuzzling at each other, smiling, whispering into each other's mouths, and then the next they're kissing, their tongues lapping at each other, flicking each other's lips. The water's lapping around their bare tits, their hands roving over each other's skin. Kacey gasps as Zen ducks down, taking her nipple in between her teeth. She licks and sucks at the dark, swollen bud of flesh, and Jake grabs hold of my arm, digging his fingers into the sleeve of my jacket.

"Fuuuuck, man. What did I tell you? They're fucking animals."

I look away, drinking the remnants of my beer and placing the empty bottle at my feet. "I'm out of here."

"Fuck is wrong with you, Moretti?" Jake's grip tightens, holding onto me as I try to stand. "Is your dick broken, or are you some kind of fucked up feminist?"

"I told you. *I'm...not...interested.*"

The other girls have all followed Kacey and Zen's lead and are undressing each other, scraps of colorful material floating on the surface of the pool. They cavort in the water, naked, performing a highly sexual, highly intense charade just for us. Their eyes are all on me, hungry, inviting, daring...

I can't see what's happening, but I can guess. Zen sucks in a ragged breath, her shoulders stiffening as Kacey dips lower in the water; I'm assuming she's touching her between her thighs, and Zen looks like she's enjoying it just a little bit too much. Her head rocks back, and Kacey laughs, kissing her neck as she—

The lounger scrapes against the tiles as I push up and away.

My feet are moving.

My back is turned.

A cold, slick, oily feeling is twisting in my stomach.

Jake hollers something behind me, but I don't turn around.

When I walk through the first door I can find back into the building, I'm met with a dozen cell phones, all being shoved into my face.

"Whoa! Hey, Alex! Alex, where the hell are you going? That's the hottest shit I've ever seen, bro!"

I don't know who says it. I cast around, searching the living room I find myself in, trying to find the owner of the voice, but there are too many lights shining in my face. Quickly, they veer away from me as the people gathered in the living room turn back to the windows that look out over the pool. They're aiming their cameras at the scene taking place out there, and it's pretty fucking obvious that they're all recording.

Just...fucking...perfect.

16

SILVER

There's no cell reception at the cabin, which is partially why I love the place. There are no interruptions up here. Just me, my school assignments, my guitar, and my books. It's so damn peaceful. Whenever I come here, I leave behind the politics and bullshit of Raleigh. There are no judgmental, suspicious eyes, following me any time I move. At the cabin, I can breathe. I can be me, without having to worry about defending myself, protecting myself, trying to think three steps ahead at all times. It's ultimately freeing.

The Nova grumbled the entire way from Raleigh to Lake Cushman, threatening to quit on me, but I talked her through it, coaxing and chiding her until she came to a relieved stop in the cabin's mossed-over driveway. Could be that she doesn't want to start again when the time comes to leave, but I'm not worried about that. If anything, the fact that Monday night could roll around and I end up stuck here is far from a tragedy. I could stay here forever, and that would be just fine with me.

It's still early enough, maybe eleven, and the day stretches out before me, full of promise. Outside, the rain hisses like the static from an old radio, the volume turned right up. With a fire crackling happily in the little wood burner Dad brought up here for me a couple of years ago, the little cabin's toasty warm and cozy; it feels like a sanctuary of sorts. One I'm always loathed to give up.

When the girls used to come here with me, things were very different. I didn't really give a shit about the cabin. I didn't pay attention to the small details of the place. I only cared about the partying. The booze we could steal away from our parents. The occasional bottle of pills Zen lifted from her Mom's purse. Diving into the lake in the middle of the night, high, drowsy and languid on Percocet, everything feeling like a dream, the black, inky water over our heads, laughing like giddy ghosts, clinging to each other on the pebbly shore. I'd sleep like the dead, not caring where I rested my head because that was unimportant.

Now, I see the scuffs and the scratches of the place and think of them as lines that mark the face of a familiar old friend, bringing them to life. The collection of small, colorful steel wind-up birds perched on the bookshelves, hiding in the corners of closets, at the back of kitchen cabinets, fallen down the back of the furniture, are totems of my childhood, reminding me of a time when I used to delight in the way they seemed to move of their own accord overnight. I would wake to find them relocated, convinced that they came to life while I slept and fluttered all over the cabin on silent wings, communing with one another in the dark. It was Mom who'd moved them, of course. She'd place them around my bowl at the breakfast table, as if they'd gathered there, waiting for me to drag my lazy butt from my bed, but the sunrise had rendered them inanimate again before I managed to show my face.

The throws that hang over the backs of chairs and at the ends of the beds are old and a little holey, but surprisingly spared by the moths. They have a smell all of their own, a little musty and dusty but comforting—the smell of faded sunlight and summers past, captured in the crocheted pinks and blues, and browns and oranges of the rough wool.

The creaky floorboards have been worn raw in some places, the varnish rubbed away by the footfall of too many sock feet, and the paint on the window sills is chipped and peeling in places. The stove in the kitchen is temperamental and likes to cut out halfway through boiling the water inside the old, dented copper kettle, and sometimes the pipes rattle and judder mid-shower, but there isn't one single detail, one single flaw that I don't cherish about this place. It's perfect in its imperfection, and I wouldn't have it any other way.

My favorite part of the cabin, though, is the deck. Out of the front bedroom, the raised wooden platform is at least six hundred square feet and seems to be both suspended amongst the trees and reaching into the water at the same time. I used to spend most of my time at the cabin sprawled out on the deck when I was a kid. I can close my eyes and still feel the rough wood beneath my belly, the sun beating down on my back, as I laid on my stomach, flipping the pages of book after book, the weeks of summer vacations passing by in a lazy, hazy blur.

I stand in the kitchen now, patiently waiting for my tea to steep, steam curling up from my grandpa's old mug, and I plan out my day: first, guitar. Then, couch time with the newest Orla Stanislavski book. Later, probably around three, I unashamedly schedule in a nap for myself. Then I'll head to the store and pick up the groceries I neglected to buy on the way up here. In the evening, I'll cook myself some dinner and relax in front of the T.V. There's no cable or internet up here, but there's something comforting about selecting a DVD from the cabin's respectable library and tucking myself up on the couch with a blanket—I usually pick '*Die Hard With a Vengeance*,' since it was Grandpa's favorite. The man loved anything with Bruce Willis in it.

I fix my tea with milk and a dash of sugar, the English way, Nona says, and I gingerly carry it up the narrow stairs in one hand, my guitar in my other, trying not to spill any liquid on the way up. Thankfully, the deck is partially covered by an overhang from the eaves so I can sit out there in an old, weatherworn rattan chair with the waist of the guitar resting snuggly against the top of my thigh and not get soaked by the rain.

It comes down in sheets over the lake, pitting the surface of the water with millions of tiny ripples. Across the other side of the lake, a column of smoke rises from another chimney, but I can't see the other house. There's someone over there, just like me, hiding from the world inside a small, warm cocoon; they're probably looking at the column of smoke rising from this cabin's chimney, trying to pick the building from the masts of the trees, too. It's so secluded here that it *is* mildly comforting to know there's someone out there. Not that I'd have a hope of finding or reaching them if I needed help, but still…

I fingerpick my way through a series of chord progressions, warming up my hands, stitching a melody together, trying to keep my mind as blank as humanly possible, but it proves difficult. I can play without any real concentration on my part, so a succession of thoughts parade through my head, one by one, all demanding my close attention.

"I'm not going to force you to fall for me, Silver. You've already been forced to do too much. But don't blame me if I try and change your mind."

Alex's words had felt like a promise. They felt like an omen of some kind. He's not just going to let this lie. He's already shown himself to be a determined person who gets whatever the hell he wants. Turning up at my place after I told him our lesson was off and hanging out with my dad until I came home? Yeah, that proved that well enough. It was there in his eyes, though: a steel will, focused directly on me, telling me in no uncertain terms that I will give him what he wants when all is said and done. Does it matter that it seems to be what *I* want to? I'm so fearful of that—my own urge to hand myself over to him, even though I know just how dangerous it is to contemplate such a thing. I've trusted before, and in turn, I've been so badly burned. My scars are all internal, but they're there, brutal and horrific all the same. He can't see them. He can't know how deep they run.

I'm too broken and too flawed. I can't get him out of my head, though. Like the oxygen bonded within my own blood, he's an ever-present constant that I can't deny myself. He's with me, listening and watching as I play, his dark eyes unknowable, his thick, wavy hair falling down across his face, soft mouth quirked up at one side in that infuriating way of his. Even as a projection from my own head, I can't figure out what he's thinking as he leans against the deck's railing in the rain, his posture relaxed and wound tight at the same time.

After thirty minutes, sifting through a litany of situations and possibilities, where I manage to overcome the damage Jake Weaving and his friends did to me and I somehow find the courage to tell Alex that I like him, I realize that I've only managed to convince myself just how impossible any of it would be. Not the outcome I was hoping for, but it seems to be the truth. I wake up panting some nights, soaked in sweat and tangled in my bedsheets, trying to fight off an echo of violence that has already taken its toll on me. For a while there, I couldn't even bear coming into contact with Mom or Dad without nearly jumping out of my own skin and dissolving into a fit of panicked hysteria.

Alex isn't safe enough to be right for me, and I'm not whole enough to be right for him, either. That's really all there is to it.

After lunch, I grab the groceries I need, grateful for the long weekend and the extra day I'll be able to spend at the cabin. The bait and tackle shop cottoned on to the idea that they were the only store within a five-mile radius of the actual lake and they expanded, turning themselves into more of a convenience store, stocking up on the essentials most holidaymakers require while they're away from home. I pick up some bread, cheese, milk... some ingredients to cook up some pasta, as well as breakfast items and snacks. Merl, the store owner, chit chats with me as he runs my card and takes my payment; I'm laughing and joking with him, helping to load my goods into a paper bag, when I feel my cell phone buzz in the back pocket of my jeans.

I've never gotten a text up here at the lake. Never. Takes me a second to register the fact that something weird just happened, though. When it hits me, I pull my phone out and stare down at the screen, trying to make sense of what I'm seeing.

"Pretty awesome, huh? They put in one of those camouflaged 5G poles on the hillside over on the other side of Whitley Hill. Now, every once in a while, we get a burst of reception and all our messages come floodin' through."

"Why?" A strange numbness is creeping into my fingertips, up my hands, sinking into my joints.

"Little girl drowned here six months ago," Merl tells me. "Such a shame. She was only eight or nine. The parents have been campaigning ever since. Said it was irresponsible that there was no way to call for help. They hold that their little girl would have survived if they'd been able to call an ambulance. Seems to me they're just trying to find someone else to pin the blame on, though. They weren't watchin' the little mite close enough. Couldn't have been if the girl slipped under the water and disappeared in the first place. You're a strong swimmer aren't you, Sil?"

I don't answer him.

I can't.

I'm too busy staring down at the video that's just come through on my phone. I don't know the number, it's not in my contacts, and it's not one I recognize. There's no message, and no name in the actual body of the text. There's only the video: Alex, sitting with Jake at the edge of a swimming pool, holding a beer in his hands. They're too far away to read the expression on Alex's face, but I can picture it just fine because, in the water, Kacey and Zen are naked, their bodies lit up by the pool lights, and they're making out like crazy.

Fuck.

Fucking *fuck*, Alex.

I close out of the video and come out of the Messages app, slipping my phone back into my pocket. Merl's still rambling on about the little girl who drowned, and the new 5G pole on the other side of Whitley Hill. "You stand on that deck a'yours, and you might just be able to get a bar or two if you're lucky. I wouldn't count on it, though. You need help for any reason, you just come on over here, okay? Don't matter what time it is. I'm awake 'til late most nights. Damn sciatica keeps me up. I don't mind answerin' the door if you find yourself in trouble, you know that."

I give him a forced smile, collecting my groceries from the counter. Over his shoulder, a rubber, mechanical fish mounted on a wooden plaque turns its head to face me, glassy eyes staring, and begins to sing, *"Don't Worry Be Happy."*

"Argh, stupid dang thing," Merle grumbles. "Never shuts up. I need to take the batteries out." He turns away from me, swatting at the fish, and I use the distraction to make my escape. I feel like I can't breathe. My eyes are stinging like crazy. Fuck, I can't fucking breathe.

Outside, I dump the groceries onto the passenger seat and watch the video again, hands shaking, heart thundering in my chest. I have no right to be angry. Alex owes me absolutely nothing. For the next fifteen seconds, I fluctuate between anger and hurt, though, feeling utterly, completely stupid.

I tap out a message before I can stop myself. Not a reply to the video. A message to Alex.

Me: Congrats on your conquest. Zen always gets what she wants. Glad you had a good night.

Almost immediately, a bubble pops up with three dots—I wasn't expecting a response from him at all, let alone so damn quickly, but Alex is typing out a reply. I sit there, staring at the screen, dread tightening like a fist in the hollow of my chest.

The three dots inside the bubble continue to shuffle, signaling that he's still typing, but then it just…disappears. I instantly kick myself. I've spent the afternoon telling myself there's no way I could ever be with Alex, and in the next fucking breath, I'm allowing myself to get sucked into this bullshit, letting myself sink into some sort of nasty downward spiral because he might have hooked up with Zen or Kacey. Or fucking both of them. God. Nope. I shudder out of the thought.

The phone chimes, just as I toss it beside the groceries on the passenger seat. I sit very still, trying to decide how I want to proceed here. I shouldn't read the message. I should drive back to the cabin and put this behind me. It's bad enough that I texted him in the first place. I should have ignored the video and fucking deleted it.

Then the phone chimes again.

Fuuuck.

I pick up the phone, hating myself.

Alex: Conquest?

And then…

Alex: Where are you?

I drop the phone, startled by the question. Why does he want to know where I am? He does *not* need to know where I am. I really am such a fucking idiot. I shouldn't have said a word. I should have kept my mouth shut and pretended I didn't care, even if the idea of him with someone else, especially one of my ex friends, did sting for a second. Now, I've tipped my hand in an awkward way that's going to be difficult to talk my way out of.

Ignore him, Silver. Do not reply. Best way to handle this is to just pretend like it didn't happen.

"Great advice, asshole," I growl at myself. "You're great at pretending, aren't you? It's your fucking forte."

I scowl at the screen, the few brief words Alex sent my way blazing there in black and white, and I can't think of anything else to do, though. I drive all the way back to the cabin, cursing at myself under my breath. When I check my phone, parked in the driveway, there are zero bars in the top left-hand corner of the screen, and I'm awash with relief. But even I know that it's stupid to be relieved, when I can't hide from him forever. This weekend might be a day longer, but Tuesday isn't that far away. I'm still going to have to face Alex at school. I delete the video, along with the text, so I can't torture myself with it anymore.

17

SILVER

"*I'm not a monster, though I do sometimes work for monsters.*"

I cram popcorn into my mouth, eyes glued on the T.V. screen. I can quote this movie word for word, but I still like to watch it with the subtitles on. Simon's big reveal that he does, in fact, have a soul, does nothing to endear him to me, as I sip on a diet coke, digging my toes beneath the cushion at the end of the sofa.

I blink and see Alex, sitting on the edge of a lounger, staring at Kacey and Zen as they rub their naked, wet bodies up against one another. Apparently, it is *not* safe to close my eyes just yet, not even for a microsecond. I try to lose myself in the explosive action taking place on the screen. It's not easy, but after a while, I'm suitably numb and warmed by the fire, and I begin to drift off.

Much later, I come to with a start, knowing that something woke me. The living room's filled with the sound of static, and the T.V. screen is all snow, the DVD having switched itself off at the end of the film. All is silent. The patter of the rain on the sloped roof is even absent, and my ears seem to ring with the tense quiet.

Something isn't right. Something…

There's a loud slam outside, the sound of a car door being closed.

I leap up from the couch, my heart rate skyrocketing through the roof. Someone's here. Someone's fucking *here*. My pulse pounds at my temples as I run to the kitchen, not knowing what exactly I plan on doing when I get there. Shit, shit, shit. Dad would have told me if he was coming to the lake. Mom never comes here, period. She's too damn busy to take a break and make the drive. It's unlikely anyone would make the trek down the two-mile-long, narrow driveway, the trees pressing in on either side of the pot-holed dirt track if they were lost and looking for one of the Airbnb cabins located along the other side of the lakefront.

No, to find yourself at this particular cabin, you have to know it's here, and you have to be looking for it specifically.

I feel like I'm going to throw up.

Hurrying back to the living room, I snatch up my phone from the couch, trembling as I open up the screen and—fuck! No fucking reception. What am I going to do? WhatamIgoingtodowhatamIgoingtodowhatamIgoingtodo?

Calm the fuck down, Silver. Just calm the fuck down right now. This is how people always die in horror movies. They panic. They lose their shit, and they wind up making stupid decisions, and then they wind up fucking dead. Do not *panic.*

Easier said than done, though. My thoughts are scrambled as I rush back into the kitchen again and look for something to arm myself with. Meat tenderizer? No. Pasta strainer? Fuck, no. Kebab skewer? Errrr no. Knife! Yes, a knife. I yank open the cutlery drawer, frantically trying to find a blade that isn't dull and pitoned with rust, but it's been a decade since we had a BBQ here. You wouldn't be able to pop a fucking balloon with any of the—

BANG!

BANG, BANG, BANG.

Fuck.

My ears are ringing. It occurs to me, after years of coming to the cabin and being entirely unafraid of the place, that coming here alone was a remarkably stupid move on my part.

Mom and Dad are used to not hearing from me when I'm here. They're not expecting me back until Monday night. Two days away. How badly can a body decompose in forty-eight hours? Are they going to find me mangled and in pieces when they finally drive up here to find out what's happened to me?

A huge weight is pressing down on me, crushing my chest, making it hard to breathe. I grab a knife, any knife, and tiptoe toward the front door, realizing, horror sending a shock wave of adrenaline through my body, that I didn't lock the goddamn door.

Fucking idiot, Silver! FUCKING IDIOT!

I'm two feet away from the door when the floorboard beneath my feet creaks.

"*Silver.*"

The voice on the other side of the door isn't posing a question, asking if I'm there. It's a statement. A declaration. It belongs to Alex Moretti.

I sag against the wood, my heart giving a hard, painful spasm below my ribs. Recognizing who it is hasn't helped, it seems; I can't decide if the knowledge is even a good or a bad thing. I'm out of breath, panting, when I speak, even though I've barely moved. "What the...*hell* are you doing here?"

"Open the door."

"*No!*"

"Open the door, Silver. It's two o'clock in the morning. I'm freezing."

My mouth falls open. Sure enough, when I look down at Mickey, his disproportionate arms confirms that it's nearly ten past two. "What the fuck are you doing, showing up here at two in the morning, Alex? Are you fucking *insane?*"

"Probably. Open the door."

I swallow, and the metallic tang of fear floods my mouth. I'm not afraid that he's here, but my fight or flight response is still taking a second to cool its jets. "Go home, okay? This is *not* okay."

Silence rings like a bell in my ears again.

"All right. I'm gonna go get in the car. I'll wait five minutes before I go. Take a beat. If you really want me to go, then stay inside. If you wanna talk, then come out."

"I'm not gonna come out, Alex. You're fucking mad!"

"Like I said. I'll wait five minutes."

I hear him walk away, footsteps moving away from the door and down the steps that lead up to the cabin's porch. A second later, a car door slams again.

Fucking psycho.

Why would he do this?

Why would he drive all the way out here in the middle of the night?

This was a bad move on his part. A stupid fucking move.

I turn away from the door and hurl the knife, grinding my teeth together. Now it's not fear that I taste in my mouth. It's just blood. I must have bitten the inside of my cheek.

"Urrgghhh! ASSHOLE!" I yell the insult, even though he probably can't hear me. Of all the dumb, shitty, cruel things he could do...

I oscillate wildly between anger and relief as I pace up and down in front of the door.

A minute passes.

I gouge my fingernails into the meat of my palms, digging so hard my hands begin to throb.

Another minute.

Another.

I'm going to fucking kill him. Dad won't be so pally-pally with him when he finds out that he came up here and scared the shit out me like this.

Another minute.

Not that I can tell Dad. If I do, I'll also have to tell him that I was here alone, and then he'll never let me come again.

Another minute.

The engine revs to life outside. Light floods through the living room window, throwing everything into stark relief, shadows climbing the walls.

Shit.

I don't even decide to do it. I act without thinking, throwing open the cabin door and storming barefoot out into the night. Alex is sitting in the driver's seat of an old Camaro, his hands resting on the steering wheel. His eyes lock onto me as I charge toward him; he remains expressionless as I pitch up at the side of the car, raise my fist and smash it into the driver's side window. Pain explodes through my hand, sharp and breathtaking, stars spangling, flaring in my vision.

"FUCK YOU, ALEX MORETTI!" I spin around, mud squelching up between my toes as I shake out my hand, walking away from the car. Fuck, that really, really hurts. I cradle my hand to my chest, holding it there, waiting for the pain to subside, but it only seems to get worse. The car door opens and closes again. Alex doesn't say a word, which is almost the most infuriating part of all of this. He doesn't even ask if I'm okay.

"You know," I hiss. "You know what happened. You know… what they did. You know how fucking *frightening* it would be…for me to have someone roll up here…in the dark, when I was alone…"

I'm crying, and I don't know if it's because my hand hurts so much, or because I'm still reeling from the fear and the panic of what might have been about to happen to me. Soon, I'm sobbing, and I can't control it. I'm straining for breath, fighting not to collapse. I can feel myself slipping, drowning, tumbling, descending into some broken kind of madness that I have never allowed myself to succumb to before. Not even after it happened.

Not even when my friends turned on me, and I found myself shunned...

I am breaking.

I am splintering.

I am finally shattered into pieces.

Alex is right in front of me, then. He's holding out his hands, dark eyes calm and steady. "*Va bene. Va bene. Respira, Argento. Respira.* Shhhh."

I want to smash my fist into his face, just like I smashed it into the car window. Instead, when he takes a slow, obvious step toward me, I fall into his arms and bawl into his chest. His arms wrap around me tight, and for the first time since that night in Leon Wickman's bathroom, I cry as I am held. The smell of laundry detergent, pine needles, and *Alex* roars inside my head as I suck in breath after breath. My hands are fisting his t-shirt, pulling hard at the fabric, but he doesn't push me away. Not even when I let go and slam my balled-up fist against his chest. Or any of the other five or six times that I hit him as hard as I can.

"Shhhh. It's okay. Breathe, Silver. Breathe. You're okay. I've got you."

He shouldn't. He shouldn't fucking have me. None of this has anything to do with him, and yet I can't manage to shrug free of him. It *hurts* too fucking much. God, I knew it did, I knew it was there, eating away at me, but I've distanced myself so effectively from the pain that I had no idea how crippling it would be when it finally overcame me.

I lose myself for a long time, and Alex doesn't falter. He stands firm, crushing me to him, whispering to me in both English and Italian as the out of control emotion gradually begins to ebb. After what feels like a lifetime, a dull, numb kind of calm settles over me, and I begin to feel stupid.

With shaking legs, I push away from him, wiping at my face with the backs of my hands. "I'm sorry. God, I'm sorry. I think...I may have overreacted a little." I try not to groan when I notice the front of his grey t-shirt is soaked, a unique Rorschach pattern of my grief staining the material. Alex's eyes are no longer calm. They're on fire, blazing, the muscles in his jaw jumping angrily as he looks down at me.

"Don't. Don't do that," he growls. "I'm the one who's sorry, Silver. I fucking..." He fists his hands into his hair and pulls, elbows crooked around his ears. He looks like he's about to hit the car window himself. "I've done a lot of stupid shit, but I've never been this fucking dumb," he mutters. "I didn't even think what would happen if I just showed up on the doorstep. Of course you'd be afraid. I scared the shit out of you. I'm a goddamn moron."

Under any other circumstance, I'd agree with him, but he's so obviously furious with himself that I don't feel the need. Still, that leaves me with nothing to say, because he *did* scare me...

He drags a hand down over his face, inhaling sharply. When he faces me, I realize that this is the first real sign of true, proper emotion I've ever seen on him. He looks like he's about to lose *his* shit now. "I'm sorry, Silver. I'm a fucking idiot. I did *not* mean to do that."

I feel small. Vulnerable. Honestly, I feel a little ashamed for having such an epic meltdown. "It's okay," I whisper.

He shakes his head, chewing on the inside of his bottom lip. "It isn't. It's not okay. None of it is. You're allowed to say that."

I can only sigh, suddenly exhausted, drained down to the very roots of my soul. "How did you even know where to find me?" I ask. Seems like the only pertinent question right now.

He looks off into the darkness, into the expanse of shadowy trees, his brows pulling together into an unhappy frown. "Halliday," he says tightly.

"*Halliday?*" A sharp pain lances through my chest. What the fuck? It makes sense that he'd be on speaking terms with Halliday, since she was there in that video, just as naked and just as drunk as Kacey and Zen. It feels wrong that she'd be talking to Alex about me, though. Out of all the girls, Halliday has been the only one who hasn't made it her sole objective to make my life a living hell. It makes me feel awkward, uncomfortable in my own skin. Alex must see the look on my face.

"She's been working at the Rock. The bar where *I* work. Your brother hangs out with her brother or something? He told her you were here. She gave me the address."

Halliday, working at a bar? She looks mature for her age, but there's no way she could pass as twenty-one. Makes no sense.

"Look, I really fucked up. I shouldn't have come up here like this. I should have waited 'til you were home or something. You weren't replying to my texts, though. I wanted to tell you—" He runs his tongue over his teeth, shaking his head again. I can feel his frustration from here. He was holding onto me a moment ago, comforting me, running his hands up and down my back, stroking my hair, but now it seems as though a gulf has opened up between us, yawning wide, and he doesn't know what to do with himself. "*Fuck!*" he yells, and the word echoes out into the forest. "I should go," he says. "This was a huge fucking mistake."

"You're here now." I sniff, pulling the sleeves of my hoodie down over my hands against the cold. "Say what you came here to say. You might as well."

He huffs. Looks like he's battling with himself, trying to figure out what he wants to do next. What he wants to say. "I just…I realized after your text that you saw that video. Jacob's been sending it out to everyone at Raleigh. He thinks it's fucking hilarious for some reason. Kacey doesn't even seem that bothered—"

"She wouldn't. She uses her body like it's a weapon. She gets naked at every available opportunity. She's probably told Jacob to send it to me."

"So fucked up," Alex whispers. "Look. I know it looked bad."

"It didn't. It looked like you were having a great time, making new friends. Why would I care about that?" God, I'm so full of shit.

Alex gives me a look that says the exact same thing. "Who are you lying to right now, Silver? Because you're not fooling anyone."

"Anyone?" I gesture to the open forest surrounding us, laughing weakly. "There's no one here but us birds."

"You're not fooling *me*," he clarifies in a stony voice. "You're not fooling yourself, either." He rubs at the back of his neck, grimacing. "Aren't you tired of this yet, *Argento*?"

"I don't know what you mean." Aaaaand the lies just keep on coming.

Alex huffs miserably down his nose. "Okay. Well…real talk. I don't like girls very often. I don't normally spend my days pissed at myself because I can't stop myself from thinking about someone. I can safely say I have never truly, really given a shit about anyone apart from my kid brother before—"

"I don't know if *that's* a good thing to be admitting."

"Just…*stop*. Quit hiding from the hard stuff. I'm not fucking hiding from it. Not anymore. If you can't just be real for one second, then I'll do it for the both of us. My life is a fucking mess right now. I have so much shit going on, and I've been trying my best to forget that you even exist, but I can't, okay? I like you. I care about you. I care that you probably think I hooked up with one of those dumb bitches at that party, when I didn't. When I walked away, disgusted at how pathetic they were being. And I know you don't want to hear any of this shit. Your life is fucked up, too. But I see you, Silver. I see you looking at me, and I can *feel* the want in you. This playing around, tiptoeing around the truth is just fucking…it's fucking pointless. You like me, too. You care about me, too. You don't know why yet, but I can show you. I'm a risk. I'm a danger. I'm not a fucking safe bet by anyone's standards. But I can be good for you if you let me. At least I think I can. You're the first fucking person in this entire world who's ever made me want to fucking *try*. And…" He runs out of steam. The muscle's ticking in his jaw again. He's trying to rein in the fire that seems to have caught in him, and he's having a tough time doing it.

Meanwhile, I'm having a hard time standing still, hearing the words that he's saying. This is not easy for me. It's been a long time since I've been spoken to like this—someone telling me the truth, on a base level, and looking to me to reciprocate.

I open my mouth and Alex stills. His eyes are slightly narrowed, his nostrils flared, hands formed into the shape of fists at his sides. He's waiting for me to deny everything he's just said, to sweep it all aside, and he's ready and waiting for it. He's not going to let me get off lightly. "I do like you," I say softly. "I shouldn't. I—I'm just—It doesn't matter if I like you, Alex. I can lie in bed and think about you all I want. I can watch you, and I can imagine…" Shit. This is too hard. I can't even find the words.

His chest is rising and falling rapidly, the tendons straining in his neck. "What do you imagine?"

"Alex, please—"

"You're not a fucking coward, Silver. I *know* you're not. You prove that every day that you show up at that school. *What do you imagine?*"

"I—" I take a deep breath. Everything is such a mess. I close my eyes and take a deep breath. "Kissing you," I whisper. "Your mouth on mine. Your hands on me. Laying my head on your chest, listening to your heartbeat…"

A harsh, pained sound escapes him. "Silver…"

"I imagine us being together. I imagine having you to myself, that you were mine. It's so easy to picture walking down the hallway at Raleigh with your hand in mine because I know it *would* be easy. It would be so much fucking better because I wouldn't be *alone* anymore. I could fall in love with you, Alex. I could see myself doing that." I nod, trying not to stumble over the terrifying words. "It wouldn't take much. But I can't let it happen."

Alex is as rigid as the statue of David. He looks struck dumb by what I've just said. I wonder if I've gone too far, been too honest, said *too* much. Guys Alex's age don't talk about falling in love. They say you're 'seeing each other' or 'talking' to avoid even calling you their girlfriend.

But he takes a slow, cautious step forward, heat radiating off him like a furnace. "Why not?" he asks. "I'm not good enough?"

"No! Of course not! God, Alex. I want you. I want all of those things! I want you to touch me. I want you to kiss me more than I've ever wanted *anything*."

"Then just give in, Silver! Stop fucking fighting so hard."

"I'm not fighting!"

"Yes, you are. You have been since the moment we met. *Before* we even met!" He huffs down his nose. "Fight the hard stuff. The wrong stuff. But stop fighting *me*. I'm neither of those things. Just...*trust me*."

I'm so close to tears. "I don't know how, Alex." If I so much as breathe right now, I'm going to fall to pieces, and I desperately don't want that.

He steps into me. A frigid breeze whips through the clearing between the cabin and the lake, and his wavy, dark hair blows across his face. It swirls around his head as the wind eddies, and I'm struck for the millionth time that he can't possibly be real. This dark, tortured soul, covered in so much ink, standing before me isn't the kind of creature to find his way into my life and somehow make it better. He was meant for other things.

A wolf and a rose—savage and wild, beautiful and tender. A dichotomy if ever I saw one. I realize for the very first time that the ink on the backs of Alex's hands really are an accurate representation of him. I stare at them as he slowly lifts his hand, and then he's carefully stroking his thumbs over my cheekbones, cradling my face so reverently that I think he's worried I might shatter against him.

His voice is filled with emotion as he sighs out his next words. "I promise. You won't even need to try, *Argento*. I'll make it as easy as breathing." He moves with infinite patience, slowly, giving me every opportunity to bolt. Somehow, despite my heart fluttering in my chest like an injured bird, I stay rooted to the ground, my feet bare in the earth, as he bows down to meet me, lifting my face to him, and he kisses me.

I've been kissed before, but not like this. Not like it means something. Not like it really is a promise. It starts slow, tentative, gentle, but I can feel the unrest in him. I know he wants to claim me with his mouth, but he holds back. He's patient with me, and I...I begin to feel the fractured pieces inside me slowly starting to hurt a little less. His fingers thread into my hair as he slowly guides my mouth open.

The moment the wet heat of his tongue touches my lips, something is kindled in me—the beginnings of a fire I already know will burn out of control if given half a chance. I'm hot all over, eaten alive by both fear and need as he pulls me to him, firmly holding me against his chest. The taste of him fills my head, cool and fresh like mint.

I surprise myself when I reach up and place my hand at the back of his neck, pulling down so he can kiss me harder. Maybe I'm proving something to myself now, meeting him in the middle, daring to slide my tongue into his mouth, too. I *can* do this. I want it more than anything I've ever wanted before. I fit against him, so much smaller than him, like a piece of a puzzle falling into place, and in one blindingly quick moment, I begin to believe in this. In him. In us. That there can *be* an us, without the fear that's been festering in me like a poison ruining everything in the span between heartbeats.

I didn't know it, but I've been waiting for him for a long time now.

When he pulls away, breath ragged, eyes wide, his pupils are blown, turning his irises almost black. "That's it then, Argento. The decision's been made. You're mine, and I'm yours. And the whole of Raleigh High is gonna know about it by five minutes past eight, Tuesday morning."

18

ALEX

"*Wake up, Passerotto. I made you something good. Alessandro, mi amore, open your eyes.*"

The smell of caramelized sugar and the sound of my mother's voice wakes me. For a drowsy, blissful moment, I am six years old, and my mother is stroking a feather along the bridge of my nose, making me squirm as I surface from my dreams. She used to do that all the time, even though she knew it made me mad and tickled like crazy. I rub at my face, scratching my nose, eyes opening slowly, and I see the full-bloomed roses, wrapped in vines, winding up my arm, and it all comes flooding back. Eleven years, rushing in, pressing down on me, replaying the greatest hits of my life, which, up until last night haven't been all that fucking great.

I wasn't paying much attention to the cabin last night when Silver showed me into a small bedroom on the ground floor, complete with bunk beds and Hulk sheets. Max's room, she told me. Turns out her brother is the same age as Ben. Now, I get up, kicking my way back into my jeans and sliding my arms into my t-shirt, noticing that this morning is the first morning in a long ass time that I haven't woken up with a stiff neck on the couch in the trailer.

There *is* a bedroom there. I could use the bed, but somehow climbing into it feels wrong. Three years, I slept on a two-inch thick mattress in Gary's converted basement. He made a point of making sure I wouldn't be comfortable, and so I made a point of getting accustomed to the cold and the ache in my bones when I woke as a fuck-you to the bastard. Now that I have no reason to mistreat my body and subject it to such uncomfortable conditions…I don't know. It's hard to stop saying fuck you to Gary, even though the motherfucker's dead.

From the way the sun's pouring in through the windows, already climbed halfway up into the sky, it must be about eleven or so. Everything looks so different in the daylight. I wander down a narrow hallway, emerging into the living room, and I catch sight of Silver through the doorway, standing in the kitchen in front of the stove, stirring viciously at something. She hasn't noticed me yet, and I take a moment to watch her. Her hair's down. I have never, ever seen it down before. The light catches at it, highlighting individual strands of honey and gold, and I remember how good it had felt to bury my hands in the thickness of it last night. Too fucking good.

She's wearing little blue shorts with ribbons tied into bows on either side of the legs, and a white t-shirt that's so big it's slipping off her, exposing one of her shoulders. She hums as she cooks, and I recognize the song. It's *'Vienna,'* by Billy Joel. So fucking weird. Weird that she even knows it. I don't want to startle her, so I clear my throat, walking heavily across the living room, making sure she knows I'm coming.

She pauses for a second, but then carries on with her stirring, whisking at something in a pan.

God, she's something else. I can't bear how fucking beautiful she is. It cuts me down to the quick. I don't even hide the fact that I'm staring at her. I'm never going to hide that she fascinates me, not ever again. "Good morning." I can hear the amusement in my tone as I prop myself up against the kitchen's door jamb. Stands to reason, since I'm highly entertained by the way today has started out—the two of us, together, in the middle of nowhere, alone. Feels fucking strange.

Aside from last night, we've never been alone like this. There have always been plenty of people within shouting distance. Other students. A teacher. Silver's father. Here, there's only me. Only her. She takes her sweet time turning around, and I can barely wait to see her face. God, I'm turning into such a fucking lovesick asshole puppy, I'm almost making myself sick. If Monty could hear me now, he'd drive his hand between my fucking legs, grab hard and squeeze, just to make sure my balls were still hanging there.

She's not wearing any make-up. Her eyes are bright and filled with nervousness, but the reckless grin she fires at me tells me that she's not going to kneel to her own apprehension today. "I'm making French toast and Crème Anglais," she informs me. "Though you're probably a bacon and eggs guy. Scratch that. You probably down a quart of engine grease for breakfast, don't you?"

I smile, scrubbing a hand through my hair, trying to make it lie flat. I know it won't, it never does, but it's worth a shot. From the crooked smile and the hiked-up eyebrows, Silver's not too sure about my crazy bedhead look. She prods a whisk in my direction. "You can eat, but then you need to leave. My parents will flip if they find a guy up here."

I try not to notice the fact that she isn't wearing a bra and her nipples are peaked beneath the material of her shirt, but I am a guy, so that's basically impossible. My poker face is unrivaled, though. "Fair enough," I tell her.

She looks deflated. "Fair enough?"

"Yeah. I plan on claiming most of your spare time, Silver. I don't want your parents ready to run me through with a pitchfork on day one."

"I thought you might put up a bit of a fight."

I give her a devilish smirk. It's fucked up how easy it is to change gear on her. Stalking into the kitchen, I approach her, keeping my thoughts from my face. Still, I'm cautious as I place my hands on her hips. "You want me to put up a fight? You got it. I'm not going anywhere. I'm staying right here with you until Monday night. And when we go back to Raleigh, I'm going to kidnap you, and have you sleep at my place. I'm keeping you for myself, Silver. I'm never letting you out of my fucking sight. Don't bother arguing. You'll only be wasting your breath."

She stares up at me with unfocused eyes, her lips slightly parted. Neither of us has commented on the fact that the whisk she's still holding in her hand is dripping some kind of yellow liquid onto the cracked linoleum floor.

"Uhhh. Okay," she says on an exhale. "Fine."

It's my turn to repeat her. "Fine?"

A quick nod. "Sure. I mean..." She shrugs. "What my parents don't know won't kill them. And my dad liked you for some reason, even though you showed up at the house uninvited."

Slowly, I lean down and kiss her. It's the lightest kind of kiss, the barest suggestion of one, our lips hardly making contact, but it seems to have a wild effect on Silver. Her eyes dance, alive and feverish. "Seems I have a bad habit of showing up uninvited," I say.

"Are you handling me like I'm a china doll now?" she asks. "You can kiss me properly. I won't break because of a kiss."

I run the tip of my index finger lightly over her forehead, down the bridge of her nose, over the biteable swell of her lips, and then trail all the way underneath her chin and down the slope of her neck until I reach her collar bone. I've wanted to touch her so many fucking times in abstract, weird ways like this. She stands still, patient, maybe a little tense, as I stroke the pad of my finger into the small hollow at the base of her neck. I pull my hand away. "There are people out there who poison themselves on purpose," I tell her. "Small doses, every day."

She's quick—doesn't need me to explain how this piece of

information is relevant to our situation. "You think I'm going to build up a tolerance to you? If you feed me small sips of you? You're not poison."

I nod, wetting my bottom lip, my eyes roving hungrily over her face. "Yes. I *am* poison. And yeah. I'm a staunch advocate for too much too quick. That's always been my M.O. but I'm willing to develop an iron will in patience to make sure I don't fuck this up."

She crooks an eyebrow at me, and I mirror her expression, making her smile.

Fuck. Me. Dead.

I made her smile.

This is the first time I've made her anything other than angry, and the rush of emotion, seeing her turn that smile on me like I fucking deserve it or something, feels like a kick to the gut. God, how am I ever going to be worthy of this girl? I have no clue, but I'm gonna figure it out if it kills me.

"I had a dream," she says quietly. It's a shy admission, which looks damn cute on her. "I dreamed we were somewhere warm. Together. In the sun."

"I'm sorry. Sun? I have no idea what you're talking about."

"Hah-hah," she says dryly. "I think it was Hawaii. We were swimming in the ocean, and all of your tattoos washed off in the water."

There's a weird tightness in my chest. I don't know if it's because she dreamed such a strange thing, or because she dreamed of me, period. I mostly only feature in other people's nightmares. "Is that your subtle way of telling me you want me to go through a hundred laborious, incredibly painful hours of tattoo removal, *Dolcezza?*"

She rolls her eyes. "I'm not finished. I dreamed they all came off in the water, but then they transferred onto me. And they were all in the wrong places."

I tug my bottom lip through my teeth, holding my hands over

Silver's face, covering her eyes. "Hmm. I'm not sure a bunch of face tattoos would suit you."

She bites back a coy smile as she takes hold of me by the wrists, the beater smearing yellow batter up my arm, and pulls my hands away. "I—" She starts. Seems like she can't finish, though.

"You what?"

"I've wondered about the rest of them. Your tattoos. How many do you have? Do they all mean something to you? Where are they?" She trails off, twin patches of red staining her cheeks. She's fucking ridiculously adorable when she's embarrassed.

Leaning into her, unable to resist the chance to make that blush spread a little further, I brush my mouth lightly against hers again. "Are you asking for a guided tour of my body, Silver Parisi? Because I will happily oblige."

The change in *her* body is very noticeable. Her back straightens, her hands tightening around my wrists. *Great job, asshole. You've freaked her out.* "I'm only teasing," I say quietly, nudging the end of her nose with my own. "I'm not suggesting we get naked and run around the cabin like animals."

Her eyes are like mirrors when she looks up at me, pale blue, almost silver. "I'm not upset. I—I *would* like the guided tour. So long as the rides are optional." She seems pretty pleased with her euphemism.

"Oh. So you're a dork? Good to know." I grab the beater from her and toss it underhand into the sink behind her, pulling her closer to me. Our bodies are pressed up against each other, and I spend all of a heartbeat trying to figure out if I should try and angle myself in a way that might hide the fact that I have a raging hard-on, but I run out of time. Silver feels it—she has to. It's digging into her fucking hip like a reinforced steel baton. I expect her to flip out, at least get a little weird, but she doesn't. Instead, she gives me a slightly scandalized open mouth smile, coolly arching an eyebrow at me.

"If I'm a dork, then you must get turned on by some pretty

weird stuff," she says breezily.

"You don't know the half of it." I gather her hair in my hands, reveling in the weight and the feel of it as I brush it back over her shoulders and I expose her bare neck. There is a line in the sand where physical contact with Silver is concerned; I made it myself, so I know how far to go and when to pull back. Kissing her neck is definitely not on the right side of the line, but I allow myself one slow, careful graze of my lips against the porcelain column of her throat. Just one…and it's enough. The identical flushed patches of red on Silver's cheeks have grown, but I don't think they're caused by embarrassment anymore.

"I'll show you my tattoos, and you can grade every single one of them," I tell her. "But I think we're gonna have to hit up that diner I noticed on the way up here to grab some more food, *Dolcezza*."

She frowns at me. I don't know if she's noticed, but her hands have found their way to my chest, palms resting familiarly against my pecs, and the contact is making me want to fucking sing. She cants her head to one side, and asks, "Why?"

"Because the French toast you were making is on fire," I reply.

She nearly jumps a foot in the air as she spins around, rushing over to the stove, swearing loudly like a sailor. "Fuck! Shit, fuck, shit, fuck, shit, fuck! Shitshitshit, nooooo…." She turns the burner off, shoving the frying pan off the ring, and then proceeds to bat at the flaming, blackened pieces of French toast with a kitchen towel. Not really a good idea. I intervene, physically picking her up by the waist and setting her down by the kitchen table, then I take the towel from her and use it to pick the pan up by the handle. The whole thing goes in the sink. I turn on the tap, blasting the contents of the pan with water, and the mini fire immediately gutters out.

Silver stands next to me in front of the sink, regarding her destroyed attempt at breakfast with morose resignation. "Probably for the best," she says. "I'm a horrible cook. I'm sure *you'd* have been the one that ended up poisoned if you'd eaten that."

19

SILVER

I pinch myself repeatedly while Alex is in the shower, hard enough to bruise. This doesn't feel like real life. I can't bend my head around the fact that he's here, with me, at the cabin, and we're actually doing this. I'm letting him in, for fuck's sake, and he...god, for some, unknown reason, he actually *wants* to be here with me.

By the time we get to the café on the other side of the lake, the heat blasting on full inside Alex's Camaro, we've missed breakfast and have to make do with lunch. People halt their conversations, forks freezing halfway between their plates and their mouths, as Alex and I make our way to a booth. No one really comes up here in October, and the café crowd today are mostly locals; they're not used to someone like Alex showing up in the middle of their BLTs and their gossip sessions.

We both order a sandwich each and two coffees. The waitress, Layla, who I've known since I was eight, shoots me a wide-eyed look as she scribbles in her notepad. I think she's trying to signal me in Morse code with her furious blinking. *Do...you...need...help?* I laugh, shrugging at her, and Alex reaches across the table and takes my hand.

Such a normal, everyday thing that people do, and yet it feels monumental to me. Alex's smile is tight when I look at him, though.

I kick him gently under the table. "What's the deal?"

"I know you're tough as old boots, but you sure you can handle this?" He dodges the balled-up napkin I throw at him in response to the boots comment.

"What? People noticing that you're a bad boy heartbreaker?"

He pulls a face. "It doesn't bother me, people looking. Never has. But it might end up bothering you if you can't even go out to grab some food without feeling eighteen sets of eyes lasering into your back."

Layla brings our coffees. I take a sip, watching, a little horrified, as Alex dumps four packets of sugar into his mug. "I think you've forgotten who you're talking to. I'm stared at way more than you are every day at school. No one thinks twice about your ink there. Well, actually, they do. They probably think it's hot. Me, on the other hand? Being a lying whore who tries to ruin Raleigh Royalty is *not* hot."

Alex's expression turns stormy. He looks out of the café window, out onto the lake, deep lines furrowing his brow. "Don't say that."

I shrug. "It's just the truth."

"You're *not* a lying whore."

"It doesn't matter whether I am or I'm not, though, right? People believe what they want to believe. They believe what everyone else believes, because they're too scared to stand apart from the crowd. In the end, I am whatever they say I am, Alex."

He picks up the salt shaker, his hand closing around it into a fist, still staring out of the window. "I'm gonna need to know exactly what happened that night," he says in a monotone voice.

My ears are suddenly on fire. I want to shrink back into the seat, or under it, or just fucking run away. I do my best to keep my voice steady when I say, "I thought you believed me."

His head whips around, eyes bearing down on me, full of wild energy. "I didn't mean it like that. I'm not trying to fact check."

Shame spirals through me. *'Don't be such a fucking tease, Silver. Show us that pretty little cunt. Come on, princess. That's right. Open your mouth. Wider. Wider. Stupid bitch. D'you wanna die for the sake of a quick fuck?'*

I jolt at the memory of the hand cracking against my cheek. Alex's eyes widen at the sudden movement. I can't bear the look on his face, so I avert my gaze, staring down at the peeling laminated menu that's tucked behind the condiment bottles. "Why then? What's the point in rehashing it all? It's all over and done with now. It doesn't matter."

For a second, Alex doesn't say anything. When I risk a sidelong glance at him, he's running his thumb along the edge of his steak knife, pressing so hard his skin has bleached white. A small, crimson bead of blood drips down onto the table. "It matters," he says flatly. "I'm gonna need to know who I have to hurt first, aren't I?"

"Don't be stupid, Alex. You're not going to do anything to any of them."

He puts the steak knife down and quickly wipes away the blood from the table as Layla approaches with our food. Once she's gone, I repeat myself, needing him to hear me. "Those guys are untouchable. Their families own the school. They own the whole town. Hell, they even own the cops. If you fuck with them, there'll be hell to pay, and it won't be any of them settling the bill. *Believe me.*"

"I believe you. But I still want you to tell me. Do you think…" He knows he's asking something really hard. He looks like he hates that he's asking it of me. "Do you think you could do it?"

"I don't know. What's the worst, most awful, brutal thing that's ever happened to you? You think you could tell me all about it in great detail?" I'm not being sarcastic. I genuinely want to know.

He gives me a hard look, jaw set, and then nods. Just the once. "My mother killed herself when I was six. I came home from school. It was a Thursday, so I only had a half day. The kitchen smelled strange, and it made me lightheaded to breathe. I didn't know it then, but the gas burner was still on. If I'd turned on a light, I would have blown the whole fucking place sky high."

I reach across the table, placing my hand over his. "Alex, I didn't mean right now."

He shrugs one shoulder, quirking his mouth up at one side, too. "Ben was only nine months old. He was in the living room, naked, with a cut on his arm. Was screaming at the top of his lungs. I knew something wasn't right, so I went from room to room, looking for my mom. I found her in the spare bedroom upstairs. She wasn't dead yet. One of her eyes was missing, and her hair was wet, full of these little white shards. Her hair was dark like mine, almost black, so I didn't know it was covered in blood until I touched it and my hand came away red. I didn't know the little white shards were fragments of her own skull.

"She was gaping at me, her mouth opening and closing like a fish. I was six, so I didn't really know what had happened. I saw the gun on the floor. It was half under the bed, and she was reaching for it, hand clasping and unclasping. She was making these awful wet, gurgling noises. I started crying, because I knew she was going to die. She was crying too, but she was crying tears of blood, and I didn't know what the fuck to do, so I tried to leave the spare room to get to the phone, but..." He swallows, then exhales a steady, long breath.

This is soul destroying. This is the most terrible thing I have ever heard, and I wasn't even there. Six-year-old Alex was, though. I rub the heel of my hand into the center of my chest, as if the physical action will ease the emotional pain I'm feeling. "Alex, you really don't need to—"

"She grabbed hold of my ankle. Wouldn't let me go. She was so fucked up, but it was surprising how tight she held onto me then. I turned her onto her back, and that's when I saw that most of the left side of her jaw was missing. She couldn't speak. She tried," he says, nodding, "but she couldn't. So, she told me what she wanted by pointing at the gun. I didn't want to give it to her, but I could see that she was in so much pain and I didn't know what else to do, so I got it for her. I gave it to her. I did."

I cover my mouth with my hands, my eyes burning like crazy. I'm too scared to breathe for fear that I'll end up bursting into tears. Alex looks at me. Looks hard. Doesn't waiver. "She couldn't close her hand around the handle. She kept on trying, and she kept on dropping it. In the end, she started this…awful wailing. I'd never heard anything like it before. She was suffering. She wanted to go, and she couldn't fucking do it, and I knew what was going to happen next, but—"

"Oh, Alex."

"The gun was fucking huge. I think it was a desert eagle or something, must have been to blow half her face off like that, but I wasn't really looking at it properly. At the time, all I knew was that it was heavy and I couldn't hold it straight, not even with both hands. She helped me. She guided it to her other temple. The one she hadn't already ruined. She closed her eyes, sighed, and it was like this…this wash of relief came over her. She nodded, squeezing her hand around the top of my thigh, digging her fingernails into my leg, and then I remember her jerking, the sound of the gun firing, the small room filling up with this horrible smelling smoke, and there being blood running down the wall. And…that was it. I called nine one one. Told them what had happened. There was a second there where they thought I'd just straight up fucking killed her. Took two days for the coroner to confirm that my story was probably the truth. They kept me in a psyche ward, locked inside this room with three fully grown crazy motherfuckers who kept trying to touch me. And then it was the system. Foster care. Bumped from home to home."

His skin has taken on this deathly hue, like a part of *him* has just died in the retelling of this dark, fucked up story. "If I'd come home earlier, I probably could have stopped her."

"It wasn't your fault, Alex. None of it."

He looks down at the food in front of him, then back up at me again. He shifts a little, laying his hands flat against the top of the table. I don't think he knows what to do with them. "You're right. I know," he says. "She did it to herself. Even in the end, *she* managed to pull the trigger. But I held it for her, Silver. *I fucking held it.*"

20

ALEX

I run the St. Christopher medallion along the chain around my neck on the drive back to the cabin, tearing myself a new one. *Way to ruin lunch, ya fuckin' asshole. Nothing like a good old gory suicide to really whet a girl's appetite.*

Beside me, Silver sits in silence, two to-go boxes full of cold food resting on her lap. I think she's fucking traumatized. *I* was traumatized as fuck for a seriously long time after that happened to me, but I've had the benefit of eleven years and a whole heap of a state-ordered therapy since then. I don't like to think about it. I sure as fuck don't like to talk about it, but I *can* if I really feel the need to.

Once we're back, Silver puts our abandoned food into the fridge for later and goes upstairs. When she comes back down, she has her guitar in her hand; she opens up the doors that lead onto the lower deck, letting the cold air inside, and goes to sit in a weathered old chair by the railing. She doesn't say anything as she begins to play. The melody is haunting and soft, filled with a sadness that makes my throat ache. She's seriously fucking talented. Her fingerpicking skills are on fucking point.

I sit myself down on the deck, back resting against a wooden post, watching her hands slide deftly up and down the instrument. I'm still only wearing a t-shirt, and the cold knifes through the material, but I barely feel it. I'm too sucked into the music that spills from her like a tortured confession of her own. To the right of the deck, the lake lies as still and flat as a mirror, reflecting the gunmetal grey of the sky, as well as the brace of trees that venture all the way down to the shoreline, their exposed roots, knotty and tangled, dipping into the water.

Time slows as Silver plays. She doesn't even seem to be paying attention to what she's doing, her fingers flying nimbly up and down the neck of the guitar. It's quite something to watch. When she finally stops, her hands falling still, I get to my feet and take the guitar from her. I'll admit, smug bastard that I am, that I'm pleased by the look of shock on her face when I begin to play, mimicking the melody, pitch and pace of the song she was just playing herself.

"You motherfucker," she says, a small smile spreading across her face. "I s'pose this is what you meant. When I asked what you were planning to do when the end of year music exam rolled around, you said you had it covered."

"Were you picturing bribery?" I ask quietly, still playing her tune from memory.

"Something like that." She chews on her thumbnail, her eyes following me as I pace up and down the deck, head bowed, expanding now on what she played, throwing my own twist on it, adding my own sorrow into the mix. That's what this song is, after all: a haunting, beautiful, painful lament. When I'm finished, I sit on the deck again, Indian style, laying the guitar flat over my legs, so it doesn't get scratched.

"I want to tell you what happened to me," Silver says. "But I worry."

"What are you worried about?"

"That you'll hear all of the gruesome, messed up details and you won't be attracted to me anymore. You'll feel sorry for me instead, and I don't want that."

"I can guarantee you, there is nothing in this world that could ever make me unattracted to you, Silver. And I'll be sorry that something so fucking horrible happened to you, but I won't *pity* you. You're too strong to deserve anybody's pity. What else?"

"I'm worried you'll do something stupid. You said something pretty disturbing in the café. You said you were gonna hurt them. And you didn't say you *wouldn't* do anything to them after that."

This is a tough one. Urgh. "I didn't take back that comment, because I don't plan on lying to you. Ever. And I *will* hurt them for what they did to you. D'you think they deserve to walk around, free, after causing so much pain? D'you think they won't do it again to someone else if they're left unchecked?"

She looks doubtful. "You forget I heard that conversation outside Darhower's office. You're on your final warning. If you do anything illegal, you're gonna end up in jail, and that's not something I can live with. Not for me. Plus, if you use violence against them, the way they used it against me, then how does that make you any better than them?"

Drumming my fingers against the top of her guitar, I consider this. The solution I come up with doesn't make me happy, but it's something at least. "What if I don't do anything illegal? Or use violence?"

"How could you possibly avoid it?"

"I'm a resourceful guy. If I have to, I'll make it work."

"I don't want to testify," she says miserably. "I can't face that. My parents wouldn't be able to live with themselves if they knew."

"They don't know? *Any of it?*"

"You don't understand. It's not as simple as just telling them something bad happened to me. They had me so young. They're good parents, but they have so much going on, Alex. They both work like crazy, and Max needs all of their focus. He's just a kid. If I tell them this, he'll fall by the wayside. Everything will be about me. Their lives will stop. I can't do that to them. I can't do that to Max."

I can see how she'd think that, but her perspective is so warped. "They're your parents, *Argento*. When they eventually do find out about this, they're going to be so fucked up. They're gonna be devastated that you didn't trust them to have your back."

She looks away, out over the lake; clearly, she doesn't want to hear this. She wants me to just understand and accept that she's made the right decision. I'm not going to get her to change her mind, so instead, I press for the offer I just made her. "How about it? All above board. A legal takedown. Not a single drop of bloodshed in the pursuit of justice?"

"And no testifying on my part."

I sigh. "Fine. No testifying on your part." She waits, considering my proposal, her eyes searching the calm water. "Come on. Don't you want a little payback? Just a little revenge, for everything they put you through?"

"Of course I do."

"Well?"

"Okay. If you think it's possible to accomplish that within those parameters, then you have my blessing. Do whatever you want. I'll give you a blow by blow account of what went down that night. But I'm not as brave as you, Alex. I don't think I can get through it if I have to say it out loud. I'll write it down, but you have to swear you'll burn it once you've read it. You have to fucking promise me, Alex. And you can't treat me any differently afterward."

Mr. Elliot, my old therapist, would have balked at this deal. He would have said it would be better for her to say it out loud, that there would be some sort of catharsis to be had that way, but shit. Who am I to argue with her? If this is the way it's gotta be, then this is the way it's gotta be. I give her a three-fingered salute. "Scout's honor. I love a good fire. You have my word."

21

SILVER

We spend the rest of the day watching movies and talking. We pretend like Alex didn't tell me the story of his mother's botched suicide, and I haven't agreed to write a fucked up essay on that one time when I got sexually assaulted. He tells me more about his brother, about how he and Ben were placed in a couple of homes together in the beginning, but that they kept getting separated over and over again when Alex began to act out and made life difficult for their foster parents. He's angry when he tells me about the woman who's looking after Ben now—a legal secretary over in Bellingham called Jackie. She makes it hard for him to see his brother, switching up his visitation days, snooping into his business, reporting him to C.P.S. whenever he puts a foot wrong.

"That woman's tried to have me incarcerated more times than I can count," he says. We're sitting on the couch. My legs are over his, covered by a blanket, and he's running his fingers up and down the soles of my bare feet, smirking every time he hits a ticklish spot and I twitch. "I deserved it back in the beginning. I was an asshole. I did plenty of shit to warrant the ten million phone calls she put in with the cops." He lets his head fall back against the sofa cushions. "I set her trash cans on fire once. I also stole her cat."

"You *stole* her *cat?*"

"Ben's allergic. His eyes were all itchy and red every time I saw him. He'd be covered in hives, and Jackie didn't seem to give a shit. For years, she and I were locked in this shitty war of attrition, neither of us backing down, neither of us giving any ground, and then I realized...I *was* the problem. I had to make some changes. Since then, Mother Theresa wouldn't have had shit on me, but Jackie's still trying to shut me out. It's been two years since I started playing nice, and Jackie'd still have me banished to fucking Alaska if she could."

I want to touch him. It's becoming more and more normal to reach out for him. We've spent the day trading casual, fleeting moments of physical contact, but I'm still nervous as hell when I slide my hand under the blanket and find his arm. His skin is smooth and hot to the touch. My fingertips buzz as I trail them up, over his bicep, slipping beneath the sleeve of his t-shirt until I hit the top of his shoulder. We're both vibrating with this frenetic kind of electricity. Alex looks like he's forgotten all about Jackie; he's staring down at his shoulder, at the point where my fingers are drawing small circles into his skin, and he's as tense as can be. Slowly, with heavy, hazy eyes, he looks up at me, and suddenly all I want to do is slide over, straddle him and rip off the shirt I'm wearing.

He has a hungry predator's eyes. Dark eyes that make promises and cut down to the quick. He's unflinching. When Alex Moretti looks at you, you feel your soul laid bare, and it's the most disturbing, thrilling thing I've ever experienced. Right now, he's looking at me like he wants to eat me.

I draw my hand out from underneath the blankets, face heated, fire singing in my veins. It's unspoken between us: after everything that happened, I can't be rushed into anything. I'm shocked by how easy this is with him, though. How much I want it. Want *him*.

"You say you've been on best behavior, but that isn't true, is it?" I whisper.

His gaze is still so unfocused. I've become so used to Deadpan Alex at school that I've learned the language of him now. I can recognize and decode even the smallest facial movement, the tiniest, little twitch. But here, alone with him, Alex isn't the guarded, hyper careful version of himself that I'm so used to. He's let down a considerable number of his walls and seeing so much of what he's thinking and feeling on his face is making me a little dizzy. He picks up my hand and lifts it to his mouth, softly placing a kiss against the inside of my wrist. "And why would you say that?" he asks.

Hard to think with his lips brushing over such sensitive skin. "You did something before you came to Raleigh. Must have been pretty bad to get you kicked out of Bellingham and nearly carted off to prison."

He smiles against my wrist. "Just ask, *Argento*. I thought we were done with the pussyfooting around."

"Okay then. What was it? What did you do that got you into so much trouble?"

He groans, smiling awkwardly, slumping back into the couch. He's suddenly very interested in the fringe trim on the ancient cushion beside him; he tugs at it, clearing his throat. "Well. The last time I got separated from Ben, I was sent to live with this guy, Gary. He was a parole officer, and he fucking haaaaated me. Told me he only took me in because he was sick of watching little punks like me get away with blue murder, and I was going to have some sense knocked into me if it was the last thing he did. And boy, did he like knocking sense into me."

It's far too late for the dread that writhes in my gut, urging me to do something, to help him—this has all taken place already—but I feel it just the same. "He hurt you?"

Alex grunts, eyes blank, fixed on the fire that's burning in the grate on the other side of the room. "I left a dish in the sink, I earned myself a swift right hook. I came back too late, I got a steel toe cap to the ribs. I played guitar too loud, I got three of my fingers broken."

"He broke your fingers?" Of all the terrible things that happened to him, this, to me, is the worst. Stealing a musician's ability to play is tantamount to stealing away their soul. Alex holds up his hand—the one with the rose inked into the back of it—and wiggles his fingers.

"Middle, ring and pinkie," he informs me. "Bastard held me down and pinned me to the side of his truck, then slammed the door on them repeatedly until I started fucking screaming. I was twelve."

"God, Alex…"

"I was lucky really." He closes his hand into a tight fist, shoving it back underneath the blanket. "They healed up straight. No real, long term damage done. They ache when it's cold and I'm on the bike sometimes, but…" He shrugs. "Gary was trying to crush my *hand*. If he'd fucked up the bones and the tendons there, I never would have played again."

"What happened then? How did you end up getting away from him?"

Alex smirks. "Puberty. I got big, and I got big quick. Fucker was content wailing on me when I was a scrawny little shit with Popeye muscles, but I started bulking out when I was fourteen, way quicker than any of the other kids in my year. I was fifteen when I started hitting back, and Gary…boy, Gary did *not* like that. Took him a while to give in, mind you. He spent a year trying to get the upper hand on me. He'd wait until I was asleep in the basement, and then he'd creep down there and start laying into me while I was unconscious. Fractured my jaw once. Eventually, that was the only way he could best me, so I just stopped sleeping. I used to lie there on the mattress, faking it, willing him to come sneaking down those fucking stairs so I could surprise the motherfucker and knock a couple of his teeth out.

"One night, he started whaling on me with this crowbar, and I fucking lost it. I took it from him and started in on him with it. Next thing I know, the cops are dragging me off, and Gary's being fawned over in the hospital, poor, saintly, selfless member of the community that he was. I was put before a judge. Told me I had to spend the summer break in juvie and do six months' community service after that. Once I got out of juvie, I was expecting to be sent to another shitty foster home, but that's when Monty showed up."

"Monty?" I haven't heard him mention the name before.

Alex nods. "Montgomery Richard Cohen the Third. He owns The Rock. He was friends with my dad back in the day. He read about me beating the shit out of Gary in the Hoquiam Gazette and petitioned the county clerk's office to take me once I was released."

"Wow."

"Yeah. Said he owed my father a debt, and he supposed it'd been paid now."

"So you went to live with him?"

"Only for a few months. The county did a couple of random drive-bys to make sure I was behaving myself and sleeping where I was supposed to be sleeping. Once they signed off on all my paperwork, Monty gave me the keys to my place now, and I've been living there ever since."

"At the Salton Ash Park?"

"You missed a word out of the title, Silver," he says ruefully. "The Salton Ash *Trailer* Park. I'm not ashamed. No need to skirt around it."

A prickle of shame bites at me, making my cheeks burn, because that's precisely what I *did* do. "Sorry. I don't even know why I did that."

He gives me a slow, almost sad smile. "Sure you do. You live in a big house with a wraparound porch and a manicured lawn out front. You have both your parents. You get to scream at your brother every morning because his bedroom is the room next to yours and he's annoying the shit out of you. Whereas *I* live alone in a doublewide on a gravel plot, and I have to fight for the chance to spend enough time with my brother that he might get the chance to annoy me."

I slump against the cushion, feeling like a grade-A asshole. "You're right," I murmur. "I'm s—"

"Don't apologize. I'm not sorry. I have freedom now. I can go where I want. Do what I want. Be who I want. And believe me, my place right now is a dramatic step up from Gary's basement. Which brings me back to my morose story. I always planned to pay Gary a visit, to let him know how much I appreciated his care and attention one last time, but I got caught up working for Monty and trying to settle back in at Bellingham, and time kinda got away from me. And then, one morning, Monty chucks the newspaper at me, and there it is on the front page." He holds up his hands, framing the imaginary headline. "'*Officer Feldman, dedicated civil servant of Grays Harbor County, killed following denied parole appeal hearing.*' He'd been escorting someone from the courthouse when a group of guys in ski masks jumped out of a van and shot him in the chest. Killed instantly. They were rescuing their buddy. As far as I know, they got away with it, too. Ironically, Gary was buried in the cemetery on the far side of this lake. When he got out of hospital after the beating I gave him, the fucker went to the detention center where I was being held and told them I'd stolen a piece of his jewelry. They let him rifle through my shit, and he took the only thing he knew mattered to me."

"Which was?"

He tugs down the neck of his t-shirt, closing his hand around the small golden medallion hanging around his throat. "My mom's St. Christopher. Gary knew I never took it off, but that I would have had to surrender it at the center, so he took it to hurt me. Then he died, and I was determined to get it back. I went to his place and tossed it, but it wasn't there. I knew the asshole wouldn't have sold it or given it away. It was the one thing he had over me, and I knew for a *fact* the sick fuck would have coveted it because of what it meant to me. So I went and dug him up. And low and behold, there it was, clasped tight in his greedy, dead little hand. A cop found me pissing on him and Tazed me. And *that* is how I ended up at Raleigh, hanging onto my freedom by the skin of my teeth."

"Jesus, Alex." Hesitantly, I touch my fingers to the fine chain where it falls across the back of his neck. I've noticed him toying with it many times since he started at Raleigh, but I haven't realized how significant it is until now. How important. "I don't blame you for doing any of that," I tell him. "I would have done the same thing."

He doesn't say anything to that. The light from the fire dances across his face, and I can't help myself: I release the chain, my hand rising up the back of his neck, a wild shiver of nerves and anticipation flying up and down my back as I brush my fingers over the closely cropped hair at the base of his skull. High, and a little higher still, and then my hand is buried in longer, wavy hair. I wind my fingers through it, curling the length of it around them, almost massaging his head, and slowly Alex closes his eyes.

"*Dolcezza*," he whispers "*Non fermarti*."

My heart trips over itself, stuttering frantically to find its lost rhythm. "You called me that earlier. What does it mean, *Dolcezza*?"

Alex's voice is rough-edged and low. "*Sweetness*," he murmurs.

A rush of adrenalin slams into me, pooling in the pit of my stomach. Sweetness. I am his sweetness. *Fuck.* "And…the other part?" I ask.

His eyes still closed, his face in profile, his features cast in gold by the fire, Alex looks like some of kind of mythical god. His chest rises abruptly, and he lets out a pained groan. "*It means don't stop.*"

He moves so quickly, I barely have time to yelp as his eyes fly open and he twists, grabbing me by the waist, lifting me from the sofa in a swift, effortless maneuver that makes me feel as though I weigh nothing at all. His hands are firm, guiding me, and all of a sudden I'm exactly where I wanted to be five minutes ago, legs either side of him, straddling him, my chest crushed up against him as his hands press urgently against my back. He shifts down a little, sliding down the sofa, and I feel him between my legs—his dick, rock solid and hard enough to dig into the underside of my thigh. For one long, paralyzing moment, I think I'm going to punch him in the throat in an attempt to flee the situation. My head… fuck, my mind is roaring. I can't…I can't fucking…

Alex takes my hands and places them on either side of his throat, holding his own hands over mine, drawing me down closer to him. I can feel his pulse hammering frantically beneath my palms. "Ssshhhh. It's fine. It's okay, Silver. I'm not going to hurt you. I'm not even gonna touch you. Relax."

"Okay. Okay." I nod up and down, breathing in through my nose. "Okay." By the third okay, the surge of panic that rose up and closed around my throat is dissipating.

"I'm never going to do anything without your permission," he says, in that low, ragged voice. "I just wanted you here, against me, your body against mine. I wanted you fucking closer, Silver. Your hands in my hair like that…" He doesn't finish. I don't think he can.

Taking my time, along with a second to catch my breath, I slide my hands out from under his and gingerly brush the tips of my fingers down the side of his face. "It felt good?" I whisper.

His eyes are bottomless and fierce in the almost dark room. "Beyond good," he grinds out. "Your hands *anywhere* on me feel good. But that…" He shakes his head, like he's trying to clear his addled mind. "No one's touched me like that before."

I see the truth in his eyes. I'm no fucking fool. Alex doesn't carry himself like a guy who's inexperienced with women. I've heard of The Rockwell, and I know of its unsavory reputation. There's no doubt in my mind that Alex hasn't been a virgin for a very, very long time, but to have him tell me that I'm the first person to touch him in such a simple, intimate way like that, rubbing his head? I had no idea I could be any sort of first for him, and that feels fucking incredible.

With one hand, I tentatively begin to repeat the motion, weaving my fingers into the thickness of his hair, pressing the tips of my fingers into his scalp, biting my bottom lip between my teeth when he shudders beneath me. He rests his hands at my hips, but I'm unafraid of the contact. I'm fascinated by the way he's looking up at me, eyes burning, jaw set, head angled back a little, exposing the column of his throat as he leans into my touch.

"Stop biting your lip," he grinds out roughly.

"Why?" God, my own voice has its own uneven step to it, too.

"Because it's driving me fucking crazy," he says.

"Now, now, Mr. Moretti. Patience is king."

"I'm patient. For you, I'll be eternally patient. Doesn't mean watching you bite that lip isn't the most torturous thing I've ever fucking seen."

I'm pleased, though I try not to be. Being pleased means I'm enjoying the fact that I can turn him on so easily. And that? That's dangerous.

When Alex shifts underneath me again, my reaction is immediate and unintentional, though. I press my hips down, rolling them once against him, and Alex goes absolutely, utterly, terrifyingly still. No sound comes out of his mouth, but I can read the word he mouths perfectly well on his lips. "*Fuck.*" A tendon strains in his neck, the muscles in his chest tensed beneath his t-shirt as he tightens beneath me.

I'm burning up. My face must be bright red from my jawline to my hairline. I feel…I feel alive, in a dangerous, reckless, insane kind of way, and for the first time since Leon Wickman's Spring Fling party, I also feel a little powerful. Like in that slight, barely-there movement just now, I regained a scrap of the power that was stolen from me. The first time I rocked myself against him might have been an accident, but the second time I do it…shit, I don't know what possesses me, but the *second* time I do it, I do it on purpose.

A flare of pleasure, intense and a little bewildering, sparks between my legs as I roll my hips again, and Alex's fingers dig into my sides, gouging into my hips, through my jeans.

"Jesus fucking Christ, Silver," he pants. In two seconds flat, I'm off his lap, on my back, the sofa underneath me, and Alex is hovering over me, holding his weight off me, his mouth less than an inch from mine. "If I kiss you now, I'm going to try and fucking consume you," he rasps. "It won't be a little sip. It won't be fucking controlled."

I take hold of the bottom of his t-shirt, not knowing what the fuck to do—if I want to tear through the thin material or just have done with it and rip the damn thing over his head. "Do it," I pant. "It'll be okay. I think...I think I'll be okay."

A brief, flicker of hesitation flashes in his eyes, but it's gone before it even really forms. Gritting his teeth, a guttural, pained sound works free from the back of his throat. *"No."* He shoves away from me, throwing himself back toward the other end of the couch, then he groans again, running his hands through his hair, tugging on it hard. "We should be smart. We should wait," he says breathlessly.

Oh, my fucking god. Silver Parisi, what the fuck is wrong with you? I am the one who was assaulted, beaten and humiliated, and yet it's *me* trying to rush into things now? "Shit. I'm sorry. I'm...fuck. I'm really sorry, Alex."

He sits there with his hands still buried in his hair. Then he falls slack, sinking back against the couch. His hands drop to his sides, then he glances at me out of the corner of his eye. "It's okay. It's not a big deal."

"But you're a *guy*," I say, wincing. "That kind of shit really *is* torture for you. Doesn't it cause serious internal damage or something? If you get turned on and then you can't do anything about it?"

Alex doesn't react to this statement the way I expect him to. He twists around quickly, facing me, grabbing hold of my hand. "You know what that is, Silver?" he growls. "That is a lie told by pieces of shit who'll say anything to get what they want. A fucking *lie*. There wouldn't be a man left alive if that were true. I'm pretty sure every single adolescent guy in the world gets a boner on the bus on the way to fucking school each morning. We're not out there, yelling at the driver, calling them a prick tease 'cause the vibrations from their fucking bus made our dicks hard. We're not being carted off to hospital because we couldn't have a moment to stroke our dicks and our balls fucking exploded. It's part of being a fucking guy. We get turned on. Nothing comes of it. We all move on. End of story. Any guy who tells you otherwise is probably gonna end up using that bullshit as an excuse for raping someone down the line."

"*Oh.*"

"Did he say that to you?" Alex snarls. "Is that the fucking line he pulled?"

"No." My chest is so tight, it hurts. That night in Leon's bathroom tries to rear its ugly head. The ugly memories try to surface, to command my attention, to take control and hurt me. I don't want to remember, though. I am so sick of fucking remembering. I'm done with being held prisoner by that night. All I want to do is be here with Alex. To feel like I felt a moment ago, when I had my legs wrapped around him, and I felt like I was in charge of my own actions. I cover my eyes, forcing the images and that all-too-familiar fear back down into the basement of my soul.

"Sorry," Alex says softly. "I shouldn't have asked that."

"It's okay. I just…I…" I can't find a way to tell him how I'm feeling right now. Or what I want. Frustration wells up inside me, tightening like a collar around my neck, suffocating me, and I know I'm on the verge of snapping. Normally, I'd retreat into myself at this point. Shut down and hide. I don't want to be that version of myself anymore, though. If I ever want to overcome this instead of it overcoming me all the time, then I have to change the way I've been doing things, because obviously the old way hasn't been working.

I'm shaking, nervous as hell as I get up off the couch. Alex frowns. He cracks his thumb knuckle, his jaw working, like he's angry at himself. "You want me to leave?" he asks quietly.

"No. Just...stay right where you are." I feel ridiculous and inexperienced as I take my shirt by the hem and slowly pull it over my head. I stand there for a second, stiff, the shirt dangling from my hand, watching Alex, trying to gauge his reaction. A fierce, tight look forms on his face. His posture's rigid, awkward, his torso twisted a little from where he was turning to look at me a second ago, but he doesn't move an inch. It's as if he physically *can't* move.

Dropping my shirt, I move onto my jeans, unfastening them and slowly, carefully sliding them down my legs. God, I want to be better at this for him. Confident and sure of myself. Kacey used to put on a show in her bedroom all the time, demonstrating the provocative strip tease she'd performed for Leon the night before, and this, what I'm doing right now? This is nothing like that. This is a simple, careful, shy undressing, and I feel like a fucking fool...

"*Silver.*" Alex's voice is a coarse, uneven whisper. "What are you doing?"

I step out of my jeans, rolling back my shoulders, convincing myself to stand tall, even though I'm wearing nothing but my underwear. If I were Kacey, I would have been sporting a skimpy matching lingerie set. I wasn't exactly planning this, though. My bra is white and lacy, my panties a pale baby pink, plain and simple. The garments are pretty, and I feel good in them, but they're definitely not doing anything to make me look less innocent. "I want this," I say softly. "I want you to see me."

"Silver, we have so much time. There's no need—"

I reach around my back, unhooking the catch on my bra strap. I'm a ball of insecurity as I slowly slip the straps over my shoulders, letting them fall down my arms. *Do it, Silver. Just fucking do it.*

I need a few deep breaths before I lower my arms, allowing the front of the bra to fall away to the floor. My chest bare, breasts exposed, I stand, letting myself get used to the idea that I'm nearly naked. Alex's eyes don't waver from my face. Not even for a split second. I wait for his gaze to dip, to look down, but they don't.

"What happened to patience?" he rasps.

I take another deep breath and finish the job, hooking the material of my panties at my hips and sliding them down. I've laid myself bare, and now I'm bathed in heat, bashful and slightly embarrassed, but also thrilled by what I've just done. *I took control. I was brave.* I realize I was unafraid, and that is a monumental step. "Fuck patience," I say. "I don't want to wait. I want to be normal. I want to feel you insi—"

Far too quickly, Alex looks away, his head whipping around so that he's looking out of the window. He's frowning deeply, expression stormy, his dark eyes hard...and I'm struck with the awful realization that *he* might not actually want this. Oh, fuck...have I just stripped out of my clothes like some stupid, naïve little girl, assuming he'll want me, when he's not actually attracted to me like that at all?

No. No that's just my paranoia talking. I know he wants me. I've felt him hard against me more than once now. He nearly just lost his shit when I was straddling him. So what the hell is his problem? I have to know, even if I'm afraid of what his answer might be. "Alex? Why won't you look at me?"

He swallows hard, his eyelids shuttering. "I can't. You're..."

"Hideous?" I laugh quietly. A little sadly.

"God, no. You're so fucking beautiful. I don't deserve to look at you." He hesitates, and when he speaks again, his voice is thick with emotion. "I'm no good fucking trash, Silver. I'm nothing. I have no fucking business being here. I sure as hell have no right to look at you like that. I can't do it. It feels like stealing something that doesn't belong to me."

I hear the truth ringing in each one of his words. Not my truth, but his. He really believes everything he's just said, and it absolutely destroys me. I step forward, taking him by the hand, and I cautiously climb back onto his lap. Every nerve ending in my body is ringing like a bell. It'd be better if I could find something to cover up with first, but I need to perform immediate surgery on this broken man's soul. He needs to know exactly how I feel about him.

"Look at me," I demand. When he doesn't, I place my hands on either side of his face, and I force him to. His eyes remain diligently locked on my face. "You are *not* trash. You're not worthless. You're brilliant, and you're clever, and I'm the one who's lucky to have you in my life. We come from different places, Alex, but that doesn't mean I'm better than you, or that you're *less* than me. I want you because of the way you challenge me. I want you because of the way you make me feel alive. I want you because you make me feel free. You're better than any painkiller. You're better than any drug. You're strong, and you're resilient, and you take what's yours. So take *me*, because everything that I am is yours, given freely, gladly and fucking proudly."

His chest rises sharply. With infinite care, he rests his hands on my bare thighs, his pupils dilated wide open. He's still wound so tight, I feel like he's going to snap any second now. "I'm far from perfect. I need you, *Dolcezza*. My hands are fucking aching for you. If I let my guard down for one fucking second, *I'm* not gonna be proud of myself. If you tell me to stop, I'll stop. If you tell me no, I'll hear you, and I'll fucking listen. But...if you don't...I won't be able to rein myself in. I'll kiss you. I'll touch you. I'll make you fucking moan. I'll sink myself so deep inside you, I won't ever want to stop fucking you, and I can't..."

My skin is on fire. My nipples are peaked so hard they're actually hurting in the most delicious, dizzying way. The nervousness I felt before has gone now. The memories that have taunted me for so long are nowhere to be seen. All I can think of, all I can see, all I want, is Alex. I kiss him, pressing my mouth down hard on his, fisting his hair in my hands.

He resists for a second. His fingers dig into my thighs, and he lets out a pained groan. The tight grip he's been holding over himself shatters into a million pieces when I yank on his hair, though. His hands slide up my back, hot and firm, pulling me to him. His tongue plunges into my mouth, and he kisses me savagely.

I may be vastly inexperienced when it comes to sex, but my body thankfully knows what it wants. I grind myself into him, rocking my hips against him all over again, and I moan breathlessly as my breasts rub up against his chest. Alex tears his mouth away, and the distant, hard edge in his eyes has disappeared, replaced by a vivid, urgent hunger that sends a hot surge of adrenalin through me. He looks at me, finally letting those impossibly dark eyes of his drop, skating down my body, and it's almost too much to bear.

"Jesus, Silver," he hisses. "You're fucking incredible." He cups my breasts in his hands, kneading my flesh, and a shudder travels through his body. I place my hands over his, encouraging him to squeeze harder, so I can fucking feel it, so that it's almost painful, and he groans again. The sound of his pleasure makes me shake with anticipation.

I shouldn't want to make him feel this way.

It shouldn't feel so good to have his hands on my body.

I shouldn't be so desperate for him that it feels like I'm about to ignite and catch on fire.

But I do.

He arches over me, leaning me back, holding me in his arms, and the next thing I'm aware of my nipple is in his mouth. He licks at the swollen, sensitive bud of flesh, then takes it into his mouth and sucks, and it feels like I've been struck by lightning, a bolt of heady pleasure firing between both my breasts, down in between my legs.

"Ahh! Holy shit!" I curve my body against him, winding my fingers into his hair, guiding his mouth down onto me, asking him for more, and Alex delivers. His teeth graze against me, fastening around my nipple, and I immediately react, rocking myself against him, needing to somehow get closer.

I had no idea it would feel like this. I had no idea I could want someone *so* much...

I'm needy and desperate as I grab at his shirt, trying to remove it from his body. He pulls away, giving me an open-mouthed, slightly dazed smile as he helps pull the shirt over his head. His eyes are so damn intense, driving into me, scouring every inch of me as he grabs me by the waist, spinning me over and lowering me onto my back by the fire.

He stands, unfastening his belt and then his jeans, kicking out of them, removing his boxers all in one go. The air seems too thick to breathe for a second, as he looks down at me, and I look up at him with matching expressions of wonder on our faces. He's the most incredible thing I've ever seen. The swirling dark ink on his chest is beautiful. It travels up over his shoulders, down his arms, around his neck—too many patterns and images to take in right now.

His athlete's physique has always been obvious even through his clothes but seeing him naked is something else entirely. His chest and stomach are ridiculously muscled, his abs tensed. The faint definition that cuts down into his groin, forming a vee shape, leads my eyes naturally down to his cock. He's hard, standing to attention, bigger than I've imagined, the few times I've allowed myself to picture it. I swallow, a buzz of electricity pooling between my legs.

"Birth control?" he asks. "Do I need to get something?"

"No. No, I take the pill."

Alex takes himself in his hands, squeezing, and I suck my lip into my mouth again. "Don't worry," he says. "It won't hurt. I'm gonna make sure of it. God, your body is..." He shakes his head, like he's having troubling thinking straight. "You're perfect in every way, Silver. Your tits are fucking mind-blowing. I can't get enough of you."

The feeling is more than mutual.

He crouches down, and I tense a little, even though I'm not scared. Not really. Alex's hands run up the insides of my thighs, reverently stroking over my skin. "Remember...just say the word and all of this stops."

I know he'll stop, too. I trust him. This is nothing like before. I loosen my limbs, consciously taking a beat to relax, and he growls at the back of his throat when my legs part. "Fuck, Silver. Your pussy looks so fucking good. Do you know how wet you are? I can fucking *see* how turned on you are."

It's a little embarrassing to think that it's that obvious, but I shy away from that feeling. I want him to know, after all. I want him to know what he's doing to me. I don't want him to doubt. He drops down onto his elbows, his chest resting against my leg, and a dizzying wave of pleasure soars through me as he uses his tongue...

"*Shit!* Oh my god!" I rest my hands on his head, not sure what to do with myself as he laves against me, his tongue finding my clit and flicking against me. It feels... I have nothing to compare this to. I've seen guys go down on women before. I've been curious. I've looked up all kinds of things on the internet, but nothing has prepared me for how *good* this feels.

Alex hums against me, and the vibrations travel through my body. "So damn sweet," he pants. "My *Dolcezza*. I've kept myself up at night, imagining what you taste like, Silver Parisi. You're fucking delicious. I'm gonna want to eat your cunt for the rest of time."

That word—cunt—sends all kinds of thoughts skittering around in my head. It's such a harsh word. So derogatory. But when Alex says it, using it like this, with his face buried between my legs, it turns me on so much I can hardly stand it. I angle my hips, opening myself to him, and he snarls fiercely against the inside of my thigh. "That's right. Good girl. Let me have you. Let me make you come. Flood my mouth, *Dolcezza*."

Oh…my…*god*.

He licks and sucks, using the flat of his tongue to sweep up and over my clit, and before too long I'm shaking underneath him. When he carefully uses his fingers to rub against the opening of my pussy, I can do nothing but hold my breath and wait.

Slowly, so gently, he pushes his fingers inside me, and my spine arches away from the floor. "Ahh! Damn it, Alex!" This isn't frightening. Far from it. It's the most intense, pleasurable thing I've ever experienced.

He moves very deliberately, the muscles in his shoulders tight, as he waits to see how I'll react. I want…shit, I want more. I rock my hips, grinding them upward, and it's all the cue Alex needs. He teases me with his tongue faster, more insistently, using his fingers inside me to beckon and coax, pumping them rhythmically, and my eyes roll back into my head as a shockwave so overwhelming crashes into my body.

"Alex… Alex…" I pant his name. It's a mantra on my tongue. A prayer. A curse. Before I know it, a bewildering, chaotic energy is building between my legs, inside me, reaching up into my stomach and my torso, spreading along my arms…

The feeling swells, so powerful and formidable, and just when I think it can't swell any further, it slams into me, rocking me to my core, white, blindingly light flaring behind my eyes. I claw at his back, trying to gasp out his name and failing.

"*Ah—oh fu—shit, Ale—Oh my god! Oh, shit, shit, shit!*"

The orgasm leaves me ruined, lifeless and limp. I'm still fluttering my eyes, trying to remember how to see straight when Alex climbs up my body and kisses me deeply. A little mortified, I realize that I can taste myself on his lips. Alex grins like a fiend when he pulls back. His grin turns into a frown, though, when I brush my fingers over his mouth, trying to clean myself from him.

"Don't you fucking dare, Parisi," he growls. "I plan on savoring every last bit of you." I try to hide my face in his chest, smiling awkwardly, but he doesn't let me. "Don't you have any idea how much that turns me on?" He takes my hand and slides it in between our bodies. My palm is closed around his hard-on a second later, and he's squeezing. I gasp at the feel of him—the firm yet silken, smooth texture of his skin as he guides my hand slowly up and down his shaft. His eyes are burning, filled with his desire as he repeats the action one last time, then tries to take my hand away.

This time I won't let him, though. I tighten my grip around him, free of his guidance, mimicking the up and down motion. His cock pulses, hardening even further in my hand, and his body locks up, going stiff. "You don't need to do that," he whispers. "This should be about you."

"It *is* about me," I whisper back. "The way you're looking at me right now…god, I want to feel you like this inside me, Alex. Please. I'm ready."

Doubt flits across his face. The vines barbed with thorns around the base of his throat shift as he swallows. "You're sure?" His lips form the words, but I barely hear him say them.

I make sure he can hear me perfectly, though. "Yes. I am one hundred percent sure. I *want* you. I want all of you. Now."

It's like watching a tide break against a shore. His indecision and uncertainty vanish, and a deep, hungry need takes its place in an instant. Shifting between my legs, he positions himself, leaning over me on his elbows, keeping his weight from my chest. His hands are sure as he cradles my face between his palms…and he pushes himself slowly inside me.

I freeze, going absolutely still.

Alex's eyes search my face frantically, looking for some sign that I'm not okay. It doesn't hurt, though. I just feel *full*, in a strange way—a pressure inside me that takes a moment to adjust to.

'Silver—"

I wind my arms around him, forcing him down onto me. Deeper inside me. I was serious just now. I want all of him. I *want* his weight on me. I want his arms around me. I want to be swallowed up by him, into his strength, because right now I feel so fucking *safe*.

He sighs, the sound rough and uncontrolled, and I can't take it anymore. I roll my hips against him, angling myself upward, and Alex bares his teeth, gritting them together.

"Fuck, Silver. That's…" His eyes are unfocused. "You feel so fucking good," he grinds out.

Carefully, he begins to rock against me, and the strange pressure inside me starts to lessen as my body learns how to move with him. Alex presses his lips against my forehead, my temple, my jaw. When he eventually uses his teeth against the sensitive skin of my neck, the feel of him inside me begins to change into something else entirely: the pressure evaporates altogether, and it begins to feel good.

"Ahh, fuck! Alex!"

He bites down harder, and I tangle my arms around him, wrapping my legs around his waist tighter, clinging onto him as fiercely as I can.

"You ready for more?" he growls into my hair.

"Yes! Yes. God, *yes*…" I don't sound like myself. I sound like someone else as I writhe underneath him. Alex gives me what I want, pulling back just enough so that he can angle his hips back and thrust them forward, driving himself into me.

Oh god…

What the hell…?

I let my eyes roll closed for a second, but they snap open again when the feeling intensifies, and I realize Alex is touching my clit. Looking down the length of my body, I see his hand is between my legs, and he's using his thumb to rub at me. I shudder, not knowing how the hell to process the sheer volume of sensation.

"Good?" Alex asks raggedly.

"Y-*yes*."

"Good." He quickens his pace, sliding all the way out of me this time and pushing forward a little harder. His eyes are all over me—my face, my breasts, my stomach, my thighs. His gaze pauses on the point where our bodies meet, between my legs, and the muscles in his jaw pop as he clenches his teeth. "Fuck. Watching you take me, Silver… You rocking against me… Your pussy…"

Lust, raw and demanding, digs its claws into me. I see a mirror of that emotion in Alex, and the look on his face sends me spiraling toward madness. I need him. I have to fucking have him. I grab hold of his other hand, sucking his thumb into my mouth, and Alex hisses. "Shit. Careful, Dolcezza."

I know why he's warning me. His movements are quickening, he's thrusting harder and faster, and I know what'll happen soon if we don't stop. There are plenty of days ahead to tease ourselves, though. Plenty of opportunity to stretch this out and make it last. Right now, the fire burning in my belly is raging out of control, and I don't want to put it out. The intense feeling that shook me so violently when Alex went down on me has returned, and I'm about to tumble over the edge all over again.

I want him to tumble with me.

I want to know what that feels like.

I lock my legs around his hips, biting down on his thumb, and I witness the moment Alex gives himself over to it. His eyes flash, and then he's falling on top of me, crushing me to him, driving himself deeper and deeper, faster and faster…

"Shit. I'm going to…I'm gonna fucking…"

"Come. Fucking *come*, Silver," he snarls into my ear. "Do it right now. I wanna feel you throbbing around my dick."

All it takes is his command. I hurtle headfirst into my climax, unable to breathe, unable to make a sound as an explosion of pleasure hits me with the force of a ten-ton truck. My back bows, and Alex holds onto me as I ride out the wave. Then he's roaring, the muscles in his arms straining, and he's coming too, crushing the life out of me as we move against one another.

It seems as though it takes a long time to come down from the high. Eventually, though, when we can breathe again, Alex rolls onto his side and then onto his back, pulling me with him. I lie on his chest, listening to his heartbeat gradually slow, and the feeling of his hand as he lazily strokes my hair is almost hypnotic.

"Is this the part where you pretend you're late for something, make your excuses and you leave?" I whisper.

Alex huffs out a shallow, soft burst of laughter. "No, *Dolcezza*. This is the part when I realize you've stolen my fucking soul and I have no chance of ever getting it back."

I laugh, too. "So, not leaving then."

"Nope."

I trace my fingers over his chest, following the lines of his tattoos, enjoying the warmth of the fire on my own skin. His torso is covered in ink, a large shield-like design spanning across his pecs, following the line of his collar bone. Sweeping down over his side, the top of his shoulder and down his left arm, a long, scaled body of a creature winds, convincing and lifelike. Sharp thorny vines wind intricately from his right arm, around his neck, down across his stomach, weaving in between what looks like a woman on her knees, praying.

"I promised you the nickel tour, didn't I?" he asks softly. "I suppose now's as good a time as any. Come on." I don't want to get up. This moment is far too perfect, but Alex seems intent as he gets up, holding out his hand to help me to my feet. By the window, he displays his hands palm-down, showing me the wolf and the rose inked there. "This is me," he says, indicating to the wolf. "And this is my mom. All of the roses are for her." He's given her his right hand, as well as his entire right arm. "She was soft, like flowers. Beautiful." He runs his own fingers over the vines, his eyes distant. "She had her sharp edges, too, though. Her own demons that plagued her."

It looks like the vines that represent those demons are wrapped around Alex's throat, as if they could press in and strangle the life out of him at any moment. "Is that why...?" I can't bring myself to ask if that's why she killed herself. Alex seems to understand my half question, though.

He nods. "She had these manic episodes. They'd last for days. She'd have so much energy, running around the house, cooking, singing, cleaning. She'd take us on these crazy adventures, walking miles and miles with us through the rain and the snow. She'd take us into Walmart and ask me to look after Ben while she got something, then she'd forget she'd even brought us there and leave. The grocery store. An auto shop once. She was always forgetting us places. She'd feel so bad afterward that she'd sink into these black moods, smashing shit, tearing the apartment up, screaming at the top of her lungs. Once that part was over, she'd get into bed, and she wouldn't get out for days. She was never diagnosed as far as I can tell, but I'm pretty sure she was bi-polar. I read when I was a kid that it's genetic. That sixty to eighty percent of cases are hereditary. I used to scare myself shitless, wondering if I was going to turn out like her, but..." He arches one eyebrow. "I can't even be sure that's what she had. And I've never displayed any of the same behaviors she did, and I've been keeping an eye out for them, believe me."

He shrugs, moving on, pointing out the tattoo of a spartan, shield and drawn swords on his other arm. "This is pretty self-explanatory. My Roman roots." He plants a hand against his chest. "This, too. It's the Moretti family crest. My own interpretation, I guess. I added the skulls and the engine parts."

I see the mechanical-looking elements now, as I look closer. The skulls, too, laughing and macabre. Different flowers bloom from the gaps in between, and red, and blue, and green—the only splashes of color in the otherwise black designs.

"Cobweb on my elbow," he says, lifting his arm, frowning a little ruefully. "Got that in juvie. Kinda wish I hadn't. And this," he says, stroking a finger across the scaled tail of the creature that's wrapped around his body, "is the Lord of the North Wind, Bahamut."

"Unusual name."

"From Arabic mythology. Misappropriated, but who gives a fuck. He's a bannerman for the weak and downtrodden. A safe refuge. Also, takes no shit," he says, grinning. "He's pretty badass, but he metes out justice if you fuck up."

"Where's the rest of him?"

Alex's quirked eyebrow rises even higher as he turns around. There, the front half of a beautiful, somber-looking dragon has been tattooed between his shoulder blades—elaborate, with swirls and curlicues, yet incredibly masculine. Above the dragon, in darker, older ink, is the word *'Fearless.'*

"You really are, aren't you? Fearless," I say.

Alex turns, bowing his head forward, letting his chin drop to his chest. He sighs, wrapping his arms around me. Leaning my forehead against him, we stand like that for a long time before Alex whispers gently into the dark. "Not nearly as fearless as you. Take me to bed, *Argento*. I wanna hold you."

22

ALEX

"He's fucked in the head, just like his mother was. Little prick. If I don't curb that shit now, he's going to end up hurting someone one of these days, just you wait and see. Yeah, yeah, don't worry. If the belt doesn't work, then my fist sure as fuck will."

I jolt awake, disoriented. A second ago I was crying in a closet, listening to Gary tell his brother what a worthless, vile little cretin I am. Now, I'm cocooned in a blissfully soft bed, staring into the face of the most beautiful fucking girl I've ever seen.

Silver's still sleeping. Her hair is loose, fanned out around her face, golden and warm in the early morning light. Her lips are slightly parted. Her eyelashes are so long that they're resting on the top of her cheekbones. From the serene look on her face, the dreams fluttering through her subconscious are nothing like mine were, and for that I am glad.

I never told her, but I vowed to myself about three seconds after I met Silver that I was going to make Jake and anyone else who had a hand in hurting her pay. I've already plotted a few unique and interesting ways to make that happen, even with the promises I made to Silver tying my hands. But none of that matters if I can't protect her from the monsters if they visit her when she closes her eyes to sleep. I can't keep her safe in there, and that makes me sick to my fucking stomach.

She stirs, nestling down into the covers. Her eyes stay closed, but I know that she's woken up. "You know how to work a Keurig, Alessandro Moretti? Or are you more for decoration?" she mumbles.

I smile. Really smile. Maybe it's easier because she can't see me with her eyes closed, but it feels natural—a normal thing to do, and not like some breach in my defenses. "Yes," I whisper, leaning in to kiss her on the forehead. "I know how to operate a Keurig. I'll be right back."

She moans, reaching after me, grabbing for my hand as I climb out of bed. I laugh under my breath all way down the stairs and into the kitchen. Without the fire burning in the living room, it's fucking freezing in the cabin. Should have put some clothes on before I came down but fuck it. As soon as I have some caffeine for Silver, I'm fully planning on getting back into bed and staying there with her for the rest of the morning. I already got my shifts covered at the Rock, so I don't have anywhere else to be.

The pods for the coffee maker take some tracking down. After rummaging through every cupboard and drawer I can think of, I eventually locate them in the freezer of all places. I fill up the water reserve on the machine and stand, hands braced against the kitchen counter as the thin stream of black gold begins to pour into the mug. It's only halfway done when I hear the rumble of an engine approaching the cabin. Instantly alert, instantly aware that I'm half fucking naked, I peer out of the kitchen window, straining to see who'd be coming up here at this hour in the morning.

I don't need to wait long. A silver van breaks through the tree line, careening toward the cabin, and a sinking feeling hits me square in the gut. *Shiiit.* I recognize the van. I last saw it parked in the Parisi's driveway as I pulled away from their house. It's the vehicle Silver was driving when she took her brother to soccer practice.

"SILVER!" I yell.

A woman scrambles out of the van. Her hair's the same color as Silver's, and her features bear a marked resemblance, too. She's young. Younger than I expected, but she's obviously Silver's mom. I'm about to bolt out of the kitchen and up the stairs in search of my clothes, already trying to figure out how I'm going to explain why the fuck I'm here, alone with her daughter, and why the hell I thought I'd get away with defiling her, when I watch the woman go down. She collapses into the mud, sinking to her knees, then landing on her ass, and she's…she's fucking *crying*.

Fuck. *Fuckfuckfuck.*

I'm out of the door and running towards her before I can assess the situation or decide if it's even a smart thing to do. The woman looks up, but I can tell she doesn't really see me. A loud, harrowing sob echoes through the trees. Her face is a rictus of pain. "Mrs. Parisi? Shit, Mrs. Parisi, are you okay? Are you hurt?"

I pat down her shoulders and arms, trying to see if she's injured or something, but she jerks away from me, tucking herself into a ball. Uhhhh…shit. I'm at a loss. I do the only thing I can think of and scoop her into my arms, picking her up out of the mud. She doesn't even question the fact that a strange, half-naked guy is carrying her inside her own cabin. She wraps her arms around my neck and clings to me as I take her up the steps, kicking open the door that almost closed behind me when I rushed outside.

"SILVER!"

In the living room, I gently lay the woman down on the sofa, and she curls up into a ball again, sobbing in a gut-wrenching, horrible way that makes me want to rip my own ears off.

Momma, why are you crying? It's all right. Everything's going to be okay. Momma. Momma!

Footsteps thunder down the stairs. Silver arrives in a whirlwind panic, her hair all over the place, wearing nothing but a vest and a tiny pair of shorts. We pose a pretty fucking damning picture, but it doesn't look like her mom's paying any attention. Her eyes are screwed tightly shut, her mouth drawn down in a mask of misery. Silver shoots me a bewildered, scared look, and I just stand there, numb, not knowing what the fuck to say.

She rushes to her mom, dropping to her knees with a loud thud, eyes still on me. "What the hell happened?"

"I don't know. She was doing seventy when she pulled up. When she got out, she was like *this*."

"Fuck, Mom. Mom, what's going on?" Silver tries to take the woman's hands in hers, but she's too hysterical to allow it.

"She's…gone…" she pants. "She's fucking…gone. She's *dead*, Silver. She's fucking *dead*."

A brief flash of confusion pulls at Silver's features, then her mom's statement must make sense all of a sudden, because I watch as realization dawns on her. "Gail? *Gail died?*"

"Yes!" Her mom sounds like *she's* dying when she pushes the word out. "It's…*it's my fault.*"

"No." Silver shakes her head, running her hands over her mom's hair, trying to soothe her. "No. Mom, it's not your fault. How can it be your fault?"

"She was angry with me," she keens. "I was chasing after her. I needed to explain. I just needed to make her stop, but…" She chokes. Barely even gives herself time to recover before she continues. "She drove straight out. Straight into the intersection. She didn't even look."

"Mom. Mom, it's okay. You're not making any sense. Tell me what happened."

"She saw me, Silver. She saw me with Dan, in his office. She wouldn't wait for me to get dressed. She…just left, and I went after her. It *is* my fault. I killed her."

23

SILVER

Mom *has* been acting weird.
Mom *has* been crying in the shower.
Mom's been having an affair with her boss.

This is the reason why she's bailed every time Dr. Coombes came to drop the boys off for their lesson. This is the reason why she hasn't been to visit her best fucking friend in the hospital. She's been riddled with guilt, it's been eating her alive, and now Gail is dead.

Alex wanted to take us back into town, but I told him I would drive the van back. He mentioned something about coming back up here later with a friend to get my car. I vaguely remember giving him the keys to the Nova. More vividly, I remember him holding me, hugging me, whispering into my hair, but after that everything's kind of a blur.

I'm numb down to my bones as I make the journey home, Mom still crying in the passenger seat. I don't even know how I made it most of the way; I'm on autopilot, shifting, stopping at lights, taking turns without really paying attention to what I'm doing. When I pull into the driveway and kill the engine, we both just sit there, neither of us moving, staring dumbly out of the window at the garage door.

"Why?" I ask. "Why did you come up to the cabin?"

She has calmed down a bit now. Enough so she can talk, at least. "I don't know. I knew you were there, and I just wanted to get away, and it just...*happened.*"

"Does Dad know?"

She blinks, shifting in the seat. Her pajama pants are destroyed, and there's mud all over the passenger door. "About Dan? No," she says quietly. "I haven't told him yet."

Great. A fucking bomb's about to go off in our house, and there will be nothing left of our happiness but a smoking crater and the remnants of my father's happiness. I can't stitch my thoughts together. Nothing's making sense inside my head. I just sit there, hands still on the steering wheel, staring into space.

I feel like I'm going to puke as an option presents itself to me—an option I do not like one little bit. I take a deep breath, swallowing down my own self-loathing as I say, "You're not going to."

"What?" Mom whispers.

"You're not going to fucking tell him, Mom," I snap. "You were selfish. You did something really fucking stupid, but you didn't *kill* Gail. It was an accident."

"I have to tell him, sweetheart. It wouldn't be fair—"

"Do not talk to me about fair!" I yell. "If you wanted fair, you shouldn't have cheated on Dad. If you wanted fair, you shouldn't have started with the lies in the first place. Now, to be *fair to the rest of this family*, you're gonna have to be a fucking adult, stop being so goddamn selfish, and you're gonna keep your mouth shut."

"Silver—"

"You get to be sad. You get to be broken up because your friend died. You do not get to tear the rest of us apart just so you can punish yourself and make yourself feel like you got what you deserved."

"I did something bad, Silver. I can't just walk around, pretending it didn't happen. It wouldn't be right."

"Shut up, Mom. Just...just shut the fuck up, okay. Enough damage has already been done. I swear to god, if you hurt Dad and Max like this, I will never forgive you. I mean it. I will never speak to you again." I get out of the car, vibrating with rage, slamming the door behind me.

Mom's hot on my heels. "Hey! Hey, get back here, young lady. I know I fucked up, but I *am* still your mother, okay. I *am* still the adult."

I turn on her, stabbing my finger into her chest. I hate that I'm crying. "No, Mom. Don't you see? You haven't been the adult in this relationship for a really long time. While you've been staying at work late, fucking your boss, *I've* been doing the cooking. *I've* been doing the cleaning. *I've* been making sure the laundry's done, and your eleven-year-old son is fed and clothed. I'm the one making sure everything doesn't fall apart, and guess what, Mom? *My* shit has been falling apart. *My* shit has *not* been okay. And then you show up at the cabin, running to me for comfort, for me to fix this fucking mess, because you know that I will!"

She just stands there. It feels as though she's looking right through me.

I can't believe I've just said all of that to her, but it needed fucking saying.

Stiffly, Mom turns to face the house...and without another word, she walks inside.

∼

Dad comes home from work, and I hear him consoling Mom. The walls of the house ring with the sound of her crying, but she doesn't tell him what she's done. Max is still over at Halliday's house for a sleepover with her brother Jamie, thank god, so at least he doesn't need to know just how dark things have gotten in the Parisi household.

Alex texts me close to midnight.

Alex: Wanted to give you some space, but now I really need to know if you're alright.

Me: Not really.

Alex: Bad, huh? What can I do?

Me: Rescue me. Kidnap me. Whisk me away.

Alex: Don't joke. I'll do it.

If only he could. I'd jump into a car with him and drive off into the sunset in a hot minute if I didn't think everything would fall apart the moment I left. My hands hover over the keyboard on my cell's screen while I think of what to type back.

Me: What's your email address? I'm going to write you.

Alex: A breakup letter on day two of our relationship. Shit. That's a record.

Me: Nothing like that. We have a relationship?

Alex: YES.

Alex: You're mine, I'm yours, remember. Hate to break it to you, but you're achieved GF status. I've already alerted the media. Email is ampasserotto@gmail.com.

Girlfriend status? I try not to grin from ear to ear, but it's a futile task. I decide to play it cool and not mention how giddy and stupid he just made me.

Me: passerotto?

Alex: Another time.

Me: I won't forget.

Alex: I don't want you to.

I planned on putting off writing my account of what happened at Leon's for as long as I possibly could, but that feels so wrong right now. I just forced my own mother into keeping a terrible secret, and I'm beginning to feel like a bit of a monster. I have to tell someone some kind of truth, otherwise I'm never going to be able to look at myself in the mirror again.

I was going to write down what happened with pen and paper, but there's so much emotion involved here; I don't trust myself to be able to write legibly once I get to the difficult parts. Starting the email is hard. Fuck, all of it is hard. It takes me two hours to put it all down into words, and by the end, I'm shaking so hard I think I'm going to pass out.

No. No, I'm not going to pass out. I'm going to throw up. I nearly don't make it to the bathroom in time. As I hug the toilet, cold sweat running down my back, my stomach churning over on itself, throat raw, the taste of vomit in my mouth, I panic. I've got to delete it. I can't send any of that to Alex. It's too much. It's all just way, way, way too much.

Making my way back to my desk, my legs feel like they're going to collapse from underneath me. My laptop screen is still displaying the pages long email as if it's just another school project or something I've been working on. The words snag, catching at me like barbs, and I'm so damn tired all of a sudden. My life shouldn't be like this. I shouldn't have to deal with any of this shit. Not on my own, anyway.

Before I can change my mind, I hit the blue button at the bottom of the email's draft screen, and my laptop chimes, signaling that the message has been sent.

Too late to take it back now.

24

SILVER

THE NIGHT OF THE PARTY...

"Stop being such a little bitch, Silver. Chug the damn drink!"

I roll my eyes at Kacey, holding the cup to my mouth. She's already four drinks ahead of me. I have some serious catching up to do, but chugging foamy beer isn't how I'd like to accomplish that. "Hey, Leon! Doesn't your dad have any vodka lying around? This stuff tastes like piss!" I call out.

Kacey's boyfriend, Leon, holds up his hands, laughing at me from across the other side of the living room. "Sorry, Sil. Blame Jake and Sam. They cleared out the good stuff before you got here. S'what you get for showing up late."

Kacey bumps me with her hip, making a disgusted sound at the back of her throat. "Fucking animals. You should have seen him when he rolled up here in his dad's Maserati. You'd think he was god's gift to mankind or something."

"Who, Jake?"

"Of course Jake. Who else has an ego the size of the State of Texas? And who else would show up to a party wearing a fucking MVP medal. Doesn't he know the season ended two months ago?"

The guy in question is standing by the beer pong table, laughing and carousing with Sam Hawthorne and Cillian Dupris; sure enough, the 'most valuable player' medal Coach Quentin awarded him at the end of the football season is hanging around his neck, resting on top of his perfectly tailored Armani blue button down shirt. He glances my way, his smile broadening when we make eye contact, and my nerves jangle like a set of wind chimes.

"Yeah, Jake loves Jake like Kanye loves Kanye. He *is* cute, though."

Planting her hands on top of the table, leaning toward me, Kacey dons her 'do not mess with me' face. "Listen, bitch. If you don't pound that beer, I'm going to walk over there and tell him just how wet he makes your pussy. And then I'm going to tell him that you're still a virgin, and you've been saving yourself for him since fifth grade."

I glare at her, the skin behind my ears and down the back of my neck beginning to prickle. "You wouldn't dare."

Kacey pouts, running her hand over her long, dark hair; it's knife-edge straight and shining like she conditioned it seven times before she came out tonight. As always, she looks incredible in a little black dress that hugs her curves in all the right places and accentuates them in others. There's a reason why she's the most lusted-after girl at Raleigh. "Try me," she says airily.

I know that look on her face. I've seen it countless times before. Usually before she decides to pull the trigger on a particularly cruel plan designed to embarrass or humiliate one of Raleigh's lesser, mere mortal students. Hastily, I tip back the cup of beer, and I chug. My throat's stinging from the cold, carbonated liquid when I slam the cup down on the table, gasping for breath. A cheer goes up around me, and Zen appears at my side, winding her arm around my waist. Her hair's braided back into cornrows, bleached blonde with pink tips. Her bubblegum pink dress is almost as revealing as Kacey's.

"Nicely done, Parisi," she says, planting a kiss on my cheek. "What took you so long? We've been waiting for you."

Kacey answers the question before I can. "*Guitar lesson.*" She says the words with the same level of disgust she might say '*Forever 21 discount rack.*' Kacey's of the firm belief that an item of clothing isn't worth shit if it isn't worth over four hundred dollars. "I don't get why you don't just quit doing that, Silly. Your parents give you an allowance, right?"

"Yeah. But I *like* teaching." We've been through this a thousand times. It would suit Kacey down to the ground if I didn't have to teach my lessons every night of the week. That way, I'd be able to go over to her place after school and we could hang out, ruthlessly criticizing the cast of The Bold and the Beautiful.

"Whatever. You're ruining your hands. They look like you do manual labor for a living."

"They're callouses, Kacey. I can't play without them."

She groans. Zen takes my hand and turns it over, inspecting said callouses. "They *feel* worse," she adds disapprovingly.

"Exactly. And how do you think Jacob Weaving's gonna feel about them when you wrap that grubby little mitt around his cock and you sand his foreskin off? I've heard he's uncut." She waggles her eyebrows, using her fingers to mimic snipping a pair of scissors. Zen explodes into a fit of scandalized giggles, while I look for the nearest deep hole to go bury myself in.

"You can stop now. I don't care about Jacob Weaving. I don't care what he thinks of my calluses, and I'm certainly not gonna be wrapping my hand around his *cock* any time soon."

"That's a shame," a voice says behind Kacey. The three of us whip around, and the chicken alfredo I ate for dinner suddenly tries to make a reappearance, rising up in my throat.

Jacob.

Standing two feet away.

Holding a glass filled with burned amber liquid.

Arching a blond, perfect eyebrow in my direction.

The amused twist of his mouth says it all.

"I've been meaning to talk to you, Parisi," he says. His head tips back, and he studies me down the bridge of his nose in an appraising fashion that makes me blush down to the roots of my hair.

"O—Oh." *Dear lord, please help me now. Do not let me trip over my own treacherous tongue.* I swallow thickly. "Why? Um. What about?"

Kacey tries to hide her smile in the veil of her hair. "God, Silver. How have you managed to make it this far without a scrap of game?" She makes a show of trying to whisper the words, but she makes sure Jacob can hear her.

"I like that about her," he says, smirking. With a practiced move, he throws back the contents of his glass, savoring it in his mouth, eyes roving over my face. He swallows, and I find I can't tear my eyes away from the muscles in his throat as they work. "Not everyone can be like you, Winters. Well-practiced and well broken in. Sometimes it's refreshing to contend with someone a little more...*innocent*."

Kacey doesn't like that. Not one bit. "Yes, well. I'm sure you wouldn't be saying that when she *blows* instead of *sucks*."

A flush of shame rockets up my spine. Even Zen's mouth drops open. "*Kay Kay!*"

Kacey slides her arm through mine, petting my hair. I love my friend to the ends of the earth, but occasionally I also want to punch her in the throat. "Oh, come *on*. She knows I'm teasing, don't you, Silly Sil? No one's stupid enough to make that mistake. You people have no sense of humor."

Jacob's eyes drive into the side of Kacey's head, boring into her, grey and unimpressed. "With friends like you, *Kay Kay*," he says, his voice full of mockery, "who needs enemies? Silver? I was gonna head out to the pool for a second. Get some air. You wanna join me?"

Oh, shit. I look to Zen, and then Kacey, my jaw practically on the floor. "Uhhh...sure. I just—"

"Actually, we were just about to pay a visit to the little girl's room," Kacey says sweetly. "You know how us women can only go in packs of three. We'll be back soon, though, Mr. MVP. I'm sure you can spin Silver one of your cheesy pick-up lines then." She already has me by the arm. She's pulling me away, stalking toward the stairs in her skyscraper patent pumps before I can even blink. We're halfway up to the first floor by the time I'm about to make my mouth form words.

"Kacey! What the hell?"

She looks back at me over her shoulder, her eyes glinting wickedly. "What? You literally just said, *I don't care about Jacob Weaving.* I thought I was doing you a favor."

"You're such a cow, Kacey. You know she wants him bad," Zen titters.

There's a line for the restroom, but Kacey breezes right past, dragging me along behind her. Perfectly timed, the door opens just as we arrive in front of it, and Kacey shoots an icy glare at the guy standing next in line—Gareth Foster: Chess team. Dork.

"You don't mind, do you?" she purrs.

Kacey's probably never made eye contact with Gareth before in her life. He looks like he just soiled himself. "Uh, no. Of course not. Go right ahead."

We're already inside the bathroom. She's already slamming the door closed. She dumps her tiny purse on the counter, opening it and rooting inside. "Look, Silver. I'm not saying I think Jacob's a jackass, but...he is. You know that, right? He definitely *is* a jackass."

God, she's so melodramatic. I use the toe of my shoe to knock the toilet lid down, then I lay a towel over it and sit down. The dress I'm wearing—one of Kacey's. She insisted—is a little too tight. I have to sit ramrod straight to avoid the fabric cutting the circulation off to my legs.

"He's arrogant, sure," I say. "But I don't know about anything else. I heard his mom paid for Jessica Birch's plastic surgery after she was in that fire last year."

"The mother's philanthropic gestures have no bearing on the son," Kacey says chidingly. "Jake probably wouldn't have pissed on Jessica if he'd been standing outside that boat shed and she'd come running out aflame. Where's Halliday and Melody?" She adds this last part as if she's only just noticed that they're missing.

"With Guy and Davis," Zen supplies. The way she hands over the information suggests our friends are up to no good.

"*God.*" Kacey hurls the lipstick she just pulled out of her purse back inside, frowning as she searches for something else. "How do they know who they're even fucking?" she mumbles.

Guy and Davis are twins. Identical twins. They've been dating Halliday and Melody for the past six months, and according to the girls, the twins do like to assume each other's identities.

"I don't think it matters this time," Zen laughs. "All four of them are in Leon's father's room, and from what *I* saw, they weren't being overly picky about who was tangled up with who."

Kacey looks up, her head rocking to one side as she processes this. "Huh. That actually sounds like it could be fun. Bummer Leon's an only child."

"There's always *Mr.* Wickman," I offer.

"*Silver!*" Kacey feigns surprise. "How scandalous. Mr. Wickman does have a certain sex appeal. There's nothing more attractive than a man who's gone after his goals and amassed a great deal of power and money in his lifetime. But no. Leon's too much of a prude to ever consider it."

I was only joking. I didn't think she'd take the suggestion seriously, but I shouldn't be all that surprised. Kacey's sexual deviant tendencies run deep.

She finally finds what she's looking for in her bag and holds the small black compact up triumphantly. "Hallelujah. Now we can finally start to enjoy this party." She flips the compact open and instead of blusher, inside is a large amount of coke. She pulls a razor blade from the back of her phone case and serves up a large amount of the powder onto the compact's mirror, cutting it into a line.

Zen goes first. She holds the back of her hand to her nose after she snorts, eyes closed, head tipped back, a slow smile spreading across her face. "Hot damn. Your stuff is always the best, Kay Kay."

"My body's a temple. I wouldn't go putting any old trash inside it. Here, Silver." She holds out the compact to me, a line ready and waiting. I was fourteen when Kacey gave me my first taste of coke. It had been a dare back then, but over the past three years, it's become more of a habit—for Kacey at least. I only use with her at parties. I'm pretty sure Kace is powdering her nose at least two or three times a day. I don't talk to her about it. The two times I've suggested that she might want to save her stash for more recreational purposes, she flipped out so violently I thought she was going to have a fucking nervous breakdown.

I'm tired. I don't really feel like getting crazy tonight, but Zen's kind of fucked me. I can't decline the drugs, because she did her line without complaint. If I refuse, they're both going to be on me, harassing me, giving me a hard time. I've learned that it's much easier to just do one line and then claim to have a headache than refuse altogether.

I hold the compact mirror to my nose, blocking off my nostril, and I inhale sharply. My sinuses are instantly both numb and burning with a dizzying wave of pleasure that spreads through my head, down into my body, down into my arms and legs. For a moment, my body is made of pure light. I'm floating up toward the ceiling. My skin's tingling, alive with sensation.

Kacey strokes the side of my face, humming under her breath. "Pretty, pretty Parisi." She takes the compact from me, cuts herself a line, and soon all three of us are flying high. She then takes the razor blade in hand, the metal gleaming wickedly under the bathroom lights, lays the sharpened metal against her tongue and licks off the powder residue. I giggle at the sight of the blade resting on her tongue—I can't decide which of them is sharper.

"Truth is, I don't think you can handle Jake, Silver," she says coolly. "You need easing into this shit. Fucking Jake would be tantamount to getting thrown into the deep. Better if you fooled around with someone a little less high-stakes first. Get yourself some training wheels."

"Careful, Kacey. You're beginning to sound like you might be a little jealous," Zen says, winking at Kacey's reflection in the mirror.

"Don't be ridiculous. Why the hell would I be jealous of a potential tryst between Silver and Jacob when I have *Leon?*" Her voice is tight, though. The protest on her lips sounds disingenuous to say the least. Holy fuck. How can I not have noticed until now? It hits me, through the drugged haze of my brain—that Kacey is jealous. Jealous that a popular guy at school is pursuing me, and not her.

∼

I'm consumed by the music. I'm covered in sweat and my heart's racing, but this, right now, is officially the most amazing moment of my life. I've never had this much fun before. *Never.* My body moves in time to the thumping track that's playing through Leon's father's top of the line speaker system, and every time my skin brushes up against someone else's body, I find myself laughing at the sheer delight of the contact. Everyone's dancing, grinding, raging along to the bassline and the beat. Kacey and Leon are practically fucking on the makeshift dancefloor; she's pressing herself up against him, his face locked in between her hands as she licks at his mouth. Zen's nowhere to be found, but Halliday bounces on the balls of her feet, grinning from ear to ear as the music begins to rise into a heady, maddening crescendo. I love that about Halliday—that she dances without caring what she looks like. She just has fun. I grab hold of her, grinning from ear to ear.

"Oh my god, this party is amazing!" she gasps, just as the beat quickens, the bassline drops, and the crowd erupts into screaming cheers. Halliday didn't partake in any of Kacey's coke, but her pupils are so blown, her entire eye is almost black, and she's chugging water like she can't slake her thirst, so I know she's on something. MDMA, probably, given the way she keeps hugging me and telling me how much she loves me.

"When we graduate next year, we need to move down to L.A. We can get a place together and become actresses. Make shitloads of money. Only sleep with fitness models. My cousin Sarah, you know, the one who got the boob job? She's been down there for three years now. She says it's basically one constant party. She sees famous people all the time. Doesn't that sound like fun?"

I wrap my arms around her neck, squealing. "Yes! We have to. Let's do it! I haven't had a tan since second grade!"

When I pull back, Halliday's blushing. She looks at me meaningfully, her eyes wide, brows rising. "Incoming, Silver."

"What?"

"*Incoming.* Hi, Jake! Wow, I really like your shirt. The blue really brings out your eyes."

I can feel the fine hair at the back of my neck sticking to my skin. I must look terrible, so flushed and red from dancing, but when I turn around to face Jake, his eyes roam over me like I'm the most beautiful thing he's ever seen.

"Thanks. Hey, you mind if I steal Silver for a moment, Hal? I just created this cool cocktail, and I wanted to show it to her."

Halliday nods a little too enthusiastically. "Take her! I've got to find Guy, anyway. Have you seen him?"

"Out by the pool," he says. God, his voice is so amazing. If football doesn't work out for him, he could always do voice over. My pulse is already racing, but it quickens even further as Jake offers me his hand. "Are you a gin girl or vodka girl, Ms. Parisi?" He smiles, and it's as if the world stops turning.

"Vodka." I take his hand, allowing him to lead me off the dance floor, and I already know this is going to be great. I've been waiting for Jake to notice me for the past two years. He was dating Olivia Jenkins, Kacey's mortal enemy and therefore *my* mortal enemy, for years. When she moved away at the end of last semester, he told everyone he was going to stay single and focus all of his attention on playing football, but now here he is, holding my hand, smiling confidently as he walks with me through the party…

It's quieter in the kitchen. There are a group of guys playing some sort of drinking game with a pack of cards. Sam Hawthorne's leaning against the counter by the sink, tapping something into his phone. His long hair's tied back into a knot at the back of his head. He grins when he looks up and sees us. "Ahhh, a pretty flower. Such a dog, Weaving. You planning on plucking this one?"

"Shut the fuck up, Sam. Be polite. Silver's not like that, are you, Sil?"

I'm not sure *what* I'm like, but I'm irritated by the smug, suggestive look on Sam's face. I've never liked him. There's something…*off* about him. Like a bad smell, he's a constant presence in the hallways of Raleigh High. Wherever Jacob goes, Sam follows. I bare my teeth in an approximation of a smile. My head's still so clouded from the coke, and it feels like there's an electric current buzzing pleasantly beneath the surface of my skin, though, so I decide not to let Sam's very obviously sexual comment bother me.

"I'm just looking forward to this cocktail," I say.

"That's my girl!" Jacob's hand presses into the small of my back, and it takes everything I've got not to burst into fucking song. I've worshipped this guy for so long. He's handsome. Charming. Funny. And it really doesn't hurt that his parents are the two most influential people in Raleigh. They've already secured Jake a place at Princeton, but surprisingly enough they're allowing him to go traveling for a year before he starts college. From what Leon told me, they're giving him free rein and access to their platinum American Express while he's on the road.

Dreamily, I'm already imagining all of the amazing, beautiful places we'll visit and see together when he realizes he's madly in love with me and invites me to go along with him.

No more running around after Max. No more cleaning and cooking at home. No more rain. Sounds like heaven.

Jacob spins a silver Boston shaker in his hand, flaring as he sets up a line of ingredients on the kitchen island: a thick wedge of orange; vodka; Cointreau; Kahlua; cream; crushed ice. He smirks at me, eyes flickering to me every few seconds as he free-pours the liquor into the shaker, adds the ice, the cream, squeezes the orange, then shakes.

Sam leans over and whispers something into Jake's ear, and Jake's eyes narrow. He nods his head. "Tell Cillian," he says. "Upstairs, though. The third floor."

I don't enjoy the way Sam's eyes crawl over me as he hurries out of the kitchen. The guy's such a smarmy prick. "What was that about?" I ask.

"Sam got some Bolivian coke from his brother. It's the purest fucking high known to man. We're keeping it quiet. He doesn't have much left. You party, right?"

"Uh, yeah. I guess. I think I've had enough for one night, though." I don't wanna break my own rule. One line's more than enough for me. The effects of the coke Kacey gave me in the bathroom are still going strong, the lights in the kitchen a little too bright, my skin burning, heartbeat a touch too quick. I'm not a heavy user like Kace. If I have any more, I'm going to be seriously messed up.

"Ahhh, come on, Silver. Don't you wanna have fun with me?" He holds out the martini glass he's just poured the cocktail into. I accept it, dipping my head.

"Sure. Of course. I'm just a lightweight. I don't wanna get too fucked up. I have to drive home, and—"

"Okay. All right. Say no more." Jake flashes me a grin that makes my stomach flip, the way it used to flip when I watched YouTube videos of One Direction when I was twelve. "I respect that. You'll still come upstairs and hang while I do a rail, though? And then we can go outside and hang by the pool. I have a lot of questions about you, pretty girl. I can't believe we've been at the same school for so long and we've barely even said two words to each other. I don't know the first thing about you."

Oh, I know plenty about you, Jacob. I try on a smile that I hope looks shy and pretty, taking a sip from the martini glass. The cocktail's strong—way stronger than I'd typically like, but it's deliciously sweet and tastes like Christmas. "Oh my god, this is amazing."

He must be used to people telling him how great he is, but I can see that he's glowing under the compliment *I've* given him, like my opinion matters to him. "Thanks. I'm glad you like it. Drink up."

There's really not much liquid in the martini glass, and I don't want Jake to think I'm a pussy, so I knock the whole thing back in one, laughing as I try to swallow.

"Nice. I like a girl who can handle her liquor. So, what do you say, Parisi? You gonna come up and wait for me?"

"Sure, let me just tell Halliday where I'm going, and—"

Jake grabs me by the hand, pulling me around the corner of the kitchen island. His hand sits on my hip, and then it's sliding around to the small of my back, rising up my spine. I'm shaking like a leaf as he leans down and presses his mouth to mine. I've daydreamed this moment enough times that I thought I knew what it would feel like to kiss Jacob Weaving. This is a little rougher than I'd pictured, a little more brash and hungry than the slow, intense burn I had in mind, but still, I'm practically crowing with delight as he pushes his tongue past my teeth and plunges it into my mouth.

God, is Halliday seeing this? Zen? Ideally, I'd prefer if Kacey isn't standing by, observing my first kiss with Jake. There's clearly something weird going on with her tonight, and I don't want the moment ruined by another of her salty barbs. One of the other girls, though. Be good if they could tell me later if I looked calm and confident as I wrap one hand around the back of Jake's neck, and I pull him down to kiss me harder.

Jake's eyes are half-lowered and hungry when he straightens, and a thrill races up my spine. I can't believe that just happened. I can't believe he just fucking kissed me. My lips feel swollen, a little raw from the stubble he's rocking. Jake slowly presses his index finger to my mouth, rubbing it along my bottom lip. "So pretty, Silver. You're so damn pretty. Come on, let's go."

He takes the martini glass and sets it down on the island, leaving it behind as he drags me toward the stairs. He seems filled with urgency, keen to hurry away from the noise and the crowd of the party. Halfway up the stairs, urging me ahead of him, he places his hand on the bare skin of my back, brushing my hair out of the way, and places a kiss on top of my shoulder.

I've never been up to the third floor of Leon's house—it's the only area of the sprawling, breathtakingly designed mansion that's out of bounds. I have no idea what to expect as Jake guides me down a long hallway with architectural plans pinned to the walls, and strange, small Japanese-looking knickknacks arranged neatly on the shelves. This is Mr. Wickman's domain. I've never met him, but from what I've heard over the years, Leon's mother's death changed the man. Made him a little unhinged. I see no sign of madness here, as I walk along the hallways, past meticulously tidy rooms with open doors. The reading nook we pass looks so inviting that I could easily pull a book from the imposing shelves to sit and read for a while, despite the churning pulse at my throat.

"There. On the end, see," Jacob whispers against my shoulder. "Terry's bathroom's insane. You're gonna freak out when you see it."

I'm feeling a little silly. A little giddy. My brain isn't focusing properly. The world's started to feel a little...*spongy*. "Does it have a sunken bath? I've always wanted to try one of those." My voice hardly sounds like my own.

"Oh, don't worry, sweetheart. We can try everything. Would you like that?"

I nod, and my brain feels like it's bouncing around the inside of my skull. The edges of my vision seem to be softer than it should; everything's a little muzzy, but I feel good. Really good. Jake ushers me into the bathroom, and I falter when I see that Sam and Cillian are already there, leaning against a huge slate grey counter, stocked with fancy looking little bottles of soaps and shampoos, along with a mountain of hand towels, rolled up, like you see in hotel spas. They look like little burritos, which, for some reason, makes me laugh.

I still don't like the fact that Cillian and Sam are here, though. Especially Sam. "I thought we were going to be alone," I whisper to Jake. I can't have whispered as quietly as I'd hoped; the other guys must hear me because they share this look, smiles curling up the corners of their mouths, their eyes narrowed into half crescents, and I try to take a step back toward the door.

"Hey, hey, easy. *Easy*. It's okay. We just came up here to have some fun, right, boys? You want to have some fun with us, don't you, Silver? I thought you liked to party." Jake's hand on my arm feels comforting. His voice is soothing. But when I look up into his eyes, they look the same as Sam and Cillian's eyes—primed, shining and excited. A cold jolt fires like a piston up my spine, like cold water. Like jumping into the lake in the dead of winter.

"Wouldn't it be more fun if Kacey and Zen were here? Or Halliday? I can...I can go and get them."

"There's only so much coke to go around," Jake says tightly. "And besides, we want to get to know *you* a little better. I hate to say it, Parisi, but your friends are all super cunts. Way too bitchy, especially Winters. If they came up here, they'd ruin the dynamic. Cillian, why don't you rack 'em? We probably don't have long."

Sam connects his cell to the Bluetooth speakers that are mounted onto the walls while Cillian preps a worryingly long line of coke along the slate counter. A creeping sense of unease keeps trying to sneak up on me, but every time I begin to worry, Jake touches me, his hand on my arm, or my back, or my side, and the attention dispels the dread.

I can't believe he likes me.

I can't believe he's finally noticed me.

I can't believe he kissed me.

I can't believe he chose to spend time with me.

'Santeria' by Sublime erupts from the speakers, just as Cillian ducks down and inhales a good three inches of the insane line he's just cut. The music seems way too loud, thumping at the back of my head, but no one else seems to mind. Cillian hands Jake a rolled-up bill, his eyes rolling wildly, a dazed smile pulling his mouth open.

"Uhhhhh, oh my god. It's good. It's good. Fuck. My face is numb as fuck," he jabbers, his words bleeding into one another. "Get in there, boss."

Jake doesn't need telling twice. He snorts just as much as Cillian, if not more. He staggers when he stands, pinching his nose, eyes tightly closed. "Shiiiiit. I think I just came," he hisses. "Holy *fuck.*"

I laugh because Sam and Cillian are both laughing. I don't stop laughing, even when Jake grabs hold of his dick through his pants, squeezing, working his hand up and down his obvious hard-on through his jeans. *He's just playing around. He's just being a jock in front of his friends.*

Sam dances along with the music as he takes his place in front of the counter for his hit. Jake has moved behind me, pressing his chest up against my back. He's stopped touching himself, but I can feel his erection butting up against my ass. His hands move to my hips, which feels good, and then they're moving up over my stomach, higher and higher; he skirts around my breasts, one hand resting around the column of my neck, stroking my skin hypnotically, while he buries the other in my hair. His breath is so hot against the shell of my ear. I'm his to puppet as he pulls me back against him, off balance, so that I'm leaning against him with most of my weight.

"Sam, take your shirt off," Cillian commands. That seems a little weird, but Sam doesn't bat an eyelid. He rips his t-shirt off over his head, exposing his muscled, tanned back. I can see his chest in the mirror—his cut abs, and his defined pecs. Sam grins like a court jester at me, his reflection making eye contact, and Jake moves his hand, taking hold of me by the jaw, angling my head so I can't look away.

"Sammy just got back from surfing in Hawaii. D'you think he's hot?"

What?

That's a really bizarre thing to ask. He must know I came up here because I'm interested in *him*, not Sam, or Cillian for that matter. "Honestly? Sam's not my type," I say in what I hope's a light, airy tone. "No offense or anything."

Sam's isn't fazed by my comment. In fact, he seems to find it entertaining. He dips, inhales sharply, groaning as he staggers back from the counter. "All right, Parisi. Your turn," Cillian says.

"Oh, no. I'm good. I think I've had enough already. Seriously. My head's thumping right now."

"Come on, Princess. Just a taste." Cillian wets his finger, dabbing it against the still foot long length of coke, collecting some on his finger. There's a devious look on his face as he stalks toward me. "Open up now."

"Cillian, seriously. I don't need any. I'm good."

"*Siiil-verrrr.*" The sing-song cadence of his voice is a taunt.

Anger finally shoves through the confusion in my head, buzzing in my ears. Spinning in Jake's arms, I try to tell him that I want to go back downstairs now, only…I can't actually turn around to face him. Jake's hands have tightened on me, around my throat again, around my waist.

"Don't freak out, sweetheart," he purrs into my ear. "We're just having a little fun."

"This *isn't* fun," I snap. "Let me go, Jake. God, you guys are such fucking assholes."

This is the moment everything changes. I'm expecting the guys to laugh at me, make fun of me for being such a spoilsport, but in my head, I'm still not entirely caught up with what's about to happen in this bathroom. I still think Jake's going to let me go. It's only when Cillian steps up and grabs the hem of skirt that I realize how badly this is going to go.

"What…what are you doing?" I pant, trying to step back, away from him. Jake's a solid wall of muscle behind me, though; I go nowhere. Cillian's hand touches the inside of my thigh, and I lock up, terror turning me into a statue.

"Why don't you just shut the fuck up?" Cillian's tone is so bewildering. He sounds like he's asking a bland, inane question that he actually wants an answer to. "You're gonna like this, I promise."

My heart feels like it's surging too hard, a lightning bolt of panic lighting up my veins as Cillian's hand rises up higher, to the apex of my thighs. "No. No more, okay. God, stop. This isn't funny!"

I lash out, kicking like a crazed animal, but the way Cillian's crouched down too close in front of me makes it almost impossible to hit him. Jake's hand locks hard around my esophagus, crushing down on my windpipe, and for the first time in my life, I feel fear. Real, terrifying, all-consuming, blinding fear.

This isn't happening. This can't be happening.

Any hope I might have had that this is all some terrible joke disappears when I catch sight of Jake's expression in the mirror. His eyes are hard as jet. Gone is the smile he was wearing downstairs. Gone is the easy, laid back set of his shoulders. This version of Jake is nothing like the version of him in the kitchen, that flirted with me and put me at ease. This Jake is a stranger. The kind of stranger you cross the street to avoid. The kind that would strike instant fear into you if you stumbled across them down a dark alley.

The man I see in the mirror is gripped by a dark, cruel, wicked excitement that speaks volumes: Jake isn't going to help me, he likely instigated this entire thing…and I am so fucked right now. So, *so* fucked.

I gasp as Cillian's hand reaches my panties. Squirming doesn't help. Twisting my body away from him doesn't work. Jake has an iron grip on me. I can't fucking breathe… I somehow manage to suck in a ragged, horrified breath when Cillian snags the material of my panties and yanks them down my legs, though.

No. No, no, no, no, nonononono….

Oh my god. I can't get…fuck…this can't be—

I still, my head falling back against Jake's chest as Cillian's fingers worm between my legs, pushing between the folds of my pussy, shoving their way inside me.

The music swells inside the bathroom, but all I can hear is a loud, desperate screaming sound in my ears. Raw. Desperate. Panicked.

With some astonishment, I realize that *I'm* making the noise. I'm screaming so loud and so hard that stars are bursting in my eyes, and my lungs feel like they're about to explode.

I'm still screaming, even when a warm, dizzying wall of pleasure begins to mount between my legs, *inside me*. God, the coke…Cillian rubbed the coke he had on his finger inside my pussy. Hot, burning shame licks at my face as I try to order my body not to react, but there's no denying the chemicals. It feels good. It feels far too fucking good for words.

The feeling spreads, rising like smoke, a sharp kind of euphoria taking over my body.

"Fuck sake. Shouldn't she be out by now, Jay? This'd be a lot easier if she wasn't trying to kick me in the balls."

Sam cackles at Cillian's grousing like a drunk hyena. Jake growls, jerking me, digging his fingernails into my skin. "I only gave her half a dose. There's nothing to her. I figured she'd be a little more docile." His teeth scrape against my ear as he hisses at me. "Try and kick one more fucking time and I will break your fucking jaw, bitch. Do you hear me? Hold fucking still."

I'm dimly aware of what he just said: *"...only gave her half a dose. Figured she'd be more docile..."* The knowledge that he's drugged me weighs heavy, pressing me down into the ground. The sluggishness. My inability to think straight. I should have known the way my body was reacting had nothing to do with the coke. The drink. He must have put something in the drink he made me. God, how fucking stupid could I have been? I should have known. I should have seen this coming.

But...

A cute guy I liked smiled at me and made me a drink. At the time, it seemed like a perfectly ordinary thing for him to do.

I feel like I'm drowning in glue. The oxygen in the bathroom is sluggish as I try and pull it down into my chest; it should be a relief to breathe, but every time I try and fill my chest, I end up coughing, choking and spluttering.

It's Jake's hand. He's...he's strangling the life out of me.

"Get her legs, man," Jake commands. Cillian obeys. I try to scream again as the room tilts, and I'm dumped roughly onto my back, but I can't make a single sound. The slate tile on the bathroom floor is freezing against my shoulder blades and the backs of my legs. Jake lets me go, twisting around, placing one foot on either side of my torso. Before he can crouch down and wrap his hands around my throat, I draw myself together, adrenalin and fear doing my thinking for me, and I holler at the top of my lungs.

I've had dreams before. Dreams where I've been in trouble, but when I've screamed for help, only the softest whisper has come out of my mouth. Well, that's not what happens this time. The scream is piercing, loud enough to wake the dead. It echoes around the bathroom, grating and high-pitched, a *help-me-I'm-about-to-be-fucking-raped!* scream. Jake cuts it off with his fist.

Pain blossoms on the right-hand side of my face as my body registers the swift, vicious right jab I just took on the jaw. I've never been hit before. Never like that. My head swims, and for a horrible moment, I think I'm going to pass out. *Don't you fucking dare, Parisi, don't you fucking dare!* I'm high, scared beyond reason, and now I'm in pain, but I know for a fact that I don't want to lose consciousness. Yes, being awake for this is the most horrible thing that's ever happened to me, but if I pass out, I'll never know what they did to me. I will only have my imagination to supply the details, and my imagination already likes to picture the worst. I need the cold, hard facts. I need to be able to hold each of them accountable for their individual actions.

A spiderweb of agony laces its fingers across the back of my head, where it hit the tiles just now. Jake sneers, face contorted, his features all warped and twisted as he looks down at me in disgust. I am seeing him for the first time. This is the *real* him, and I suddenly have no idea why I've wasted the better part of the last two years lusting after him. He's so damn *ugly*. All the anger, and the hate, and the loathing he's wearing on his face is enough to make him the most hideous creature I've ever seen. He grabs my face by the jaw in one hand, holding me steady, and slowly purses his lips, letting a string of saliva fall from his mouth. I try to turn my head away, but it's no good. His grip on my skull doesn't waver for one second. The only thing I can do is close my eyes as the wad of spit lands on my cheekbone, rolling into the well of my eye socket.

"God, you're a fucking mess, Silver." I whimper when his thumb presses down on the top of my eyelid. I have no idea what he's trying to do for a moment, and I imagine the worst—that he's about to gouge my eye out. Quickly, I comprehend what's really happening, though; he's smearing my eyeliner down my face. Not quite as awful as losing an eye but humiliating none the less. His thumb shoves into my mouth, and I do the only reasonable thing: I bite down as hard as I can, until I feel my teeth scrape against bone.

His howl of pain is almost as loud as the scream I let out a moment ago. Another blow hits me in the temple and blackness seeps in, threatening to swallow me up in its oblivion. "Stupid *bitch!*" I've never heard anything that comes close to the rage in Jake's voice as he grabs a fist full of my hair and yanks my head up, smashing it back down onto the tiles. "Looks like you need to learn a few lessons, Parisi. Who do you think you are? Mmm?" Again, he smashes my head down, and I open my mouth, stunned by the shockwave of disorienting pain that floods my being. "You're nothing. Worse than nothing. You're a piece of meat, put here on this earth for *our* pleasure. Don't you know how this works, you dumb fucking cunt? Me and my boys? We're from different stock. Purebreds. We do what we want. Say what we want. Take what we want. You should be fucking grateful we even deigned you worthy of our attention."

He's dripping blood onto the floor, a red, gory circular welt around the knuckle of this thumb. The sight of the wound I gave him does something to me. I should stay quiet. That's what I should do. I should ride this out, keep my mouth shut, and hope they'll go easy on me. Be a good possum and play dead. But...I can't. It's just not in me to lie down and take something like this. I will fight them every step of the way. I will kick, and scream, and bite, and I will cause as much chaos as possible, if it means that this won't be easy for *them.*

"If you're waiting for me to show gratitude," I spit, choking on the word, "then you're gonna be waiting a hell of a long time, Jacob

Weaving. I am *not* nothing. I have a voice, and I will use it. I do not give you permission to touch me. *Let...me...go.*"

Jake's had my arms pinned by my sides all this time. He snatches hold of my wrists and pulls them roughly up high over my head, a dangerous, malicious, crazy light in his eyes. "Hmm, that's it, is it? Pretty Princess Silver. Too good for all of us. Too fucking special. Don't bite. Don't kick. Don't scream. Spread your legs and keep your mouth shut, bitch, and we'll see if we can make this quick."

Setting my jaw, even though it hurts, and my teeth feel like they're shattered, I look him dead in the eye. The drugs are still there, churning around my system, making it difficult to focus, but in this moment everything becomes crystal fucking clear. He wants more than my body from me. More than my pain. He wants my *fear*. He, alone, is so much stronger than me, but with Sam and Cillian thrown into the mix, I don't have a hope in hell's chance of fighting them off. They're going to do what they set out to do. I've pissed Jake off, so he *is* going to make this hurt. But there's one thing I can do, one thing I can keep from him, and that's my fear. I won't fucking give *that* to him.

Jake's sickening smirk deepens as he leers, eyes roving down to pause on my chest. "Sam, what the fuck are you doing, dude. Get over here. Take her hands. Hold her tight. Wait. Are they scissors over there?"

"A razor blade," Sam says, holding up a blade that's identical to the one Kacey used downstairs to cut her drugs. "You want it?"

"Yeah. That'll do nicely." He takes the blade from Sam in exchange for my wrists. If anything, Sam's grip is even harsher, grinding the bones of my wrists down into the floor. It hurts. It feels fucking terrible to be so vulnerable, at their mercy, but I draw in a breath, holding it in my lungs. Then I force my face to go absolutely blank. It would take more control that I possess right now to stop pulling and straining, trying to get free, but my face I *can* control.

I barely even blink as Jake makes a show of holding the blade the material of the dress I borrowed from Kacey, slicing easily through the fabric. He tears and rips at it, pulling away handfuls of black, his eyes glinting with frenzied expectation. "What you staring at, Parisi? You like this after all?" he growls. In no time at all, the dress is gone. I don't even flinch as he greedily saws through the pretty red bow between the cups of my bra. My breasts spring free, and frightening tension begins to mount in the room.

"Shit, Silver. You've been holding out on us," Cillian says thickly. "Who knew you were hiding those bad boys underneath your clothes all this time. Fuck, look at her nipples. They're so fucking pink."

Sam uses a knee to pin my hands, reaching for me, cupping me in his hands, his fingers pinching painfully at my nipples, rolling them as he grins down at me. "God *damn*. And here I was, thinking this'd be a waste of time. If I put my dick in your mouth, Parisi, are you gonna suck it for me?"

Jake punches him hard in the shoulder. "Wait your fucking turn, asshole. I brought her to the table. I get to fuck her first."

"All right, man. All right! No need to get shitty." Sam leans back, his weight on my wrists, and the pain is excruciating. I breathe in deep through my nose, trying to compartmentalize it, distance myself from it, but it's just too much. Jake's gaze crawls over my skin, feasting on me. He sits back on his heels, looking at me, and I'm dreading what will come next, but I don't look away. I meet his gaze, burning my hatred into him.

"You're blocking the view, man," Cillian complains.

"Shut the fuck up," Jake snaps. "We've got all night, haven't we?"

Cillian mumbles something inaudible and unhappy in return, but Jake ignores him. Getting to his feet, he shrugs out of his letterman jacket, removing the button down shirt I admired downstairs, slowly unfastening his belt, and then his jeans. It's probably not the smartest move on my part—definitely not the smartest move on my part—but I let out of a bark of laughter when I realize that he's planning on leaving his MVP medal on.

Jake falters, glaring down at me. "What the fuck is wrong with you?" he hisses. "Don't you have any sense of self-preservation?"

"Don't you have any *pride*?" I fire back. "Is this the only way you can get a girl to fuck you, Jake? Do you have to force yourself on women 'cause none of them will voluntarily climb into bed with you?"

"You would have happily climbed into my bed an hour ago, you pathetic piece of trash. You would have parted your legs for me just like that." He snaps his fingers. "You don't understand. We're given everything we want. The world bows down and lays itself at our feet. It's *boring* being given so much, Silver. Sometimes, to know the depths of your own true power, you've got to *take…*" He unzips his fly, pushing his boxers and his pants down in one go, and then he stands there, as if he's expecting me to swoon at the glory of his body.

I've seen a penis before. He's acting like he's unveiling the eighth wonder of the world, though. I look down at him, terrified to the marrow of my bones, my panic an insidious thing, working its way into each and every cell of my body…but, somehow, I find the courage to laugh again. At him. At the hard, straining appendage hanging there between his legs, looking like some comical design flaw. "God, Jake. Now I get it. If that's what you're working with, then it makes sense that you'd need two guys to pin a girl down."

Jake's face turns a frightening shade of purple. He's shaking as he sinks to his knees, kicking Cillian out of the way. I try to twist out from underneath Sam one more time, frantic, the opportunity to escape flashing before my eyes, but Jake's too fast. He moves quickly, forcing me back onto the tile, the weight of his body bearing down on me. "You're going to regret that," he snarls. "You're gonna wish I'd cut out your tongue with that razor blade, so you couldn't have said something so fucking stupid."

I'm already regretting it. I don't know what I was thinking, but I fucked up. He's going to kill me. He's going to fucking kill me. I whimper, struggling, hating myself for cracking, for letting any sign of fear through, but none of it matters. Jake roughly shoves his way between my legs, baring his teeth in a savage rictus of hate as he drives his hips forward, his erection butting up against the inside of my thigh. "Fucking *cunt!*" he seethes. "Fucking dirty, disgusting *cunt!*"

A sharp, breathtaking moment occurs, suspended in time, and Jake stills on top of me. His pupils are blown, dilated wide enough to have swallowed his irises. He's inside me.

He's...

God...

I bite the inside of my cheek, reviling the new stab of pain between my legs. The signal that I've lost something I will never get back. "Oh, Silver. Silver, Silver, Silver. This tight little pussy of yours has just made all the hassle and trouble you've caused worth it. Fuck me, but you're tight. Does it feel good? Am I making you feel good?"

Hot, burning tears streak from my eyes, but I don't make a sound. I just look up at him, my face blank again, though this time from shock.

I can't believe...

This isn't...

It can't be...

Jake begins to undulate on top of me. I can feel him pulling out of me and driving back up and inside, a fresh wave of pain coursing through me with every roll of his hips. My stomach is rioting, threatening to eject its contents, and I do nothing to hold it back.

"Don't look at me like that, Parisi," Jake snaps. "I'm doing you a fucking favor."

In my head, I laugh. I laugh that he could ever think that, because he does. He really believes this lie. On the outside, I remain closed off, numb, my eyes boring into him as he thrashes, quickening his pace on top of me.

"Look away," he commands.

I don't.

I won't.

If he plans on continuing this violation of my body and my soul, then he's going to have to bear the weight of the judgment in my eyes as he does it. Jacob Weaving, captain of the Raleigh Roughnecks, one of Raleigh's most respected, influential students, grunts, gouging his fingers into my breasts as he fucks me against my will. Sam makes a guttural sound at the back of his throat, his eyes dancing with amusement as he watches Jake writhe on top of me. I pay him no attention, though. I only have eyes for Jake.

Frustrated, furious, his hand swings down to connect with my cheek, and I taste blood. "I said look away!" he yells.

Again, I don't.

Time stretches and slows, taunting me as each second drags by. Jake bites the top of my shoulder, hard enough to draw blood. He bruises me, gouges, digs, twists, pinches. He fucks me harder and harder, and I see the mad lust in his eyes changing into something else. Something that resembles desperation. I don't know how long he continues for. I wrestle for each breath. I struggle and pull. I do everything in my power to get away—which is to say I can do nothing. And every time he pushes himself inside me, grunting and sweating, I make sure I'm glaring at him with, cold, dead eyes.

Eventually, he snaps. Dropping down, shoving his face into mine, he roars into my face. "I SAID FUCKING LOOK AWAY!!"

I...

can't...

fucking...

breathe...

Jacob slams his fist into my side, and my ribs scream, agony ripping through my torso, tearing through every last nerve ending. I have no choice in the matter now. My body convulses as I try and roll onto my side, vomit rising up in my throat, but Sam's still holding me in place. Jake reels back, though, and I see what I felt between my legs—his sad, flaccid dick, hanging pathetically now, stuck to the inside of his thigh, covered in blood.

Now, he reacts with shame.

Now, because his friends have seen that he couldn't fucking finish.

That he couldn't keep his dick hard enough to humiliate me by coming inside me.

"Don't just fucking sit there, staring." He snatches a towel from the counter, wrapping it around his waist, then wipes his nose with the back of his hand. "Get on with it, for fuck's sake. It's early. There's a party still going on downstairs."

Sam doesn't need a second invitation.

He climbs on top of me and does what Jake could not.

Cillian follows.

When they're done, they release me…

…and one by one they take turns in spitting on my cold, bloodied, naked body.

The sound of their laughter rings in my ears as they leave the bathroom.

Jake pauses a second in the doorway, revulsion raging like a storm in his eyes. "If you tell anyone that I couldn't," he whispers, "I'll make your life a living hell, Silver Parisi. I'll make your life so unbearable that you'll do us all a favor and kill yourself before *I* have to do it fucking for you."

25

ALEX

It must be nearly dawn. The light in the trailer's grown progressively brighter as the hours have slipped by, but I haven't moved an inch from my spot on the couch, elbows digging into the tops of my thighs, my balled-up hands pressed against my mouth. My retinas are probably burned beyond repair from the amount of time I've spent staring at the laptop screen, but I haven't been able to look away. I haven't been able to blink for fear that even that small movement might send me into a fit of rage so dark and bottomless that I'll never be able to pull myself out of it.

Silver's email took a while to read, but now her words are scorched into the barren wastelands of my soul forever. They've sparked a maelstrom of toxicity inside me that I can barely breathe around. For the past four hours since reading through the email, not once or twice but countless times, all I've done is sit here and talk myself out of breaking the promises I made to Silver. I should never have sworn I wouldn't hurt those motherfuckers before I knew the full story. It was going to be bad, it was *always* going to be bad, but reading the minutia, diving into every single tiny detail that took place that night...fuck, I felt like I was there, in that bathroom, on my knees, hands tied behind my back, being forced to watch as those sick motherfuckers took turns hurting my girl.

It's with a weird sense of calm that I realize I have officially lost my mind. A temporary kind of insanity. The same kind psychiatrists diagnose people with when they snap and lose all control over themselves and their actions. The only thing keeping my brain from breaking apart and sending me into a fit of incomprehensible insanity is the knowledge that Silver will never speak to me again if I don't honor her wishes.

There will be recompense, though. There will be an atonement for their sins, I'm going to make sure of it. There has to be a workaround that will allow for those fuckers to bleed for what they've done.

And Jacob Weaving...

Oh, Jesus, Jacob. You have no idea what you've done. Nine months ago, when you took a drugged, vulnerable girl into a room with the intention of causing her pain, shaming and humiliating her, stealing her virginity, you clearly weren't thinking of the future. You didn't consider for a moment what was going to happen today.

You didn't see me coming.

If you had, you would never have laid a finger on Silver Parisi. You wouldn't have allowed yourself to even think her damn name.

I'm vibrating with rage, floating outside of myself as I make myself a coffee. No way I'm going to sleep at all now. We're not back in school until tomorrow, so I'll go and see Silver later. In the meantime, I plan on getting the ball rolling on this situation, and I know just the man for the job.

I fill up the bike at the gas station closest to the bar, and a guy honks at me, trying to get me to hurry. I want to grind my knuckles into his face. Hit him until he begins to cry like a little bitch. I wanna break his fucking neck.

I've been angry for most of my teen years—at Gary, for using his strength and his size over me. At Jackie for keeping me from seeing Ben. At Maeve, Rhonda and a whole line-up of other social workers, who have all made my life way harder than it needed to be. At my mom for fucking dying. But I have never, never been *this* angry before, spilling over with rage, panting and breathless, rendered mentally incompetent because of it.

I sit on the bike in a parking spot, stewing over everything, thoughts like the blades of a blender, whipping around so fast and so sharp that the inside of my skull is in chaos. Five minutes later, the punk in the white button-down and the pressed khakis who honked at me emerges from the gas station, and I climb off the bike, heading toward him with a tire iron in my hand.

He runs across the gas station forecourt, bolting for his Durango. "What the fuck? *You fucking psycho!*" He dives into the vehicle, slamming the door and locking it swiftly behind him.

I'm three seconds away from smashing the tire iron into his window when the attendant comes rushing out of the building with a phone in his hand. "Hey! Hey, asshole! Get out of here before I call the fucking cops!"

The taunt sits heavy on the tip of my tongue, burning like battery acid: *Go ahead, motherfucker. Call them. See what happens.* But I know how that'll go. They'll show up here en force, tires screeching as they peel onto the forecourt, guns already drawn, aimed at my fucking head. They'll cart me off in cuffs. It'll be on the news. 'Local thug arrested for attempted assault.' All of Raleigh will know about it before lunchtime, and Silver will be hysterical. She won't forgive me. I told her I could handle the truth from her. I can't let her down at the very first hurdle by pulling this kind of stupid shit.

My pulse pounds like a runaway train in my temples as I stalk back to the bike and climb on, starting the engine and roaring out of the station.

This is not good.

This is *not* fucking good.

I need to *do* something.

At the bar, I find Monty in his office, going over surveillance footage at his desk. His expression darkens when I burst in without knocking. "The fuck's got you so riled up?" he asks, halting the feed on the screen.

"I need a favor," I grind out. I'm calmer than I was when I had the tire iron in my hand, but I am a far cry from actually *being* calm.

"Does this favor involve murder? 'Cause you look like you're about to kill someone."

"Maybe," I say grimly.

"Jesus. It's only Monday morning, Alex. Can't we at least make it to Thursday evening without a need for homicide?" He jerks his head at the seat opposite him. "Sit. Tell me what's happened."

I don't want to sit but I know he won't appreciate me prowling up and down in his office with a face like thunder, so I slump down in the chair and lean forward, holding my head in my hands.

"You even shower this morning? You look like shit," he says.

"No. I did not shower. I had other things on my mind."

"If this has anything to do with that tasty little treat from Raleigh High that you brought in here the other night, please know I am not going to be happy."

I roll my eyes. "No. Not her. Another girl. My *girlfriend*," I add on the end, gingerly…because I know he's gonna give me shit for—

"Girlfriend? Since when?" I don't even get to finish the thought. Monty's already smirking like the bastard that he is, kicking his feet up on his desk like he's settling in for a juicy bit of gossip. "You knock her up the first time you stick your dick in her, Moretti? 'Cause that would be some dumbass bullshit right there."

"Fuck you, man," I growl. "My dick isn't the problem here."

"But it *is* a dick problem."

"Three guys from the Raleigh football team raped her. It was really fucking bad."

Monty's grin takes on a sour, displeased look. "Well. That does sound like a problem, doesn't it?" He leans forward, swiping his pack of smokes up from the edge of his desk. He lights one, narrowing his eyes at me. "Should never have gotten kicked out of Bellingham, kid. A Bellingham girl would have carved 'em up before letting 'em pull that kinda shit. Raleigh's too touchy-feely. Makes the kids too soft to stick up for themselves."

"I'm not really interested in arguing the pros and cons of Raleigh High. I just want some fucking justice."

"For her, because they hurt her? Or for you, because they broke one of your toys?"

Monty's done a lot for me since I got out of juvie. More than anyone else would have done. But at the moment I feel like knocking his fucking head off. Common sense prevails, though. He's my only ally in all of this. I still give him a look laced with enough vitriol to let him know what I think of his question. "She's suffered long enough, having to see those fuckers day in and day out. She shouldn't have to."

Blowing out a cloud of smoke, Monty regards me. "She go to the hospital? Take a rape kit?"

I grip the arms of the chair, growling low, like a dog. "She's not making it up, asshole. You don't know her, man. She's not like that." She's nothing at all like the girl Jake tried to paint when I first started at Raleigh. That was all subterfuge. So much smoke. Groundwork on Jake's part, prepping me for the time when Silver told me what he did, so I'd think she was a liar right out of the gate.

"I'm not saying she's lying. Though high school girls do do that, y'know. I'm merely wondering if there's any kind of evidence to this crime. Something the cops can work with."

Bitterly, I shake my head. "She was too fucked up. Hasn't told her folks. She told her friends, and they cut her out. Shunned her."

"And the school?"

"The teachers heard about it. Called her in. Called him in, too. Made them do some conflict resolution counseling and swept the entire thing under the rug. They look at her the same way as all the other students do. Like she's some trouble maker, out to cause issues for their golden boy."

"You said there were three of them. You keep on talking about one guy, though."

"He was the one who drugged her. He's the one who orchestrated the whole thing. He's their fucking ringleader. They all need to suffer…but Jacob Weaving needs to suffer the most."

Monty's eyebrows rocket, shooting upward. "Weaving? Caleb Weaving's kid?"

"I don't know who his father is." That hardly seems important, but the look on Monty's face says otherwise.

"Caleb Weaving used to be one of my biggest clients. Owns half of the farmland in the county. Richer than sin."

"And what? That means Jake shouldn't be held accountable for what he's done?"

Slowly, Monty smiles, stubbing out his cigarette in an overflowing ashtray. "No, Alex. It means, if we *are* talking about Caleb's kid, then I will happily help you bring the little fucker to his knees. Caleb's screwed me over more times than I can count. It's about time someone taught that family a hard lesson. When were you hoping to mete out this justice of yours?"

"Today? Yesterday? As soon as humanly fucking possible. Why?"

"Because…if you're willing to stay your hand for a couple of weeks, a couple of months, even, then I think I know just the thing that'll strip that little fucker of his crown."

"I don't know, man. *Months?*"

"It'll be worth it. Trust me. By Christmas, Jacob Weaving won't be bothering your little girlfriend any longer."

~

Silver's car doesn't sound healthy at all. On the drive back from the cabin, I make a mental note to give the engine a once over as soon as possible. Monty drove me over to the lake to collect it, and said no more about what his plan to punish Jake involved, but he played Lynyrd Skynyrd the entire way there—his thinking music—and wore a wolfish, smug smile that meant he was plotting something genuinely vile. I thanked him, told him I'd make sure I showed up for my shift on Wednesday, grim in the knowledge that he'll probably want me to do another run for him. When we pulled out of the cabin's long driveway, I took a left back toward Raleigh, and he took a right, disappearing off to god only knows where.

Now that I'm close to Silver's, I message her to let her know I'm heading her way.

> **Me: Almost at your place. Gonna leave your beater. Should I knock?**

I'm turning onto her street when she answers.

> **Silver: I resent that. My car is not a beater.**

> **Silver: I feel rude as hell, but would you mind dropping it off and going? Things aren't good over here.**

> **Me: No problem**

> **Silver: You have plans tonight?**

> **Me: At your mercy. Have something in mind?**

> **Silver: What's your address? I'll come over after ten.**

My nerves revolt, making me feel nauseous. Silver, coming to the trailer? I told her I wanted her to come over when we were at the cabin, but I didn't really think about all that that entailed. The place needs more than a little TLC.

Me: 1876 Bow Hill Rd. You know which park?

I arrive at her place while she's still replying. I make it quick, pulling into the driveway, parking, killing the engine. I get out, looking up at the house—beautiful, serene, ivy climbing up the fascia, roses planted in the beds. The kind of house I dreamed of living in when I was a kid—and then I spy her, standing at one of the upstairs windows. My poor Silver looks like a ghost up there, alone, pale behind the glass. She really is so fucking beautiful. She raises a hand, pressing it against the window, a small, sad smile on her face, and I want to kick in the front door, race up the stairs and take her into my arms right this second.

She said now wasn't good, though, which means the shit must be hitting the fan in there. I hold up her keys, making sure she can see what I'm doing as I place them on the Nova's dashboard. She nods, just once, and then she vanishes out of sight.

I could call an Uber to take me home, but it seems like a waste of time. The trailer park I call home is four miles away, but I'm no stranger to walking. I don't care about the cold or the fact that it's just starting to rain. I need to clear my head, and four miles should give me plenty of time to think.

26

SILVER

He didn't mention anything about the email in his texts. Not one word. I don't blame him, either. If I were him, I'd probably want to pretend like I hadn't read such a crappy, terrible story, too. He probably doesn't even know what he's going to say to me.

I make my way downstairs, feeling sick to my soul. I have plenty of regrets, but I regret sending that email more than anything else I've ever done. I have no idea what tonight's going to be like with him. I'm hoping it won't be an awkward disaster, but—

I run into Dad the second I hit the bottom step. "Holy hell!" He clutches a hand to his chest dramatically, staggering back until he hits the wall. "I thought you'd moved out. There were rumors some sort of nocturnal creature had taken up residence in your room. I was gonna start charging it rent."

"One day, Dad. I've been up early every other day for the past year. Feel free to cut me some slack."

"I know, I know," he says, throwing an arm around me, guiding me into the kitchen. "I'm just messing with you. Figured you could take it, but I can see you're feeling a little sensitive. I was surprised you came back yesterday. I thought you'd be making the most of every last second at the cabin. Mom said you weren't feeling good. Everything all right?"

Wow. Guess I shouldn't be too surprised that Mom's been lying again. I told her to do it, after all. I'm kind of glad she came up with this excuse, though. Would have been hard to explain my early return otherwise. "Yeah, yeah. I'm just feeling a little under the weather's all. Decided it'd be smarter to head home before I came down with a full-blown head cold."

Dad releases me, making a cross with his index fingers, like he's warning off a demon. "If ye be infected, keep thy germs to thyself, lest the whole household succumbs to thy plague," he says, feigning horror all over again. He is such a damn dork. "You want huevos rancheros? Extra spicy, just the way you like 'em. Might destroy whatever's ailing ya before it can take hold."

"Sure. Thanks, Dad."

He gets to work, clattering around the kitchen, pots banging on the counters, noisier than ever. I take a seat at the breakfast counter, watching him make a mess. "Your mom's taken Max to the movies," he says. "I know she told you about Gail. She's been crying all morning. I told her to get out of the house. Shame you're sick. Max is all well and good, but I think she'd have rather had you to hang out with today. Another girl, y'know."

Oh, I'm sure she would rather have gouged her own eyes out than spend the day with me. I'm the only other person in the world who knows her dirty little secret. As a rule, I've learned that people don't like spending extended amounts of time with the people who know all about their misdeeds. Seeing them only serves to remind them of their crimes, and they'll do anything to avoid facing *those* at all costs. "Yeah, it is a shame. I feel so bad for Dr. Coombes right now," I murmur.

"Yeah, poor bastard. Don't know what I'd do if I ever lost your mom. God, it doesn't even bear thinking about."

Normal, everyday statements like this have already begun to take on much deeper meanings for me, and I fucking hate it. I despise that I've been put in this position. My father has no idea how close he is...or was...to losing Mom. Not to a car crash, though. To a guy named Dan, her boss, who has sat at our dining table with his wife and eaten dinner with us more times that I can remember.

Does Dan's wife know anything about the fact that her husband's been fucking my mother? And what would Dad actually do if he *did* find out? A part of me thinks he'd leave her. Another part of me suspects that he'd stay, though, try and save their marriage, because that's just the kind of guy he is, and that just breaks my fucking heart for him.

He'd be crushed. He'd be in pain, and yet he'd stay, for Max and for me, and for all the years he and Mom have shared together, but every time he looked at her, he'd see it all in his head, imagining every last little kiss and caress that was shared between *them*, and it would eat him alive.

"Sil? Earth to Silver? What's wrong? You look like you're about to burst into tears. My cooking really isn't *that* bad."

"Oh, I know. I—it's just—it's my sinuses, that's all." I scrub at my eyes with the backs of my hands, glad I caught myself in time before I actually started crying. "The onions probably aren't helping. My head feels like it's about to explode."

"Joking aside, why don't you go back up to bed, honey? I can bring this up to you when it's ready. You probably should rest."

I want to be able to stay here with him, listening to his dumb jibes and laughing at how absolutely lame he is in the best possible way, but I honestly can't trust myself. I feel like I'm going to dissolve into a puddle of misery, and that would be really, really bad. "Thanks, Dad. You're the best."

I get up and head for the stairs. It's stupid and feels a little too obvious, but I pause at the foot of the first step, glancing back at him over my shoulder. "Hey, Dad?"

"What's up, kiddo?"

"I love you."

His eyes round out, as big as silver dollars. "Shit, Silver. You really must be sick."

I'm slipping into my bedroom when I hear him yell up the stairs after me. "But I love you, too, sweetheart!"

∼

Mom and Max get back from the movies around five. I don't go down for dinner. I just…I can't force myself to convincingly sit there and pretend. I would fail. Snap at her or something, and Dad would lose his shit. No way would he be okay with me giving Mom attitude when, as far as he's concerned, she's grieving over the death of her best fucking friend.

If I'm being fair, she *is* grieving over her friend. She's just also feeling guilty as fuck because she feels responsible for the accident that killed Gail, and she's been revealed to be an adulterous monster at the same time. I can appreciate what a head fuck *that* must be at least.

She goes to bed ridiculously early, shutting herself away in their bedroom. At nine, I head downstairs and knock on Dad's office door, knowing he'll still be at his desk, working hard.

"Enter at your own peril," he calls.

Inside his office, he rubs at his eyes, the light from his computer screen casting a blue glow over his face. "Feeling better, kiddo?" he asks.

"Mostly."

"Well, if you want money, it had better be for something good. Beer. A handgun. A brick of coke."

He's joking, because he trusts me implicitly, and he knows I'd never have anything to do with illegal firearms or hard drugs. Shame cuts at me, a cold, unforgiving knife under my skin. I'm exactly the good girl he believes me to be now, but that hasn't always been the case. Far from it. He'd have a heart attack if he had any idea the shit I used to get roped into with Kacey. "I don't need money, Dad. My savings account is looking pretty healthy as a matter of fact. I wanted to ask for something else."

He peers at me, sitting back in his chair. "Sounds ominous."

"I want to go spend the night at Alex's place." I blush furiously as soon as the words are out. God, this was a bad idea. What the hell was I thinking, blurting it out like that? My father looks like he's having trouble swallowing.

"I'm sorry? *Alex*? Your guitar student? The one with the motorcycle and all the prison ink?"

"It's not priso—never mind. Yes, the guy who came here the other day. He and I...we're together now."

"Aaaand..." He shakes his head, puffing out his cheeks. "You tell me this on the back of a request to go and spend the night at his house?"

"Yes. I know. I'm insane."

He laughs, but I can tell he's uneasy. "How long have you been seeing him?"

"Not long. A few days."

"God, Silver. Come on, what do you expect me to do here? You really think I'm going to agree t—"

"He lives at Salton Ash Park. By himself. In a trailer."

"Jesus fucking—"

"He's had a couple of run-ins with the law. But nothing bad. Nothing terrible."

"Silver, if you are trying to make your request sound any less crazy, then you are heading in the *wroooong* direction."

"Just laying all the cards on the table, Dad. Giving you all the information, no matter how damaging, seems like the smartest option. It's a radical approach, I'm aware. I'm just hoping you'll appreciate the honesty and trust that I know what I'm doing."

He gives me a troubled, torn look, bordering on annoyance.

"Fuck, Sil. Can't you just lie to me like any normal teenager? Ignorance is bliss sometimes."

This hits me like a ten-ton weight. *Ignorance is bliss sometimes.* Would he still say that if he knew what Mom's been up to? I have no idea. Am I so candid with him now because I've forced Mom to lie to him and I'm feeling guilty as fuck, though? Absolutely, one hundred percent, yes.

"Seemed like I owed you an honest explanation," I murmur.

"And if I say no? Are you gonna be plotting some great escape and clambering down the trellis at three in the morning? 'Cause I don't wanna have to worry about setting up some makeshift perimeter alarm this late in the evening."

"No, Dad. Jeez. I'm not that limber, and you know it."

He huffs, giving me a scowl. "This is some kind of karmic kick in the ass because of all the shit me and your mom got up to when we were in high school, isn't it?"

"I bet you weren't asking Nona and Gramps for their permission."

He laughs. "No, I was *not*, and neither was your mom. We were ninjas, Silver. *Ninjas.* They never suspected a thing."

"At least *you'll* know exactly where I am," I say, shrugging weakly. He wants to say no. He really wants to be the strict, firm dad, who wraps his daughter in cotton wool and triple bolts his front door at night, trying to keep the Big Bad World out for as long as he possibly can. Poor guy; he looks like he's aged ten years in the last ten minutes. I'm honestly surprised when he sighs and throws up his hands.

"All right. All right, you can go."

"Seriously?"

"Yes! But…Jesus, Silver. You know as well as I do, the picture you just painted of the guy doesn't look good. If he starts getting handsy, if he starts acting pushy, if he so much as looks at you the wrong way or scares you, you call me immediately and I'll be down at that trailer park in a heartbeat with a goddamn sledgehammer in my hand."

He's so serious, he means every word. His eyes have grown distant—I can tell that he's imagining how that would play out, the drive over to Salton Ash, the weight of the weapon in his hands, how it would feel to swing it up over his head and break the knees of the boy who made me cry.

Little does he know, he's already nine months too late for any of that.

It was a boy with a clean record, a winning smile and a glorious halo who broke me. Ironically, it's the boy with the rap sheet, a body full of ink and the dangerous glint in his eye who's putting me back together.

27

SILVER

I've driven by Salton Ash plenty of times, but I've never actually taken the exit and entered the trailer park's grounds before. In seventeen years, this is the first time I've ever known anyone to live here, and I'm surprised by how well kept and pretty the grounds are. My nerves feel like they're going to get the better of me as I drive slowly down the wide, paved road, scanning the numbers on the trailers, searching for the trailer that belongs to Alex. Eventually, I see his motorcycle and know I've found the right place.

Unlike some of the other trailers, there are no potted flowers, plastic windmills or little gnomes sitting on the front steps in front of his trailer. The small grass patch to the right of the front door looks like it's actually been mown, though, and the exterior looks clean and well-maintained, even in the dark.

There are lights on inside. I get out of the Nova, slamming the door behind me before I can heed the anxious voice in the back of my head that's telling me this is a dumb idea and I should go home. I can barely stand still as I wait at the top of the steps, trying to gather the confidence required to knock on the door. The music inside dips suddenly, though, and I hear movement on the other side of the door.

Alex's voice—a little muffled, though perfectly audible—is a little teasing when he speaks. "Come on, *Argento*. You've made it this far."

"You're seriously going to make me knock?"

"Only polite."

"Jerk," I groan. "Open the door."

The door swings inward, revealing Alex in a pair of black jeans and a plain black t-shirt. His dark hair is swept straight back, highlighting the shaved sides of his head. God, the longer, usually wavy strands are wet. He looks so, so unbelievably sexy. A fresh, clean smell hits me, stronger than ever, and I realize that he must have just gotten out of the shower.

I'm woefully unprepared to deal with this kind of shit. Next level *'Alex-Moretti-is the-finest-fucking-thing-to-walk-the-face-of-the-earth'* shit. I've never been one to succumb to hormones or lose my head over a handsome guy, but with him standing in front of me now, the side of his face bathed in the warm glow coming from inside the trailer, I discover what it means to be rendered speechless by the mere sight of someone.

He smirks, mouth open a little, the tip of his tongue pressing against his front teeth, and my traitorous knees nearly go out. "Get your ass in here before one of my neighbors steals you," he says, placing a hand on my hip, pulling me up the last step into the trailer.

I formed a pretty clear picture of what his place was going to be like on the way over here, but, stepping into his home, I learn just how wrong I was. The place doesn't reek of dirty socks, for starters. It smells clean, just like him. The living room I've stepped into isn't a bomb site, cluttered with clothes, empty take out cartons, and dirty dishes. There are no posters of half-naked women draped over motorcycles on the walls, either. A large sectional couch fits along the wall and into the far corner of the room, and on my left, there's a shelf, stacked with row upon row of tatty, worn, well-read books.

The music I heard playing from outside is coming from a record player on a side table underneath the window, underneath which is a staggering amount of vinyl. The television isn't as big as I would have thought. A collection of photos, framed and mounted beside it, take up most of the real estate on the largest wall. I'd prepared myself for a ratty, sticky carpet, riddled with cigarette burns, but there are polished hardwood floorboards beneath my feet instead—and they look like they've been freshly swept and cleaned.

"No need to look so surprised," Alex whispers into my ear. I didn't even notice that he'd crept up so quietly behind me.

"I'm not *surprised*. I just, well…okay. All right. I'm surprised. But can you blame me? A guy's parents go away for the weekend and the place ends up destroyed. You live on your own permanently. I figured your place would be…"

"Disgusting?"

"Yeah. I did. I thought it was gonna be disgusting." It's a relief to laugh. It kills the tension that's been climbing up my spine since I got out of the Nova. Alex spins me around, wrapping his arms around me.

"The kitchen can get turned upside down," he admits. "But don't worry. I cleaned out all the dead flies and rat shit in honor of your visit."

"You are not serious."

"No. I'm not." Hesitantly, he leans down and places a gentle kiss against my mouth. "I'm just fucking with you," he murmurs. "The park doesn't have rats. And Oscar catches and eats all the flies."

"Oscar?"

"The cat."

"You have a *cat*?"

"No. He's *the* cat, not *my* cat."

"What's the difference?"

Alex shrugs. "Sometimes he lives here, with me. Sometimes he lives at one of the other trailers. He's a cat slut, keeping his options open. Come on. I'll show you where everything is."

The kitchen isn't quite spotless, but it's damn near close. The counters are clean, and there are no dishes in the sink. Small, spiny cactuses sit on the window sill over the sink, and my brain nearly melts. Even a cactus requires some level of attention, and I just can't wrap my head around Alex Moretti caring for something like that.

The bathroom's small, but the grout in the shower isn't black with mold, the mirror isn't streaked with watermarks and flecked with toothpaste, and the actual toilet bowl is glowing white.

Alex pauses, faltering in front of the last remaining unopened door in the trailer. "My room is…uhhh…" He rubs at the back of his neck—the very first sign that he might be suffering from a few nerves himself. "I don't sleep in here much. It's not exactly palatial." He opens the door and enters, bracing himself like he's stepping into a room full of angry wasps. He hits the lights, and I follow after him.

The room's a decent size. Probably the same size as my room at home. The walls are bare. Dark grey curtains at the windows. A shelf on the wall displays a series of framed pictures, drawings actually, hand sketched in pencil. The same woman features in all of the drawings—dark hair, dark, soulful, wounded-looking eyes, pouting mouth. She looks heartbreakingly beautiful and heartbreakingly sad at the same time. Her resemblance to Alex leaps out of the drawings and grabs me by the shoulders, shaking me, leaving no doubt in my mind that she is his mother.

A large, king bed dominates the room. The duvet cover is plain white, as are the sheets and pillowcases beneath it. "Bought the covers this afternoon," Alex says awkwardly. "I didn't know what color to get, so I said fuck it and got white. The woman in the store said it'd look clean. Maybe I should have gone with black. Or red."

"White's good, Alex," I whisper. Suddenly, the bed feels very big and very intimidating. I've already slept with him. I know what his body feels like against mine. I've had him inside me…but I suddenly find it very hard not to feel shy when confronted with such a large bed. My palms are sweating like crazy. I turn away from it, moving to stand in front of the drawings, studying each one of them closely, trying to calm my racing heart.

"My father drew them. Before I was born," Alex says behind me.

"Where is he now?" After the harrowing story of his mother's suicide, I'm almost afraid to ask.

Alex grunts. "Who knows. Prison, probably. He skipped out on us after Ben was born. I hardly remember him. He wasn't around much in the first place."

I brush my fingers against the closest drawing, a heavy sadness tugging at me. My dad's always been there, no matter what. I can't imagine what it would have been like to grow up without him. Without knowing that he always had my back. "Not many people can draw like this. He was very talented," I say.

"His only real talent was letting people down. I barely remember him. I look at these pictures, and I see her, not him."

"You miss her," I say softly.

Alex replies, voice dipped low, scraping the barrel of his chest, hushed, like he's afraid someone from the cruel, harsh world outside might hear him admitting his one and only weakness. "Sometimes, I miss her so much sometimes, I forget how to fucking breathe."

28
ALEX

I've had plenty of girls want to come hang out at the trailer, but I've never let any of them inside. I've never even given anyone my address before, so having someone here now is really strange. Monty came here with me the day he gave me the keys, but apart from that I've kept this place to myself. Quiet. Private. Mine.

Silver moves around the kitchen, opening the drawers, taking mugs out of the cupboard, putting water into the kettle and prepping the coffee filter, and I lean against the kitchen wall, watching her like a hawk, chewing on my thumbnail. She looks like she belongs here. She has no idea where anything is, but she looks so damn *right* searching through my stuff in my kitchen that every beat of my heart feels labored and fucking painful.

This is so damn confusing.

I've guarded this place so fiercely that I'm not sure what to do now that she's here and I want her to stay. She doctors my coffee, heaping four teaspoons of sugar into my mug, then pouring in a healthy splash of milk and handing it off to me.

"Thank you." Jeez, even saying fucking thank you to her feels weird. I've had to fight so hard to earn or accomplish anything in this life that I'm usually very reluctant to be polite about it when I win. I can't remember the last time someone did something as simple as make me a coffee, though, and the gratitude I'm hit with is genuine. Pathetic, but I don't know how to fucking handle it.

I wince as I take a mouthful of the coffee, pretending not to notice how sweet it is. I never told her that I was just nervous at the diner by the lake; I emptied those packets into my cup because I just needed something to do with my hands. I actually take it black, too, but it doesn't matter. I will down every last drop of the liquid in this cup, because Silver fucking made it for me.

Everything's been normal up until now. If I don't say something to her soon, it's gonna get weird, though, and I don't want to spoil however much time we have to spend with each other tonight. Grabbing Silver by the hand, I take her back into the living room and sit her down on the couch. She knows what's coming; she looks like she's about to bury her face in the couch cushions and hide when I clear my throat, trying to think of how best to begin.

"You read it," she rushes out, before I can even open my mouth. "The email. And now you think I'm tainted goods, and you wanna trade me in for a less broken model."

I arch an eyebrow at her. "Is that really what you think I'm gonna say?"

She smiles weakly. "I don't know. Probably. Most guys would run a mile..."

"The guys you've had dealings with are obviously disgusting pieces of shit, Silver. A guy like Jake would run. And I am *nothing* like Jake. You know that, don't you?" If she doesn't, it's going to fucking gut me. We'll never make it if she doesn't know *that*.

"Of course I do. You couldn't be more different from him if he tried. I guess I'm just...afraid. I don't want you to think about me and see the ugliness that I wrote about in that email."

"Silver, when I think about you, I see the girl who stripped in a cabin for me and drove me fucking insane. That's all I've been seeing at the moment, period. You have no idea how fucking hot that was. It'll be burned into my brain for the rest of fucking time, so you don't need to worry about that."

She smiles a little sadly, looking down into her coffee mug. "But?" she says. "It sounds like there's a but in there somewhere."

"No buts. That's it. I think you're sexy as fuck, and that's never going to change."

She looks at me, and the blue of her eyes is as crisp and clear as Lake Cushman. "And…you don't think it was my fault? For going up there with Jake? You don't think I lead them on?"

I suddenly feel like I'm burning up. Anger roils in my gut. "*No. Fuck no.* Don't ever think that. If someone's told you that, I will fucking destroy them." She laughs softly, dismissing the comment. She has no idea how serious I am. "I spend a lot of time with a lot of dangerous people, Silver. I could have Jake buried up the side of a mountain in less than three hours, and they would never find the body. If you say you don't wanna use violence, that's fine. I'll respect that. But I'm never going to judge if you tell me you want him to hurt the way he hurt you. All you need to do is say the word and it'll be done."

She seems to shrink in on herself, her shoulders rounding in, gripping her coffee cup so tight her knuckles go white. She stares silently at the edge of the coffee table for a minute, and I let her think. I know her well enough to know that she's going to reject that offer out of hand. I still want to let her know it's a real option, though.

"What would you do?" she asks quietly.

"You already know the answer to that question." She can see it in my eyes. She knows I'd have already dismembered those motherfuckers and tossed their mangled corpses into the ocean. I would have had no fucking mercy.

She nods slowly. Her eyes don't meet mine when she speaks. "I don't know what to do. Everything's gotten so confusing and complicated. I honestly don't even want to think about it anymore. At least not tonight. I just want to be here with you."

This is a plea. Now that we've acknowledged the email, she wants it to be done with. She doesn't want it looming over us for the rest of the night. I get it. I understand. I also just wish she'd give me the green light so I could jump on the back of the bike, go and find every single one of those motherfuckers and mess them up so badly they'll never walk again. That'd be satisfying beyond words. I'm not going to push the matter, though. It was a massive leap of faith for her to tell me what happened in the first place. "All right. Done. No more email talk. We can save the dark stuff for another time. Or never. It's your call. When's your curfew? If we have time, we can throw on a movie?"

"Actually..." She pauses. Looks a little awkwardly around the living room. "There is no curfew. I'm free for the night. I was hoping I could crash—"

"You're staying here? Tonight?"

"If that's okay with y—"

She squeals as I lunge for her, lifting her off the couch. "I have no idea how you pulled that off, *Argento*, but you just made my week," I growl into her hair.

"Alex! Put me down! What the hell?" She's laughing. The smile's right there on her face, so I know she's not mad about the fact that I'm dragging her off toward the bedroom, but I still need to want to make sure...

"You wanna help me break in that bed, Dolcezza? 'Cause I've never even slept in it, and I've wanted to tear your fucking clothes off since you walked through the front door." I really have wanted to get her naked since she arrived, but I'm not a monster. I could wait. I'd be happier than a pig in shit if she wanted to curl up on the couch and watch a movie, but I don't think that's what she needs right now. She needs to know just how bad I fucking want her. She needs to see for herself just how attractive I think she is.

How that email isn't going to affect my need for her in any way, shape or form.

Silver winds her arms around my neck, digging her fingernails into my shoulder blades. Her eyes shine brightly as she reaches up to kiss me. She runs her tongue over the seam of my mouth, tugging on my bottom lip between her teeth, and my dick begins to throb, screaming for attention. Needy bastard. I come to a halt outside the bedroom, resting my hand on the doorknob. "Say the word, and we can eat ice cream on the couch and watch Seinfeld."

"Or…?" she asks breathlessly.

"I take you in here, and I eat *you* until you come."

Her color is high, a small, dazed smile on her face. "Open the door then. Seinfeld can wait."

I'm crowing in my head as I kick the bedroom door open and carry her inside. Silver yelps again, laughing, as I throw her down onto the bed. I have her shoes off, her jeans down, her panties on the floor and my fingers inside her before she can even draw breath. She grabs my wrist with both her hands, catching hold of me, stilling me so I can't move. Her eyes have doubled in size, and her mouth is hanging open…

"Oh, fuck. *Alex!*"

God damn, she is so fucking beautiful. Everything about her is perfect. In the small hours of the morning, when the prospect of the future has kept me from sleeping and I've laid there, considering what will probably come of me, the life I've pictured for myself has been far from promising.

Stuck working at the Rock for starters, putting in years for Monty. Maybe joining the M.C. Doing runs, dropping off guns, or drugs, or dirty money whenever the need arises, not asking questions, keeping my head down. When I've felt optimistic, I've allowed myself to imagine Ben here. That I've gained custody of him, and I'm a good role model to him. I keep him safe. The one thing I have never, ever imagined, though, is a girlfriend or a wife. I never thought I'd meet anyone I'd want to factor into my life…

but now there's Silver. I'm almost panicked by the idea that she might like me as much as I like her. I don't want to mess this up. I don't want to hurt her. I don't want to risk fucking losing her…

Fuck, what the hell are you doing to yourself, Moretti? Now's not the time to be worrying about that stuff. Just kiss the girl. Make her feel good. Make her fucking come.

I take my own advice and shut all thoughts of what could be out of my head as Silver pants on the bed. She looks like something out of a fucking dream, her hair spread out over the new duvet cover. Her eyes are locked onto my hand between her legs. She's staring at it, as if she's fascinated by the fact that I'm actually touching her.

"Fuck, Alex. Oh my god, that feels so good."

She's already turned on and ready when I begin to pump my fingers inside her. Her pussy's wetter than wet. I had just my middle finger inside her, but I add my index finger, sweeping them up and toward myself in a beckoning motion, and Silver lets go of my wrist, grabbing hold of the duvet cover instead, fisting it in her hands.

"Shit. Ahh, shit. *What…the…hell?*"

Her head is rocked back, her eyes closed tight, so I allow myself a smug little smile. If she thinks that feels good, she has no idea what I have planned for her. We both wanted each other so badly back at the cabin that it was pretty much impossible for either of us to hold back. I still really want her now, but I'm going to keep a tight leash on myself this time. I plan on bringing her to the edge of insanity tonight. I've already given her a taste of how good it can be between two people if they care about each other. Now, she's going to get the full experience.

She whimpers, eyes flying open when I remove my hand from between her legs. She watches me, a little stunned as I slide my fingers into my mouth, sucking the slickness of her pussy from them. "Fuck me, Silver. You taste so fucking good. You're gonna be the death of me." My voice is rough with need. My dick is urging me to hurry the fuck up, hulk out of my clothes, shred her shirt and her bra from her beautiful body and sink myself inside her, but that's not how it's going to go tonight. I take a couple of breaths, waiting for my heart rate to even out, and then I begin to *slowly* take off my clothes.

Silver watches, transfixed. I still can't believe I'm lucky enough to have a girl like her look at *me* like that. It just doesn't make any sense. She's so good. So strong. So innocent in so many ways, and I'm nothing more than the dirt beneath her fucking feet. I shrug out of my shirt and stand there, looming over the bed, looking down at her with ravenous eyes.

Her legs are fucking phenomenal. She arches her spine, taking hold of her shirt and pulling it up over her head, shedding it in a quick movement. I was planning on undressing the rest of her, but I can't seem to find it in me to stop her as she unhooks her bra and tosses it onto the floor.

I spend a lot of time around strippers, so I've seen a lot of naked women. I don't even really *see* them anymore; I've become desensitized to the sight of so much bare flesh when I'm working at the Rock. It's not the same with Silver, though. Her tits are fucking amazing—flawlessly proportioned with the rest of her body, the perfect shape, not too big and not too small. Her nipples are a faint blushed pink color, very pale. Her skin is the color of fresh poured cream. I can't tear my eyes away from the slight rise of her hip bones, and the way the moonlight flooding in through the window plays over her body, casting shadows across the flat plane of her stomach and up her throat.

"Feels like I'm breaking all the rules, having you here like this," I rumble. I meant for the words to come out light and easy, but they come out hard and coarse; I want her so fucking bad, I just can't keep the desire from my voice. "I never thought I'd get to see something so beautiful."

"Alex," she whispers. "Don't just look. I want you to touch. I want you to lick. I want you to taste. Please. I *need* you..."

God fucking damn it. Does she have any idea how hard it is to hold myself back when she says something like that? I grind my teeth together, sucking in a calming breath as I unbuckle my belt and lose my jeans. It's probably best if I keep the boxers for now—

Silver sits up, positioning herself on all fours, edging down the bed. Her tits sway as she crawls toward me, and I have to bite back a groan. "What are you doing? You're not leaving those on," she says.

"I'm *not?*" She's so damn sexy. She sits back on her heels, hooking the material of my boxers beneath her index fingers, slowly wiggling them down over my hips.

"Nope. I want to look at you. I want to be able to see every last millimeter of you."

She's a hell of a lot more confident than she was back at the cabin. There's still a hint of nerves in her eyes, though, as she—

Holy fucking shit!

"Ahhh! Fuck, Silver. Jesus!"

I was expecting her to work my boxers down my legs and then lay back on the bed. I sure as hell wasn't expecting her to take hold of my cock, press her lips to the tip and suck it into her fucking mouth.

She looks up at me, eyes searching my face as she slowly slides her mouth down onto my dick. A string of curse words flies out of my mouth. I have no idea what I say, though. My brain has seized. All I can do is watch as Silver carefully takes me deeper into her mouth, deeper and deeper, until I can feel the head of my cock butting up against the back of her throat.

She bobs her head, slowly moving up and down my dick, and I can't—I have to stop her. Jerking my hips back, I pull out of her mouth, and my cock makes a wet popping as it springs free from her lips.

"Did I do something wrong?" she pants.

"No. But I wanna fuck your mouth so badly, Silver. I want to grab hold of your hair and shove myself all the way down your throat, and I'm trying to be a fucking gentleman."

She smirks, glowing a little, looking a little pleased with herself. "I take it that's why you were swearing in Italian?"

I laugh, noting with vague amusement that I sound a little shaky even to my own ears. "I didn't even realize I had."

"Sounded very aggressive. You're gonna have to teach me how to say some of those…"

"Anything. Fucking anything. I'll give you whatever you want if you lie on your back and let me see that perfect, pretty little pussy."

She tries to act cool, tries to pretend that she isn't blushing as she rolls over onto her back and spreads her legs, but I see the bright spots on her cheeks. They make her look so damn innocent.

I fall on her like the savage monster I am, grabbing her thighs and closing them around my head as I sink my tongue into her pussy. She pants and shakes against me, writhing, rocking her hips, screaming out a few curse words of her own by the time she comes.

It nearly fucking kills me to show some restraint, but I accomplish what I set out to do. Silver surrenders up two more orgasms before she literally begs me to fuck her. I make her come once more on my dick before I finally allow myself to ride out the wave of my own climax, holding her tight in my arms, shuddering against her, and she clings to me, sighing out my name like a promise.

For a long time, I bury my face into her neck, and I just breathe her in. She smells like summer, like gardenia, and violets, and bright spring mornings. Eventually, I stroke back her damp hair from her face, pulling her close to me and catching her up in the circle of my arms. "This the part where you make your excuses and leave?" I whisper against the crown of her head.

She laughs quietly, pressing a kiss against the ink on my chest in return. "No. This is the part where I realize you've stolen my fucking soul, and I have no chance of ever getting it back."

She borrowed my line, but I don't mind. If it's the truth, if I *have* managed to lay a claim on her like that, then she can borrow as many of my lines as she damn well wants. Fuck it, she can have them all. We fall asleep, wound up in each other, spent, exhausted and delirious on endorphins.

29

SILVER

"What the hell do you want me to do with that?"

The next morning, I look down at the helmet in Alex's hand like it's about to jump up and bite me. I woke up tangled in his arms, and for the first time in a string of seemingly endless, torturous days, I wasn't immediately crushed by the knowledge that I'd have to go to school alone and face Jacob and Kacey. I knew I'd have at least one ally roaming the halls of Raleigh High, and that, along with the surprisingly crisp, unexpected sunlight flooding in through the bedroom window of Alex's trailer, had me feeling surprisingly upbeat about the day ahead.

Now that same sunshine means I'm supposed to ride to school on the back of Alex's bike, though? He laughs mercilessly. "No getting out of it, *Argento*. It's a nice day. No ice on the road."

I wrinkle my nose, eyeing the bike. "I don't think so."

"What? You don't trust me?"

"Sure, I trust you. It's all the other people on the road I don't trust."

Alex takes the helmet and places it on my head before I can

stop him, pushing it down firmly. "Don't worry. I got you. I'll take care of you, I promise. Now get on the damn bike."

He throws his leg over the motorcycle, the blacked-out visor on his helmet hiding the highly entertained look on his face, and starts the bike, gunning it so I can feel the throb of the engine through the soles of my feet.

If my mother knew what I was about to do…urgh, who am I kidding? She probably wouldn't mind. Dad had a motorcycle in high school, and she rode around on the back of that thing for years. It'd be reassuring to think there was someone out there, willing me not to follow Alex's command, and that they'd be highly disappointed by my reckless actions, but I think even Grams would tell me to stop being such a pussy and get on.

I mimic Alex's easy leg swing, and though I'm sure I look a hell of a lot less graceful than he did, I manage to get on without falling flat on my face. I feel rather than hear Alex laugh when I wrap my arms around him as tight as possible. The guy's gonna end up with bruised ribs by the time we arrive at Raleigh, but it'll serve him right for insisting I do this. I bite back a shriek of surprise when he kicks back the stand and we surge forward. My fears are forgotten the moment he pulls out of the trailer park and hits the main road, though.

The wind pulls at my jacket, rushing through the open vents on the helmet, and a feeling of pure exhilaration sweeps over me. Alex leans into a corner as we hit the winding road that leads down into the valley toward Raleigh, and I let my body lean, too, resisting the urge to fight gravity…

…and it's fucking amazing.

We're flying, the bike rumbling between my legs, and I finally get it: this is what freedom feels like.

I release my death grip, throwing my hands up into the air, whooping as we reach a straight, flat stretch of road and Alex opens up the throttle. By the time we arrive at school gates fifteen minutes later, I'm enjoying myself so much that I want to tell him to just keep on driving.

The colors and sounds of the parking lot are heightened as I jump off the back of the bike, pleased that I somehow made it look as though I've performed the maneuver a thousand times before. The old Silver would have panicked when she pulled off the helmet, irritated that her hair had been ruined and was sticking up all over the place, but now I don't give a shit. I don't even attempt to tame it as I thump Alex in the arm, beaming from ear to ear.

"Oh, man, you are so screwed. You have to teach me how to ride one of these things."

When he takes off his helmet, the guard that Alex always wears around Raleigh is firmly in place, but I can see how pleased he is from the small smile that tics at the corner of his mouth. "Can't do that, I'm afraid," he tells me, his face perfectly serious. "I can't have a girlfriend who's cooler than me. Not my style."

"I've always been cooler than you, Moretti."

Alex reaches out, taking a piece of flyaway hair and tucking it behind my ear. His hand cups the side of my face, and I lean into his touch. I feel so damn light. Like I could lift up off the ground and just...float away. "I think you may be right," he says under his breath.

"What the fuck is this?"

The sour, angry note to the voice at my right brings me crashing back down to earth. It's Zen. And behind her, Kacey...

Both of them are wearing their cheerleading skirts, white socks pulled up to their knees, and matching expressions of disbelief. "Alex?" Zen says sharply. "I thought after the other night, you and *I* might be spending some time together." She sounds reproving, like she's telling him off. Alex looks to me, eyebrows raised, like I might be able to explain why the fuck she's speaking to him like that.

"Don't look at me," I say, laughing quietly. "This one's all you."

"Was I even speaking to you, *slut?*" Zen sneers.

In a heartbeat, Alex's back is straight, shoulders drawn back, anger flashing like liquid mercury in his eyes. "Watch your fucking mouth," he growls. "Call her that again, and we're gonna have issues."

Zen's mouth falls open. She looks stung. Hurt, even. "But…I'm sorry. I don't get it." She screws her eyes closed, shaking her head, curls bouncing. "Silver's *scum*, Alex. She's a fucking *nobody*. Everyone at this school knows she's poison. You can't seriously want *her* over me."

"I'd take just about anybody over *you*, but that's beside the point. Silver's fucking magnificent. She has more brain cells in her little finger than you spiteful, nasty little cunts have to squabble over between you. The fact that she'd even look at me twice makes me the luckiest bastard in the world. Now kindly fuck off. We're bored of looking at your average, ordinary faces."

Holy fucking *shit*. Alex can't know much about Kacey and the girls I used to call friends, but he couldn't have thrown a better insult if he'd tried. Average? *Ordinary?* Fuck me. Kacey's spent every waking moment of her life doing everything in her considerable power to make sure everyone around her sees just how extraordinary she is. She glowers at Alex over Zen's shoulder, her fury twisting her features into a mask of hatred.

"You really shouldn't have said that, Alessandro. You're a lowly piece of trash we decided to pick up off the side of the road out of the goodness of our hearts. Most guys at Raleigh would have ripped their own right arm out of the socket to be given a front row seat at that show we put on for you. *You* do not reject *us*."

"Funny. I seem to recall rejecting you over…and over…and over…"

Kacey grabs Zen by the arm, digging her fingernails into her skin. She looks like she's about to go nuclear. "You have no right to insult my friend."

Alex's expression is blank, untroubled, as he steps forward and leans down, shoving his face into Kacey's. His voice is frighteningly calm as he says, "The insult was for the both of you. That's a nice act though, playing the good little friend. I've heard all about how you really stand up for the people around you. I thought you were more of a *leave-'em-broken-and-bleeding-in-the-gutter-after-the-boy-you-like-raped-'em* kinda girl."

Oh no. *Oh no, no, no.* I don't want this. I won't be able to handle this if he says one more thing about...

"I mean, what kind of lowlife does *that?*" he snarls. "Who's jealous of a girl for being assaulted, for fuck's sake? There must be something seriously wrong in that coked-out brain of yours, Winters. I almost feel sorry for you. I can only imagine the therapy bill..."

"You're *dead*," Kacey snaps. "Fucking dead. Jacob's going to fucking murder you when he finds out what you just said to me."

Alex tuts under his breath. "You think I haven't dealt with worse than you and Jacob Weaving, little girl? You people may have money. Your parents might be stuck up assholes who think they're too good for the rest of this town, but do you honestly think you can beat me down with an empty threat? Jake isn't gonna do shit to me. He's going to end his campaign against Silver. He's going to give her a wide berth if he knows what's good for him. And while Silver's deciding if she wants to change her mind and have me permanently disfigure him for what he did to her, you psychos are going to avert your eyes any time either one of us walks by you in the hallway. *Do...you...hear...me?*"

Kacey blinks rapidly, shrinking back on herself. To be fair, she doesn't look away, but the set jaw and her defiant sneer aren't fooling anyone, least of all me. He's obviously scared her. It's a miracle that I'm even capable of such emotion, but...I feel sorry for her. Students have gathered around in fives and sixes, all watching the exchange, and no one has come to her aid. Some of my classmates are even laughing behind their hands, whispering to one another with smiles in their eyes.

This is what it's like, Kacey. This is what humiliation feels like. Stings, doesn't it?

Zen's the one who pulls Kacey away. She spits and curses, shoving me out of the way, dragging Kace behind her. Kacey yells back at us, though, ever the one to get the last word in.

"You wouldn't have dared to speak to me like in front of Jake. He'll hear about this! You're through! You're gonna be locked up before nightfall, motherfucker!"

∼

Jake hears about it all right. Sheriff Hainsworth shows up at Raleigh just before lunch, along with a tall guy in a tailored suit, who climbs out of a flashy Maserati and storms toward Principle Darhower's office wearing a face like thunder. Not long after that, I'm called to Darhower's office myself. In a sour mood, Karen barks at me, ordering me to sit down and wait outside to be called.

When the door to Darhower's office opens, Jake emerges first, looking like the smug piece of shit that he is, followed by Kacey. Her face is splotchy and red, her mascara smudged, and I know for a fact it was smeared with her fingertip in the girls' bathrooms before she went in to put on her performance. She flips me off as she sails past, pretending to sniffle into Jake's shoulder.

"Ms. Parisi. Inside, please," Darhower calls. Jake's father's still in with him, leaning against a bookcase filled with encyclopedias, looking like he owns the damn place. Sheriff Hainsworth's standing at the window with his back to the room. Alex is nowhere to be seen. "Sit," Principle Darhower orders. I do so, dread spiking in my veins. "Some very grave accusations have been made against yourself and another student, Silver. It's my duty to investigate the legitimacy of these accusations and act accordingly, based on their veracity. Is there anything you'd like to tell me about what happened this morning?"

"Really? This is actually, *really* happening?" I laugh, unable to stop myself in time.

"Young lady, you will take this seriously or lose the right to give your version of events at all," Mr. Weaving snaps.

"Actually...no. That's not...we can't do that, Caleb," Principle Darhower says wearily. "There are protocols in place for this type of thing. They have to be observed. Silver, just get on with it and tell us what happened. We all have things to be getting on with here."

"Okay. I arrived at school with Alex—"

"That's Alessandro Moretti, correct?" Sheriff Hainsworth asks stiffly. He doesn't turn around.

"Yes."

He grunts, and I feel like, in confirming Alex's name I've basically just signed some sort of confession of guilt. "Continue," Principle Darhower urges.

I give him a run-down of everything that happened, bar any mention that was made about my assault. With Jake's father in the room, seems like a prudent plan. It takes all of five seconds to recount the petty spat that took place in the parking lot. When I'm done, Principle Darhower bridges his hands in front of him, frowning deeply. "So, there were no threats of physical violence made by Alex? Toward Kacey?"

"I'm sorry? *What?*"

"Ms. Winters is claiming that Alex Moretti pulled a knife from his bag and brandished it in her face. She said he told her he was going to slit her throat from ear to ear if she didn't leave *you* alone."

What the hell did he just say? I heard the words, but he could *not* have just said that. "That is a flat-out *lie*, Principal Darhower. Alex did tell Kacey to leave me alone, but he didn't have a knife. He sure as hell didn't stick it in her face."

"Jim, Kacey's been dating Jake all summer. She was at my house, with my family every single day for weeks. I know that girl, and she's sweet, kind, and thoughtful. I'm telling you. She wouldn't lie about something like this."

I burst out laughing, even as Principle Darhower rolls his eyes at Caleb Weaving's preposterous statement. "Caleb, come on now. We all know that's not true. Kacey's been known to spin a yarn in the past if it's helped get out of hot water. She's no saint."

"What about everything else she said?" Caleb hisses. "That Alex Moretti punk threatened my son, too."

Principle Darhower ignores Mr. Weaving, but still—tiredly—gives him what he wants. "Kacey claims Alex threatened to hurt Jacob, Silver. She said he swore he and his biker friends were going to jump him and break every single one of his ribs."

Oh…my…god. This is getting more and more ridiculous by the minute. "Alex said nothing of the sort. This is all just…fuck, it's a complete fabrication!"

Darhower rocks back into his chair. Caleb Weaving stabs a finger in my direction. "See! Listen to the language on her. You're going to believe this little upstart over *my* son and his girlfriend?"

I have had enough of this bullshit to last me a lifetime. I narrow my eyes, digging my fingernails into my palms. "Why is *he* even here right now? Shouldn't *my* dad be present if I'm being accused of something?"

"I fund this entire school, young lady. I own this building down to its crumbling foundations! Don't you dare presume to—"

I ignore the bastard, looking Darhower square in the eye. "Alex did *not* have a knife. He did *not* threaten to hurt Jake, either. I mean, what would he possibly have to gain?"

Revenge.

Justice.

Satisfaction.

"Jake already told me this kid wants his spot on the team, Jim. He's already tried to hurt him during practice. Poor sportsmanship. Late hits. Whispering all kinds of foul nonsense in his ears. I don't like it. I want that boy *gone*."

"There was no knife on him when we searched him," Sheriff Hainsworth interjects. "And his story matches up with the girl's. Can I get the hell out of here now? This is not a police matter."

"You're not going anywhere," Mr. Weaving snarls. "This most definitely *is* a police matter. That little shit's broken the rules of his probation."

"By telling a prissy little rich girl that she's a prissy little rich girl?" He clucks his tongue disapprovingly as he shoves past Mr. Weaving, headed for the door. "Fortunately, callin' a spade a spade ain't illegal in the fine State of Washington just yet. If he sets something on fire or actually starts stabbing people, then you give me a call. In the meantime, I'm gonna release him and let him get back to class. I'm sure you two gents can handle an argument between two teenagers without me holding your hands."

I watch him go, horrified. "Release him? What did he mean, *release him?*"

Principle Darhower rubs at the lenses of his glasses, clearly very over this meeting. "Sheriff Hainsworth detained Alex in the back of his squad car. Just for a moment, while we talked in here."

"He *arrested* him?"

"Detained," Darhower repeats. "Now. Since no weapon was found on Moretti and it's just his and your word against Kacey and Zen's, I'm afraid measures must be taken if all of you are to remain at Raleigh. You and Kacey used to be thick as thieves, Silver. Obviously, something happened to cause a rift between the two of you. You're both going to have to attend joint counseling sessions with Ms. Landry, twice a week to iron out your differences. No, don't even bother, Silver. This is non-negotiable."

"And the deadbeat on the motorcycle?" Mr. Weaving demands. "You have to suspend him, preferably for the rest of the semester. He has to learn a lesson, Jim! His type needs a firm hand to rein them in and show them who's boss."

"No way! That's weeks' worth of work. If you do that, there's no way he'll be able to catch up. He'll have to re-sit the entire year!"

Darhower slams his open palm down on his desk. The loud burst of sound nearly makes me jump out of my skin. "Alessandro Moretti is *not* being suspended. His attendance has been good, and his grades, despite the motorcycle, have been exemplary. Jesus, why the hell is everyone so bent out of shape about the kid's goddamn mode of transportation."

"He *cannot* be allowed to play on the team," Mr. Weaving says, voice rising with his anger. "That, I simply will not allow. Jake's worked too hard and too long to have his dreams of playing for state crushed because of some orphaned, violent thug with an ax to grind. Do not test me on this, Jim. Believe me, I will make things very difficult—"

"When *don't* you make things difficult," Darhower mutters under his breath.

"*Excuse me?*"

"I said fine, Caleb. Have it your way. Alex is banned from playing on the team for the rest of the year until graduation. He can play basketball or something else instead for all I damn well care. Now that's an end to it. Silver, back to class. Caleb, honestly, it's been a pleasure as always."

∽

Alex's fumes like a smoking volcano as he burns across the lot, threatening to blow any second. Two identical red rings cuff his wrists, the skin broken and stained with dried blood. I have to jog to keep up with him, dodging around all of the other students pouring out of the building, heading toward their cars.

"He told me to '*take the rest of the day off*,'" he growls, fishing in his pockets for his keys. "Like I'd earned myself a little break or something. I swear, I want to fucking murder Jake Weaving right now, *Argento*. Him and his arrogant son of a bitch father."

"Alex. Alex, it's okay. You're not gonna lose the credit. It's still early enough to get you on another team, okay? Darhower said so himself. Hey. Hey, look at me." I have to step up onto the low brick wall next to the bike so I'm the same height as him; taking his face in my hands, I hold him in place until he has no choice but to stop prowling up and down like a lion with a sore head and has to stand still.

"I warned you hanging out with me would have consequences," I say softly. "You can take this all back, y'know. Me and you. If they fuck with you again and do something to ruin your chances of getting custody of Ben, I'll never forgive myself."

He meets my gaze with a fierce, unrelenting fire in his eyes. "You think I'll give you up because some dumb assholes wanna make life hard for us? No fucking way, Silver."

Guilt nips at me, biting at my conscience. "I'm sorry you had to deal with that. Fuck, I'm sorry you had to deal with *any* of that. Hainsworth definitely shouldn't have thrown you in cuffs over some stupid high school argument."

"He could have done worse," Alex says, tensing as he looks over my shoulder at something behind me. From the way his eyes are flashing, I'm willing to put money on it being Jake and Kasey burning out of the lot in her matte black G-Wagon. "Hainsworth's patience with me is generally stretched pretty thin," he says. "He could have thrown my ass in a cell, no questions asked. I'm sure Jake knew that. Things could have been much, *much* worse."

"My parents think I have cheerleading practice. You wanna go somewhere for a couple of hours? Cool down?"

The creases on Alex's forehead remain, but the agitation in his eyes dims a little. "Did you have somewhere specific in mind?"

"Yes, actually. I've seen where you live, Alex, but I still haven't seen where you work. I want you to take me to the Rock."

"Uhh...I don't know, *Argento*. The Rock isn't exactly an ideal spot for date night. It's... There's..." He's grasping at words, clearly trying to find a way to explain that his workplace is a den of iniquity worthy of biblical renown.

"I've lived here my whole life, Alex. I hear plenty of things. I know what the Rock is. I've always been curious about what goes on behind those heavy wooden doors, and now I have a handsome boyfriend who works there to sneak me in unnoticed. Come on, don't you think it'll be fun?"

Alex considers. He stares off into the dark forest that borders the Raleigh High parking lot. *He doesn't think it's a good idea. He's going to say no. He's—*

"All right. But just because it's the middle of the afternoon, doesn't mean anything at the Rock. It's a shit fight no matter what time of day it is. If you're ready for some incredibly loud music and lots of drunk people, and you're okay with the fact that you're gonna come face to face with a fuck load of strippers…then sure. I'll take you."

∼

The imposing, looming double doors of the Rock are infamous in Raleigh. You can see them, the burning torches mounted on either side of the thick, weathered wood, from up on the road that takes you out of town toward Iron Springs. Besides the Rock, there's nothing of note between Raleigh and the coast. If you're seen pulling off of that long, winding road through Grays Harbor County, it's pretty damn obvious where you're going, and there are plenty of people in a small town like Raleigh who'd love to judge you for it, should they just so happen to recognize your license plates.

There's no one around to see us peeling away from the road, though, as Alex steers the bike down a narrow, darkened driveway, the boughs of the trees forming a sinister looking tunnel over our heads, blocking out what's left of the weak afternoon sun. Loud, thumping, grinding music reaches my ears before the building's even in sight. And then, there it is, a single story, squat looking structure, constructed out of stone and rough-hewn rock, massive and quite possibly the ugliest building I've ever seen.

Alex navigates a path through the haphazardly parked vehicles in front of the bar, going around the side of the building, where he pulls into a narrow bay reserved for staff only. I feel so alive as I climb off the back of the bike, humming from the excitement of the ride. Alex takes the helmet from me, grinning. "I really have created a monster, haven't I?"

I nod, grinning back. "Looks that way. I've been thinking about using the money I was saving to fix up the Nova to buy my own deathtrap now."

"Uhh, the Nova's gonna need some TLC real soon by the sounds of that engine," Alex says, poking me in the side. "Maybe you should make do with borrowing my bike instead."

"*You'd let me borrow your bike?*" The fake-surprised teasing in my voice makes him smile.

"You're already holding my damn heart *and* my soul hostage, *Argento*. You might as well take everything else."

These things slip out of his mouth so effortlessly, like they're so easy to confess. Most guys his age would rather bite off their own tongues than admit they felt any emotional tie to a girl. Alex, of all people, who is so stony and withdrawn from the world most of the time, has no problem admitting whatever he's feeling to me, though. There's a surprise around every corner with Alex. I still have to pinch myself whenever he looks down at me, and I see the longing his eyes, like I'm something of value, to be treasured, to be adored.

"My dad told me this place was commissioned by one of the scientists who worked on the U.S. nuclear program during the Second World War. He was paranoid, so he had this place built. It was designed to survive the fall out if Seattle were ever hit by a nuke dropped by the Nazis. Does it really have an underground bunker?"

He tells you that you own his heart and soul, and you start talking about the fucking Nazis. *Way to go, Silver.*

"Yeah," he replies, chuckling under his breath. "But trust me. You don't want to go down there."

"Why? Are you nervous, bringing me here?"

He takes me by the hand. Laughing, he leads me toward an emergency exit at the rear of the building that's been propped open with half a brick. "You don't want to go down there because it's a sex club, *Argento*. And no. Why would I be nervous?"

Sex club? Lord. I do my best to hide my surprise at *that* revelation. "Because this is where I find out how many strippers you've fucked?" I'm only half serious, half joking, but it has occurred to me—Alex might only be seventeen, but he easily looks twenty-one. Not to mention the fact that he's hot as hell. There's no way he hasn't been involved with the women who dance here.

"I haven't fucked any of the strippers, Silver," he says ruefully. "Most of the girls who dance are also available for *extra* services. Private services. And I don't sleep with girls who fuck for a living. I respect their choices, it's their decision to make, but I also respect my dick. I don't want it to fall off."

"They're running a *brothel?*"

Alex shakes his head, no. "The girls might meet or find a client here, but they cater to them at home. Or in a hotel room. Whatever. The owner, Monty, will fire any girl on the spot if he finds out she's been screwing the customers on his property."

"Right. So, we're not going to stumble across anyone fucking in a hallway then." Cue nervous laughter.

Alex winks, ushering me inside, through the emergency exit. "Don't worry, *Argento*. As long as we stay above ground, I promise you there will be no fucking."

30
ALEX

This place is and always has been a dirty little secret. It's been renamed a thousand and one times in a thousand and one ways. The bank; the grocery store; the post office. When a guy's wife asks him where he's been, he'll say he was at the game. When a woman has to explain to her husband why she smells of stale booze and cigarette smoke, she'll tell him she was pulling an extra shift on the casino floor. Very few people tell the truth and admit to spending time at the Rock, though. It's tantamount to saying: *I cheated on you; I fell off the wagon; I stole the housekeeping money; I broke a promise I swore I would never break.*

When the door swings open and someone new arrives at the Rock, the customers already at the bar or snuggled into the booths all hold their collective breath, heads turning in unison, squinting into the dark to see if (horror of horrors) it's someone they might know.

We walk through the winding hallways, past Monty's empty office, and through the 'Staff Only' door into the bar. Fifty pairs of eyes turn on us as the patrons take a beat to assess the newcomers. It only takes a half a second for the regulars to recognize my face.

In the far corner on the stage, a Led Zeppelin cover band is murdering *"A Whole Lotta Love.'* On the narrow catwalks that protrude out onto the bar floor, two of Monty's favorite girls are already down to their bikini tops and G-strings.

I'm so used to this place that nothing about it surprises me. What the hell is Silver making of all of this, though? I try to see the place through her eyes, to imagine what she's thinking right now, but it's impossible. I'm jaded and rotten down to my core, and Silver is a fucking innocent. She's *good*. We're too dissimilar for me to piece together what might be going through her head as Jasmine, the stripper closest to us sinks slowly to her knees, arching her back, eyes heavy-lidded, glossed lips parted, and she slides her hands beneath her bikini top, cupping her own breasts. When one of the loggers sitting at the edge of the catwalk drops three dollar bills in front of her, she teases the material of her bikini top aside, exposing her tits, squeezing them in her hands, her pierced nipples on display, and Silver tenses beside me.

"Moretti! What the fuck, dude!"

Ah, shit. I scan over the top of the crowd, searching for Paul, the owner of the loud, obnoxious voice that just called out across the bar. Takes me a second to find him behind the altar on the other side of the room. Taking Silver by the hand I steer her toward him, doing my best to keep my face as emotionless as possible.

When we reach the bar, Paul—one of Monty's nephews, the tallest, skinniest guy I've ever come across—glares at me, anger simmering in his eyes. "You fucking kidding me right now?" he hisses. "You know you can't be here unless you're on shift. No underage drinking at the Rock."

"Fuck you, Paul. I'll come here whenever I want. And you'll shut your goddamn stupid, ugly, dumb, moronic..." I can't keep it up any longer. He's already started to smile, his eyes crinkling at the corners, and once he starts, I can never keep my shit together. I laugh, dropping the act as he leans across the bar, holding his fist out for me to bump.

"What's up, man?" Paul arches his eyebrow, jerking his head none-too-subtly toward Silver. I know it's absolutely killing him not to openly point at her and demand to know who she is. Paul's barely three years older than me, attempting to graduate college this year if he can get his grades up, but he acts like he's still in high school.

"Paul, this is Silver. Silver this is Paul. No, no, I wouldn't do that." I grab hold of her arm before she can shake the hand he's offering to her. "You don't know where he's been."

Paul lowers his hand, throwing a bar rag over his shoulder. "Asshole. I'm cleaner than you."

"Doubtful. Paul lives here above the bar, which means he probably pops anti-virals like most people pop daily vitamins. Monty's not in?"

Paul pulls a face at me in return for the jab. "He went out on a run. Be back in a couple of hours. You need him?"

"No. Just saw he wasn't in his office."

"You want a drink then, or are you pretending you're a good boy in front of your beautiful friend?"

"Hah hah, dickhead. No, I think we're go—"

"Tequila," Silver says, leaning her elbows against the bar. "Shots. Two, please. And Alex doesn't have to pretend to be anything around me. I know who he is."

My dick is immediately hard, throbbing against the inside of my thigh, partly because of the way her ass is sticking out, looking perfectly fucking biteable in her tight black jeans, but also because of the sassy confidence she's emitting as she watches Paul place the shot glasses down on the bar.

"On me," Paul says. "I knew I was saving my promo tab for a good reason. See me if you want another round. Colleen's fucking PMS-ing. She tried to choke out the new bouncer 'cause she caught him looking at her ass. She'd probably charge you double for your drinks right now sooner than comp them. Oh, and...no offense," he says, grimacing at Silver. "About the PMS thing. I'm a total feminist. But seriously, it's a real *thing* here. The girls all sync up. It's like fucking Armageddon one week out of the month."

"Throw down the shovel, man. Walk away. You're not doing yourself any favors," I laugh, picking up one of the tequila shots. Silver hardly seems bothered by Paul's comment. The savage little smirk on her face says she's enjoying watching him squirm, though. Paul slides us two wedges of lime on a cocktail dish and then heads off to serve someone else, flipping the bird at me over his shoulder as he goes.

"He seems nice," Silver offers. She's holding her shot, the back of her hand already salted.

"Didn't realize you were such a hardened drinker, *Argento*. You look like a semi-pro right now."

"Yeah, well, you forget. I was friends with Kacey for a long time before I was cut from their little squad. And Kacey Winters will drive anyone to drink, friend or otherwise. Come on. Down in one." She licks the back of her hand, and I can't fucking help myself. I grab her by the back of her head, hand fisting in her hair, and I kiss her. Her lips are so damn soft. She sighs into my mouth, breath sweet and warm, and I have to convince myself it'd be a bad idea to tear her clothes off and fuck her up against the bar right here and now.

Using the flat of my tongue, I stroke it against her own, stealing the salt she just licked from her hand, and my mouth aches with the taste of the sea, of a childhood spent running up and down Black Sand Beach with an icy wind pulling at my clothes. She moans, a quiet, tense pant of pleasure, and my hands almost get to work on the button of her jeans.

Silver opens her eyes and looks up at me, pupils dilated, her cheeks flushed, and I realize a little too late maybe that my thumb is rubbing along the addicting curve of the underside of her breast.

"Alcohol," she whispers, dazed. "Shit, let's do the shot before I embarrass the crap out of myself and climb you like a tree, Alex."

I can't tear my eyes away from her. I keep her in my sights as I throw back the tequila, the burn lighting me up from the inside as the booze floods my chest. I'm fucking fascinated by the way the shot glass presses against her bottom lip. The way the muscles in the graceful column of her throat work as she swallows. The tiny wrinkles that form on the bridge of her nose as she shakes her head, wiggling her fingers as the tequila hits her.

Oh, holy fuck. You stupid son of a bitch, Alex.

How can I not have realized until now? Feeling more than little slow on the uptake, it occurs to me that at some point, I became so enthralled with Silver Parisi that there isn't a part of her I'm not completely and utterly in love with.

She wipes her mouth with the back of her hand, cringing when she notices me staring at her. "What? Did I spill it all down my face?" she asks. "You didn't do the lime."

"I don't need the lime."

"Of course you do. It's the rule. You do the shot, and then you—"

"Silver?"

"—do the lime. We have to get ano—"

"*Silver.*"

She finally stops talking. Looks up at me, eyes a little bright from the tequila. "Yeah?"

I lean into her, brushing her hair back behind her ear. Only she can hear me when I whisper into the shell of her ear. "I'm in love with you. Did *you* know that?"

She stiffens, her breath catching in her throat. When she looks at me out of the corner of her eye, her smile is gone, and she... fuck, why does she look afraid?

"Yes." Her voice cracks on the word. "I did."

"Why didn't you tell me?" I stroke the back of my index finger over the smooth, porcelain of her cheek. Fuck, she's so fucking beautiful, it makes me want to scream. To trash the entire bar and set the whole place ablaze. I can't fucking take how perfect she is.

"It's not my place to tell you your feelings, Alex." She's putting on a brave face on it, laughing lightly, trying to be glib, but her hand, still holding her shot glass, is shaking. I take hold of it, closing my own around it, steadying her.

"I know plenty about lust. There's very little anyone could tell me about want. There hasn't been a day in my life when I haven't *needed* something or someone. But love? Shit, I hardly know anything about love, Silver. I'm out of practice. You're gonna need to help me out *a lot* with this one."

"Who's to say I know any more about it than you do," she asks. The bar's loud as hell, the band striking up another song, laughter and chatter all around us, but I hear her as clearly as if we're standing in a silent room, quiet enough to hear a pin drop. "Who's to say I'm not going to need just as much help?"

My chest feels like it's splitting open. My heart's a fucking ruin. "Why? What does that mean, *Argento?*"

"It means...god, Alex. Don't you know that I love you, too? That I have no idea what the hell I'm doing either?" Her playful smile has disappeared. Her eyes are shining even worse than before, only now the burn from the tequila is gone, and it looks as though she's about to burst into tears.

I cradle the side of her face, cupping her cheek in my hand, brushing my thumb against the line of her cheekbone. "Fuck," I whisper. "Is it too much? Loving me? If the answer's yes, then I'll take you home right now. I'll change schools. I'll go, and you'll never have to see me again. I don't ever, *ever* wanna cause you pain."

She catches hold of me by the wrist, turning toward me, a look of panic on her face. "No. Alex, *no*. Don't you dare let me go. Loving you is the only thing that makes any sense right now. It's everything else around us that's fucked up beyond belief."

I'm suddenly aware of someone standing next to us, on the

other side of the bar. Paul's returned and he's got a fresh bottle of tequila in his hand. The roar of the bar comes crashing back down around us, people pressing in on all sides. "Looked like the one shot wasn't gonna cut it," Paul says, smirking. "Thought you guys might appreciate some bottle service." He gestures for our glasses. I give him mine, and Silver slides hers robotically toward him over the sticky countertop. Neither of us speaks as he tops us up and winks. "I know we just met," he says, addressing Silver, "but I will tell you this. This guy has never brought a girl here. And I have never seen him look at anyone the way I just saw him looking at you. I had to run to the bathroom and throw up before I could bring this over. It was positively disgusting. That said, if he's done something to upset you, I already like you enough to take him out back and tan his tattooed hide for you. Just say the word, and it's as good as done."

"Fuck you, asshole. You're dreaming if you think you could," I say, scowling at him halfheartedly.

Silver just smiles shyly. "It's okay. He hasn't done anything wrong. In fact, he did the opposite. He just made me really, really happy."

~

SILVER

We drink, we dance, we talk, and then we dance some more. Once we're sick of the noise in the bar, Alex takes me to a flat, dry spot on the hill behind the Rock, and we lie there for a couple of hours, freezing, looking up at the stars, talking about Ben and Max. The fresh air works wonders, and by the time the Uber pulls up in front of the house to drop me off, I'm stone cold sober. The windows are all in darkness, apart from one: Dad's office window. He told me to be home by midnight, so it was safe to assume he was going to wait up for me and make sure I abided by his curfew.

A wishful part of me had been hoping he might have just said fuck it and gone to bed, though. I see the blinds twitch and curse between my teeth.

I get out of the ride and let myself into the house, bracing for the litany of questions that will be coming any second now. In three…two…one…

"Silver?" he calls from his office.

Damn. No sneaking up the stairs unnoticed then. I close my eyes, take a deep breath, then walk down the hall and stand in the doorway. "Hey, Dad."

He takes his glasses off and sets them on his desk. "Three minutes past twelve, kiddo."

"Are you gonna cane the back of my hands?" I say, grinning at him.

"For three minutes? I should think only a light beating's in order. How was your night?"

I sigh, hiking my backpack up on my shoulder. "Ahh, y'know. Drunken debauchery. Half a bottle of tequila. Running around naked, howling at the moon. The usual." It's a low blow, using the truth to throw him off guard. I don't' feel good about it, but it's better than an outright lie.

"And the car?"

"Hmm?"

"You rolled up in an Uber. The Nova crap out on you?"

"Yeah…it's been acting up for days. I left it at Alex's. He says he's gonna take a look at it for me in the morning."

"Well, I guess having a boyfriend who knows his way around an engine has its perks. Tell him to come over for dinner tomorrow night. Your Mom and I want to get to him know him a little better."

"Dad—"

"How about you drag the guy over here tomorrow night without a fuss, and I won't make a stink about the fact that I can smell all that booze on you from fifteen feet away, hmm?"

I chew the inside of my cheek, knowing defeat when I see it. "Well played, sir. Well played."

He turns back to his computer, sliding his glasses back on. "Don't wake your brother up on your way to bed," he says in a sing-song voice. "Otherwise I'll be forced to rethink my very forgiving mood."

I laugh softly under my breath. "Night, Dad."

31
SILVER

I wake up to a throbbing, thumping drum beat, pounding somewhere right behind my head. I'm gonna fucking kill my brother. Since when did he start listening to house music? And what the fuck time is it? The kid needs to learn some goddamn manners. Cracking my eyes open, I find my watch on the nightstand and peer blearily at Micky, blinking rapidly when I see that it's nearly seven fifteen.

"Fuck! *Fuck fuck fuck.*" I am so screwed. Like, definitely-going-to-be-late-for-first-period-if-I-don't-fucking-move! screwed. My bedroom pitches as I sit bolt upright, and the thumping gets even louder, pulsing through my extremities and rattling against the inside of my skull. I realize, misery sinking in, that there is no music, and the pounding is actually my own heartbeat, hammering at my temples.

Just…fucking…awesome.

I haven't had a hangover in a long time. The effects of all the tequila I drank yesterday might have worn off by the time I sank into bed last night, but was I smart enough to chug a liter of water before I fell asleep? Nope. I was not. I'm so dehydrated, my tongue feels like sandpaper as I peel it from the roof of my mouth.

"I'm coming in, Sil," my mother calls from the other side of my bedroom door.

"No! Mom, I'm not dre—"

She enters before I can complete the protest. She's fully dressed, way smarter than usual in a full suit and salmon pink silk shirt. Her hair's tied back into an intricate braid, and her makeup is on point. Generally, at this time of morning, she's still rushing around in her pajamas, trying to locate her keys, or a report, or one of her shoes.

She's holding a tumbler in her hand with what looks like a raw egg inside it. She crosses my room, shoving the glass in my face, and says, "Down the hatch."

"Thanks. I'm good."

"Don't be a baby. Just pinch your nose and swallow it in one. It'll make you feel better."

"Or make me hurl," I counter.

"Either way, you'll feel better."

I take the glass, hoping she'll leave, but she doesn't. "Fine. Have it your way." I nearly wretch when I force the raw egg down the back of my throat, gagging on the texture. She takes the glass from me, folding her arms across her chest.

"You're only gonna get so many hall passes, y'know. Don't think I've forgotten about the guy in the boxer shorts at the cabin."

"You mean the guy who carried you inside, covered in mud and soaked from the rain, because you were having a nervous breakdown? I haven't forgotten about him either. Dad wants him to come for dinner tonight."

Mom's expression falters. She came in here with the tough parent act, ready to try and reassert her position of power over me, but now she's back to Worried Mom Keeping Secrets again. "That might not be a good idea," she mutters.

"Tell me about it. Don't worry. He won't mention the fact that the two of you have met before."

"Silver, this can't go on. There has to be some sort of—"

I don't want to hear it. Not from her. Not this morning. I hold a hand up, cutting her off. "Why are you dressed like that?"

"I have an interview at nine. I didn't think it'd be appropriate to keep working at the firm after…"

You had an affair and slept with your boss? I glower at her, daring her to try and play it down. She clears her throat uncomfortably.

"Anyway, I gave my notice yesterday. I applied for an auditing position at the mayor's office. If I get the position, it'll be a big step up. Better all 'round. More money. More time off." She smiles hopefully, rolling the empty glass between her hands—I think she's waiting for me to say something positive.

"Well congrats, Mom. Failing upwards. Great job. I suppose I should be grateful Mayor Reid's a woman, right? At least I won't have to worry about you fucking *her*."

The sound of the slap registers in my ears before I feel the sting of it against my cheek. Mom's face is a picture of rage. Her expression quickly transforms into one of shock, though. She covers her mouth, taking a step away from my bed. "I'm sorry, Silver. Shit, I shouldn't have done that."

"No. *You shouldn't.*"

"Let me grab some ice—"

"Why, so you can avoid having to explain the huge red welt on my face to Dad? Don't bother. I'm gonna be late for school." I storm into my bathroom, sliding the lock closed behind me, quickly turning the shower on. Mom calls my name through the door, but I don't answer her. Standing in front of the bathroom mirror, I clasp my hand to my cheek, letting out a shuddering breath. There's no stopping the tears. I sob silently, staring at myself in the mirror, my heart breaking in two as I try and figure out who I hate more this morning: My mom, for hitting me, or myself, for being such a spoiled little bitch.

∼

"Thanks for dropping the car off again. And picking me up. And for listening to me rant," I groan. Alex isn't even slightly hungover—a fact that I'm incredibly jealous of, since I still feel like I'm going to throw my guts up any moment.

We're already at my locker, having made it successfully into school and through A.P. physics without encountering Kacey, Jake, or any of their minions. The bell's about to ring for second period any moment. "You're welcome," Alex says, leaning against the locker next to mine as I rummage around for my English textbook. "And I'm happy to listen to you rant. Families are tough. Moms are tough."

"You think I should go easier on her, don't you?"

He thinks about this. "No. She betrayed you and Max too, when she cheated on your dad. She probably deserves a rough week or two. But *you* think you should go easier on her, don't you?"

How? How the hell can he read my mind like that? I shove my textbook into my bag, sighing heavily as I slam my locker door closed. "I really hurt her this morning. I saw it on her face. And I *wanted* to hurt her so fucking bad, but…"

"But she's your mom, and you love her," Alex finishes. "It's okay to forgive her, y'know. The world won't stop turning."

"But it's not up to me to forgive her. That's Dad's job. But he can't, he's never even gonna get that opportunity, because I told Mom to keep her mouth shut. And now the air inside the house feels so fucking toxic, I can't even breathe in there, and it just seems like everything going to *explode.*"

CRACK!

On my last word, a loud, sharp explosion sounds at the other end of the hall, and my heart fucking stops.

I frown at Alex. "What the fuck?"

I know what that loud bang sounded like, but there's no way…

Not here. Not at Raleigh.

A chorus of screams go up outside the entrance to the cafeteria.

Alex grabs hold of me by the top of my arm. His eyes are huge in his face. He's craning over the top of the students crowding in the hall, trying to see what's happening. That's when the second loud crack rips through the air...and all hell breaks loose.

"Shooter," Alex hisses between bared teeth. "There's a fucking shooter."

Shooter?

"Fuck. Come on." He yanks me by the arm, pulling me along the line of lockers, heading toward the exit. My legs follow along automatically, but my body's twisted. I'm trying to face the other way, trying to get a clear image of what's going on behind us. What the hell is he talking about? Alex said *shooter*, but the word makes no sense. Even the panic on my classmate's faces doesn't make any sense, as they begin shoving down the hallway, shouting, dropping books and bags in their attempts to flee for the double doors that lead out toward the parking lot.

"Alex?"

God, I'm...my head is spinning. The edges of my vision are blurring, smudging the posters on the walls and the faces of the other students together in a streak of too-bright color.

Alex doesn't look back. His fingers are gouging into my arm, his nails digging into my skin—the bone feels like it's going to shatter as he urges me along with him, but I don't want him to let go. I need to stay with him. *Please don't leave me, please don't leave me. God, don't fucking leave me...*

CRACK! CRACK!

Two shots, this time. The press of bodies heading for the door becomes suffocating as everyone rushes forward, trampling on those who have fallen, the smell of fear and acerbic gun powder thick in the air.

"They're locked. The doors are locked!" The shout goes up at the front of the crowd. A kid I recognize from the chess team,

Gareth Foster, is frantically pulling on the doors, trying to force them open, but they aren't even budging.

Alex stops dead, his mission for the doors abandoned. Turning to me, his eyes flash cold as he takes hold of me by the chin and speaks in a calm, even tone. "The music rooms, Silver. What's the quickest route to the music rooms?"

"The...music rooms?"

"Concentrate, *Argento*. Think. How can we get there without having to push through all this?"

"Oh my god! Korra! Korra's been shot!" Terrified wails go up in the hallway, deafening, and tear-streaked kids blunder, fumbling to get the classroom doors open.

I watch, stunned, as Laughlin Moss, one of Raleigh's best linebackers, slams a girl out of the way, knocking her to the floor, as he bulldozes his way into Mr. Biltmore's history classroom.

"Silver. *Silver!*" Alex's hands are on my shoulders. He shakes me roughly. "Silver, I know this is really fucked up, but I need you to listen to me right now. How do we get to the music rooms from here? Is there a way, other than the main corridor?"

"Uh...yeah. Uh, the back stairs. Through the science block. You can go through that way."

"All right. Good girl." He presses a hard kiss against my forehead, hugging me to him fiercely. "Go. Go up to the music rooms and lock yourself in the sound booth, you hear me? You'll be safe there until the police get here."

Fear closes around my heart, squeezing too tight. "What? Alex, no. I'm not leaving you. I'm staying with you."

"I need to try and find the guy with the gun."

The school's P.A. system buzzes, a high-pitched tone shrieking from the speakers.

"ATTENTION. SCHOOL LOCKDOWN IN FULL AFFECT. ALL FACULTY MEMBERS, CODE ORANGE. I REPEAT, CODE ORANGE. ALL STUDENTS, REMAIN IN

CLASSROOMS AND BAR ALL DOORS. DO NOT COME OUT UNTIL AUTHORIZED BY POLICE OR SCHOOL OFFICIALS."

Oh my god. This is happening. This is really fucking happening.

Alex braces my head in his hands, forcing me to look up at him. "Okay, okay. Stay calm. It's okay. Shhh, I'm coming with you. I'll come with you. Go. Let's go."

The hallway's half-emptied already. At the far end of the hall, I see a body laid out on the ground, pens scattered everywhere, and the white floor is stained with stark, bright red streaks of blood.

Alex takes me by the hand again. He drags me behind him, heading for the stairway up toward the science block. Which means we're actually heading toward the body…

"Alex, no. No, no, not that way." I try to pull my hand free, but his grip tightens.

"Keep down. I'm not gonna let anyone hurt you. Stay close. Hurry, hurry, hurry."

I duck down, sticking close to his heels, following his instructions. I've thought about what I'd do in situations like this. We've prepped. Drilled. Practiced.

I thought I'd be calm.

I thought I'd be clear-headed.

I thought I'd be okay.

I thought wrong.

CRACK!

Alex shoves me to the ground. I can feel him over me, his body on top of mine, his chest up against my back. His ragged breathing is so loud in my ear.

"*Sarah! Oh my god. Sarah. Sarah, no, no, no!*" The petrified shrieking cuts me down to the bone. I know the voice… "*Oh, shit. Shit, please! Don't fucking…just…*"

CRACK!

"We need to move," Alex pants. "I need you to run, Silver. I need you to run toward that stairwell, up, up, up and through the science block. Do not stop. Do not look back. I'll be right behind you. Can you do that for me?"

"I don't know!"

"You can, Silver. I know you can. You're brave, and you're fucking fast. Come on. We have to get out of here, right now."

I scrunch my eyes closed, trying to grab hold on the terror lashing around in the pit of my stomach. It takes every scrap of willpower I possess, but I manage to calm myself. "Okay."

"Okay?"

I nod beneath him.

"All right. One…two…THREE!" Alex has me by the back of my shirt. He lifts me up off the floor and onto my feet, and then his palm is against my back, shoving me forward so quickly I can barely get my legs to move fast enough. I hurtle toward the stairwell, jumping over two girls who are hunkered down, covering their heads with their backpacks.

"Up! Let's go, let's go!" Alex hisses. His hand is gone from my back. He told me not to stop. He told me not to hesitate, but I do…

Then he's right behind me, the girls, Alicia and Sophia, being herded along by his side, their faces stained with eyeliner.

"RUN!" Alex's roar echoes down the hallway. A strangled scream comes right after, cut off by the loud, terrible report of another gunshot.

My lungs are burning. My legs are burning. I take the stairs three at a time, tripping, struggling to stay on my feet. There are footsteps behind me, screaming and shouting—

I take a turn in the stairwell, surging up the second flight of stairs.

"He's coming. He's fucking coming!" Alicia yells.

"Faster, Silver. Go faster!" Alex hollers.

There's a skidding, a thud, but I keep going forward, keep

trying to pull air into my lungs. The door to the first science lab crashes against the wall as I hurl myself through it. The lab is empty. Deserted. I run for the interconnecting door, flying through that, into the next lab and then through the next again.

My backpack snags on something. I rip it from my shoulders, dropping it, still running...

Out of the last science lab, I nearly fall down the stairs that lead toward the music rooms. Oh god, where's Max? Where the fuck is my brother? Through the chaos whipping through my head, for a second I don't even have the sense to realize that Max is at his school. He's not here. He's not here...

Everything is noise, and color, and panic.

Blood on my tongue.

My pulse racing in my ears.

I'm going to fucking throw up...

"Left! Left, Silver! Through the door!" Alex shoulders the music room door open, grabbing me and yanking me after him. Alicia and Sophia cling to each other as we race for the sound booth. A second later, Alex has *that* door open, and he's pushing us all inside.

His fingers dig painfully into my shoulders again. His face is ashen. "Close it after yourself. Lock the door. Do not open it for anyone, you hear me? I don't care who it is. You lock that fucking door, and *you do not open it.*"

"ALEX, NO!"

It's too late. He's ripped himself free, and he's elbowed me inside. The door slams closed, the sound ringing in my ears like yet another gunshot. "Lock it, Silver! Do it! Right fucking now!"

I don't want to. I want him inside the booth, next to me, holding me in his arms, but I'm too numb. I do what he told me to. I lock the door.

"Good girl. Good girl," Alex pants. "Stay inside. Stay safe. I'll be back."

32
ALEX

Raleigh's an old school. Its systems are outdated. There should be automatic locks on all of the classroom doors, preventing them from opening before the code has been cleared and the all-safe has been announced, but they don't. There are no fucking safety measures in place, which means the place is wide fucking open right now.

I stave off the immediate urge to go back, grab Silver, smash a window and get the fuck out of here. I saw the guy with the gun in the main hallway, though. When I covered Silver with my body, shielding her from the horror of what was happening ten feet away, I saw the guy, standing there with a bleak look on his face and the array of weapons he had strapped to his body. He wasn't planning on emptying one clip and then calling it a day. No, he came to school this morning planning on taking down as many people as possible, and he came armed to do so. There would have been no sneaking into a classroom and bolting out of one of the windows. He would have killed us first.

A rattle of gunshots in the main hall confirms this; the shots come from a semi-automatic. A cold wash of dread settles over my limbs as I creep down the stairs from the music rooms, heading back toward the hallway. I nearly have a fucking heart attack when someone bursts around the crashes right into me.

It's Karen, Darhower's assistant. Her shoes are gone, stockings ripped, her knees all scraped and bleeding. Wildly, she grabs hold of me, sobbing silently.

"All the exits are locked," she whispers. "Chained on the outside. There's no way out. He said he was going to kill me, but I ran…"

"It's okay. He won't. He's not going to kill you. Where is he?"

"I don't—" She jumps, spinning around, as if she thinks the shooter might suddenly be right behind her. "I don't know. I think…I think he went toward the library."

Great. The library only has one entrance. If he has gone there, then everyone inside is fucked. He'll be able to stalk from one stack to the next, putting down whoever the hell he comes across until everyone's fucking dead. "Stay out of sight," I tell Karen. "Find a room with a lock. A closet. Anything. Just stay hidden until someone comes and finds you."

I leave her behind before she can beg me to stay with her. My heart's fucking galloping as I sneak out into the hallway. Packed only minutes ago, the place is now deserted…apart from the six bodies lying dead on the floor.

One of the kids looks like a freshman. Half her fucking face is missing. Her cell phone's still clutched in her lifeless hand, lit up, a call coming in. The name *'Mom'* repeatedly flashes on the screen.

Jesus fucking Christ.

There are faces at the classroom doors, timid, scared shitless, as I hurry down the hall. The entrance to the library's fifteen feet away, up another flight of stairs. Another round of shots rings out, coming from that direction, confirming Karen's suspicions.

Fuck, this is so fucking stupid.

Fly away, Passerotto? *Find cover. Find someplace safe. Don't be a hero, baby.*

My mother's voice whispers into my ear as I begin to climb the stairs. I grind my teeth together, tensing, wishing I could fucking heed her words, but I can't. I just can't. If I do, more people are going to die.

At the doors to the library, I see it: a gun, discarded on the floor. Stooping, I pick it up, checking the clip as a fresh hail of gunfire erupts from inside.

"God, what the hell are you doing, man! Fuck! Stop! I'm gonna fucking kill y—"

CRACK!

The fearful, strained voice is cut off, dead.

The gun's clip is empty. Goddamnit, this is so fucking stupid. What use is an empty gun? I'm gonna end up shot myself at this rate. But Silver… she's upstairs, trapped inside that sound booth. There's no way in hell I'm letting someone roam the halls of Raleigh, picking off people until he finds her. I will die trying to bring him down first. I'll fucking kill him before he can get to her.

Passerotto, *go. Find the police. Be smart. Be safe.*

I pretend I'm not shitting myself as I toe the library door open. I pretend I'm not picturing own my own death as I step inside.

Almost immediately, I nearly trip over yet another corpse. It's Cillian Dupris, one of the motherfuckers who hurt Silver. His eyes are blank, mouth yawning open, surprise on his face as he gapes up at me.

Gingerly, I step over him, crouching down, hurrying toward the librarian's desk, taking cover behind it. Blood, so dark it's almost black, pools on the floor there. I risk a quick glance around the side of the desk and find Mrs. Peters lying on her stomach, arm stretched out in front of her, a frightening amount of blood oozing out from her chest. The left lens of her glasses is shattered, her dark eyes staring off into spa—

She blinks, and I fall back on my ass, nearly colliding with an overstocked book cart. "*Fuck!*"

Her hand opens and closes, reaching for me, and I hold my

index finger to my mouth, miming for her to stay silent. Her eyes close anyway, a wet rattle coming out of her mouth, and she falls still.

"You don't have to do this," a female voice whispers, close, maybe only two or three stacks away. "I'm sorry! I really am. I didn't...I didn't even think you cared."

A male voice responds, hard and cold. "Didn't think I *cared*? That's the problem with you, isn't it? You never fucking think. You just do whatever the hell you like, and fuck how your actions might affect anyone else. You're so fucking self-centered."

"Come on. Just listen, okay. Okay. Yeah. We can go back to how things were. Nothing has to change. It'll be the same as last year. We'll go on that trip—"

"SHUT UP! Just shut the fuck up, you stupid bitch! You think I'd take you back after what you did?"

I can barely differentiate between heartbeats as I hurry out from behind the desk, skirting around Mrs. Peters, in the direction of the voices. It takes everything in me not to charge around the stack and launch myself, fists flying, but I need to see. To assess the situation. I could end up ruining my only chance at surprise if I fuck this up. I straighten, holding the empty gun in my hand, and I peer around the tall stack, holding my breath.

Kacey Winters is in a heap on the floor, her back pressed up against the wall, her face red, trembling so hard her shoulders are visibly shaking. Around her, a puddle of yellow liquid is spreading, soaking through her cheerleading skirt. She sees me, her eyes going wide...

...and then the guy with the semi-automatic hunting rifle pointed at her head curses, spinning around to face me.

I react, throwing up the gun *I'm* holding, even though it's empty. "Steady. Steady, Leon. Just take a breath, man. We do *not* have to fucking do this."

33

SILVER

"He's not coming back. He's the only one who knows we're in here, and he's not coming back. We're all going to fucking die."

Sophia hasn't stopped freaking out. Neither have I, but she's too loud in her panic, and she won't shut the hell up. The sound booth is small—nothing more than a cubicle, really. The three of us are all trying to pace at once, frantically trying to get our cell phones to work, but none of our devices can get a signal. The entire network seems to be down.

"He will come back," I say tightly. "Alex won't just leave us here. He'll come back for us when it's safe."

"He's probably already dead. You heard all those shots just now."

"Sophia, I swear to god, if you say one more thing about anyone dying, I'm going to kill you myself," I snap.

Alicia gasps, hugging Sophia into her side, giving me a baleful look. "Threats aren't constructive here. Neither is talking about Silver's psycho boyfriend dying. We all just need to stay quiet. We need to stay calm."

"I know. I've been saying that for the last ten minutes. Can you...fuck, *both* of you. Can you please just sit down? The three of us bouncing around in here is making me crazy."

"You're moving about just as much as us," Sophia moans around her tears. "it's not like—"

DUM DUM DUM!

The loud thuds fill the sound booth, and all three of us shriek, grabbing each other's hands. From outside comes a demand that sends panic skating up my spine: *"Let me in!"*

"Are you the police?" Alicia yells.

"No, I'm not the fucking police! I'm standing out here in the wide open. Let me in, for fuck's sake!"

I recognize the voice. It's been haunting me for the past nine months, forcing me to relive the most traumatic thing that's ever happened to me every time I've heard it in the hallways of Raleigh.

"That's *Jacob*," Sophia says, sniffling. "Jake, is that you?"

"Yes!"

"Prove it," Alicia demands.

"God, do you want me to slide my fucking driver's license underneath the door? Open up."

Alicia and Sophia almost climb over each other in their haste to unlock the door. I step in front of them, the tiny room spinning like a merry go round, blocking their path.

"What are you doing?" Alicia hisses. "Let him in. We'll be safe if he's in here with us."

I stand firm. "How do you know that? What if *he's* the shooter?"

The girls pause, uncertainty all over their faces. "Well...why would he sound so panicky if he was the one with the gun?" Sophie reasons.

God, this girl would be the first to fucking die in a horror movie. "To trick us into opening the door obviously!"

"Who's in there?" Jake shouts through the door.

"It's me, Allie. Sophia and Silver, too," Alicia answers back.

"Why did you tell him that?" Sophia growls, slapping her friend's arm like she's a naughty little child.

Alicia rubs at her arm, feigning hurt. "What's the harm in him knowing if he can't get in?"

A thick, heavy silence has fallen in the music room beyond the sound booth. Jacob's obviously realized how little chance he has of being admitted into the booth now that he knows *I'm* inside.

I allow myself a sick, twisted moment of satisfaction.

"Silver? Can you hear me?" he says softly. "Silver, please. If you don't let me in and I die, what do you think's gonna happen to your family? My father'll know you shut me out. He'll ruin them. You know it's true. Be better if you let me in so I can wait this out with you."

It's a ridiculous thing to say. He's grasping, trying to concoct something that'll scare me into giving into him, but it's not going to work. "Really? You really think threatening me is an appropriate tactic?"

Another loud thud crashes against the door, this time bordering on violent. "Let me in, Silver, or so help me I'll—"

"You'll what, Jake? Hurt me? Humiliate me? Bully me? Destroy my entire fucking life? You already did that, remember?"

"Silver, *please...*"

Below us, in the library, a jarring, thunderous round of shots sound out, shaking the floor beneath our feet.

"See. Jake can't be the one with the gun if they're shooting down there," Sophia says. "What the fuck is your problem. Let him in."

"*Please, Silver.*" On the other side of the door, Jake sounds like he's about to break down and start sobbing.

For all that he's done, I should not open the door.

The initial assault was reason enough to leave him out there to be shot, but add the months and months of psychological abuse I've suffered at his hands within the very walls of this school? Jacob Weaving deserves whatever brutal death awaits him.

He tried as hard as he could, but he didn't succeed in truly breaking me, though. He stole so much from me, but he didn't take my humanity. A part of me almost wishes he had, as I reluctantly unlock the door to the sound booth and let him in.

He rushes inside, collapsing to his knees, shaking just as severely as Sophia was a moment ago. He cowers, holding his head in his hands, and a strangled sob fills the cramped booth. Alicia and Sophia look down at him, shock and concern developing on their faces, and I allow myself the smallest moment of victory.

"You really think he's going to protect you now?" I ask bitterly. Stooping low, I scoot down so that I'm level with Jacob, eye to eye with the bastard who pinned me down and raped me. "I don't think so. See, you've always been a fucking coward, haven't you, Jake? Your strength and bravado are a pathetic act. Deep down, you've always been...*this*."

He flinches at the raw disgust in my voice.

He doesn't deny it. He doesn't deny a single thing. He casts his gaze down at his hands, and he silently weeps.

34
ALEX

"I'm afraid you've caught me in the middle of a crisis," Leon says, laughing shakily. His hands are steady on the rifle, though. They don't waver an inch. The gun remains firmly aimed at my forehead. "Kacey and I were just ironing out a few issues, weren't we, Kace? I was just letting her know how much I fucking hate her for dumping my ass via text after four years of dating. Coming to my house, acting like she still belongs there, draping herself all over Jacob fucking Weaving. Thought it was hilarious, didn't you, Kacey? Go on. Tell Alex what you did at the party after he left. I'm sure he's just *dying* to hear."

Stall, stall, stall. The longer I can keep him talking, the longer I can keep him from killing anybody. "I could use a story," I say evenly. "What d'you do, Kacey?"

The girl who threatened me in the parking lot only yesterday looks at me with pleading, desperate eyes. "That's not important right now, Leon. What we really need to do is get you out of here before the cops show up."

She just pissed herself, but it appears Kacey still has enough fire in her veins to try and manipulate her ex. Leon knows her better than anyone, though. He dealt with her for four years; he sees straight through the act without missing a beat.

"Oh, *please*, Kay Kay. You'll be shoving me in front of a firing squad the second you get. You're a horrible fucking actress. Always were. Tell Alex what you did after he left the party or I'll shoot you in that vicious, ugly face of yours and I'll tell him myself."

"I—I slept with my boyfriend. At a party. Big deal, Leon. People hook up at parties all the time."

"WHERE!" Leon screams. "*Where* did you hook up with your boyfriend?"

"In your bed," she whispers.

Leon's eyes are full of madness. He nods violently. "And there you have it. You fucked Jacob fucking Weaving in *my* fucking bed."

"It was supposed to be funny, Leon. Jesus, it was a joke."

"Funny? What kind of fucking psychopath are you? What kind of sick, twisted mind do you have, if you think something as spiteful and shitty as that would be *funny?*"

"Everyone…*everyone* thought it was funny," she pants.

Leon stills. He's staring at me, dead in the eye, but his focus is most definitely on the girl behind him. "Exactly. You *told* everyone. You used me as a source of entertainment. You ridiculed me, made me look like an idiot, and everyone laughed along with you because you're Kacey fucking Winters, and if they're not laughing along with you, then you're singling them out and tearing their lives apart. Don't you realize? You think people worship the ground you walk on in this school, but they don't. They fucking hate you. They're afraid of you. They walk around on eggshells, hoping you don't even notice them, because you are a vile, vindictive, spiteful *cunt*."

She can't keep her tongue in her head. She just can't help herself. "You think anyone's gonna love *you* after this? You're the fucking psycho, Leon! You've killed half the fucking school!"

"I've killed eighteen people, actually. You never were any good at math," Leon spits.

"Leon, it's seriously fucked up that she did that," I say, inching closer. "You and I both know Kacey's a piece of trash, though. Is she really worth all of this? Is she really worth any more violence?"

Leon narrows his eyes, adjusting his grip on the rifle. For a second, I'm hopeful—he looks like he doubts himself—but then he clenches his jaw, his shoulders tensing, and the moment has passed. His finger shifts on the trigger. "I thought you of all people would understand this, Alex. You're with Silver. Cillian, Sam, Kacey...they all hurt her, y'know. How can they hurt anyone else if they're all fucking *dead*? How can any of them laugh at someone else's pain again, if they're not around to see it?"

"Man, you're right. These guys should all be punished for what they've done. But that doesn't mean you should arm yourself and go on a...on a..."

"Killing spree?" His brows rise. "It's okay. You can say it. I know exactly what I've done."

"How are you going to live with all of this?" I whisper. "When you're finished, and you've painted every single wall in this building red? How are you going to reconcile yourself with that?"

"Don't you watch the news, Alex?" he says bitterly. "The troubled kid who murders half his classmates never *lives*. I don't plan on being the exception to the rule."

"Leon. Leon, please, man. Let's just take a step back for a second. We're traveling at a hundred and eighty miles an hour right now. No one's thinking clearly."

"I am. I stood up for the first time in my life and said enough. Enough is enough. This is the clearest I've been able to think in a long, long time. I have no issues with you, Moretti. You've only been stuck at Raleigh a month. You seem like a decent guy. You should just leave now. Get the hell out of here. Be the last man standing."

"Fuck, I'd love to do that, I really would. But there's a girl inside this building who I love more than life itself, and I can't just let you hurt her. And all of these other kids? They might be assholes, and they might treat other people like shit, but they have people waiting outside who love them. Would I be a decent guy if I turned my back on this and let it happen? How many hearts have to break? How many people have to—"

I've been so focused on trying to get through to him that I haven't noticed Kacey. She's not sitting on the floor in a puddle of her own piss anymore. She's on her feet, and suddenly she's rushing at Leon, screaming…

Leon spins, firing the rifle into the stack of books as he turns, spraying a hail of bullets in his wake.

Fuuuuck!

I charge him, grabbing for the rifle. The metal is warm and deadly in my hand, unrelenting. Leon has a firm grip on it, though, the weapon braced into his shoulder, locked against his body. I drop the empty gun, freeing up my other hand, and I drive a right hook into his ribs, trying to wind him. I wind him, all right, but Leon's a stubborn bastard. He doesn't let go. Staggering backward, he slams himself into the book stacks behind him, and Kacey screams out in pain. She falls to the floor, whimpering, scrambling away as I kick out at Leon's legs, trying to take him out at the knees.

For someone so resigned to die, Leon sure puts up one hell of a fight. He's desperate as he twists his body, struggling to aim the rifle at Kacey.

"Just her," he grinds out between his teeth. "She's the only one that really matters."

"LEON, STOP!"

Everything happens in a blur.

The deafening bang.

The blow to my ribs.

Leon slumping to the ground.

The cold, wet chill that spreads outward across my chest.

I stagger back, stunned at the sight of Leon sprawled, glass-eyed, on the floor.

"What the...fuck?"

I look at Kacey, and her mouth is open, tears streaming down her face. She's holding the gun I dropped in her hands. "God, I'm sorry, I...I don't know what happened. I shot him. I shot *him!*"

I hold my hand to my chest, and...it comes away red.

The pain kicks in, just as I look down and see the small, smoking hole in my sternum.

Turns out I was wrong.

The gun Leon dropped outside the library wasn't empty after all.

I just forgot to check the chamber...

35
SILVER

I've been climbing the walls, straining to listen, to hear anything for minutes now. Long minutes that have surrendered nothing but silence. At some point, not long after I let Jake into the booth and I watched him whimpering on the floor, I realized that I couldn't let my fear control me anymore. Alex didn't fucking blink before he went back down there, determined to help. What good am I here, locked away in a glorified closet, when he's out there, risking himself for us?

"Fuck this. I'm not waiting here another second. It's been quiet for too long. Something must have happened." I head for the door, but Jake jumps to his feet, barring the exit. "You're not going anywhere. We have to stay here and wait for the cops," he growls.

I realize something else, as I look up at him, into a face that has scared the shit out of me for so long now. I know that I'm not scared of him anymore. "Don't worry, Jake. No one's expecting *you* to go out there and act. If anyone asks, I'll be sure to tell them how bravely you handled all of this. Now get out of my way."

"Sit down, Silver."

I won't sit down. I won't listen to him anymore. No way in hell am I going to let his cowardice prevent me from trying to help in any way that I can. I stand my ground, folding my arms across my chest. *"Move."*

Jake looks at the other two girls. Funny how he doesn't seem so untouchable now. "She's right, Jake. It's been quiet for too long. Something must have happened. We should go and look." Sophia's the last person I expect to say this, but she seems a lot calmer now. She comes and stands beside me. Alicia swears unhappily, but she joins her friend. Then it's us three girls against Jake.

"You're all fucking insane," he spits, moving out of the way. "Be my guest. Go out there and get yourselves killed. See what difference it makes."

He doesn't follow us out. The door slams closed behind us, and the king of Raleigh High locks himself back in the booth without another word.

We tiptoe through the music room and down the stairs, and that's where we see the first cop. Relief surges through me, making my legs turn to Jell-O; I've never been so happy to see a badge and a gun in all my life. "Any of you hurt?" the guy calls, hurrying toward us.

"No. No. But there are others," Alicia says. "The library. Have you checked the library? We heard most of the shots in there."

"The EMTs are in there now, dealing with the casualties. Head outside, girls. There are blankets and more ambulances. You're probably in shock. Your parents are on—hey! Hey, where the hell are you going?"

I'm not heading outside. No fucking way. If most of the shooting took place in the library, then that's where Alex would have gone. I'm running at top speed before I even make the decision to bolt. Alicia and Sophie both shout after me, but I don't hear a word they say.

I have to find Alex.

If he's hurt, I need to be with him.

I crash into a firefighter on the stairs up to the library. He tries to grab hold of me, to stop me, but I duck around him, pressing forward...

..and then I stop.

The library's a blood bath. Everywhere I look, bodies lie in strange, unnatural poses. Some of them are covered with grey sheets, body bags laid out on the floor beside them.

Fuck.

Where is Alex?

WHERE IS ALEX?

I see Sheriff Hainsworth, standing grimly by one of the stacks, his head bowed, hands on his hips, and I make a beeline for him. "Sheriff Hainsworth? Sheriff Hainsworth, have you seen Ale—"

The question freezes on my lips. At the sheriff's feet, three EMTs are working frantically over a body. The floor is slick with blood. So much blood. It's everywhere.

Then I see the hand thrown out lifelessly to one side. A glimpse of the fierce wolf tattoo on the back of it. The sharp, thorny vines that are wrapped around the wrist.

"Oh, God. God, no, that's not...that's not *him?*"

"Silver, get outside with the others. There's nothing you can do here," Sheriff Hainsworth commands, trying to push me back. I rip myself free of him, struggling forward, determined to prove to myself that I was seeing things just now. That the body on the floor does not belong to Alex.

"He's coding," one of the EMTs grinds out, scrambling around in the small red bag beside her. "There's too much blood. Airway's collapsed. We need to intubate. Damn it, where the fuck is the epi!"

She shifts out of the way, and my heart stops dead in my chest.

Alex.

It *is* him.

"No! *No, no, no, no, no!*"

His t-shirt's been cut away, exposing his chest. And there, just below his left pec, a tiny, perfectly round hole is leaking blood all over his tattooed skin. His face is so pale, his dark eyelashes resting against his cheekbones. He doesn't cry out in pain as one of the other EMTs sticks him with a needle. He doesn't respond at all.

"Still in v-fib. Prep the paddles. Forget the trach kit. If we can't get a rhythm, it won't matter if he can't breathe anyway."

The dull roaring in my ears mutes the words they're firing back and forth to one another. The world is crashing down around me. "Save him! Oh my god, you have to save him. Please!"

"For Christ sake, someone get her out of here," someone snaps.

Hands close around the tops of my arms. I yank myself free again, spinning on the police officer I saw back in the hall. "Don't fucking touch me! I'm staying!"

The EMT who stuck Alex moves quickly, placing two gel pads on his chest. "Charging to two hundred. Clear." She discharges the defibrillator next to her, and Alex's back arches off the ground. The next second, he's still again. Lifeless.

"No good," she says, her fingers pressed against the side of his throat. "Again. Charging to three hundred. Clear."

I cover my mouth with my hands, biting down on my lip so hard that the metallic, sharp taste of blood coats my tongue. Alex's body jolts again, then slumps back down to the ground.

"Anything?" the first EMT asks.

The woman operating the defibrillator rechecks Alex's throat for a pulse...then shakes her head.

"Nope. Nothing. Flatline. I'm afraid he's dead."

...

Dorme, Passerotto. *That's right, mi amore. Shhh. Rest. It time to go to sleep...*

36

SILVER

I've never looked good in black.

Even before, when I used to hang out with Kacey, and it was all she ever wanted us to wear, it used to wash me out too much. I'm too pale as I stand in front of the mirror in my bedroom, fiddling with the high-necked collar of the dress Mom picked out for me. We called a truce after the shooting. With so many announcements and funerals, so many damaged parents mourning dead children, it felt wrong to be angry with her over Dan. There'll come a time at some point in the future when she's going to have to tell Dad what happened—I know that now. It was wrong of me to try and force her into keeping it a secret—but for the time being, we're standing united as a family while Raleigh grieves.

In the mirror, I see her standing in the doorway to my bedroom. She's already dressed in her funeral clothes, and there are dark, bruised shadows under her eyes. "You haven't eaten anything," she says.

"Can you blame me? I'm not really feeling hungry this morning."

She smiles sadly, her mouth pulling into a tight line. "I know, honey. I just thought I'd try. Your dad and Max are already waiting downstairs."

"Okay. I'll be down in a minute."

She leaves, and I tug at the collar again, this time trying to loosen it. It's too tight. Too restrictive. I can't fucking breathe. I give up eventually. No matter how much I pull and tug at the damn thing, I'm never going to feel comfortable in it.

We're silent in the van on the way over to the cemetery; it was decided that it'd be better if there was no actual church service, since no one in town was likely to come.

The ground's covered in snow, the world too white and bright, after the first really heavy flurries of winter rolled in late last night. Max is somber next to me on the back seat, his face drawn. He looks wrong in the suit Dad took him to get fitted for—like he's a little adult now, old enough to handle something like this, when he most definitely is not. As Dad pulls into the lot and parks up, I take Max's hand and give it a squeeze. "You want to wait here in the car?" I whisper. "It's okay. You don't have to come. No one's gonna think badly of you."

He grimaces, looking down at his polished shoes. "I don't wanna be rude, though."

God, I just want to hug him so hard. I want to hold him so tight and protect him from this kind of shit. This kind of violence was never supposed to rear its ugly head in a town like Raleigh. Max should have been sheltered from this kind of horror. "Honestly. It's okay, Bud," Dad says, reaching into the back and giving him a squeeze on the knee. "Wait here. It's no big deal. The service won't be long. Take a nap or something, kiddo."

At any other time, this would be a strange suggestion to make, but in the ten days since Leon shot up Raleigh High, no one's been sleeping very much, Max included. He's been getting most of his rest in during daylight hours, when his nightmares seem to leave him alone for the most part.

I walk between Mom and Dad along the pathway that's been cleared in the snow toward the gravesite with my heart in my throat.

Jesus, I can't do this. It's too fucking hard. I can't take another moment, feeling so torn open and raw inside. I've cried so much, it's a miracle my tear ducts even work anymore. My legs threaten to give out as we turn a corner and I see the priest standing there over the open grave. I want to turn back. I want to go and sit this out with Max in the back of the car, but I can't. I *wanted* to do this, but now that the time's come…it's just so difficult.

As if he can read my thoughts, Dad puts his arm around my shoulders, tucking me into his side. "Sure you don't wanna go get a milkshake at Harry's instead?" he asks quietly.

"No, no, I'm fine. I'll be okay." I don't think I will be okay, though. This is going to be brutal.

The priest looks up from his open Bible, smiling tightly at us when he sees that we've arrived. I look down into the grave, swallowing back bile. The casket that's already been lowered into the frozen ground is simple, plain, and inexpensive. There's no brass plaque on the top of it like the one Mom had engraved with a quote for Grandpa when he died. There are no flowers, except for the two large sprays of white calla lilies we've brought with us. Mom and Dad set the arrangements down at the foot of the grave, bowing their heads respectfully. The priest begins immediately.

"In the name of God, our Father, we are gathered here today to commit the body of this young man to the peace of the grave."

Pain lances through my chest, so spectacular and blinding that I have to press my hands against my ribs.

"You gave him life, Oh Lord," the priest continues. "Now we beseech thee to receive him unto your rest. Though the path be straight and narrow, often your servants wonder. The gift of this life is challenging, filled with love and laughter, but also with much hardship and sorrow. We pray to thee to stand beside us in our grief. Bring comfort and understanding into our hearts—

At first, I pay no heed to the rumbling in the distance. It's not until the rumbling turns into a roar that I lift my head, frowning.

"...we plead for your mercy, Father, and pray for the soul of your troubled servant..."

The roar becomes a throaty snarl, echoing around the cemetery, so loud now and so close that my heart skips a series of fluttering beats.

It can't be...

"...accept Leon Wickman into your heart, Lord. May he find in Heaven the peace he could not find here on earth..."

I look up at Dad, about to beg for *his* forgiveness, only to find that he's already smiling at me. "Go on, kiddo. Go find him. It's all right. We'll stay."

I'm bolting, kicking off my shoes and running barefoot through the snow before he can even finish his sentence. My pulse races, arms pumping, legs burning, feet stinging against the cold, but I don't stop. I run faster, as fast as my legs will carry me. And then, breathless, struggling to catch my breath, I reach the top of the snowy rise by the entrance of the cemetery...and there he is.

Still straddling his bike, helmet in his hands, he looks up and sees me, and a slow, wicked smirk spreads across his handsome face.

"Alex Moretti, as I live and breathe," I call down to him. "You weren't supposed to get out of the hospital until tomorrow afternoon."

He shrugs. "Hospital food's the worst, *Argento*. And besides, I had to see you. I may have performed an elaborate and highly professional escape from the recovery ward about an hour ago."

I slide all over the place as I throw myself down the embankment toward him. When I reach him, he catches me up in his arms, grunting a little as he hugs me to him. I realize too late that I've probably really hurt him. "Fuck, I'm sorry. I keep forgetting..."

He dismisses my apology by kissing me, his mouth against mine, hot and persuasive. He tucks a piece of my hair back behind my ear when he's done with me. "How the hell can you forget, with the badass scar I'm rocking these days?" he asks.

After Alex had officially been pronounced dead, the lead EMT had charged up the defibrillator again and given it one last shot. A final Hail Mary. Screaming in a heap on the floor, I'd been too hysterical to notice the fact that they were all still working over him, but I sure as hell heard that EMT when she announced that they'd regained a sinus rhythm.

The bullet had traveled straight through Leon and buried itself deep in Alex's chest, perforated one of his major arteries, caused both of his lungs to collapse, along with all kinds of other damage to his body. The eight-hour surgery that saved his life has left him with a nine-inch-long scar from the base of his throat to his mid-torso, and he's convinced it's ruined the tattoo of his family crest.

"I'm glad you came here today," he says, whispering into my neck. "It doesn't make any sense, I know, but…I liked Leon. Until he started killing people."

"I know. I did too."

"I heard the nurses saying his father checked himself into the psych ward."

"Yeah. There's a for sale sign up at the end of their driveway. Dad says they're probably going to have to pull it down though. Apparently, the fact that a mass murderer used to live there is gonna affect the house's resale potential."

"Fuck. How did any of this even *happen?*" Alex shakes his head sadly. "No one fucking saw how broken he was. I sure as hell didn't when *I* hung out with him. I had no clue."

"I don't know. Leon was Kacey's puppet. When she shut me out, he did, too. I never blamed him for it. Not really. But I wasn't close to him for nearly a year. I wish I'd noticed the change in him. I would have *tried* to help…"

"And now Kacey's been sent to Seattle under a cloud of shame, Leon's gone, and eighteen other people are dead."

"Don't forget that *you* nearly died," I remind him.

He pulls a bored face, like that part's not important. "And they're reopening Raleigh in a week. Savage bastards. You'd think they'd give us all a little more time to recover."

"We'll all have to re-take our senior year if they did, and I, for one, would prefer to get it over with and move the hell on."

"Oh? And where does that leave me, *Argento*? You, so quick to try and leave town and all…"

"I don't care all that much about leaving Raleigh anymore. Just high school. But it would be nice to go to college somewhere less cold? And I was kind of hoping you might…"

Alex firmly shakes his head. "I can't. I can't go to college. Monty will never let me live it down if he ever finds out I can read and write properly."

"You are coming to college!" I say. "You're coming with me, wherever I end up going, and you're going to love it. You have to promise."

He observes me with a pensive, serious look in his eyes. He's far too pale after everything that he's been through, but he already looks so much better than he did. "All right, Silver Parisi. If that's what you want, then fine. I'll go to college with you. I'll follow you to the ends of the fucking earth if it'll make you happy. But there *is* something we need to do first."

"And? What's that?"

"We have to actually *graduate* first."

EPILOGUE

SILVER

There are days in your life that are more than a series of hours strung together. Days that start off the same as any other. You eat breakfast. You struggle to find your keys. You're mad at your mom, or your dad, or your brother, or your friend. You couldn't find the shirt you wanted to wear, and it feels like the world is ending. And then something happens. Something so terrible and so catastrophic that suddenly the fact that you were running late doesn't matter anymore. A literal or metaphorical bomb goes off, and all of the tiny little annoyances that were driving you crazy are thrown into stark relief, revealing them for what they are: unimportant. So inconsequential that you're humbled by the size of the universe and how little control you have over absolutely anything in your life.

I have already lived through two such days in the past twelve months. The ground has been pulled out from underneath me, I've been blindsided, and the context of the world around me has altered so dramatically that I've looked around and not recognized what was once familiar. But, the thing about these nightmare days, the thing that continues to surprise and confound me, is that a series of days will follow right after them, when things slowly but surely seem to return to normal, and life? It just goes on regardless.

I sit on the bleachers inside Raleigh High's gym, surrounded by three hundred other students, and I'm awed by the way that people are already somehow finding it in them to laugh. Yes, there are tears. Yes, there are hugs, and there are empty seats, but I also see the hope in people's eyes, and I hear their words of encouragement and comfort. I feel a sense of community amongst my peers that I used to feel every day before I was trapped inside a bathroom with Jacob Weaving, and that...*that* is what enables me to sit straight, chin high, and endure the pain of what happened at our school two weeks ago.

Of course, it helps that I have someone here with me to hold my hand. Someone I didn't see coming. According to the letter of the law, the person sitting next to me is still an adolescent, and for that I am eternally grateful; if the powers that be had seen him as an adult a little over a month ago, he'd currently be sitting in prison right now, and I would never have crossed paths with him. Perhaps more importantly, there's a chance many more Raleigh students could have lost their lives when Leon Wickman stalked through these familiar hallways and opened fire. Who knows what could have happened. All I *do* know, is that when it counted, Alex Moretti was a *man* and he stepped up to the plate.

I nestle into his side, deeply inhaling, soaking up the scent of fresh pine needles and cold winter air. He smells like freedom, like the wind that whipped past us as he drove us here on his motorcycle, risking one last ride before the snows set in for the next few months. I used to hate the brutal, oppressive Washington winters, but now every time I step out into the snow and rain, I'm instantly reminded of the guy who swept into my life on the very first of Raleigh's sleet flurries and altered my life forever. See, in truth, I've had three of those *bombshell* days. It's not just the nightmare events that catch us unaware and unprepared. Mercifully, there are days, unremarkable days that seem to follow the status quo, that start out with lost keys and engine trouble, and detention…and then you see someone for the first time. You catch their face in profile, and you see the hint of a wicked smirk on their face, and it begins: you're stumbling, tripping, losing your footing, and the world feels like it's ending all over again. Ending the very best of ways, to start all over, fresh and anew, and you're falling. But this time, falling isn't so scary after all. You're falling in a good way, and the journey over the edge of the cliff you were standing on is the turns out to be the most exhilarating ride of your life.

Alex presses his lips against my temple, kissing me softly, and my heart swells to the point of bursting. "How many more, *Argento?*" he rumbles into my ear.

I smile, laughing softly under my breath. "One less than yesterday."

"Humor me."

So, I humor him. "One hundred and thirty-two. One hundred and thirty-two more school days until we're free."

"But in between, there's Thanksgiving. And Christmas. And New Year's. And *prom.*"

I groan, turning my face into his chest, enjoying the deep, bassy rumble of his laughter. "God, let's not talk about prom. *Please.*"

"Really? You don't care about prom? I have it on good authority that someone's planning on asking you."

I look up into his face, arching an eyebrow. "Oh yeah?"

He nods, a glimmer of amusement dancing in his eyes. "I heard Gareth Foster on this phone with his *mom* in the parking lot. He said you have hair the color of spun gold. I could see his boner through his chinos."

"Great. I've always had it bad for Gareth. He's a great dancer. Maybe prom won't be so bad after all."

Alex wraps an arm around my shoulders, growling into my ear. He's being playful, but the sound sends a shiver up my spine that isn't entirely appropriate for this setting. "You realize I will cut anyone who even looks twice at you between now and the rest of time, right, *Dolcezza?*"

He makes me feel so good it fucking hurts. "I had a sneaking suspicion that might be the case," I whisper back. "But it's a girl's prerogative to consider her options when prom comes around, *Alessandro*," I say teasingly.

His eyes travel over my face, pausing on my nose, my chin, roaming over my cheekbones before they come to a stop on my eyes. Goddamnit. The way he looks at me, so serious, so…*at peace*, his face so full of emotion. I don't know how to tolerate the intensity of his eyes sometimes. I feel like I'm about to crack apart and fall open in his hands at any moment. I would typically hide at this point, embarrassed and too overwhelmed by him, but I've been fighting that urge recently. I want to show up for these moments. I *have* to. There are people in this world who never have someone look at them the way Alex looks at me. I am one of the lucky ones.

"What? No, '*It's Alex*,'" reprimand today," I ask.

He pauses, his eyelids lowering just a little, and then he shakes his head. "No. Not today." He speaks quietly, so only I can hear him. "She used to call me that. My mom. I've always hated it when someone else uses that name. Feels like they're taking a razor blade and cutting down into me as deep as they can. But…not *you*, *Argento*. When you call me Alessandro…" He huffs, looking down at his hands, studying his own tattooed fingers that are interlaced with mine. "When you say it…it feels the same as when *she* said it. It feels like…" He seems to be battling with something too deep and too raw to process right now. He laughs, shaking himself out, shrugging out of the tense moment we just found ourselves in. "It feels good when you say it," he says briskly. "That's all."

I know what he wanted to say, though. I know, because I know him, and I know how his heart works now.

When you say my name, it feels like love, *Silver.*

When he says my name, it feels like love too.

"She had a nickname for me," he says, eyes casting around the gym. "She used to call me *Passarotto*."

"Ahh, yes. That was in your email address. You promised you were going to tell me what it meant."

A shy, rueful smile flickers at his mouth, there one second, gone the next. "It means *little sparrow*," he says reluctantly.

"Little *Sparrow*?"

He bumps me with his shoulder. "Laugh and suffer the consequences. It's common in Italy. It's more like…precious. And I was a scrawny kid. All knock-kneed and weird looking. I think my head was too fucking big for my body."

I reach up and run my fingers through the ends of his wavy hair, pretending to assess his head. "*Hmm…*"

He leans back for me to get a better look at him. "Well? What do you think? Did I grow into it?"

I angle my head to one side, squinting.

"You are skating on *such* thin ice right now," he growls.

"All right, all right. Yes, everything's in proportion now. You're lucky. You would have looked real weird riding around with an extra, *extra* large motorcycle helmet."

We quietly joke with each other, our shoulders and our legs pressed up against one another, neither of us able to get close enough to the other person. After a while, the atmosphere in the gym changes, the air vibrating with tension, and the smiles fade from everyone's faces.

Principle Darhower enters and walks stiffly toward the small microphone stand that's been set up in front of the bleachers. His face is pale, and his hands shake as he reaches inside his suit pocket and pulls out a square of paper. You could hear a pin drop as he unfolds it and begins to read.

"When I was a kid, my father was my idol. He was a stock car racer, and every weekend my Mom would sit with me in the stands, and we would watch him race. In high school, I decided I wanted to be just like him. I wanted to be a Nascar driver, and that's all there was to it. It was seriously all I could ever imagine myself doing." His voice rings out, clear and loud, reaching every corner of the gym. "I didn't care about math, or science, or history. I never paid attention in my language classes, and I didn't care about my GPA. I didn't need any of that to be a Nascar driver, so I didn't even try. My father knew how badly I wanted to follow in his footsteps, so he suggested I get my GED and take an internship with his sponsor, learning how the industry worked, learning how to build and fix engines, and most importantly learning how to drive. But I decided not to get my GED."

He pauses, taking a breath. His hands are shaking so badly now, the paper in his hands shakes too.

"I stayed in high school because I actually *loved* showing up every day. I loved my friends. I loved my teachers. I loved feeling like I was at a place that *mattered*, even if I didn't particularly want to give my studies my all. School, for me, was a safe place, where I felt at home, and I didn't want to miss any of it.

"My father died when I was the same age as many of you are now. Five days after my seventeenth birthday, another stock car crashed into him on a corner, and he went hurtling into the barricade at ninety-three miles an hour. He was killed instantly. I was there, sitting in the stands with my mother as I always was whenever he raced, and I watched that day as my hero died. It was… officially," he says, his voice breaking, "the *worst* day of my life.

"A week later, I went back to school, and *I* was a wreck. I couldn't breathe. I couldn't function. I was a zombie, stumbling through my day, a war raging inside me because I now hated something that had consumed my entire life. I didn't want to be a Nascar driver anymore. I didn't know who or what I wanted to be. All I wanted was to have my father back.

"Grief was a long, lonely road for me. I didn't want to be consoled. I didn't want to feel better, because feeling better somehow felt like I *cared* less, and that..." Principle Darhower dashes at his eyes with the back of his hands, and my throat begins to ache. "I didn't want to do *that*. Eventually, when the grief became too much, it nearly finally broke me, and it was my friends and my teachers at school who I turned to for help. They consoled me. They held me together. They *saved* me. It was then that I decided to teach. To help continue on a legacy of support and care that had been shown to me at a time when I needed it.

"Two weeks ago, one of the students at this school, one of *my* students, did something terrible. People were hurt. Lives...were..." He clenches his jaw, his nostrils flaring. "Lives were taken," he rushes out. "Many of you lost friends. Many of you are feeling the same way I felt after I lost my father, crippled with grief and alone...and I am standing before you now...humbly apologizing to each and every one of you. The world has changed so much since I was at school, but that is no excuse. It was *my* burden of responsibility to ensure that this school was a safe place for *you* to come to every day, and...two weeks ago, I failed you. This tragedy never should have happened. It should have been prevented long before any of my students ever felt the need to harm others. What he did was wrong. There's no excuse...ever...for the kind of violence we suffered through here. But I became complacent. My vision became narrowed by years of routine and ritual, and I wasn't looking for the unexpected. And I am profoundly and deeply sorry for that.

"Today, we return to Raleigh with heavy and broken hearts, but please know...I will never allow anything like this to ever happen to our community again. I promise to keep you *safe*. I promise to do *better*. Now, let's go and shine...and let's help each other remember how to breathe again."

~

SILVER

I don't think I've ever been this nervous. Alex has been to the house before, but never under these circumstances. Never as the boy I'm dating. Not as my official *boyfriend*. God, it's still so weird to think of him in those terms. It feels stupid. Childish. Immature. Alex was shot not too long ago and nearly died. Seems to me there should be a weightier title for him now.

"Silver! Can you remember where we put that photo album with that one picture? Y'know, the one with you hiding behind the couch, taking a shit in your diaper?"

Dad is *loving* this.

In turn, I have learned that it's possible to love a parent but also want them to writhe in pain. Nothing serious. A broken toe would be nice. Or surprise root canal surgery.

I almost trip over my own feet in my haste to make it down the stairs and into the dining room. Mom's laid out the table with all the fancy cutlery and dishes, six places set around the massive, formal dining table that only gets used at holidays and for special occasions. I gape at the set-up, holding out my hands just as Dad enters the room. "What the hell is *this*?" I demand.

Dad takes a bite out of an apple. "Your mother went *mad*."

"We're not Catholic. We *aren't*, are we? Why does it look like the Pope's coming for dinner?"

"We've lapsed," my father confirms. "But, sidenote. *I've* recently taken up praying again. Funnily enough, my renewed faith coincided with the night you asked to go spend the night with a guy who looks like something out of Sons of Anarchy."

"Dad. Please shut up."

He holds his hands in the air, still brandishing his half-eaten apple. "All I'm saying is, I think I'm greyer than I used to be. If I start clutching my chest at dinner and I slump over my plate, face-down in my stroganoff, it's because I'm faking my own death and I can't live with the knowledge that I basically gave that little punk permission to defile you."

"DAD! Oh my fucking god. *No!* Don't ever open your mouth again. Especially not in front of Alex."

He laughs like the evil monster that he is as he turns around and heads into the kitchen. I pace anxiously up and down the hallway for the next thirty minutes, worrying at my thumbnail with my front teeth, trying to come up with a decent excuse to call off the entire dinner. I come up with plenty of solid reasons, but every time I pull out my cell to text Alex, I realize how stupid I'm being and talk myself out of it.

At six thirty on the dot, the doorbell chimes. I just so happen to be banging my head against my bedroom door at the time, so Max gets there before me, screeching like a banshee at the top of his lungs. "ALEEEEEXXX! IT'S ALEX!"

I'm hissing every dark, vicious curse word I can think as I thunder down the stairs, running to get to the door before Max can say anything to embarrass or humiliate me. When I arrive, however, Alex is standing with his tattooed hands resting on the shoulders of a very pale, wide-eyed young boy, introducing him to my brother.

"Ben's eleven, too. You guys are in the same year," Alex says. He looks up at me, and my heart stops dead in my chest.

Holy fucking Christ on a bike.

He's wearing a button-down black shirt, the top button popped, that is tailored and fits him perfectly. I nearly faint at the sight of his sleeves rolled up, cuffed around his elbows—what the hell is it about rolled up sleeves? *I swear to god...*

His black jeans are brand new, minus the usual rips and tears, and his Stan Smiths look like he spent a considerable amount of time scrubbing at them with a toothbrush. There isn't a speck of dirt on them. Alex smirks ruinously at me, biting down on his bottom lip. He begged me not to do that the first night we spent in the cabin because it was driving him crazy. I wonder if he's aware that the action has the exact same effect on me when he does it.

"Silver, this my brother, Ben. Ben, this is Silver," he says. There's a cautious edge to his voice. Usually, he's so confident and unshakable, but right now he seems downright nervous. It's kind of adorable. I hold my hand out to the little boy, my breath catching in my throat when I look at him properly, square in the face, and I find a small, timid version of Alex staring back up at me. The shape of his face, the cheekbones, the straight, no-nonsense nose. Even his chin looks identical to Alex's, and for a second I'm taken aback.

Alex would have looked a lot like Ben when does now when he was six. When he walked into the house and found his mother lying on the floor in a pool of her own blood. Except he was even smaller, five years younger, and the mental image that conjures itself in my mind makes me want to burst into tears.

He doesn't just look like Alex. They both look so much like *her*.

Instead, I whisper out a greeting as Ben uncertainly takes my hand and shakes it. "I'm so pleased to meet you, Ben."

"Pleased to meet you, too," he mumbles in return. When I let go of his hand, he slips it underneath his other arm, tucking it against his body like he's protecting it. He looks up at Alex, big brown eyes wide and unsure, and Alex nods, smiling down at him.

"S'okay, man. It's just dinner. That okay? Silver told me Max likes to play Halo. Is that true, Max?"

Max's never been shy a day in his life. He nods enthusiastically, grabbing Ben by the sleeve of *his* super smart blue button-down shirt. "I have my own room for gaming. There's a forty-two-inch screen in there. Dad got it to watch the baseball, but it's basically mine now. Have you got Red Dead Redemption two? I got it last week, but I'm not allowed to play it until I finish Halo. Which school do you go to?" He chatters the whole way down the hallway, leading Ben toward the game room. Alex leans against the door jamb, stuffing his hands in his pockets as he watches them go.

"He'll be fine as soon as he gets some sugar in him," he says.

"Well, there's plenty of that down there. Max has a number of gummy bear caches hidden in the cupboards that he thinks Mom doesn't know about." I step back, making room for him to pass me. "You coming in?"

"I don't know. I brought the kid as a human shield to use against your dad, but that you just disarmed me I'm wondering if it's safe…"

"I have excellent hearing!" my father yells from the kitchen.

"You are *so* screwed."

I flinch, screwing my eyes shut. "He's basically going to be unbearable all night," I admit. "Just don't pay any attention and you'll be fine."

"Hey, Alex? Any idea what cyanide tastes like?" Dad hollers.

Alex glares over my shoulder. "Is he serious?"

I try not to laugh, but I give in in the end. If I don't laugh, I'm only going to end up crying. "If he asks, it's probably better to tell him you slept on the couch when I came over the other night. Just…act natural."

"No one in the history of being told to act natural has *ever* acted natural," Alex fires back. He does step into the house, though, essentially sealing his fate. He wraps his arms around me, stealing a kiss. I'm flushed and a little breathless when he releases me, holding a finger to my lips, pretending to shush me.

I pretend to bite that finger in return. "I'm glad Jackie let you bring Ben."

"Yeah. Well. She's actually been okay with me recently. I know.

Shocker. Still insisted on coming to pick him up from here, but I've got him until eight-thirty."

"And after that?"

Alex shrugs. "I'm yours to torture as you see fit."

My pulse quickens as I look up into his eyes, bracing myself for what I want to say next. He can't have had any idea, but I do have something planned for after dinner, and it really *is* going to be torture. I'm panicking, my anxiety through the roof, my—

Alex cups his hands around my face, frowning deeply. "Hey. Hey, what is it? What's wrong?"

He's so damn attuned to me. I'm pretty sure my expression is still under control, but he can tell I'm freaking the fuck out. "I—I want to talk to them. About…what happened at Leon's party. Tonight."

Alex's eyes round out. "*Oh.*"

"And…" Jesus Christ, this is hard. "I was wondering…"

"You want me to stay with you. You want me to be there," he says quietly.

"Yes. I'm sorry, I know it's a lot to ask. It's definitely not going to be fun, but—"

He cuts me off with his mouth. The kiss is light and gentle, designed to reassure and calm. Pulling me to him, he presses me up against him, and suddenly I'm safe in the circle of his arms. Sweeping a piece of hair back behind my ear, he rests his forehead against mine, his eyes fierce and firm. "Silver, you don't need to ask. I will *always* be wherever you need me to be. I will sit right beside you. I will hold your hand. I will carry you out of here and steal you away if that's what you want. *I'm not going anywhere.*"

I've made it through so much recently without crying. The days I spent sitting in a chair next to Alex's hospital bed, not sleeping, not eating, hoping and praying every second that he was going to be okay, were the worst days of my life, but I was determined to be there every time he opened his eyes. I was strong for him because he needed me. Now, it's me who needs him once again, and boy is he showing up. "*I love you, Argento.* Don't worry. Everything's going to be okay. Just you wait and see."

And I do believe him. I trust him. I know that he's right. He's *always* right because he's Alessandro Moretti…and despite everything, despite seemingly insurmountable odds, he managed to accomplish something that I told him couldn't be done.

The Rebel of Raleigh High managed to pull down the moon… and now *nothing* is impossible.

A NOTE FROM THE AUTHOR...

Dearest Reader,

Thank you so much for reading The Rebel of Raleigh High. Some pretty tough subject matter was covered within the pages of this book, and I know it might have been hard for some of you to read. I apologize for that. I tried my best to handle such sensitive topics with care and compassion, and I truly hope that came through in the story.

This isn't a story about violence and hatred, though. It's a story about strength and resilience, and at the end of the day I really have to hope that that shone through in the words.

Silver and Alex's story is far from over. The Rebel of Raleigh High started out as a standalone story, but as I neared the end of the book it became very apparent that they weren't done telling their tale. In light of this, there will be a further book coming out (fingers crossed) in late June.

If you're interested in finding out what Alex and Monty have planned for Jacob Weaving, and if you want to know what happens with Ben, then keep an eye out for the cover reveal and title announcement that will be coming soon on facebook and other social media platforms. I promise I won't keep you waiting long.

Once more, thank you for reading this book. It was a labor of love to write, and I adored these characters and connected with them on such a base level. Their struggle and their plight to overcome resonated with me as I wrote, and it's my sincere hope that it spoke to you in some way, too.

All my love,

Callie x

P.S. Keep on turning the pages for a VERY special surprise!

SURPRISE!

Yes, that's right! Coming in late August, Zeth Mayfair will be getting an entirely new book, and this chapter in his journey is going to blow some minds!

Want a little taste? Who am I to refuse…

Enjoy!

PROLOGUE

The acrid tang of Gasoline bites at the back of my nose. Tonight, death lingers on the cold mid-winter Seattle air. Somewhere, across the snow-laden winter city, a woman is dying in a pool of her own blood. She's alone, her fingers half-curled around a crucifix, her dark hair spun out around her head like a sheet of rumpled black silk. The light in her eyes is fading, the pulse fluttering in the hollow of her throat gradually slowing. Her cheeks, normally flushed with all the brightness and enthusiasm of youth, are leeching of color, turning waxy and sallow.

It's within my power to save this woman.

It's possible to stem the flow of her vital life force before it evacuates her body beyond the point of no return.

I'm the only person who can bring her back from the brink.

But I don't.

I turn my back on the steaming, surging, churning city, and I face the mountain at my back instead. I've been standing still for so long that the leather of my jacket crackles with ice as I twist around and look up into the looming darkness.

Not too long ago, a house stood on the side of this mountain. A woman lived there. A doctor. I somehow came to find myself there, too, pulled out of the filth and the muck of my own miserable existence and allowed to exist within her orbit, a miracle I never envisioned for myself. We had a life together there, within that house. A strange, off-kilter, chaotic kind of life, but also peaceful. Also, wonderful.

We *created* a life there.

Not just a routine, or a home.

An actual *life*.

Ten fingers.

Ten toes.

Intense, fierce brown eyes, and wild, dark curls.

A tiny body, bursting with so much potential and promise.

All of it gone now.

All of it shade, and dust, and ashes, and smoke...

Yes, on the other side of the city, with shards of ice forming within the narrow canals of my veins and the marrow of my bones gripped by frost, I ignore the pleas of my conscience and I allow a woman to die.

She deserves her fearful, sour, undignified death.

She deserves so much worse.

My hand closes around the gun in my pocket, the metal lamenting as my grip tightens around the handle; it's as if the weeping steel knows what comes next. As if it somehow senses all of the pain and destruction I am about to cause with its sleek, cool, heavy form in my grasp.

It can't know, though. How can it? It's just a gun. It's enough that *I* know what will happen over the next few hours, and days, and weeks.

Men will die.

Mothers will lose their sons.

Children will be orphaned.

Even more blood will flow, until the snowdrifts of the mountainside and the heaped white snowbanks of the winter city are marred and stained a brutal shade of red.

No matter the cold. The whole world will burn before I'm through with it.

There will be no rest.

There will be no hesitation.

There will be no mercy.

For the black-hearted few who took that most precious from me…I am the apocalypse. I am the darkness. I am the night.

I am the storm that will *not* be weathered.

CHAPTER ONE

ZETH

Once upon a time…

That's how all good fairytales start. A princess lies asleep for a hundred years, awaiting the kiss of her one true love to waken her from her slumber. A beautiful young woman is cruelly oppressed by her evil step mother, only to be rescued by a fairy godmother and a magical glass slipper. A child visits her ailing grandmother, bringing her food and drink, only to discover an interloper masquerading as an old woman in her bed.

This story is far removed from those tales of whimsy. For starters, there's no magic here. None of what follows hereafter is make-believe. Good does not always win out. The righteous do not always overcome. The vile and the wicked are not always punished.

Will there be a happy ending? Who knows? Our rough accounting of what happened in Seattle this winter has only just begun and not yet reached its climax. But one thing's for certain: this story will deliver everything and nothing, depending on your heart's desire.

Let's start it off right, and in a true and proper fashion.

Once upon a time…
…there was a murderer named Zeth Mayfair.

******

All organized crime syndicates possess a figurehead. All gangs, mobs, and families are led by one power hungry, vicious tyrant who calls the shots and makes the decisions. And at that man's side stands another. A right hand. A tool, both blunt implement and finely-honed weapon, carrying out their boss' every violent wish and savage desire. I was that man, that tool and that weapon. I killed, I stole, I kidnapped, I broke bones, and I did not give a fuck about the consequences.

Many people would be ashamed of a past like mine, but sometimes I like to look back on those days with an abstract kind of fondness. Yes, it was a life of chaos. Did my lifestyle see me injured and hurt? Sure, every now and then. Was I in danger of losing my liberty and my freedom? Of course. Fuck, I *did* end up in jail once, though ironically not for a crime of my own doing (prison royally sucked. I wouldn't recommend it). But that kind of a life has its benefits. You keep your fucking mouth shut. You do what you're told, and you don't ask questions.

Simple.

Easy.

No worrying. No making the hard decisions for yourself. Everything is black and white. Yes and no. A list of tasks that must be completed in order, and at the end of it all a hefty payday lands in your lap.

But then…I met *her*: a woman with hair the color of molten chocolate, honey, cinnamon and gold, and eyes as dark and incomprehensible as a bottomless pit. Some people might say Sloane Romera, resident at St. Peter's of Mercy Hospital, saved my life. Others might say she ruined it. I suppose it all depends on your perspective. Either way, I fell for her, against my better judgement, knowing everything would change and nothing would ever be the same again. The man who had pulled my strings for so long no longer controlled me. The murdering ended.

And then, all of a sudden, out of fucking nowhere, I was a father.

In.

Out.

In.

Out.

In.

Out.

In.

Out.

My breath catches in my throat.

He's not breathing. *He's not fucking breathing.* Leaping to my feet, I close the space between the chair I was sitting in by the window and the small crib on the other side of the room, my heart a pulsing, thumping lump of meat trying to climb its way up my throat.

The child lies on his back, hands balled into tiny fists, thrown up on either side of his head. His lips are parted, his cheeks stained a rosy red, his dark eyelashes fanned out against the pale white plumpness of his cheeks. There are tiny little lions with shaggy manes on his onesie. I stare at his narrow, still chest with the intensity of fifty thousand burning suns, adrenalin making a racetrack of my circulatory system—feels like the goddamn Indie 500's taking place beneath my ribcage—and I will his chest to move. My palms are slick with sweat; I'm gonna have a fucking heart attack. Where the hell is my cell pho—

In...

Out...

In...

Out...

I nearly fucking keel over and weep when his fingers spasm and he takes another deep, steady, even draw of breath.

Jesus fucking Christ.

God...

I swallow down the panic that just rose up and closed its fingers around my throat, shaking myself out, but my body won't seem to comply. I've never known relief like this before. I thought I'd be crushed and I would die under the weight of the relief whenever I held Sloane in my arms and I knew that she was safe, but this is something else altogether. Fatherhood has wrought a dangerous change in me. The earth's still spinning around the sun. As far as I know, the universe is still expanding at a terrifying speed, rushing outward in every direction, larger, vaster with each and every second, too immense for my mind to even comprehend.

But these scientific facts might as well be fairytales to me these days. The earth will do as it will, but I am locked within the gravitational pull of the small child sleeping peacefully in this crib. The universe can continue charging away from itself, speeding into the unknown, but *my* universe is shrinking by the day. Now, it seems as though my universe is comprised of the space occupied by just two human beings.

And it's right where I belong.

ALSO BY CALLIE HART...

FREE TO READ ON KINDLE UNLIMITED!

DARK, SEXY, AND TWISTED! A BAD BOY WHO WILL CLAIM BOTH YOUR HEART AND YOUR SOUL.
Read the entire Blood & Roses Series
FREE on Kindle Unlimited!

WANT TO DISAPPEAR INTO THE DARK, SEDUCTIVE WORLD OF AN EX-PRIEST TURNED HITMAN?
Read the Dirty Nasty Freaks Series
FREE on Kindle Unlimited!

LOVE A DARK AND DANGEROUS MC STORY? NEED TO KNOW WHAT HAPPENED TO SLOANE'S SISTER?
Read the Dead Man's Ink Boxset
FREE on Kindle Unlimited!

ALSO BY CALLIE HART... | 341

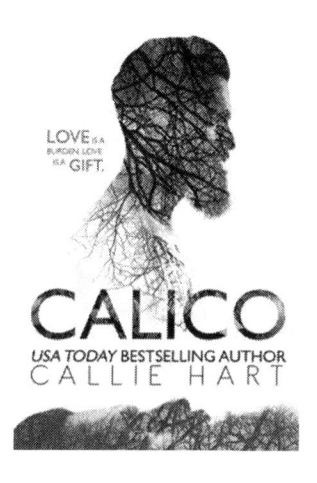

WANT AN EMOTIONAL, DARK, TWISTED STANDALONE?
Read Calico!
FREE on Kindle Unlimited

WANT A PLOT THAT WILL TAKE YOUR BREATH AWAY?
Read Between Here and the Horizon
FREE on Kindle Unlimited!

ALSO BY CALLIE HART...

WANT A NYC TALE OF HEARTBREAK, NEW LOVE, AND A HEALTHY DASH OF VIOLENCE?
Read Rooke
FREE on Kindle Unlimited!

KEEP READING TO MEET FIX MARCOSA...

Face of an angel. Body of a god. And a mouth so dirty he could make the devil blush...

ONE

LIBERTY FIELDS

SERA

"Ma'am, I don't give a fuck what your GPS is telling you to do. The road's closed. We have power lines down all over the goddamn place and water up to our necks. Now turn around go back the way you came before I have your car towed."

The man wearing the high visibility vest, leaning in through the window of my rental, looked like he was about to burst a blood vessel. His name was Officer Grunstadt, and he'd eaten curry for dinner; I knew this because he'd been blasting me with his spicy breath while I'd been arguing with him about the state of the road up ahead for the last ten minutes. The twitch in his left eye was a recent display of his frustration. The rain had fogged up his glasses, and large, fat water droplets coursed down his face as he, once again, pointed back in the direction I'd just come from. "Liberty Fields is only thirty miles away. There are two motels there and a bed and breakfast, though I think the bed and breakfast was already fully booked the last I heard. You can figure out what you want to do tomorrow, once the storm's died down."

"I can't go back to Liberty Fields. I have to get to Fairhope, Alabama, in two days, or I'm going to miss my sister's wedding."

"I don't know what to tell you, sweetheart. Catch a flight."

"Every flight out of Rawlins and Laramie is canceled until further notice. I need to keep driving, officer. You have to understand, I—"

"I do understand, miss. I understand perfectly well. You're a pretty young millennial with a bad case of *'I always get my way.'* You're not used to being told no, and you want me to break the rules. Unfortunately, I have a twenty-one year old daughter, and I'm used to all this…" He reaches out his hand, gesturing at my face, "…*nonsense,*" he finishes.

Asshole. Rude, small town punk asshole. "Firstly, sir, please do not gesticulate in my general direction like I'm a piece of trash you found at the side of the road. Secondly, I am *not* a millennial. I'm twenty-eight years old. I'm a successful business owner. The reason why I'm successful is because I've worked my ass off, not because I've pouted, sulked, or convinced anyone to break rules for me. I know the storm's bad, but the winds are calming down, and Waze does say the road is open and clear just another mile up ahead. You have no idea what stresses I'm dealing with, or the consequences I'll have to face if I don't make it to this wedding on time. *So just let me through the damn blockade.*"

Officer Grunstadt gave me a tight-lipped smile and pointed through my car, out the passenger window, to the other side of the road, where an overweight guy in a yellow plastic rain jacket was eating a sodden Subway foot-long. "See Jo over there? Jo gets four hundred dollars from the state to tow cars. That's why he comes and stands out here on nights like tonight, come hell or high water. If I wave Jo over here, it's gon' cost ya an extra two-fifty on top of that four hundred to get your car outta his lot, and that's after the twenty-four hour holding time is up. So, Miss…?"

"Lafferty," I said, sighing heavily.

"So, Miss Lafferty. Is sitting here, arguing with me worth six hundred and fifty dollars to you? Or would you rather just turn back, get dry, get a good night's sleep, and hope the fallen power lines have been dealt with by the time you wake up?"

God, this guy was a real piece of work. I forged a smile, digging my fingernails into the rental's steering wheel, begging myself not to say anything that would get me into trouble. It had happened before. "You're right, Officer Grunstadt. A night in a shitty motel does sound perfect right now. Thanks *so* much for your assistance."

The road back to Liberty Fields was narrow and winding, turning back on itself a hundred times before I even saw another car. The whole world seemed deserted. I'd tried to convince Grunstadt the wind was dying down a little, but the truth was it buffeted and rocked the car like crazy as I drove through the hammering rain; I had to focus to keep the thing from careening off the road and into the dark line of trees that bordered either side of the single-lane highway.

"Should never have left Seattle," I grumbled to myself. "Should have just stayed home and watched Shark Tank, for fuck's sake. Wyoming is the worst."

My sister and I had always wanted to road trip across country. Sixsmith, my father, had forbidden us from doing it, which made sense. Sixsmith hadn't wanted us driving off, because he'd known full well we'd never have come back. He would have had no one to torture and manipulate. He'd have had no one to cook his meals and clean his house. He'd have had no one to beat on when he came home drunk and bored.

So I'd waited. I'd waited until Amy was eighteen, a legal adult, before I'd packed up our bags, stole Sixsmith's red Chevrolet Beretta, and got us both the fuck out of Montmorenci, South Carolina, for good. We'd worked in bars and as temps in offices, scraping enough money together to go to community college. Amy had studied languages, and I'd studied business management. Once we'd completed our degrees, unbelievably, Amy had moved out to South Carolina with her boyfriend, Ben, and I'd relocated to Seattle with dreams of creating my own consulting firm. It hadn't been easy. There'd been many months when I couldn't make rent, and many months when I'd thought about giving it all up, becoming a waitress, and living from pay check to pay check. I'd thought about that a lot, but I'd stayed the course. My persistence had finally paid off six years ago, when I'd landed a huge corporate account with a private lender. After that, I'd had more clients than I knew what to do with. I'd had to take on three new members of staff just to cover the workload.

My H.R. department—namely a perma-harrassed woman in her late forties called Sandra—had insisted I take time off to drive to Amy's wedding. If only I could wrap my hands around Sandra's neck right now, I'd throttle her. It would have taken six hours to fly to Alabama. Maybe a couple of hours in a car on top of that to reach Fairhope. But now, here I was, after three days on the road, stuck in the middle of the biggest flash flooding the state of Wyoming had ever witnessed, instead of being tucked up, comfortable and warm in a fancy hotel.

Goddamnit.

As I pulled up outside the Liberty Fields Guest House and Artisan Art Gallery, I mourned the fact that the place certainly did *not* appear to be a fancy hotel. Fat lot of good my Hilton Rewards points were going to do me out here. The guesthouse looked like a derelict, abandoned farmhouse, perched on the side of the highway embankment as I pulled into the packed parking lot. My teeth rattled together as I traveled over a series of giant potholes, invisible in the near perfect darkness, and I swore colorfully under my breath. I didn't want to be here. I didn't want to be dealing with any of this. It didn't seem to matter what I wanted, though. The car rocked from side to side as I slid my arms into my thick winter jacket, preparing myself to face the weather. Through the windshield, the trees on the other side of the parking lot were bowed, their branches waving like outstretched arms, reaching for help. God, it looked fucking miserable out there.

Opening the car door, I swung my legs out, and my feet disappeared up to my ankles in frigid, inky black water. "Ffffffff—" I stopped myself from swearing. This night just couldn't get any better. Seriously.

There were so many cars parked haphazardly in the lot that I had to walk a solid hundred and fifty feet to reach the dimly lit entrance to the guesthouse. The rain seemed to come down harder as I half ran toward the building, my teeth grinding together. I had no idea rain could actually be this cold. Shit, I needed to get inside. I needed to get inside. The rust-flecked handle on the front door of the motel threatened to fall off in my hand as I yanked on it. A blast of heat hit me in the face as I hurried through the entranceway, and strains of Jonny Cash's 'I Walk The Line' flooded my ears. The left hand side of the lobby wall was fitted out with a stand—

the same kind of stand you'd find in any normal hotel, where local businesses and tourist attractions advertise themselves—but the slots on this stand were all notably, depressingly empty. Liberty Fields was a black hole in the center of the State of Wyoming, zip code: nowhere.

The motel lobby smelled like damp and mildew. A puddle the size of Lake Michigan had collected in front of the rickety looking front desk; it was impossible to avoid the vast body of water as I made my way to the counter to ring the brass bell. Not that it mattered, of course. My feet were already soaking wet, right along with the rest of me. I hit the top of the bell for service, and nothing happened. No sound. No cheerful, inviting, *I-need-help* chime. Nothing.

"For fuck's sake." I looked around, searching for the night manager, but no one was to be seen. I leaned over the counter, hunting, hoping and praying for a savior to come along and tell me they had a secret, exclusive retreat out back that I hadn't noticed on my way in, but all I found were stacks of rotting newspapers, a metal dog bowl with food encrusted around its rim, and a mouse trap butted up against the wall. Very encouraging indeed.

On the other side of the lobby, I spied a public payphone. Pulling a handful of quarters out of my jeans pocket, I took advantage of the opportunity and I called Amy.

"God, Sera. It's nearly two in the morning," she groaned when she picked up.

"I know, I know, I'm sorry. I just—fuck—I'm still stuck in the middle of nowhere. I have another twenty-four hours to drive, and it looks like tomorrow's going to be a complete wash out. I don't know if I'm going to make it." In my experience, it was better to rip the Band-Aid off as quickly as possible, especially with Amy. She was hardly a no-nonsense woman, but if you strung things out with her, she tended to get a little hysterical.

"What do you mean, you don't know if you're going to make

it?" Her voice was a little groggy when she picked up a second ago, but now it was sharp with accusation and worry.

"There's a huge storm, Amy. The roads are all closed. I'm stranded in Liberty Fields."

"Liberty Fields? Where the fuck is *Liberty Fields?*"

"I—god, *I* don't know. It sucks, though. I can tell you that much."

Behind me, the guesthouse door chimed, and a loud groan drowned out Johnny Cash for a second. I glanced over my shoulder, hopeful that it was the night manager entering the building, but when I saw the guy who stooped through the doorway to enter the place, I immediately knew he didn't work here.

A creature like that simply didn't exist in a place like this. Tall. Square jaw, lined with a swathe of black stubble. Bright, intelligent eyes—so damn pale, like quicksilver—traveled over me as the newcomer took in the lobby. The black suitcase in his hand appeared to be designer. Definitely not something a night manager would be carrying around with him. He looked like a character right out of Reservoir Dogs. Our eyes met, and there was absolutely nothing. No greeting smile from a fellow, weary traveler. No relief at finding someone else waiting in the lobby. Absolutely no flicker of emotion whatsoever.

"*Sera*. You do know what'll happen to you if you're not here on Saturday, right? I will disown you and never speak to you again." Amy's voice rattled down the phone. I turned back around, pressing the receiver harder against my ear.

"Yes, yes. Disowning. Eternal silence. I'll do everything in my power to make it, I promise."

"Don't promise me you're going to try! Promise me you're going to be here!"

"*Okay*! I promise. If I have to get up in two hours and break through the road cordons, I'll make sure I get there. How's Ben?"

"I don't know. Drunk?" Amy said pathetically. "Who has their bachelor party two nights before the wedding?"

"Hmm. I'm sure he's fine," I replied. I wasn't really paying attention, though. The guy who'd just entered the guesthouse was standing at the front desk, and he was about to ring the bell.

"It doesn't work," I told him.

His back was to me; he didn't turn around.

"Sera, we can push the ceremony back to later in the afternoon, but that's it. The weather's not going to hold into the evening. We have to make sure we're inside by five."

"I know." I pinched my brows, trying not to groan. "Everything will be perfect. Please don't stress."

I recognized the manic edge to my sister's voice. The vein in her temple would be visibly pulsing right now. "Oh, okay. My maid of honor's telling me she might not make my wedding, but I shouldn't get stressed. I'll just start popping those Valium Ben's dad pre—" The line crackled, and I couldn't hear Amy anymore. Static flooded down the line.

"Amy? Hey, Aim?" Nothing. The static grew louder, roaring, drowning out the thunderous rain hammering against the lobby windows. I pressed my forehead against the side of the payphone, slowly closing my eyes. Perfect. She was gone. No surprise, with the weather being what it was. I must have seen four or five downed telephone poles on the way into Liberty Fields. It was a miracle I'd even managed to make the call in the first place. God...

She was going to be freaking out so hard.

I turned away from the payphone, resting my back against the wall. The guy with the suitcase had moved away from the front desk and was stabbing at his cell like he was trying to force it into cooperating by sheer force of will alone. "Good luck," I muttered under my breath. "I had service until I turned around on the highway, then...*poof!* Gone."

The guy glanced at me sideways, and once again I was startled by the intensity of his pale blue, silvery eyes. His mouth lifted up at the corner into half a caustic smile. "You don't say?" His voice was the snarl of a chainsaw: rumbling, low and raw. He'd probably smoked a pack a day for fifteen years to get a voice like that.

If I hadn't already been frozen solid, I would have melted from the wave of heat that exploded across my cheeks. Turned out Mr. Black (as I'd named him in my head) wasn't so friendly. He slid his phone into his pocket, straightened his spine, allowed his head to tip back, and then cracked his neck.

He looked like he was about to say something else, then apparently thought better of it. He rubbed his hand through his dark, wet hair, sending a shower of water droplets up into the air. He was dressed head-to-heel in black, nothing too out there or ostentatious, but it was clear the plain shirt and the plain pants were brand name. His shirt was soaked at the shoulders, and his leather shoes were splattered with mud, but other than that he was very well turned out. His facial stubble wasn't due to neglect. It was the perfect length—not too long, and not too short. His neck and his throat were trimmed neatly, too, showing that he obviously took care of his scruff on a daily basis.

The men in my line of business were a little more showy with their wealth, their clothing, and their personal hygiene. A couple of the guys at the law firm opposite my offices had even started wearing makeup, believe it or not. I certainly had *not* believed it when Sandra told me she'd found a guy touching up his eyeliner in the elevator mirror one morning. It had taken seeing the exact same guy, doing the exact same thing, a couple of weeks later for the idea to really take root in my mind.

Mr. Black definitely wasn't wearing any eyeliner. His eyelashes were dark enough already, inky against the paleness of his skin. Perfect, really. The kind of eyelashes a woman would lynch a sales rep at Sephora for. I quickly glanced away when he turned to face me. Had he noticed me looking? Fuck, I hoped not. That really would have been the perfect way to end an already shitty day: busted checking out a particularly cold, frosty character in a crappy motel lobby.

"You're in the doghouse, then," the guy said. Once again, his unique, devastatingly deep voice caused a relay of electricity to run up and down my spine, lighting up my nerve endings.

"I beg your pardon?"

He pointed an accusatory finger at the payphone.

"Oh. Oh, right. Yeah. My sister. Her big day's on Saturday."

"And you're stranded in the middle of nowhere, in the middle of a giant rain storm."

"Yeah. Bad luck, I know."

He shrugged, scratching at his jaw. "Or bad planning."

I'd been told in the past that my death stare could literally eviscerate a man at twenty yards. Mr. Black didn't wither and die under the weight of my cold look, though. If anything, he seemed to be enjoying the attention. I buttoned my lip, choosing to ignore his barb. Yeah, sure, I could have made better arrangements. I could have checked the weather ahead of time. I could have used common sense and caught a goddamn plane, and yada yada yada. Just because he was right and I did land myself in this particular predicament through my own lack of foresight, didn't mean he got to chide me like I was a complete moron. But I could take the high road. I could be the bigger person and not sink to bickering with a stranger.

"You're upset," he offered.

I flared my nostrils, exhaling slowly down my nose. "I'm fine. I just want to get a room, get some sleep, and get out of this shit hole. Just like you, I'm sure."

Mr. Black laughed silently, propping his black suitcase up against the threadbare, heavily stained couch that had been positioned beneath the large picture windows by the front door.

"Not at all. *I* plan things very well," he informed me. "I'm right where I need to be."

"You came here *on purpose?*"

I was met with stony silence and a flat, indecipherable stare. "Liberty Fields is an historical landmark. Why not?"

I'd been out of the habit of rolling my eyes for well over a decade, but I felt prompted to give the ceiling tiles a once over in this instance. This guy was something else. He was baiting me, being difficult on purpose, and it didn't look like he was going to quit any time soon. "All right, buddy. Well, I hope you have a stellar Hicksville vacation."

"I'm here for work, actually."

If this conversation had been a text message, I'd have given him the big blue thumbs up by now. Being passive aggressive was a nuanced art, and far easier via emoji, especially when you didn't *actually* want to start a fight with someone. Mr. Black didn't seem to care that he was being kind of hostile, though, so why the hell should I? "Let me guess. Playing in an emo 80's cover band? Vampire coven gathering? Tarantino cos-play convention?"

Mr. Black's smile was cool and unruffled, though he seemed to be spitting sparks of ice from his eyes. His irises were the color of winter. The color of early morning skies in February. They reminded me of being very, very small. Smoke on my breath and stiff, unresponsive fingers. Stomping my thick rubber soled boots against hard-packed snow, trying to regain feeling in my toes.

It was amazing how visual or auditory cues affected me sometimes. I could be waiting in line to buy popcorn at the movies, and then the next second I was being dragged backward through time, to fifteen years earlier, when my very first boyfriend tried to make me touch his dick in the back of his pick-up truck.

Every time I saw the ocean in person or even on TV, I immediately smelled the peachy, light, fragrant scent of my mother's perfume, instead of the briny, salty sharpness of the water. My mind played tricks on me all the time.

"I'm a hitman. I took a job here in town," Mr. Black said nonchalantly. He ducked down, unzipping his suitcase, and pulled out an iPad, which he turned on. The white flare of the screen as it powered up briefly lit up his face before it dimmed. I jabbed my fingernail into the rubbery seam that ran down the side of the public payphone, considering his last statement.

"I hear it pays well. Being a hitman."

"It does." He was distracted, not really paying attention.

"So, you roll up on a dark and stormy night. You secure a base for yourself. Then you sneak across town while the place is in chaos, and you..." I made a gun out of my hand, pretending to take aim, "...*pull the trigger.*"

"Pretty much. Something like that. Though, I'm going to wait until morning. Roads aren't safe right now. Wouldn't want to end up being responsible for an accident or something."

That made me snort. "So you're going to kill someone, but heaven forbid you cause an accident while you're at it."

"If I'm gonna kill someone, it's because I'm being paid to do it. Not because the roads are treacherous and I can't control my vehicle."

Wow. This guy was good. He didn't even flinch as he spoke of murder. Most people wouldn't have been able to keep up the pretense. They would have laughed, or winked, or pulled a face, but not this guy. He lied as if he was speaking the truth. Looked like he believed it one hundred percent.

The lobby entryway opened, and a blast of wind howled through the door, pelting the couch and the small, peeling veneer coffee table with rainwater. A short, rotund, sour looking man wearing a cheap, plastic waterproof poncho bustled inside, swaying a little as he fought to get the door closed behind him. Mr. Black didn't help him, but then neither did I. We both just watched as the strange, oddly shaped figure belted the bottom of the door with his booted foot, slapping his palms against the doorframe, as if he were trying to reshape the woodwork with his bare hands.

"*Stupid...fucking...motherfucking...*"

The door closed, and the man stopped swearing. He turned around, panting, his wide frame shuddering as he looked from me to Mr. Black and back again. His eyes were a watery blue—inconsistent and weak—and his cheeks were marked with a spider web of ruptured blood vessels and thread veins. "You're outta luck," he said, slurring a little. Shoving away from the entrance door, he pushed himself forward toward the front desk, as if he needed the momentum to help get himself there. "No more rooms!" he cried. Instead of raising the hatch in the counter, walking through and lowering it behind himself again, he ducked down and scurried underneath it, growling unhappily as he struggled to heave himself upright on the other side. I crossed the lobby and leaned against the desk, being very careful not to raise my voice.

"I'm sorry. There *are* rooms available. Your vacancy sign's lit up in the parking lot."

"So what? Sign's always lit up, no matter what." The man, in his late fifties and reeking like a stale bar rag, flashed me a yellow smile rotten enough to turn my stomach. "Besides, I ain't had no time to turn the damn thing off. I been run off my feet, checking you people in and out all over the place. Don't know if you're comin' or goin', none of you."

Mr. Black appeared beside me and leaned across the counter, taking something from the night manager's hand: a long, scuffed, brass fob attached to a dangling key. On the brass fob: the number twenty-seven. "So you *do* have a room," Mr. Black said, holding up the fob.

The night manager tore the cheap plastic poncho over his head, exposing a broad section of dimpled belly fat as his shirt rose up; he growled under his breath as he wadded up the waterproof poncho and tossed it into the overflowing trashcan behind him. Above his left shirt pocket, the name 'Harold' had been stitched in black thread.

Harold staggered a little as he turned to face Mr. Black. "I ain't checked that key back into the system. So, no. It ain't free." He lunged to snatch the key back, but drunk as he was, he ended up grasping at thin air and nearly hitting the counter face-first. Mr. Black cleared his throat, flipping the key over in his hand.

"How much to expedite the process of securing this room from you, Harold?"

"Hey! I was here first. If anyone's gonna bribe him for the room, it's going to be *me*." I was far more successful in wrenching the key from Mr. Black's hand. The handsome stranger standing next to me didn't see me coming, or maybe he didn't expect me to hurl myself at him. Either way, I yanked the key from his grip and shoved it into my pocket, hurling a vicious look at him, just in case he was thinking about trying to get it back.

With the strangest expression on his face, he whispered a word that made my blood run hot and cold at the same time. "*Hellcat.*" His entire body pivoted to one side, away from me, as he curled a finger, motioning for Harold to lean in and speak with him. "I probably have way more money than her. What's it gonna be, cowboy?"

Harold, clearly a little discombobulated, just frowned. "The room's forty-nine ninety-nine for the night."

Mr. Black smirked. "Yeah. But if you give it to me, I'll pay you two hundred."

God, what a bastard. "I'll give you three hundred, Harold."

Mr. Black huffed down his nose, his smirk now a full-blown smile. "Five hundred, Harold. And a box of Cuban cigars. The good kind, not the cheap shit you can buy at customs."

Harold's eyes had glazed over a while back. He didn't seem to be taking any of this in. I grabbed hold of Mr. Black by the arm and tugged him forcefully away from the check in desk. "Look. You heard me on the phone just now. I have to get to my sister's wedding in Fairhope by Saturday. If I let her down, I'll break her damned heart. I'm the only member of family she'll have at this stupid fucking ceremony. Now, please… I need to drive out of this dump first thing in the morning, and to do that I need to fucking sleep. Please! Just let me have the fucking room!"

"You know you say fuck a lot?" he whispered, leaning into me, as if imparting a piece of information I might not yet be aware of. His snowstorm eyes flashed at me, filled with amusement.

"Lady, what's your name?" To my left, Harold scratched at his temple with the chewed end of a ballpoint pen. Oh, thank god. The guy had seen reason. I'd been the first person waiting for a room, so therefore I got it. Fair was fair. I breathed a sigh of relief, releasing my grip on Mr. Black's arm.

"It's Sera. Sera Lafferty.

Harold stuck out his tongue, his brow furrowing as his hand weaved toward what looked like a guest ledger. I risked a victorious sidelong smirk at Mr. Black, but I wasn't rewarded by a look of dismay plastered across his face. The bastard was still smirking, himself.

"And you. What…?" Harold hiccupped. "What's *your* name?"

"Felix Marcosa."

Of course his name was fucking Felix Marcosa. It suited him down to the ground. What an asshole. Harold obviously agreed with me. He groaned, shook his head, and then scribbled something sideways in the ledger. "I entered you into our state-of-the-art database as Mr. and Mrs.…" Hiccup, "…*Jones*. Twenty-seven's got two beds. Figure it out. Now…" He squinted at me and then at Felix, narrowing his eyes. "What did we agree? Three hundred from *you*," he said, pointed at me. "And five hundred from *you*. Plus…a box of Cuban cigars."

Felix Marcosa wasn't smiling anymore.

But then again, neither was I.

CLICK HERE TO KEEP ON READING!

FOLLOW ME ON INSTAGRAM!

The best way to keep up to date with all of my upcoming releases and some other VERY exciting secret projects I'm currently working on is to follow me on Instagram! Instagram is fast becoming my favorite way to communicate with the outside world, and I'd love to hear from you over there. I do answer my direct messages (though it might take me some time) plus I frequently post pics of my mini Dachshund, Cooper, so it's basically a win/win.

You can find me right here!

Alternatively, you can find me via me handle @calliehartauthor within the app.

I look forward to hanging out with you!

Callie
x

37
DEVIANT DIVAS

If you'd like to discuss my books (or any books, for that matter!), share pictures and quotes of your favorite characters, play games, and enter giveaways, then I would love to have you over in my private group on Facebook!

We're called the Deviant Divas, and we would love to have you come join in the fun!

ABOUT THE AUTHOR

USA Today Bestselling Author, Callie Hart, was born in England, but has lived all over the world. As such, she has a weird accent that generally confuses people. She currently resides in Los Angeles, California, where she can usually be found hiking, practicing yoga, kicking ass at Cards Against Humanity, or watching re-runs of Game of Thrones.

To sign up for her newsletter, click here.

Printed in Great Britain
by Amazon